Praise for *New York Times* bestselling author B.J. Daniels

"Daniels is truly an expert at Western romantic suspense."

—*RT Book Reviews* on *Atonement*

"B.J. Daniels is a sharpshooter; her books hit the target every time."

—#1 *New York Times* bestselling author Linda Lael Miller

"Daniels is a perennial favorite on the romantic suspense front, and I might go as far as to label her the cowboy whisperer."

—*BookPage*

Praise for author Nicole Helm

"An intimate, rewarding romance with a hot hero whose emotional growth is as sexy as his moves in the bedroom."

—*Kirkus Reviews* on *Want You More*

"Nicole Helm has done a great job of writing three-dimensional characters.... This is a super beginning to this series. I look forward to the next book in the series, *Wyoming Cowboy Protection*."

—*Harlequin Junkie* on *Wyoming Cowboy Justice*

STAMPEDED

NEW YORK TIMES BESTSELLING AUTHOR

B.J. DANIELS

Recycling programs
for this product may
not exist in your area.

ISBN-13: 978-1-335-40649-1

Stampeded
First published in 2011. This edition published in 2021.
Copyright © 2011 by Barbara Heinlein

Stone Cold Christmas Ranger
First published in 2017. This edition published in 2021.
Copyright © 2017 by Nicole Helm

For questions and comments about the quality of this book,
please contact us at CustomerService@Harlequin.com.

Harlequin Enterprises ULC
22 Adelaide St. West, 40th Floor
Toronto, Ontario M5H 4E3, Canada
www.Harlequin.com

Printed in U.S.A.

CONTENTS

B.J. Daniels is a *New York Times* and *USA TODAY* bestselling author. She wrote her first book after a career as an award-winning newspaper journalist and author of thirty-seven published short stories. She lives in Montana with her husband, Parker, and three springer spaniels. When not writing, she quilts, boats and plays tennis. Contact her at bjdaniels.com, on Facebook or on Twitter, @bjdanielsauthor.

STAMPEDED

B.J. Daniels

This book is dedicated to Deb Lorene Mallory, a fan and fellow writer who has become a good friend. Thanks again for being such a wonderful guide that weekend in Billings. I had a great time and it was a treat to get to know you better.

Prologue

"Alexa? Alexa, wake up."

The five-year-old came awake with a start to find her mother beside her bed. Her heart thumped in her tiny chest.

"What is it, Mommy?" she asked, her voice breaking. Just the sight of her mother beside her bed in the middle of the night filled her with panic. She struggled to come out of her sleep. Had she been screaming in her sleep with another nightmare?

Sometimes when she had nightmares, she would wake up to find her mother beside her bed, standing motionless, staring down at her. Like now, her mother would have that strange, eerie look in her eyes, the one she got when she was working with her clients.

"Honey, I need you to sit up and do something for me."

Alexa loved her beautiful mother with her long, curly

black hair, her wide violet eyes so like her own and the
face of an angel. But she couldn't help the shiver that
ran through her. Sometimes her mother scared her.

She rubbed sleep from her eyes and pushed herself up,
blinking at the shaft of golden light that spilled across
the floor from the hallway. Her mother always left the
hall light on and the door cracked open a few inches because of Alexa's nightmares. The light from the hallway
illuminated the empty, dark walls of her cavelike room.

"What were you thinking, Tallulah?" Alexa's father
had demanded. "She's a child, a little *girl*, she should have
a room painted pink with stuffed animals on the bed and
clouds painted on the ceiling—not horrible black walls."

"The black walls will keep away the nightmares,"
her mother had argued.

But they hadn't. And her father had finally given up
arguing and left before Alexa's baby brother had come
along, and he'd never come back.

"It wasn't his spiritual path to be with us," her mother
had told her when Alexa cried for her daddy. She missed
the way he would hold her when she was frightened, the
way he would smooth her long, wild dark hair with his
big hand and the way he would rock her with soothing
words until she fell back to sleep.

He used to call what Tallulah did for a living total
nonsense. "Don't let it scare you, Alexa. It's all just
mumbo jumbo, stuff your mother makes up for the fools
who are silly enough to pay her."

"Alexa?" There was impatience in her mother's tone
now.

She loved her mother and would do anything for her.
The last thing she wanted was to disappoint her.

But she had seen how happy it made her mother when everyone commented on how much Alexa looked like her. Tallulah Cross wanted her daughter to be just like her in every way, and that was what frightened her more than the nightmares.

"Honey, I need you to look down at the end of your bed. What do you see?"

Her tiny stomach turned. She sensed how important this was to her mother. But Alexa didn't want to look. She wanted to close her eyes tight and make her mother and whatever might be at the end of the bed go away.

But she always did what her mommy asked her. She was her mommy's good girl, her precious girl.

Alexa sat all the way up and took a breath, wrinkling her nose. The air smelled funny and she felt the way she did when she rubbed a balloon on her hair—her skin tingly, the space around her filled with static. Her body began to tremble under the covers as she slowly turned to look toward the end of her bed.

Tallulah Cross made her living in a small room at the front of their house. She told fortunes to the tourists who came through town by looking into the future and talking to those who'd gone to the other side. Dead people.

Alexa had overheard her mother telling her friends that her greatest hope in life was that, along with her beauty, she had passed her "gift" on to her daughter. For a long time, Alexa hadn't known what gift she was talking about.

Tonight, she knew. Just as she understood that this was a test and that if she wanted to be her mommy's "precious little girl," she must not disappoint her.

"What do you see, sweetie?" her mother asked, hope and something close to desperation in her voice.

Alexa tried not to flinch as she looked at the man standing at the end of her bed. He was tall. He stood funny, as if one leg was shorter than the other. But it was his face she would never forget, awake or asleep. Half of it was gone.

"You see the man, don't you, sweetie?"

A sob caught in her throat. "No, Mommy." It was the first lie she'd ever told and she instinctively knew it would come at a very high cost. But she didn't want to be just like her mother, even though it would mean she was no longer her mommy's special girl.

Alexa couldn't bear to see her mother's disappointment. Her heart ached as she closed her eyes, lay back down and pretended to go to sleep. It wasn't until she heard her mother leave the room that she opened them again and looked toward the end of her bed, knowing the man was still there. Nor had he been fooled.

He stared at her with that one dark eye, then he gave her a conspiratorial wink and vanished.

Alexa shut her eyes tight, fighting tears. She didn't want to see dead people. She didn't want them to talk to her. She told herself she wouldn't see them again. Nor would she see the future.

And she didn't for twenty-three years.

Chapter 1

Marshall Chisholm was no carpenter. He was learning that the hard way, he thought. He put down his hammer for the day and turned to gaze out at the Montana landscape through what would one day be his finished bay window.

While he spent most of his days on the back of a horse herding cattle, he'd fallen in love with this house the moment he'd seen it. Not that there was anything special about it—or even the view. The house was a two-story farmhouse that had been built in the late 1930s. But it had good bones, as they say, and it had spoken to him the moment he'd walked in. Not that he would ever admit that.

There was something about the place that appealed to him even though it had been vacant for many years.

He'd known it would take a lot of work, but he'd been eager to get started on it.

Along with the house, Marshall liked the view of the rolling prairie. It stretched out across this vast part of Montana as if endless. Out here, he felt on top of the world. Through every window he could see to the horizon with nothing to break that view on three sides but sagebrush and Black Angus cattle—his family's cattle.

The Chisholm Cattle Company ran more head of cattle than any other in the state and that took a lot of country. He also liked that as far as he could see, this was Chisholm land, most of it running to the horizon.

On the fourth side, the side this upstairs bedroom window faced, there were rolling grain fields and pasture, with only one structure on the horizon.

Marshall squinted as he noticed something different about the old three-story mansion in the distance. He'd looked at it many times since moving into this house. But this time he saw something odd.

Someone was over there.

That was such a rare occurrence that he picked up the binoculars he kept by the window and, peering through them, brought the huge mansion into focus.

He'd heard there had once been a small settlement around the mansion called Wellington, but all the other buildings had been gone for years. The only structure that remained was the monster of a mansion, or Wellington Manor as the locals called it.

The massive, old place must have dwarfed the other buildings that had been there years before and would have been ostentatious even in these times, let alone a hundred years ago. He'd heard stories for years about the family and the house, though he'd never believed them. People liked to think that old places had ghosts.

The last resident of Wellington Manor had died a year ago, an old spinster niece of the original owner, Jedidiah Wellington. Marshall had heard the place was tied up in an estate.

He frowned as he noticed there was a small red sports car parked under the cottonwood trees that flanked the house. The cottonwoods were fed by a small spring-fed creek that ended in a pond at the end of the row of trees. Marshall liked to swim in the pond since it was halfway between his house and the mansion.

As he scanned the scene, he saw that there was also a dark-colored large SUV parked behind the sports car.

How odd, he thought as he lowered the binoculars. Was it possible someone had bought the place? Or could it be squatters? His father had told him that drug dealers coming out of Canada would often stay in abandoned farmhouses, but he'd never seen anyone around Wellington Manor in the past year since it had been empty. The Canadian border was only about thirty miles away. The closest town to the south, Whitehorse, was another twenty miles. So the dirt road up to this part of the county didn't get a lot of traffic—let alone tourists. He supposed it could be drug runners.

Marshall took one more look through the binoculars and saw yet another vehicle coming up the long tree-lined drive to the mansion, this one a small white SUV.

He didn't know anyone who'd even been inside the mansion. Apparently Jedidiah Wellington and his family kept to themselves, and so had the old-maid niece who'd been the last one to live there.

His curiosity piqued and tired of carpentry work for the day, Marshall decided to saddle up and ride over to see what was going on.

Alexa Cross pulled up to the monstrous house with growing unease. The house looked like a hotel, looming three stories up with wings off four sides—not what she'd expected at all. When her brother had told her at the wedding that he and his new bride were remodeling her family's old house in Montana, she'd pictured something smaller, set in the mountains with lots of rock and wood. Not this ugly monstrosity.

As she stared at the house, she thought of his recent call saying he needed her to come out for a visit. She'd heard something in his voice that had scared her.

"What's wrong? Is it Sierra?"

"No," Landon had said, clearly irritated. "My wife's fine. *We're* fine."

Alexa wished now she'd never voiced her misgivings about her brother's hasty marriage. But she couldn't help worrying that he'd made a mistake and was now realizing it.

Both university students, Landon and Sierra had met while working in Yellowstone Park for the summer and had fallen in love. Alexa hadn't even gotten a chance to meet Sierra before the wedding held at the old hotel at Mammoth Hot Springs until the day before the ceremony.

Sierra Wellington wasn't the woman Alexa would have chosen for her brother, but she'd seen at once what had attracted Landon to the petite, pretty blonde. Landon, like Alexa, had taken after their mother. He had the curly, dark hair, the dark eyes and olive skin of what was rumored to be fortune-telling, gypsy ancestors.

The contrast between Landon and Sierra, Alexa was sure, had been part of their attraction for each other. That and a common denominator called Montana. Both had a tie to the state. Landon's father had allegedly been born here—at least that was what their mother had told them. Neither Alexa nor Landon had ever met the man. Nor had their mother apparently bothered to get the man's last name at the time of Landon's conception.

Sierra's roots ran deeper in Montana, with several generations of Montanans and a family house that still stood in what had been a town named after her great-great-grandfather.

"It's this house," her brother had said on the phone. "There's something wrong with it." When Landon had told her about the idea he and Sierra had to turn the mansion she'd inherited into a bed-and-breakfast, Alexa hadn't shared their enthusiasm.

"You mean structurally?" she'd asked, relieved it was nothing more earth-shattering than a construction problem. Neither her brother nor his wife knew anything about running a bed-and-breakfast, and Alexa questioned the feasibility when the closest town was Whitehorse—apparently a small western town with a declining population. Not to mention that this wide-open prairie part of Montana wasn't the one most tourists came to see.

She'd kept her reservations about their plan to herself though, fearing alienating her brother, who seemed as excited about the prospect as his wife.

"I know this is asking a lot, but I need you to come out here," Landon had said. "I want you to see the house and tell me what you think. What do you say, sis?"

What could she say? He was her only family, since their mother had died a year ago. She would do anything for him and he knew it. Also she felt honored that he wanted her opinion.

"I'll drive out this weekend." It was a ten-hour drive from Spokane, Washington, where she lived and worked as a reporter. She could get a few days off from the newspaper without any trouble, and she hadn't seen her brother since the wedding and was worried about him.

"It might take more than a weekend," Landon had said, adding, "It's a big house."

The mansion was indeed big, she thought as she looked up at it. Big and ugly as if built by someone who wanted not to just impress but shock. There was nothing engaging about the structure. All she could hope was that it was more hospitable inside, since she didn't like old houses. As she stared at it, she feared coming here might have been a terrible mistake.

Alexa climbed out of her white SUV as the front door opened and her brother, Landon, came out to her. He looked so happy to see her that she shoved aside her misgivings.

"It is wonderful to see you," he said as he hugged her tightly. "Thank you so much for coming."

She drew back to study him, thinking how much she loved him. Sometimes she forgot how handsome and sweet he was. Their mother had called him her "little prince." Both of them had adored Landon, but somehow he hadn't grown up spoiled.

If anything, he was too generous with his money and his love, Alexa thought, as Sierra appeared in the wide doorway.

"Welcome to Wellington Manor," Sierra said with a grand gesture. "That's what the locals call it and I think it fits the place. You're early. Supper's not quite ready. The others are either napping or in town for supplies but should be back any minute."

"The others?" Alexa asked her brother.

"We have friends helping get the house ready for guests," Landon said as he reached into the back of her vehicle for her suitcase. "Only one suitcase?" He looked disappointed as he hooked the strap of her bag over one shoulder.

"I travel light," she said with a smile and reluctantly let him lead her toward the mansion. She could feel tension between her brother and his new wife and suspected it hadn't been Sierra's idea to invite her to come for a stay.

She wondered whose idea it had been to have these friends help get the house ready for guests; after all Sierra and Landon had given up their honeymoon to come here and get started on the bed-and-breakfast.

As they walked toward the front entry, Alexa noticed something that hadn't registered minutes before. Her brother was rubbing his left arm.

"Did you hurt yourself?" she asked and saw him glance toward his wife before he answered.

"Just me being clumsy." He put his other arm around Alexa and smiled at his wife in the doorway. Sierra smiled back and disappeared into the house, leaving

Alexa with the distinct impression that her brother was hiding something for Sierra's sake.

The moment she stepped into the house, she felt the cold. It instantly crept into her bones and made her shiver.

"It's a bit drafty," Sierra said, no doubt having witnessed Alexa's reaction.

She could see that both Sierra and Landon were defensive about the house. She fought not to show the effect it was having on her. The mansion had once been opulent, from the marble foyer to the huge sunken living room with its massive stone fireplace to the ornate stairway that swept upward to the floors above. Hallways ran from the living area like spider legs, disappearing in the dim light.

"Isn't it beautiful," Sierra gushed. "I just love it. Can't you see it as a bed-and-breakfast? Wait until you see the rest of it."

Alexa smiled at her sister-in-law's enthusiasm. The house had recently been cleaned but there was still a musty smell as if the rooms had been closed up—even though someone had been living here. Only a little light bled through the high leaded-stained-glass windows. Heavy velvet curtains hung next to the lower windows and while the glass had been recently cleaned, even the summer sun seemed to be having a hard time getting through.

"I'm sure you're tired after your long drive," her brother said, apparently wanting to talk to her alone. "Why don't I show you to your room."

"Oh, you'll want a tour first," Sierra said, sounding both surprised and annoyed at her husband's suggestion.

"I would love one later," Alexa said quickly. "Landon's right. I would like to freshen up first."

Sierra looked disappointed. "I've just been so excited to show you the house. My great-great-grandfather designed it, you know." She gave a little pout but said, "I guess I'll see how supper is coming instead. I think I hear the others pulling in now."

"I'd love to see it after we eat, thank you," Alexa said, relieved her sister-in-law hadn't insisted. She sensed Landon's need to talk to her, and whatever this was about, he hadn't wanted Sierra to hear.

He was quiet as he led her upstairs through what seemed like a maze of hallways before stopping at an end room. Opening the door, he stepped back to let her enter.

"Sierra got the room ready for you," he said, pride in his voice.

Alexa was reminded how much her brother loved his wife and how careful she had to be around Sierra so she didn't hurt his feelings. She knew she wasn't being fair. She barely knew the woman and chastised herself for not giving Sierra more of a chance.

"It's beautiful," she said as she entered the room. And it was.

The wood floors were buffed to a golden shine, and the huge canopy bed was adorned in white linens. An array of pillows were piled against the carved wooden headboard. An antique vanity stood against one wall, with two matching highboys and a loveseat and overstuffed chair on the other.

"The house came filled with furniture," Landon said. "There is even more up on the third floor. The last resident used that floor mostly for storage. The place really is huge, isn't it?"

He sounded nervous and while she was anxious to know why he'd gotten her here, she warned herself not to push.

"Sierra chose this room because of the view and the peace and quiet," Landon said. "It's the farthest from where the construction work is going on. We're remodeling some of the lower rooms that were built as servants' quarters."

"The view is wonderful," Alexa said as she stepped through the open French doors onto a small balcony. The land seemed vast and endless—just like the clear blue sky overhead. She'd never been to Montana before, but all the stories she'd heard about it seemed to be true. It really was amazing country. She could imagine what it must have been like when thousands of buffalo roamed it.

As she stared out, a cowboy on a horse came into view. Something in her froze. She stood transfixed as he rode from the stand of large cottonwood trees and into the sun and sage. For a moment she'd thought she'd conjured him up from her imagination because he looked so at home in the saddle with this landscape in the background. He wore jeans, boots, a red-checked western shirt and what she thought must be a Stetson resting on his longish, raven-black hair. A brown-and-white mutt of a dog ran along a few yards off to the side of his horse.

Alexa held her breath, wanting him to turn and look in her direction. She desperately needed to see his face.

Just when it appeared he would ride by without looking in her direction, he glanced up at her.

Chapter 2

Only two of the vehicles were still parked in front of the old Wellington mansion, the red sports car and the white SUV, Marshall Chisholm noted as he rode his horse by the house. The former street was no more than a narrow dirt lane with rows of huge, old cottonwood trees on each side.

The sports car had California plates, while the SUV was licensed out of Washington State. Neither rig looked as if it might belong to drug runners out of Canada hiding out here. The expensive sports car had a Montana State University sticker on the bumper. College students?

As he came out of the trees, he got his first close-up view of the house. He'd never paid much attention to the old place. Truth is, there was something about it that had always put him off. That and no doubt the stories he'd heard over the years.

Even up close, the mansion still didn't draw him. There was nothing in its design or the size of the place that made him want to stop and look. It was the three vehicles he'd seen here that had him curious. He wondered where the black SUV had gone.

As he circled around the place, he looked up at the blank windows, thinking he should probably just go knock at the huge front door and introduce himself as the only neighbor.

He was chewing on that idea when suddenly a young woman with long, dark, curly hair, wide violet eyes and the heart-shaped face of an angel appeared on a second-floor balcony.

But it was what he saw behind her that startled him. His horse suddenly snorted and jerked her head, eyes wild as she reared up. His western hat fell off as he fought to stay seated. He'd never seen the mare react like this before and knew he was lucky he hadn't been bucked off.

As he regained control of his mount, he glanced up again. The young woman was still standing there, but the image he'd seen behind her was gone.

She stood in the morning light, lithe, wraithlike against the darkness behind her. A vision. Her hair floated around her face, falling about her shoulders in stark contrast to the white of the blouse she wore.

His dog, Angus, barked, making him start again. Everything about being here was making him jumpy as hell. He told himself he was letting his imagination run away with him. That and the stories he'd heard about the mansion—even though he'd always said he didn't believe a word of it.

"Hang on a minute, Angus," he said, glancing at the impatient mutt before looking back at the mansion window. The woman was gone.

Marshall felt a knot form in his belly as he continued to stare at the window for several long moments, trying to assure himself he hadn't imagined her any more than he'd imagined that other image standing behind her.

He wished to hell she would reappear just to prove to himself that she'd been real though.

You don't really believe that was a ghost you saw.

Of course, he didn't. But still there had been something about her, something ethereal, angelic. While what he'd seen behind her... He spurred his horse, chuckling at the strange trail his thoughts had taken. He didn't believe in ghosts or haunted houses. Or evil spirits.

But as warm as the summer morning felt with the sun hot on his back, he felt a chill.

"Alexa, did you hear what I said?"

She stepped back into the room, but she couldn't shake the rush of sensations she'd felt when she'd seen the handsome cowboy's face. A strange, wanton desire—and darkness.

Both frightened her by their intensity. She recalled how desperate she'd been to see his face. How she had needed him to look at her.

She shuddered, shocked by what she'd felt as much as by the force of it. Often she got sharp first impressions, but she'd convinced herself that other people got them too and often didn't recognize them. Everyone met people and in an instant decided if they liked them or not, and never questioned why.

Plain old intuition. She'd even convinced herself that her mother had probably merely been good at reading people, so of course her daughter had picked it up as well. Alexa wanted to believe that rather than the other possibility.

Since she was a girl she'd been haunted by the memory of waking to find her mother standing over her, telling her to look at something at the end of her bed.

Just the thought of it after all these years gave her chills, but she'd convinced herself that what she'd seen was nothing more than her imagination. Or part of a bad dream.

Unfortunately sometimes she felt things, sensed things, she didn't want to know about. She'd found it easier not to get too close to anyone. As long as she kept her distance and her defenses up, she could live blissfully oblivious about the people around her and their fates.

None of her earlier sensations, though, had ever been as powerful as what she'd felt when she'd seen the cowboy's face. Desire and darkness.

"Are you all right?" Landon asked as he touched her arm and she flinched.

"Yes." She shook her head as if she could shake off what she'd felt moments before. It had been so potent. "I'm just tired. It was a long drive."

"I hated to ask you to come...."

"No," she quickly reassured him. "I'd been wanting to come for a visit." Her brother reminded her of light.

There was something so pure and innocent about him. He was loving and devoted, open and trusting.

Unlike her brother, she had never been open or trusting.

"You sounded strange on the phone," she said as she drew him over to the loveseat between the two highboys. "I was concerned." Alexa still worried why he had invited her here, almost pleading with her to come.

"I didn't mean to trouble you," he said, but looking at him she could tell something was wrong and said as much.

"Like I told you on the phone, it's the house."

"If you don't want to remodel it for a bed-and-breakfast then—"

"It's not that." He seemed to hesitate, his gaze locking with hers. "You're the only person I can tell this to who won't think I'm crazy. The house is trying to hurt me," he said dropping the words like stones into the room.

"What?" Alexa said, thinking she must have heard him wrong.

"You asked about my arm? A cabinet fell on me, but there have been other near misses since we got here."

"Landon, do you realize what you're saying?"

He nodded. "Do you remember when we were kids and Mother used to ask you if you saw…things that the rest of us couldn't see?"

As if she could forget. Alexa got up and moved to the open French doors again. There was no sign of the cowboy she'd seen earlier. "Landon, I've told you. I don't have the sight."

"Mother was convinced that you blocked it. That you were simply afraid of it but that if you let yourself—"

"Mother was wrong," she said, turning to face him. "This is all her fault," she continued with a wave of her hand that encompassed the house. "If not for her beliefs, then you would never be thinking that because of some isolated accidents…" The rest of her words died in her mouth as she saw her brother's crestfallen face. "This is why you got me here? To tell you whether or not this house is haunted?"

Her brother suddenly looked so young, so vulnerable, her heart nearly broke for him. "Something is wrong in this house," he said with obvious fear.

Before she could question him further, there was a knock at the door.

"Please don't say anything about this to my wife," he whispered hurriedly.

Alexa felt sick to her stomach. She couldn't believe this is why he'd gotten her here.

"So how do you like your room?" Sierra asked as she stuck her head into the doorway.

"It's lovely," Alexa told her, though still upset from her conversation with her brother. She was angry with him for getting her here under false pretenses and, at the same time, worried about him. Landon was scared. But he also had enough of their mother in him that he was prone to overreaction and flights of fantasy. His hasty marriage to a woman he barely knew and getting involved with this white elephant of a house were two perfect examples.

"You did a beautiful job," she said to Sierra. "I really think you have a talent for this."

Her sister-in-law beamed at the compliment. "I can't tell you what that means to me." She let out a pleased sigh. "Supper is ready. Afterwards I will give you a tour of the house. You really have to see it to appreciate how amazing it is."

Landon followed his wife out of the room, hesitating only long enough to say to his sister, "We'll talk later."

As Alexa stepped out into the hallway, she felt a winterlike draft that stole her breath. She suppressed a shudder as she saw her brother watching her and realized Sierra was also intently focused on her.

Of course her brother would have told his wife everything about his family—Alexa included.

"Has anyone heard anything about the people who are staying at the old Wellington place?" Marshall asked as casually as possible during supper at the Chisholm ranch that evening.

While he and his five brothers all had their own houses, they still had breakfast most mornings at the Chisholm Cattle Company main house—and were always expected for supper unless they were out of town *or* dead.

Their new stepmother, Emma, had a hard-and-fast rule about them being at the table on time, showered and shaved and without any manure on their boots. So tonight they were all seated at the table, his father, Hoyt, stepmother, Emma, and his five brothers, Dawson, Colton, Zane, Logan and Tanner.

"I heard something in town about a bunch of hippies moving into it," Colton said as he helped himself to more roast beef from the huge platter in front of him.

"You want Halley to check on it?" Deputy Halley Robinson was Colton's fiancée.

Marshall chuckled at the hippie remark. Anyone from California with relatively long hair was considered a hippie in this part of Montana. The word covered a lot of territory.

He thought of the woman he'd seen at the window. "I think they might have bought the place."

"That's news to me," his father said, frowning. "I'd have known if it had come on the market. I've been trying to buy it for years and was told the family wasn't interested. Since the old woman who lived there died, the place has been tied up in the estate."

"I wonder then if the people I saw over there might be related to the original owner," Marshall mused.

"What is your interest anyway?" Zane asked, studying him.

"Just curious," Marshall said, feeling all eyes at the table on him. He was a terrible liar and they all knew it. "I can see the place from my house. I noticed activity over there, three cars, and just wondered what was going on. As I was driving in for supper, I passed a local hardware truck headed out that way with a lot of supplies in the back."

"You think they're remodeling it?" Hoyt said. "I can't imagine anyone wanting to live in such a huge place. Unless they have something else in mind for it."

"Are you talking about that old mansion north of here?" Emma asked. "I'd hate to have to heat that place in the winter. Why, it must have thirty bedrooms."

"I heard the old woman who lived there last stayed

in just a small part of the house, boarding up the rest," Hoyt said, still frowning.

"Was it once a hotel or something?" Emma asked.

"That might have been the original plan," Hoyt said, "but the community of Wellington died when the railroad came through twenty miles to the south. I still can't believe anyone has moved in there with the idea of staying."

In the silence that followed, Tanner said, "The place has a dark history. I had some friends who went out there one night. They said they heard a baby crying and when they left they were chased by a pickup truck that disappeared at the edge of town. Just disappeared."

"I've heard stories about the Phantom Truck," Logan said.

Emma laughed. "Oh, posh. You aren't trying to tell me that the place is haunted or something silly like that." She glanced around the table. "Hoyt?"

Her husband sighed. "Let's just say that if a building can be haunted, it would be that one. The Wellingtons had their share of tragedies."

"Ghosts are said to have been born out of tragedy," Logan added and grinned mischievously.

Emma shook her head and turned to Marshall. "What do these people who have moved in look like?"

"I only saw one of them," he said, then remembered the image he'd seen behind the woman and felt a chill snake up his spine. "She *could* have been a ghost."

Emma shot him a disapproving look. "I'm asking if they seem like decent enough people and if they do, I think as their only neighbor you should go over there, introduce yourself and be neighborly. I'll bake something for you to take." She was already on her feet.

Hoyt was shaking his head. "You might want to get the lay of the land before you do that. Who knows who might have moved in there? We've had trouble with drug runners from Canada, escaped prisoners from Deer Lodge, criminals crossing the border through some barbed-wire fence and heading for the first house they see. Until you know who you're dealing with—"

"Hoyt!" Emma chastised. "I'm sure all those instances were rare. I've read the local paper. There is hardly ever any crime up here. And Marshall is no fool. He'll go over and meet them and make up his own mind. I'm sure they're fine people if they're remodeling the place and determined to live here."

They all loved Emma's positive attitude, no matter how naïve. But Marshall found himself poking at his food, his appetite gone as he remembered how his horse had spooked—not to mention his own reaction to what he'd seen just inside that balcony.

Supper at Wellington Manor was served in the warm kitchen at a long, old table with mismatched chairs and dishes. The casserole that Carolina had fixed was delicious, and Alexa did her best to relax.

Carolina was a twenty-something, soft-spoken, pretty woman with blond hair, green eyes and porcelain skin. Her father, Sierra had said by way of introduction, had made his fortune in the hotel business. Carolina seemed shy and clearly embarrassed by Sierra's introduction.

Her husband, Archer, was boisterous and big, a body-builder who apparently had been a football star until an injury had sidelined him. His father was a producer in Hollywood, his mother a lawyer.

The other couple, Gigi and Devlin, seemed cut from the same expensive cloth, both with parents who had retired to Palm Desert, California. Gigi's long white-blond hair was pulled up in a ponytail, making her blue eyes seem even larger, her tiny nose all the more cute. A slender, athletic-looking young woman, she was in her twenties but could have passed for sixteen with her sweet, innocent face.

Her husband, Devlin, was a beach-boy blond with blue eyes. He laughed when Sierra introduced him as a rich kid whose parents owned a couple of vineyards in northern California. He'd had some wine shipped from home, which he poured with enthusiasm.

The lone wolf of the group was Jayden Farrell, whose father was an unemployed actor in Los Angeles, according to Sierra. Unlike the others, he was thirty-something and apparently hadn't been raised privileged. But he was as movie-star handsome as the others, maybe even more so because there was intelligence behind his blue eyes that Alexa found both appealing and disturbing.

Not only that, Jayden also seemed to set himself apart from this group, watching them almost with amusement. Alexa doubted the rest of them had noticed the disdain for them that she glimpsed in his gaze. What was this single man doing here with these married couples, especially when she sensed he didn't like them?

As the group around the table talked and joked, she and Jayden remained silent, she noted. She listened to them talk about their many university degrees, extended

European trips and the benefits of growing up in sunny California.

None seemed to have professions, at least no jobs that kept them from helping their friends Sierra and Landon with their mansion, Jayden again being the exception. He'd made a point of saying that he'd studied business finance and would have to leave this fall to pursue his career.

The others seemed to see this Montana bed-and-breakfast venture as a lark, a great adventure, something to tell their friends about when they returned to their real lives. Jayden was more serious, which made Alexa all the more curious about his motives for being here.

Through all the laughter and camaraderie during the meal, Alexa found herself studying her brother. If she hadn't known Landon so well, she might have thought he felt at ease with the assembled group, even though his roots were nothing like theirs. It was clear that Sierra had come from their world, though, rather than the one Alexa and Landon had grown up in. This made the reporter in Alexa curious, since Sierra had said she had been raised by a single mother in what she made sound like the Los Angeles projects.

Something was definitely wrong with that story, Alexa thought as she watched Sierra interacting with her friends. There was a gaiety to their stories. These young people had no worries—unlike her brother who seemed to be working hard not to show his.

Alexa also sensed tension within the group but couldn't pinpoint exactly where it was coming from. All she knew for sure was that her brother's forced merriment tonight didn't fool her for a minute. If only their mother was here. Tallulah Cross would have sized up this bunch in an instant and known exactly what was going on.

Alexa hated that she felt bombarded by conflicting sensations in this house. Something was trying to break through the wall she'd built to keep these kinds of sensations out. For years, she'd feared she'd lied as much to herself as she had to her mother and brother. She felt things, things she didn't want to feel. But if she truly had her mother's gift, she was terrified of it, didn't know how to use it and had done everything she could to block it for so long that she had no control over it.

Coming here had been a mistake and yet even as she thought about leaving, she knew she couldn't abandon her brother. Not when she knew something was wrong in this house. He'd said he'd already had a series of accidents. What if he was right about something—or someone—wanting him out of the mansion?

By the time supper was over, Archer had the flushed face of a man who'd consumed more wine than anyone else. Sierra was in a friendly debate with Carolina and Gigi about the best sushi restaurants they'd ever gone to outside of California. Archer and Devlin excused themselves, saying they were going to try to catch the baseball game on television.

Alexa rose to help with the dishes.

"It's Gigi and Landon's turn to do the dishes," Sierra insisted. "Come on. I want to show you the house."

"Go on," Landon said. "I'll catch up with you later."

Alexa had hoped to talk to her brother after supper and wished the two of them could have done the dishes together, but Sierra was determined to show her the house.

"You have to see this," she said as they passed through the huge living area. She pushed open two large carved wooden doors. "The library," she announced with a grand gesture. The books on the shelves had been moved and stacked as if someone had gone through them, the thick layer of dust that coated the room disturbed.

"We have so much to do before the house is restored," she said. "But I love this room and can't wait to get to it."

Closing the doors, Sierra led her down a hallway, pointing out the servants' quarters, most of the rooms empty except for one that Jayden was using. In another wing there was a music room with an old piano, and finally the ballroom.

All of the rooms looked as if a little work had been done in them. Alexa had the feeling, though, that not much was getting done—at least from what she'd seen so far.

"Let's take the back stairs," Sierra said and led Alexa up to a wing of the second floor.

Alexa felt a little turned around and said as much.

Sierra laughed. "It does get confusing. That's why I ask that you not go exploring on your own. It is too easy to get hurt, and who knows how long it would be before anyone found you?" She laughed as if delighted by the size of this place.

Alexa thought of her brother's accidents and wondered how long it had been before he'd been found.

"We are in the north wing. Your room is in the east

wing, Gigi and Dev have a room on the west wing, Carolina and Archer are on the south wing, Jayden's on the first floor in the servants' quarters. His choice," she added quickly. "We decided we might as well stretch out and have our own space."

She remembered at supper how she'd felt the others occasionally studying her with interest. She realized with a start that Sierra had probably told her friends about Landon's sister's "sight." She groaned inwardly at the thought that everyone in this house would be watching her now.

"Jayden's kind of a loner."

Alexa mentioned her surprise that he had wanted to be here with three couples, as Sierra led her along a long, dark hallway.

"He's one of the gang," Sierra said. "I guess I was a little surprised too that he came with us. But we all loved him the moment we met him. Isn't the house in great shape for how old it is?"

"Some relative of yours lived here most recently?" Alexa asked.

"My great cousin lived here until she died," Sierra said. "I never knew her. Most of the rooms were closed off while she lived here. She stayed in one of the maids' rooms downstairs, where Jayden is on the first floor." She chuckled again. "The old maid in the maids' quarters. It's pretty funny. I doubt she even came up to these rooms."

Alexa couldn't help but wonder why Jayden preferred one of the small rooms for maids rather than the opulence—not to mention the views—of an upstairs bedroom. Maybe he didn't hold himself apart only at supper.

As they left the catacomb of rooms and hallways to return to the main hall, she saw that the kitchen was empty. Gigi and Landon had finished the dishes. Alexa couldn't wait to get him alone to talk to him again.

"Do you know where I can find Landon?" she asked.

Sierra shrugged. "I'll tell him if I see him before bedtime."

She got the feeling Sierra had no intention of telling him. "Thank you for the tour."

"My pleasure, although I do wish you had waited until the house was done before coming for a visit," Sierra said.

"Landon asked me to come now."

Her sister-in-law raised a brow. "Did he? I wish he'd discussed it with me first." She smiled and let out a small, humorless laugh. "I guess it isn't that big of a deal. I just wanted everything to be perfect the first time you saw it."

With that, Sierra gave a wave and disappeared down a hallway.

Alexa looked around the huge living room, thinking that her brother had made a mistake calling her. Not only had he upset his new bride, but also, she thought, spotting a Ouija board on the coffee table in front of the huge fireplace, he'd called the wrong person.

Landon would have been much better off trying to reach their mother.

Chapter 3

Sheriff McCall Crawford knew it had been impulsive and no doubt a fool's errand, especially coming here after work. It was dark and late as she pulled into the parking lot at the state mental hospital.

Her husband, Luke, had tried to dissuade her, but after the call she'd gotten from the doctor, she had to make sure for herself—not to mention for the safety of the Chisholm family.

"Why did you fail to mention the extent of Aggie Wells's alcoholism?" the doctor had chided her on the phone when he'd caught her at work earlier. "We almost lost her last night. Had we known of her problem, we would have eased her off the alcohol with the use of drugs—"

"Doctor, I'm sorry. I was completely unaware that

Aggie Wells had an alcohol addiction. Are you sure she wasn't…faking it?"

"You can't be serious! One look at this woman and it would be apparent to anyone that she was most certainly not 'faking it,' as you so delicately put it. A blood test confirmed that the woman is an alcoholic. We don't assume anything around *here*."

McCall had felt confused. "Are you sure we're talking about the same patient?"

"Agatha Wells."

Still something was wrong and McCall felt it.

Now as she climbed out of her car and started into the state mental hospital, she had to see for herself what Aggie Wells was up to. Aggie hadn't exhibited any signs of alcoholism when she'd been in the Whitehorse jail over the past few months.

The doctor didn't know how smart and manipulative this woman was. Nor was he aware of the extremes Aggie would go to in an attempt to get what she wanted. McCall did though, since she'd been the one to arrest her.

A former insurance investigator, Aggie Wells had taken pride in exposing anyone who tried to defraud the company she worked for. But something had happened on one of her first cases, more than thirty years before. It had been the life insurance case of Laura Chisholm, first wife of Hoyt Chisholm, of the Chisholm Cattle Company.

Aggie hadn't been able to accept that Laura Chisholm's drowning had been accidental. And while she couldn't prove it, she also wouldn't give up. When Hoyt's second wife was killed in a horseback riding accident, Aggie again tried to prove murder. Failing that, she'd only become more obsessed. A few years later, when he'd remarried once again and his wife had disappeared, Aggie Wells was determined the woman had been murdered—to the extent it was now believed that Aggie had killed his third wife herself to prove Hoyt Chisholm a murderer by framing him.

Hoyt had gone years after that without marrying, turning all of his attention to raising the six boys he'd adopted. A few months ago he'd met Emma McDougal at a cattlemen's convention in Denver and fallen so hard, that the two ran off to Vegas and married.

Even though she'd lost her job at the insurance company because of her obsession with the Hoyt Chisholm case, Aggie Wells had come back into his life, determined that he wouldn't get the chance to kill another wife. She'd bugged his house, tried to frame him for the murder of his third wife, after her body had mysteriously turned up, and she'd abducted Emma, his new bride.

Fortunately, McCall had stopped her before Aggie could harm Emma. After taking Aggie's statement following her arrest, she claimed that Hoyt Chisholm's first wife, Laura, was still alive, and it was Laura who had killed his other two wives and would soon kill wife number four unless the sheriff didn't set her free to save Emma.

After hearing Aggie's testimony, the county attorney had finally ordered a mental evaluation to see if Aggie Wells was fit to stand trial, and sent her to the state hospital.

"I'm here to see Aggie Wells," McCall said as she

showed her identification at the front desk of the hospital. "Dr. Barsness is expecting me."

"The third door on the right," the receptionist said, pointing down a long hallway.

At her knock, a male voice on the other side told her to come in. A balding, short man looked up from his untidy desk as McCall entered the small office. Dr. Barsness looked busy and irritated. It was clear he thought her visit was a waste of his time and hers. She thought he might be right.

But if Aggie Wells had a drinking problem so extreme that she'd almost died from withdrawal at the mental hospital, then McCall wanted to know why none of them had suspected it during her stay in the Whitehorse jail. Unless Aggie had somehow talked someone at the jail into getting her alcohol behind McCall's back. And if that was the case, the sheriff was bound and determined to find out.

"I won't take but a few minutes of your time," she said as the doctor got to his feet with a heavy sigh. "I just want to see Aggie for myself."

With a shake of his head, he led her down the hallway through several locked doors into a noisy ward and finally to a room at the end of a hall.

He opened the door with a key. "Miss Wells? You have company."

McCall looked into the narrow room. The only furniture was a bed bolted to the wall. A figure lay in the bed, covered with a blanket, face to the wall in a fetal position.

McCall remembered the woman she'd arrested for abducting Emma Chisholm and suspicion of murder.

Aggie was a tall, slender, attractive woman. Also a very intelligent woman with a lot of resources at her disposal and enough knowledge about illegal things to make her dangerous.

"Aggie?" McCall asked as she stepped in. The room had an odd smell to it and she was reminded of a homeless man her deputies had put up in a cell for the night last winter. He'd had that smell. *"Aggie?"*

The woman in the bed rolled over and squinted. "What?"

McCall took a step back, shocked by what she saw. Alcohol and a hard life had ravaged this woman's face, making her appear years older than she was. "You aren't Aggie Wells."

"Yes, I am. My name is Agatha Wells," the woman said. "I used to work as an insurance investigator...."

The sheriff turned to the doctor. "This is not the prisoner I sent you for a mental evaluation. This woman has obviously been coached. Where is Aggie Wells?"

Even as she asked it, McCall was reaching for her cell phone. If Aggie Wells was on the loose, then she had to warn the Chisholms—especially Emma.

Her mother was on her mind as Alexa got ready for bed. Since Tallulah Cross had died a year ago, Alexa's greatest fear had been that her mother would try to contact her from the beyond. To her relief, she hadn't. But in this house she felt vulnerable so it was no wonder she was thinking of her mother, she told herself. She hadn't been able to talk to her brother again. According to Sierra, there was some sort of water leak in the basement and he and the other men had gone down to fix it.

Sierra had said that the "girls" were going to build a fire and have a few drinks before bed. Alexa had excused herself, feigning exhaustion from her long drive. She *was* exhausted but not from the drive. She told herself it was from being in this house with all these people and worrying about her brother.

The truth, she finally admitted when she reached her room, was that her brother was right. This house had a dark history that had been coming at her like a battering ram. While she couldn't say what it was exactly, she could feel the unrest of a house that had known its share of tragedy.

As Alexa turned on a light, chasing the dark shadows back into the far corners of the room, she fought the urge to pack and get away from here as fast as possible. She didn't want to know what was going on in this house. She wanted to go back to her life in Spokane, where no one knew that her mother had been Tallulah Cross, the fortune-teller and infamous psychic.

But she knew she couldn't go anywhere tonight. Tomorrow, she would try to talk her brother into leaving here. If she could get him away from the house…

Her head ached as she stepped through the open French doors to the balcony and looked out on the peaceful landscape. She breathed in the sweet, summer's night air and tried to calm herself. Landon would never leave his wife without reason. Which meant Alexa couldn't leave until she knew that reason or was sure that her brother was safe.

These accidents he'd been having—wasn't it possible that's all they were?

Of course it was. Her brother could be overreacting because of their mother's profession and his DNA. While he apparently hadn't inherited what he and their mother called the "gift," he still had the same genes.

Alexa started to move away from the window when she saw a light in the distance. Another house. Was that where the cowboy lived whom she'd seen earlier?

At a sound outside, she quickly extinguished the lamp. Two figures moved through the deep shadows of the trees out to what appeared to be a pond. She could see the faint moonlight shimmering on a portion of the water's surface through the thick-leafed branches of the trees.

She could make out the shapes of the figures. A man and a woman walked side by side, not touching and staying in the shadow of the trees. Was it only her imagination that they avoided the moonlight because they didn't want to be seen together?

Standing in a dark corner of the balcony, Alexa watched the two stop under a tree. They were talking, facing each other. She couldn't hear their words—only read their body language.

They were arguing. She wondered if it was Archer and his wife. Carolina hadn't seemed happy with all the wine he'd consumed at supper.

But as she watched, she realized the man was taller than Archer and slimmer. Jayden. The argument was growing louder and more violent. Alexa caught snatches of the conversation.

"Stop worrying...no reason to panic."

"You smug bastard."

"Keep your voice down."

"Don't tell me what... I don't know why I ever..."

She heard what sounded like a slap, then another, followed by a small cry. The woman started to leave, but Jayden pulled her back. The two dark figures melted together and the night grew silent again.

Who had the woman been? Alexa hadn't been able to recognize her voice from the distance and hearing only snatches of the conversation. Gigi? Carolina?

With a start, Alexa reminded herself there were three women in this house—all of them about the same size—and all blond.

The woman she'd just seen in Jayden's arms could have been Sierra—her brother's wife.

Marshall had a hell of a time getting to sleep after he got the call from his father about Aggie Wells being on the loose again.

"Are you sure you don't want me to come spend the night at the main house?" he'd asked after hearing that no one knew where Aggie was. The woman was believed to be a killer. She'd abducted his stepmother and done her best to frame his father for murder. Marshall couldn't believe that she'd somehow not just gotten away, but paid some woman to pretend to be her at the mental hospital.

"Don't worry," his father had said. "The doors are locked and the shotgun is beside my bed. Emma and I are fine. The sheriff has a deputy parked outside tonight."

Still, Marshall had felt restless after the conversation with his father. Aggie Wells was crazy. Who knew what a crazy woman would do next?

He'd stood for a long time just looking toward the

east and the faint glow of golden light from Wellington Manor.

"Speaking of crazy," he'd said to his dog, Angus, remembering his earlier impressions. He'd assured himself that the woman he'd seen was real and what he'd seen standing behind the woman at the window had been a trick of the light, no more than a shadow, and that tomorrow morning he was going to ride over there and introduce himself. Emma had insisted on baking a batch of her gingersnap cookies to take before he'd left the house earlier.

He'd finally gone to bed and felt as if he'd only just drifted off when he was awakened with a jolt. Lying in bed listening, he wasn't sure what had brought him out of his sleep so suddenly. He glanced at the clock, surprised it was only an hour or so before daybreak, then glanced toward the open window and darkness beyond—and saw his dog standing there, looking out, the hair on the dog's back sticking straight up. Angus let out a low growl.

"What is it, boy?" Marshall whispered as he slipped out of the bed and padded quietly over to the window. A sliver of moon hung on the edge of the horizon, golden among the canopy of stars. The breeze was scented with the smells of August, golden grasses heavy and ripe with grain.

He loved this time of year because he knew how fleeting it was. Montana was a place of seasons that changed with little notice. One day could be hot and beautiful, the next the temperature would drop and that season would be over. Or after an unusually long winter, the snow would suddenly melt and the air would smell of spring.

His thoughts surprised him because there was almost regret in them. Another summer almost gone. He could feel his life slipping away. Part of the problem, he knew, was that three of his brothers had fallen in love and were talking marriage. He hadn't been aware of a time when all six of them weren't sowing their oats, the wild sons of Hoyt Chisholm.

"I don't see anything," he told the dog and started to head back to bed, no longer concerned about what had awakened him.

The scream made him spin around to the window again. He realized it was what must have awakened him and had Angus on alert.

His gaze went to the Wellington mansion, but all he saw was darkness at first. Then a flash of white caught his eye. A woman was running across the pasture toward his house.

Marshall felt a chill wrap around his neck and tighten at the sight of the same ghostlike woman he'd seen earlier in the second-story window of the mansion.

Unable to move at first, he stood watching her approach. She ran as if the devil himself were at her heels and yet he could see no one, nothing, chasing her.

Hell, he wasn't even sure *she* was real. Maybe he was just dreaming her.

But Angus thought she was real. He let out a bark and tore downstairs as the woman turned to look behind her, stumbled and almost fell and another terrified scream burst from her throat.

Pulling on his jeans, Marshall raced downstairs and

out onto the porch as she emerged from the field and into his yard. He bolted down the porch steps as she stumbled and fell on the patch of grass in front of his house.

She was breathing hard, huge gasps and sobs emitting from her, her body quaking from exertion and whatever had her so terrified. Angus had stopped partway out into the yard and stood as if frozen in midstep, a low growl coming from his throat.

"Stay!" Marshall ordered the dog as the woman staggered to her feet. She wore a thin, white nightgown, her lush body silhouetted against the moon and starlight and more beautiful than he thought possible.

As he rushed to her, she looked up, but her eyes had a strange emptiness to them, as if whatever she was seeing wasn't really there.

Marshall wasn't even sure she was real until she fell into his arms and he felt the weight and warmth of the flesh-and-blood woman.

The nightmares had always been waiting for her the moment Alexa closed her eyes. They had terrified her when she was a child. As she got older, she'd come to accept them, telling herself they weren't real.

But of course they were. Her mother knew, that's why Alexa had often found Tallulah standing over her at night as if gazing at the nightmares like a horror film on television.

"I'm always watching over you," her mother used to say, the words giving her no comfort.

"Why don't you wake me up and hold me like my father used to?" she'd wanted to know. When her father had touched her, she had always awakened from the horrors of her dream.

"They're *your* nightmares, Alexa. You must learn to control them. You have the power—if you choose to use it." Her mother would give her that look that said she suspected Alexa had lied about not having the gift.

Just as the nightmare would end the moment her father awakened her, this one ended the moment the cowboy took her in his arms.

Alexa looked up into his face, felt the lingering effects of her nightmare, the exertion of her run across the pasture toward the only light she'd seen, the shock of finding herself in the cowboy's arms and fainted.

When she came to, she was lying on the cowboy's couch with a cool, damp washcloth on her forehead. His dog, the one she'd seen with him earlier that day, was sitting in front of her, staring at her.

She sat up abruptly, making her head swim, the blanket he'd covered her with falling to her lap.

The dog growled.

She quickly pulled the blanket back up over her thin cotton nightgown, aware of how naked she was beneath it and how big his dog was.

"Don't let Angus scare you," the cowboy said as he came into the room. "I told him to watch you while I got you something to drink." He had a glass of water in one hand and a bottle of beer in the other. He must have realized her fear wasn't just of the dog because he stopped midway into the room.

"I thought you might like some water," he said and stepped forward to offer her the glass. He'd put on a shirt and boots since she'd last seen him. She recalled the feel of his broad, warm, bare chest before she fainted. Just as he must remember the sheerness of her nightgown.

She felt her face heat with embarrassment. She wasn't overly modest but she did hate anyone knowing about her nightmares, and she wasn't in the habit of visiting neighbors half-naked.

"Or you're welcome to the beer," he said. "I don't know about you, but I could use a drink."

She couldn't help but smile at his gentle manner and kind, almost embarrassed, expression. She accepted the glass of water with a "Thank you," and took a sip as he sat down in a chair across from her.

"I see you've met Angus," the cowboy said. "He seems pretty taken with you. I apologize for his manners. But he only stares at people he likes."

She could tell he was trying to make her feel at ease. It was working.

He held his bottle of beer as he looked at her, then as if remembering it in his hand, he took a long drink.

"I'm glad to see you're feeling better," he said, wiping his mouth with the back of his hand self-consciously and she realized she was smiling at him again. There was just something about him. She loved the dark sheen of his longish straight, black hair, the deep, rich hues of his equally dark eyes. His skin was a warmer mocha than her own—hers descending from Gypsies, his, she guessed, from a Native American mother or father.

It surprised her that she wasn't the one feeling self-conscious, since she had on less clothing than he had and had obviously awakened him in the middle of the night, dragging him into one of her nightmares. And yet she didn't. She felt strangely safe here with him. Even the house felt inviting. Is that why she'd run to him in her nightmare?

She'd never been able to remember anything about her nightmares when she'd awakened and had always been glad of that.

"You need to try to remember your dreams," her mother had said many times. "They signify something important either from your past or your future. Stop being afraid of them."

That only had made Alexa more terrified of the nightmares, since she didn't want to see into the future. It also had made her all the more determined to keep them from her conscious mind. She'd become very good at it. Like tonight. She had no memory of what had sent her out into the night.

"I'm sorry. I must have frightened you," she said as he took another drink of his beer and she realized that he was shaken by what had happened. "I must have been screaming?"

He nodded.

Alexa had often awakened in the middle of a blood-curdling scream. The horror and pain in the sound had made her all the more terrified. What in her sub-conscious could frighten her so much? She could only imagine, given the kinds of things her mother used to tell her about the people she read fortunes for.

"Bad dream?"

She nodded, took a deep breath and let it out slowly as she felt her strength coming back into her. The nightmares took something out of her. When she was younger, she sleepwalked a lot, waking up in strange, frightening places.

It had been years, though, since she'd taken off in her sleep. She didn't need to think hard to figure out what had caused the relapse as she glanced out the window and saw Wellington Manor in the distance. The sun was starting to come up, the horizon a fiery red, shafts of light streaking up into the big, dark sky above it.

She turned to look at the cowboy again. "You don't happen to have another one of those beers, do you? I think I could use something stronger myself."

He chuckled as he got to his feet and took her water glass, returning with a bottle of beer and a clean glass. She shook her head when he offered her the glass and noticed his large, callused hands as he twisted off the cap and handed her the cold bottle.

Alexa took a swallow. She couldn't remember the last time she'd had a beer. Especially just before daybreak. It tasted better than anything she could remember ever drinking. "It's wonderful."

He smiled at that as he sat down again. She could see that he wanted to ask her about the nightmare, but was either too polite or too shy. Or maybe too afraid of the answer.

"I suppose we should introduce ourselves," she said, thinking this had to be the strangest way she'd ever met a man. "Alexa Cross."

"Marshall Chisholm," he said, leaning forward to shake her hand. "Nice to meet you." His rough hand felt surprisingly warm even though it was the one he'd been holding his beer bottle in. His dark eyes held that same warmth.

She took another sip of her beer and said into the silence, "I'm a reporter from Spokane visiting my brother, Landon. His wife, Sierra, inherited the Wellington house. He and some of their friends are helping her remodel it."

It was the reporter in her that had her sizing up the situation in as few words as possible, known in journalism as the "nut graph."

Taking her example, he said, "My family runs the Chisholm Cattle Company. I saw you over at the house when I went for a horseback ride yesterday. You were standing on one of the upstairs balconies. I thought you were a ghost."

Alexa laughed. "Then I can well imagine what you thought when you heard me screaming and saw me running across your field."

She had a great laugh and Marshall found himself relaxing as the sun came up behind her through the window and they drank their beers.

He waited, thinking she might tell him about what had sent her out into the night like that, but she didn't. There was something almost exotic about her, the wild, curly dark hair, those amazing violet eyes that pulled him in like a well-thrown lasso, that heart-shaped face. He couldn't help but remember the body he'd seen in the moonlight and starlight.

She was beautiful and she'd ended up on his doorstep. He felt privileged and smiled to himself when he saw that Angus seemed just as smitten with her.

He could have warned the dog though. There was something inaccessible about Alexa Cross. He recognized it because he was like that himself. He was no stranger to the walls that people built to protect themselves. But last night he'd felt as if a part of those walls had come crashing down when she'd stumbled into his arms.

"I should get back before I'm missed," she said as she finished her beer.

He got up to take her empty bottle. "I'll drive you." He could tell she didn't want to put him to any trouble but also didn't want to make the trek back across the pasture. "I've also got some clothes that might fit you...."

"Thank you. I'd appreciate that."

He left her on the couch with Angus watching over her and went upstairs to rummage in his bureau, returning to find her still wrapped in the blanket he'd put over her earlier. As he handed her a flannel shirt, a pair of his jeans, a belt and some knitted slippers someone had given him for Christmas, he pointed to the bathroom off the kitchen.

"I'm sorry, but the clothes are going to swallow you," he said as she, still in the blanket, padded barefoot to the bathroom. "I apologize. That's the smallest I could find."

She came out of the bathroom a few minutes later and handed him his blanket, now neatly folded, along with his jeans and belt. He couldn't help but smile at the sight of her. She'd rolled up the sleeves of his flannel shirt but the hem dropped past her knees.

The knitted slippers were a little floppy but would work. He knew her bare feet had to be sore after running through the pasture the way she had. Just a bad dream? That was a hell of a long way to run in the middle of the night because of a bad dream.

"I couldn't keep the jeans up," she said. "But I will borrow your shirt and slippers. I'll see that you get them back though."

"No hurry," he said, looking forward to seeing her again, even though he'd been around long enough to know that there was something going on with this woman, more than bad dreams.

Chapter 4

The house was quiet as Alexa let herself in. She'd feared that the front door might be locked. Or that someone in the house had heard Marshall's truck as he dropped her off.

But as she stepped inside, she heard no sound of life. It wouldn't have surprised her to learn that the occupants weren't early risers. She hurriedly mounted the stairs and walked the long hallway to her room, making as little noise as possible.

Once inside her room, she finally let out the breath she'd been holding. The last thing she wanted was to have to explain where she'd been or why some neighboring cowboy had brought her home at daybreak with the smell of beer on her breath.

She smiled at the thought of how her brother would react—let alone Sierra—as she started to take off the shirt Marshall had lent her. She caught a whiff of his male scent and slowly lifted the sleeve to her face, breathing him in, her smile widening at the memory of the sweet, bashful cowboy.

Reminding herself of her first instincts about him, the wanton desire and the darkness, she quickly stripped off the shirt, her nightgown and his slippers and headed for the shower. She couldn't explain either sensation she felt. But standing under the spray she let herself admit how much she'd enjoyed the handsome cowboy, his home and even his dog.

Later, after she'd dressed in a blouse and skirt and sandals, Alexa made her way downstairs to the empty kitchen. She'd barely gotten a pot of coffee going when Sierra walked in wearing a robe and slippers. She looked as if she'd just woken up and Alexa couldn't help but notice that her eyes were red and puffy as if she'd been crying.

She was reminded of last night and the fight Jayden had had with one of the women from this house out near the pond.

"Good morning," she said to her sister-in-law.

As Alexa handed her a cup of coffee, Sierra gave a small grunt and dropped into a kitchen chair. Alexa joined her at the table, cradling her cup in her hands and watching Sierra through the steam.

Was it possible her brother had gotten her here under the pretext that the house was haunted and trying to hurt him, but something else entirely was going on and he knew it? Or at least suspected it?

After a few sips of coffee, Sierra seemed to stir. She

blinked as if only then aware of Alexa's presence. "So how did you sleep?"

"Fine." She could feel Sierra's blue eyes boring into her. Did she know about her nightmare last night or her excursion to the neighbor's?

"I put a down comforter on your bed. Was it warm enough?"

"It was perfect."

Sierra nodded and took another drink of her coffee, seemingly content with the answers, but Alexa could tell that something was bothering her. What had made her eyes puffy and red this morning?

Alexa got up to refill their cups. When she came back to the table, Sierra was pulling a tissue from her robe pocket and blowing her nose. "Allergies," she said when she saw Alexa looking at her.

Feeling relieved, she started to fill Sierra's coffee cup, but her sister-in-law quickly put her hand over the top to stop her.

"Can you read coffee grounds?"

Alexa felt as if she'd been slapped. She'd suspected Landon had told his wife not only about their mother, but also his suspicions about her as well. Now there was no doubt, was there?

"No."

Sierra looked disappointed. "What about tea leaves?"

"I'm sorry, but I don't read anything but printed words," Alexa said as she refilled her own coffee cup, then motioned to Sierra's, who reluctantly moved her hand to let her fill it. She was trembling with indignation as she took the pot back over to the counter. She knew she shouldn't be so upset, but she couldn't help it.

No one in Spokane knew about her mother or the world she'd come from, and Alexa liked it that way. She had made a point of putting that life behind her the moment she'd left home. Now she felt betrayed by her brother and hurt. She should have realized that he didn't have the same kind of abhorrence about growing up with a fortune-teller for a mother that she did. His friends probably found it amusing, his background unique.

"Landon said you were touchy about your powers and didn't like using them, but I thought since we were family…" Sierra said, pouting.

Powers? Sierra made it sound as if Alexa was a superhero. She started to tell her that there were no "powers" and that knowing too much was a curse. Just like knowing that Sierra was the wrong woman for her brother. But Carolina and Gigi came into the kitchen, followed close behind by Archer and Devlin. As Jayden came in and plopped down in a chair across from Sierra, Alexa watched the three women for a reaction.

Sierra didn't even bother to look up. She was still pouting. Carolina began to pour all of the men coffee as Gigi made herself a piece of toast.

Whoever had been down by the pond last night with Jayden must have patched up things with him. But he'd been with one of them and Alexa had seen how intimate the argument—and the making up—had been.

One of these women was cheating on her husband.

But which one?

With Landon running scared, Alexa feared what she'd witnessed last night was at the heart of what her brother had to fear in this house.

* * *

Emma Chisholm sat across the table from the sheriff, telling herself she wasn't all that surprised that Aggie Wells had managed to get away. Next to her, Hoyt was trying hard to contain his anger. He was scared. She was too.

"I just don't understand how this could have happened," he said to the sheriff.

"That's what we're trying to figure out. Aggie managed to make the switch before the van reached the hospital. That means she had help."

"Who?" Hoyt demanded.

"We don't know yet," the sheriff said.

"This homeless woman who Aggie substituted for herself, she's admitted that she was paid to pretend to be Aggie?" Emma asked.

The sheriff nodded. "Aggie told her exactly what to say. The hospital had no reason to question that the woman wasn't who she was supposed to be. As far as they knew, we sent them a homeless alcoholic named Aggie Wells. If she hadn't gone through alcohol withdrawal and almost died, it is hard to say how long it would have been before we discovered she wasn't Aggie Wells."

Emma shook her head. "You're afraid the real Aggie will come back here."

In the heavy silence that followed, Hoyt said, "If she isn't already here."

The sheriff looked uncomfortable. "I can't keep deputies watching the house."

"Of course you can't," Emma said, cutting off whatever her husband was about to say. "Nor can we live with a deputy parked outside our door."

"There's the chance that Aggie will run as far away as possible," the sheriff said. "I have been in touch with Aggie's brother and niece. They swear they haven't seen her, but I think the niece has. She's just a high school student, so I'm sure she had nothing to do with the switch with the homeless woman, but I think she gave her aunt money to get away. The brother definitely didn't help her. He promised to call if he heard anything from Aggie. I believe him."

"Someone helped her. I've worried all along that she has an accomplice," Hoyt said.

"Aggie made a lot of…maybe not friends, but people she helped over the years. She could have gotten any one of them to help her," the sheriff said. "Her brother said she used to brag about all the people who owed her and would do anything for her if she asked."

Hoyt swore under his breath.

"I'm following up on a lead concerning the driver of the mental hospital van who picked Aggie up in White-horse," the sheriff continued. "He was recently employed at the hospital. Apparently they go through a lot of staff. They had checked this driver's references and they were fine. But when they tried the numbers again, they'd been disconnected."

"Aggie really is incredible, isn't she," Emma said, awed by how Aggie had maneuvered her way out of this. She doubted there was anything the woman couldn't do if she set her mind to it. Including killing her. But if her original intent had been to frame Hoyt for the murder,

B.J. Daniels 63

she was going to have a much harder time doing it herself, given the trouble she was in.

"I just don't believe she wants to harm me," Emma said.

Hoyt scoffed at that. "She's crazy. Who knows what she'll do." He put a protective arm around his wife. "Find her," he said to the sheriff. "Find her before she strikes again. In the meantime, I'm not letting Emma out of my sight."

Emma groaned inwardly at the thought that she was now a prisoner in her own home.

At the breakfast table, Alexa studied her sister-in-law, torn between hoping it wasn't Sierra whom she'd seen with Jayden last night by the pond—and almost wishing it was. The sooner Landon got out of this house—and this marriage—the better off he'd be.

She hated that she felt this way and reminded herself that Landon adored Sierra. It would break his heart if his wife was cheating on him. But she couldn't help wondering if his "accidents" could have something to do with whatever Jayden was up to.

Alexa could feel even stronger undercurrents in this house this morning. Whatever had been at the edge of her consciousness gnawing to get in seemed even more determined as she excused herself and went to find her brother. She feared he needed more help than even he knew.

Sierra had said that she and Landon had taken a room on the north wing of the house, so she headed in that direction, hoping to talk to Landon alone. This house was such a maze of hallways that she quickly got turned around and wasn't even sure she was still headed north. She stopped to get her bearings and froze as she heard crying.

The desolate cry sounded like a woman sobbing her heart out. Goose bumps rippled across her flesh as she moved down the hall, the mournful wail growing louder, until the hallway ended. Stopping at the dead end, she stood listening. The crying seemed to be coming from inside the wall.

In this part of the house, a variety of woods had been used as a wainscoting that rose three-quarters of the way up each wall, with a very ornate, flocked wallpaper pattern on the upper part above it. Alexa touched the wood. It felt like a block of ice. She quickly drew back her fingers, unable to suppress a shudder.

Suddenly the crying stopped as quickly as it had begun. She took a step back and let out a startled yelp as she bumped into someone. Panicked, she spun around, half expecting to see the woman she'd heard crying.

"You heard her, didn't you?" Landon asked as he reached out to steady Alexa.

"Who?" Her heart was pounding. For twenty-three years she'd avoided seeing dead people. Alexa didn't want that to change and yet, in this house, she feared that gnawing presence would win if she didn't get out of here soon.

Her brother gave her an impatient look. "The Crying Woman."

"The Crying Woman?" she repeated, trying to slow her racing pulse.

"That's what we all call her. We've all heard her at one time or another."

Her cynicism won out over her earlier fear. "But none of you have ever seen her, right?"

Landon swore. She could feel anger coming off him in waves and felt her own rise in her. His betrayal still stung. He'd gotten her here under false pretenses, and he'd told his wife and friends about her and their mother.

"How can you mock something you obviously heard as well?" he demanded furiously. "You do realize why you have to pretend it isn't real, don't you? It's like whistling in the dark. Well, sis, there's really something evil out there and you can whistle all you want, but that isn't going to save you. Or me."

She hated how much he sounded like their mother. "Could I have a word with you alone before you go down to breakfast?" She didn't like standing out here in this hallway. Not because she believed there was some crying woman ghost, but because she didn't want their conversation overheard. It was bad enough that the people in this house already knew their family secrets. She didn't want to add fuel to the fire.

He nodded, still clearly angry, but opened a door behind them and led her into the room he shared with Sierra. Like her own room, this one had been decorated with some of the same touches. Only this one had a fireplace, one that had been used recently. She caught the faint hint of smoke and saw that some papers had been burned. The lower corners of several sheets that hadn't fully burned could still be seen in the charred remains.

As she turned, she noticed her brother was limping. "What's wrong with your leg?"

He gave her an impatient look. "Another *accident*."

Her heart lodged in her throat and all her earlier

resentment and anger toward him evaporated. "What happened?"

"I went down to get a glass of milk last night and I fell down the stairs." His tone made it clear that there was more to the story.

"Are you telling me someone pushed you?" she demanded.

"More like some*thing,* but what would be the point in telling *you*? You wouldn't believe me."

"Landon—"

"Alexa," he said, pleading suddenly in his voice, as well as fear. He stepped to her and took her shoulders in his hands. "You can exorcize whatever is wrong in this house. Mother used to—"

"It was a trick. Mother couldn't—"

He pulled free of her again, his face twisted in anguish. "You have always lied about your talents. Don't lie about Mother's. I saw her do amazing things time after—"

"It was all just illusion, Landon." Even as she said it, she knew it wasn't true. But she wished it was. If her mother had no gift, then her daughter couldn't have inherited it.

He stared at her in disbelief. "How can you discredit something that our mother believed in so strongly? It wasn't just what she did for a living." He moved to the window, turning his back to her as if he couldn't bear to look at her. "She wanted you to have what she did. She really did see it as a gift. While you…" He turned to face her again, his face twisted in pain. "You mock something I would give anything to have."

"Don't say that." She hurriedly crossed herself, the motion, like the words, coming before she could stop them.

His eyes narrowed. "You're afraid of it. That's why you block it. You think it's something evil."

"No, I told you—"

"Stop lying. You profess to be such a skeptic, a true cynic, but you just proved otherwise. What else are you lying about?"

"Landon—" Alexa reached for her brother, but he took a step back.

"I got you here because I desperately need your help. Don't even bother to tell me that you don't have the sight because I have *never* believed you. Maybe you fooled Mother—"

"Wouldn't that prove that she couldn't see as well as she pretended?"

He continued as if she hadn't spoken. "I know you, Alexa. You are the only person who can help me. Are you going to keep denying that you can't until it's too late?"

"Landon, I can see that something is wrong, but are you sure it isn't something more personal going on in this house?"

"Personal?" His face twisted into a mask of pain. "You think this is about Sierra and me? You think she had something to do with my accidents?" He let out a choked laugh. "I know that you don't like her. That's it, isn't it? But that you'd think she would try to hurt me..."

"Landon—" Alexa reached for him again but he quickly sidestepped pass her and stormed out of the room.

She started to go after him but Sierra suddenly appeared in the doorway, blocking her exit.

* * *

Marshall felt a little guilty for what he was doing. But he couldn't quit thinking about last night and Alexa Cross. She worried him a little. No, more than a little.

"Don't be looking at me like that," he said to his dog lying a few feet away. Angus sighed and closed his big, brown eyes as if to say, "Do whatever it is you have to do and leave me out of it."

"Oh, come on, you were as taken with her last night as I was," Marshall reminded the dog as he typed Alexa Cross into the computer and held his breath. Her name came up dozens of times. To his relief they were all pertaining to articles she'd written as a reporter for several newspapers during her career, including in Spokane, Washington, her latest job.

He felt relieved. She *was* a reporter, just as she'd said. Had he thought she'd lied about that? No. So what was bothering him?

Marshall laughed at the thought. A woman comes screaming across your pasture out of the darkness in the middle of the night dressed only in a thin—very thin—nightgown and faints in your arms. You have to wonder, right?

He moved the mouse down the list, taking note of the articles she'd written. Interesting, but nothing unusual or odd about any of them. In fact, the ones he called up and read were heartwarming stories about people. She had a nice writing style; he felt her compassion in the words she used.

She'd just had a bad dream last night, as he'd suspected.

His relief slipped away like fog as he recalled the

first time he'd seen her. He could keep telling himself that it had just been a trick of the light. That there hadn't been anyone standing behind her. And if there had been, there was nothing…evil lurking there.

But he'd seen something that wasn't…of this earth.

And so had his horse. They'd both reacted to it. So how did he explain that away?

Marshall logged off the computer and checked his watch. He'd already wasted most of the morning, and he did have the cookies Emma had made to take to his new neighbors.

Grinning, he headed for the shower. Wouldn't hurt to take a day off. His father and brothers wouldn't miss him and it was only neighborly to stop over at the Wellington house and make sure Alexa was all right.

As he stepped under the warm spray of the shower, Marshall couldn't shake the feeling that Alexa was in some kind of trouble and that, more than a bad dream, it was what had sent her running across the pasture last night—as if running for her life.

Sierra stepped into the room, closed the door and leaned against it, making it clear that neither of them was going anywhere.

"What are you doing here?" she asked.

"Landon let me in—"

"Not this room. This house. Montana. What are you really doing here?" Sierra asked. "Did he tell you the house is haunted and you've come to exorcise our ghosts?"

"Don't be ridiculous. My brother—"

"Is it so ridiculous?" She raised an eyebrow. "I saw

your reaction to the house. You might be able to fool Landon, but you can't fool me."

Alexa took a step toward her. "I'm not having this conversation with you again."

Sierra didn't move. "You shouldn't be here. Landon and I are technically still on our honeymoon."

Alexa almost laughed. "And that's why you invited five other people along?"

"They're friends."

Alexa felt her ire rise. "And I'm family."

"Yes, but it is clear that doesn't mean as much to you as it does to some," Sierra said. "I wouldn't say anything but you're upsetting Landon."

"He was upset before I got here. How many *accidents* has he had while in this house?"

Sierra rolled her eyes. "Who knew he was such a klutz, but then it is an old house and dangerous if you don't know what you're doing. Landon doesn't have much experience when it comes to handyman work."

As if the rest of this bunch were card-carrying finish carpenters.

"There isn't anyone here who might want to hurt him?" Alexa asked.

Sierra met her gaze with a steely-blue coldness that chilled Alexa to her soul. "I hope you didn't come here to cause trouble for me and your brother."

"I think there is already trouble enough in this house."

Her sister-in-law sighed. "I just came up to find you and inform you that breakfast is ready. You'd hate yourself if you missed out on Gigi's margarita pancakes." With that she turned and left the room.

Alexa stood for a moment, trying to still the apprehension she felt for her brother. He had no idea whom he'd married. But Alexa feared she did.

Emma had been going crazy ever since the sheriff had told them that Aggie Wells was missing. They didn't need to tell her that Aggie might be dangerous. The woman had abducted her only a few months ago.

But Emma couldn't live her life in fear, and she especially couldn't stand her husband hovering over her all the time. She knew Hoyt must be going crazy too. He needed to be out on the ranch working with his sons. It's what kept him young.

"Just let me go to the grocery store alone," she'd pleaded after the sheriff left; but, of course, he wasn't having any of it.

By the time they'd reached town, though, she knew she had to talk him into dropping her off at the grocery store while he ran his errands.

"It's the grocery store in broad daylight," she'd argued. "You don't really expect Aggie Wells to attack me in there, do you?"

"I don't know what she might do and neither do you," Hoyt said. "I told you I didn't want you out of my sight until she's caught."

"And what if she is never caught?"

He shook his head. "I just don't want anything to happen to you."

"I know," she said, touching his handsome face. "I appreciate your concern." What she didn't add, but wanted to, was that she couldn't keep living like this.

This wasn't Hoyt's fault. Not unless you believed that he'd killed his other wives, which she didn't.

Even Aggie Wells, the former insurance investigator who'd been after him all these years, no longer believed Hoyt was a killer. Instead, she had another theory— one that had almost gotten her locked up in the mental hospital. Aggie was now convinced that Hoyt's first wife, Laura, had faked her accidental drowning and, being the jealous woman she apparently was, had become determined that Hoyt would never find happiness with another woman.

And that was why everyone thought Aggie was crazy. With the exception of Emma, who thought that was as good a theory as any.

The sheriff and Hoyt, though, believed Aggie was several bricks shy of a load and a dangerous, deranged murderer.

As Emma pushed through the doors into the town grocery, she shoved all thought of Aggie to the back burner and grabbed a cart. It just felt so good to be alone for a few minutes.

The town was small enough that she felt safe. She started in the produce aisle. The selection was pretty basic, but she loved fresh vegetables and began to load the cart. She nodded at other shoppers, spoke to a few and, after getting everything she needed plus some junk food she shouldn't have, she started through the check-out.

Suddenly she felt someone watching her. As she looked out through the large plate-glass window at the front of the store, she felt a jolt of shock rocket through her.

Aggie Wells was standing across the street, staring right at her.

Her heart dropped—along with the half gallon of milk she was unloading from her cart—as her gaze locked with Aggie's.

A van went by, blocking her view. Her initial shock changed into anger. As long as Aggie was on the loose, Emma was going to be a prisoner in her own home and she was sick of it.

Stepping over the spilled milk, she ran out through the exit and into the parking lot. As she started across the street, she was almost struck by a pickup. The driver hit his brakes, missing her by inches, as she rushed across the street to where she'd seen the woman watching her.

Aggie was gone.

Emma stood, breathing hard, heart racing. She leaned over to catch her breath, hands on her knees, telling herself how foolish she'd been to chase after Aggie alone, when she saw the envelope lying at the edge of the sidewalk.

Written on it was one word: *Emma.*

Emma looked around, thinking Aggie couldn't have gone far. But there was no sign of her.

She picked up the envelope from the ground and stuffed it into her pocket as Hoyt drove up in the ranch pickup.

He gave her a surprised, questioning look that quickly turned to panic. Hoyt was out of the pickup in an instant and pulling her in his arms. Emma felt sick with guilt that she had resented this man's protection.

His gaze scanned the parking lot. "Where is she?"

Emma shook her head. He'd known the moment he saw her so there was no point in trying to lie her way out of it. "She got away."

He lowered his gaze to his wife and swore under his breath. "And the groceries?"

She glanced toward the store where a handful of people were gathered at the window, staring out at them.

"Everyone is going to think I've lost my mind," Emma said.

"They aren't the only ones," Hoyt said as he gripped her arm. "Let's go get our groceries."

Alexa had no interest in margarita pancakes, but she feared that if she didn't go down for breakfast, it could make things worse for her brother. She knew Sierra would use anything she could to put a wedge between her brother and her. The woman felt threatened. No doubt because Alexa saw through Sierra's act and she knew it.

She had worried for some time that part of Landon's allure had been the money their mother had left them. Remodeling this huge, old place was going to cost a fortune—even with free labor. Although Alexa hadn't seen much work getting done so far.

As she started to follow Sierra into the kitchen, she saw her brother seated at the kitchen table, his head down as he cut into his pancakes. He looked up as Sierra slid into a chair next to him and put her hand on his arm.

"Is everything all right?" he asked.

Sierra gave a little pout then looked over at Alexa.

Landon frowned as he followed her gaze, making it

clear that he knew his sister had said something to hurt his wife's feelings.

Alexa felt her stomach roil as she saw how easy it was for Sierra to manipulate her brother. Love was definitely blind.

The loud doorbell startled everyone, including Alexa. Everyone looked toward the front door with a mixture of surprise and suspicion. Apparently they didn't get many visitors.

Since she was closest to the front door, she went to answer it. As the door swung open, she saw Marshall standing on the front step, looking up at the house and clearly giving it a mixed review. She felt herself smile, relieved to see him, and completely agreeing with his sentiments about the house that were written on his expressive face.

"Hello," she said, breathing in the morning air and his freshly showered scent.

He smiled. "Hello again." He removed his Stetson and handed her a small basket filled with what smelled like gingersnaps. "From my stepmother. A housewarming present." He turned the brim of the hat in his fingers, looking more than a little nervous. She liked his large hands, the strong, well-shaped fingers, the pads callused from hard ranch work.

She saw him look past her, peering into the house almost warily and yet with obvious curiosity. "I'd invite you in, but I was just on my way into town to pick up a few things." Not exactly true, but once said, she realized how badly she needed a break from this house and everyone in it. Also she knew Sierra would have a fit if she invited him in. And, even if she had wanted to share him, she had a pretty good idea of what the others' reaction would be to this cowboy.

Marshall brightened. "Great, how about lunch then?"

Her first instinct was to turn down his offer. She tended to keep people at a distance. It was easier that way. "Well, I do owe you after last night," she said, keeping her voice down so the others in the kitchen wouldn't hear.

He grinned. "I actually had a good time last night."

"Me too," she said, realizing that as strange as it was, it was true. "All right," she agreed. It was almost lunchtime and the last thing she wanted was margarita pancakes. "Why don't I follow you into town? Just give me a few minutes?"

As she glanced toward Marshall's pickup parked next to the house, she saw his dog sitting in the passenger seat and found herself smiling as she ran up to get her keys. There was nothing quite like a man and his dog.

"I'm having lunch in town," she said, sticking her head into the kitchen. She got the impression they'd all been holding their combined breaths, listening to every word anyway.

"You're missing margarita pancakes," Sierra said.

"My apologies to the chef," she said to Gigi, who obviously couldn't have cared less what Alexa had to eat.

But Sierra was pouting again. Alexa shot a look at her brother. How could Landon not notice his wife's obsessive need to control everyone around her?

Chapter 5

Alexa put her sister-in-law out of her mind as she drove through the rolling prairie, the morning sun warm, the sky a breathtaking blue. When she'd driven through Whitehorse yesterday, she hadn't been paying much attention. Landon had given her directions to Wellington Manor, and she'd been more worried about missing her turn than looking around the small town.

Now, though, as she drove in behind Marshall, she took in the small Montana town. It seemed a lot like others she'd driven through on her way here.

Situated around the railroad, the main drag faced the depot. She saw several bars, a clothing store, a hardware store, and a bank and electronics shop before she parked diagonally across from the depot and small town park.

"We had a fire last winter," Marshall said, when she

asked about a newly graded area between two of the
buildings. "Took out five businesses."

"That must have been a devastating blow to a town
this size," she said.

"Fortunately, they all relocated into vacant buildings.
Unfortunately, the population's dropping every year,
like most small towns in this part of Montana," he said
as he led her down the street to a restaurant. "But we
also had a couple of new businesses start up this year,
and some young couples are coming back because it's
such a great place to raise a family."

Alexa smiled at his obvious love for this town. She
could feel his close relationship with the land and this
part of Montana. She liked that about Marshall Chisholm. She liked him.

The sign over the door of the restaurant read Northern Lights. He held the door for her and she stepped in,
instantly assaulted by wonderful smells.

A young woman stuck her head out of the kitchen to
tell them they could sit anywhere they liked.

"Thanks, Laci," Marshall said and explained on the
way to their seat that Laci Duvall and her husband,
Bridger, owned the restaurant and now had two young
children. Her twin sister, Laney, also had two children
pretty much the same ages and the rumor around town
was that they were both pregnant again. "It must be a
twin thing," he finished.

They walked over to a table by the window in time
for Alexa to see a passenger train stop on the tracks
just across the street in front of the small depot. By
the time they'd sat down, the train had already loaded

the half-dozen passengers waiting by the tracks and chugged off again.

"So how are you doing today?" Marshall asked.

"Better than I was last night. I apologize for waking you up and scaring you," she said.

"You looked more scared than I was."

She nodded and chewed at her lower lip for a moment. "I get nightmares sometimes, especially when I sleep in strange places."

"Nothing much stranger than that house your brother lives in."

She laughed. "You don't know the half of it."

A young waitress brought them menus and told them about the lunch special, which they quickly ordered: trout ravioli with the Northern Lights famous marinara sauce, salad and homemade garlic bread.

The owner sent out a carafe of red wine on the house, calling to Marshall to give his family her best and enjoy their lunch.

Alexa did. Both the food and company warmed her and she found herself opening up to this man she'd only just met. It wasn't like her. But last night had definitely made her drop her guard around him.

"You have *five* brothers?" She couldn't imagine what that must be like and said as much.

"It's just you and your brother?"

"He's my half brother. We have a mother in common." She looked away, hoping he didn't ask about their mother.

"All six of us are adopted, three of us having the same mother and father," he said. "My mother was Norwegian, my father Assiniboine. Three of my brothers are triplets. They're blond and blue-eyed. We make quite the family."

She loved hearing what it was like growing up in a large ranch family. "It must be wonderful."

He laughed at that. "You haven't seen the way we fight. But let anyone else pick on one of us and he'll have all six to contend with."

At his prompting, she told him about her job at the newspaper. "I love interviewing people, writing their stories. Mostly I do feature writing, no hard news." She liked upbeat stories and was glad to let someone else write about fires and crime and misery. "Don't laugh, but I've always wanted to write children's books."

"I'm in awe," Marshall said. "I hate to write a check."

They both laughed and he asked, "So where did you grow up?"

"California." Fortunately the waitress brought them Laci's famous flourless chocolate cake for dessert and Alexa was able to change the subject. "I haven't eaten this much ever," she said as she took another bite of the cake. "It was all so delicious."

"Laci will be glad to hear it. Where in California?"

"The Laguna Beach area. So tell me about the Chisholm Cattle Company," she said, steering the conversation away from her once again.

But she had the feeling that Marshall wasn't fooled. Nor had she curbed his curiosity. His interest in her both flattered her and scared her. She had learned the hard way that once men found out who her mother had been, they suddenly felt uneasy around her and didn't call again.

She liked Marshall, but she was only here for a few

days and she had her hands full back at the house. She warned herself not to get too close. Or worse, let him.

"I really need to get back to the house," she said at the thought of the trouble her brother was in.

Marshall looked disappointed, but quickly asked for the check. "Maybe we'll see each other again. I'll pick up more beer at the store in case you have another bad dream. Or just want to talk some night."

Alexa felt the pull of this man and quickly thanked him for lunch. "Please thank your stepmother as well for the cookies." As they left the restaurant, she told herself she wouldn't see Marshall Chisholm again before she left town, and it was probably just as well.

She recalled her first impression. Desire and darkness. While she felt drawn to him, she didn't want him getting involved in whatever was going on at Wellington Manor. The desire she felt scared her. But the darkness terrified her. She feared it was because he had crossed her path.

As he tipped his Stetson, climbed into his truck next to Angus and pulled away, she couldn't help feeling a sense of regret.

Marshall glanced back in his pickup's rearview mirror. Alexa Cross was still standing next to her car, watching him drive away. Something in her expression reminded him of the first time he'd seen her standing at the window—and whatever that had been behind her.

He also recalled the way she hadn't invited him in this morning. That hadn't been like her. Just as she had seemed to want to get away from that house as quickly as possible.

"Something's wrong over there," he said to Angus, who'd curled up on the seat for his usual nap on the ride home.

He didn't like the idea of Alexa staying at that house, but he reminded himself that it wasn't any of his business. He had cattle to help move today and a list a mile long of things to do at his house later, and yet his thoughts kept returning to her.

"What do you even know about this woman?" his brother Tanner asked as they moved cattle that afternoon. It was one of those amazing August afternoons when the sky is a crystalline blue stretched from horizon to horizon, with only a few white clouds moving in the breeze.

The sun felt hot against his back as they rode across the same rolling prairie that thousands of buffalo had once roamed. Marshall took off his hat to mop his brow with his sleeve. What *did* he know about Alexa Cross?

"She's a newspaper reporter, won some awards for her writing, has a half brother who's married to a Wellington." That was the extent of what he knew—at least on the surface.

He also knew her laugh, knew the way she felt in his arms, knew that she was up for a beer at sunrise and that something had her running scared.

"I like her," he said defensively.

Tanner laughed. "I gathered that since she's all you've talked about this entire cattle drive." He shook his head. "I never thought I'd see the day you'd get hung up on a city woman, let alone a *reporter*."

"She wants to write children's books," he called after

Tanner, as his brother spurred his horse and took off in a cloud of dust after a couple of straggling calves.

Marshall sat back on his horse, watching the undulating ocean of Black Angus cattle moving across the prairie. Tanner thought he had fallen for this woman? Marshall laughed at the thought, then sobered as he realized he'd never felt this way about any other woman— or so quickly. Both thoughts sent up red flags.

He'd dated, like his brothers, sowing his wild oats but never getting serious about anyone. Then one by one, his brothers were starting to fall in love. He was a little insulted that Tanner had thought he would never see the day that Marshall fell in love.

"All it takes is meeting the right person," Emma had said once about how she and Hoyt had fallen in love. "You know immediately."

Marshall heard a shrill whistle, saw his brother Dawson pointing to some calves that had fallen behind. He spurred his horse to ride after them, embarrassed that he'd been sitting on his horse woolgathering instead of working. He'd get a ribbing about it later.

But as he thought about Alexa Cross, he knew he had worse problems than a little ribbing from his brothers.

Alexa felt better after her lunch with Marshall. He was so down-to-earth, so…normal. She smiled at the thought. She'd aspired to be normal, or what she had thought of as a child as normal. She really hadn't had much to base it on—other than her father.

He had been so normal, though, he hadn't been able to take living with Tallulah and her "gift" any longer. Is that another reason Alexa hadn't wanted to be like her mother? And why she kept her past life secret? Because she doubted any man could live with a woman like that.

As she drove up the tree-lined lane that led to Wellington Manor, she felt her earlier calm evaporate.

There was an ambulance parked in front of the house.

She pulled her SUV up next to it and hurried toward the front door as an EMT was coming out. "What's happened?" she cried, thinking of her brother and his recent series of accidents.

"Just a minor concussion," the EMT said as he loaded his gear into the back of the ambulance. "He's going to be fine."

A minor concussion? Alexa ran into the house, crying her brother's name. She came to an abrupt stop as Landon stepped out of the kitchen with half of a sandwich in his hand and a frown on his handsome face.

"Why are you screaming for me?" he demanded.

"I thought..." The rest of her words died in her throat. She took a shaky breath as she saw several of the others looking at her as if she'd lost her mind. "I saw the ambulance."

Her brother seemed to realize exactly what she'd thought, and said, "Jayden. A pipe fell in the basement. He has a slight concussion. He'd just come over to help me when it happened."

She had the feeling he was enjoying her fear, now that he realized it had been for him. But his look also said, "It could have been me, no thanks to you."

"So you're still working on that leak in the basement?" she asked because she couldn't think of anything else to say.

"Upstairs bedroom. I got it fixed," Landon said and

turned back to the kitchen where everyone had been having a late lunch.

She wondered how they ever got anything done as she tried to still her racing pulse. She'd been so sure the ambulance had been here for her brother. As she let out a breath, she felt guilty for her relief that it hadn't been Landon.

"Is Jayden all right?" she asked.

"He'll live," Archer said with apparently little interest. He was reading a book and eating a sandwich and didn't bother to look up.

As she glanced around those sitting at the table, Alexa saw that along with Jayden, the only other person missing was Sierra. She started to ask about her but her brother cut her off.

"Sierra took the first shift to make sure Jayden doesn't fall asleep," Landon said. "So how was *your* lunch?"

"Good." No one at the table seemed in the least bit curious but she continued, "Marshall took me to Northern Lights. The owner makes the best ravioli I've ever had."

"Marshall Chisholm?" Gigi asked, looking up. "Sierra said he had a house on the other side of the pond. So he's a real cowboy?" she added with a smirk.

"His family ranches. The Chisholm Cattle Company," Alexa said, wanting to defend Marshall but also not wanting to be baited into it.

"That's a big operation," Devlin said with awe. "I heard in town it's the largest working cattle ranch around here. So was your date the owner?"

"One of six sons."

He looked disappointed for her as if she'd missed a real opportunity. Gigi wasn't smirking anymore, at least.

"I need to get back to work," Landon said as he finished his sandwich.

"Oh, I was hoping we could visit for a moment," Alexa said as he started past her.

"Archer and I promised Sierra we would have the bathroom done before supper," he said as Archer got to his feet as well. "Find something to amuse yourself. We can visit later."

"Don't forget," Gigi spoke up. "Sierra said she had something fun planned for tonight after supper."

Alexa had to bite her tongue not to groan. "Why don't you come up to my room when you get done with your jobs. Maybe we can talk before supper," she said to her brother.

She could tell he was still angry with her. Unreasonably, she thought with irritation. But then another person had been hurt in this house. Jayden this time. She wondered though if the *accident* had been meant for Landon. Or if that was all it had been, an accident.

As she watched her brother head off down the hall toward the servants' quarters, where his wife was telling stories to Jayden to keep him awake, she knew he'd gone to check on Sierra before going upstairs to work in the bathroom.

How could she make him see what she suspected was going on in this house? She realized there was only one way.

As she started up the stairs, she saw a bucket of tools someone had left in the corner. Taking a few items she didn't think would be missed, including a flashlight, she hurried up the steps to the second floor.

Alexa suspected that someone in this house wanted everyone to believe Wellington Manor was haunted. For what reason, she had no idea yet. But for now, it was time to expose the Crying Woman for the fake she was. At least it would be a start in exposing whatever else was going on inside Wellington Manor.

Emma felt badly about not telling Hoyt everything after how scared he'd been at the grocery store. But she told herself she didn't want to upset him further. He'd hardly said a word all the way home, and she could tell he was stewing in a brew of anger and fear, all of it directed at Aggie Wells.

When they reached the ranch house, he said, "Stay here. Keep the doors locked. I want to check the house."

Emma started to argue but one look at his expression warned her to keep her mouth shut.

She watched him take the shotgun from behind the seat in the pickup, close the truck door and stand outside until he heard her lock the cab, before he walked toward the house.

Emma waited until he went inside before she pulled the envelope from her pocket. Her fingers were trembling.

All the way home from Whitehorse, she'd been going over what had happened and what it all meant. Aggie was still in town. She'd taken a huge chance showing herself the way she had. What if Hoyt had been in the parking lot and seen her?

Had Aggie followed them from the ranch? How else

would she know where they were going? With a start, Emma realized that she had become a creature of habit, shopping every Wednesday after lunch when the ads came out in the newspaper.

Emma recalled what Aggie had told her about why she'd been such a good insurance investigator. "I become my subjects. I learn everything about them. I dress like them, listen to the same music, wear the same perfume."

That was why Aggie had known Emma would run out of the grocery store after her. That frightened Emma more than anything else, because there was a good chance she was dealing with a murderer who knew her too well.

Emma carefully opened the envelope and took out the single sheet of paper. Had Aggie planned to hand this to her? Or had she always planned to leave it on the sidewalk?

Not that it much mattered. Aggie had taken a huge risk getting it to her. That alone showed an unsettling desperation. This woman was a wanted, escaped criminal who just wouldn't give up in her quest.

And that quest apparently was either to save Emma or kill her. No one knew for sure which it was, Emma included.

She unfolded the page of plain white paper.

Emma,
I've found Laura Chisholm. I can prove it. We have to talk. But if you go to the sheriff or do anything that will alert Laura, it will mean your life.
Aggie

Under her name she had written what Emma recognized as a local cell phone number.

The front door of the house opened. Emma hurriedly refolded the paper and stuffed it and the envelope into her jacket pocket as Hoyt returned to the pickup.

"The house is empty," he said as he put his shotgun back up on the rack behind the seat. "Are you all right?"

Telling herself she just wasn't ready to talk to him about this, she said, "I guess it is just starting to sink in."

He nodded, looking relieved. "The woman is crazy and dangerous and I wish I didn't have to keep telling you that."

Emma nodded as she got out of the pickup. She wished she wasn't so stubborn and independent and hard to get along with too.

"She thinks my first wife is still alive," Hoyt said as if Emma didn't know that as well.

"What if she is?" Emma said and instantly regretted it when his face clouded over.

"I saw Laura go into the water," Hoyt said, pain making his voice sound hoarse. "She hated water, didn't know how to swim well and with the storm and the waves…" His voice broke. "I saw her go under, Emma. I almost drowned trying to save her. There is no way she could have swum to shore from the middle of the Fort Peck Reservoir…." He ran out of words again and gave her an impatient look before stalking into the house.

Emma told herself he was right, of course. But she reached into her pocket to make sure the note was still there. But she couldn't help thinking about what Aggie had written. She had *proof* Laura was alive. What if it was true? What if Aggie wasn't the killer at all? What if it really was Hoyt's first wife back from the grave?

What scared Emma was that while Hoyt was trying to protect her from Aggie Wells, there could be someone more dangerous out there who wanted her dead—and none of them would see Laura Chisholm coming.

Alexa ran her fingers along the expensive wood of the wainscoting, starting from the place where she'd first heard the Crying Woman and moving down the hall to where it ended—and the crying had stopped.

She told herself that someone must have activated the crying with some sort of device this morning after she'd said she was going upstairs to see her brother, because she heard nothing now. But then no one knew she was up here.

But who had turned it off? Or was it on a timer? Either way, someone in this house had set up the device. Not hard to believe, given this new generation that was raised with computers and all the other high-tech toys.

But why would anyone go to the trouble? Why make her and the rest of the people in this house believe it was haunted? She feared the reason had something to do with Landon. He believed the house was trying to either scare him away—or kill him.

Alexa knew someone in this house wanted him to leave. Sierra? That made no sense, since she was the one who was pushing to remodel the house and run it as a bed-and-breakfast. Unless she'd decided the marriage wasn't going to work out and she knew about Landon's inheritance. Their mother had left them a lot of money.

Knowing her brother, he'd probably told Sierra about it long before their nuptials.

Alexa moved quietly down the wall, feeling her way along. She wasn't even sure what exactly she was looking for. There didn't seem to be anything along the wall. Nor were there any doors on this side of the hall other than one at the very end. She tried the door. Of course it was locked. Why have a locked room?

She was about to find out. Using the screwdriver, she was able to open the old skeleton-key lock. The door swung in as if on a gust of wind. The room appeared to be a broom closet—at least at first.

Alexa stepped in and, turning on the flashlight, searched for a secret door. She found the panel in the wall easily enough, since she knew it had to be there. It swung in. Musty air wafted out.

As she shone the flashlight into the dark, dusty space, she found a long, narrow aisle that ran adjacent to the hallway outside this room. What surprised her were two sets of stairs—one that went up to the third floor, the other down to the ground floor and a door outside. A secret passage—and another way out of the house.

Sierra hadn't taken her up to the third floor during her tour. She'd made the excuse that it was unfinished and full of spider webs and storage items. Alexa would have loved to see for herself, but she had to find the Crying Woman first.

At a sound from the hallway, she froze, listening. When she didn't hear anything more, she shone the flashlight down the narrow aisle behind the stairway. No spider webs, but footprints in the dust. She wasn't the first person to squeeze through the opening and into the space behind the wall.

Alexa hadn't gone far when she found the wires and small speakers. She was looking for what was being used to operate the Crying Woman, when she heard the same sound from the hallway she'd heard earlier.

Only this time, she realized it wasn't coming from beyond the wall. It was from a person in the space with her.

She swung around with the flashlight, but too late. The blow knocked her into the wall. She smacked her head hard, stars dancing in her vision as the flashlight fell from her hand, hitting the floor with a thud just an instant before Alexa joined it.

Chapter 6

Alexa woke in her bed to find everyone standing around her. Her brother was holding her hand and looking scared.

"I'm going to have to insist you not explore this house alone again," Sierra said, her voice shrill. "You could have been killed. If Archer hadn't found you…" She looked as if she was going to cry.

Landon put his arm around his wife but still held tight to Alexa's hand. "Alexa's all right," he said, trying to reassure his wife, but he looked at his sister for confirmation.

"I'm fine," she said, although her head ached and for a few moments, she couldn't remember what had happened. As it came back, she said, "Archer found me?"

The big man nodded. "I was coming down the hall when I saw you lying on the floor at the end of it."

"You found me out in the hallway?" she asked, knowing that couldn't be true. The last thing she remembered was that she had been behind the wall.

"I can't imagine what you were doing in the north wing to begin with," Sierra said.

"I'm sure she probably just got turned around. Are you sure you're all right?" Landon asked again as he saw her check her clothing.

Just as she'd thought, she was covered in dust. As she looked up, she saw all of them watching her. One of them had carried her out of that space behind the wall and left her in the hallway to be found. She wanted desperately to ask Archer how it was he had just happened along when he did. Either he was lying or someone had sent him up to that hallway knowing he would find her.

"I'm just a little tired," Alexa said, not wanting to question Archer in front of the rest of them.

"You're sure she doesn't have a concussion?" Sierra asked her husband.

But it was Jayden who answered. "I checked her pupils. They seem fine. Nothing like mine yesterday."

"Remodeling this house ourselves was a mistake," Sierra cried. "I can't bear to see anyone else get hurt. Landon, I should have listened to you. It's too dangerous."

"Don't you dare back out now," Carolina said. "Everyone is fine and this is *our* project. We've done too much work for you to make us stop now."

"She's right," Jayden said. "We're all invested in this old place. Let us finish."

Alexa saw Sierra weaken and suspected she hadn't been serious to begin with. "If I hired contractors, they would kick us all out until it was finished," she said. "And we do love that our closest friends are a part of our adventure."

Landon looked as if he wanted to object, but it was already decided. Everyone started to leave the room to go back to work. Her brother let go of her hand to follow them out.

"Landon, can you please stay for a moment?" Alexa asked.

He hesitated. Sierra had turned at the door waiting for him. "I'll be down in just a moment," he told her.

Sierra shifted her gaze to Alexa, anger flashing in her eyes, then she smiled a weak smile. "Make her promise she won't be wandering around the house anymore," she said and left.

"Close the door," Alexa said quietly to her brother.

He studied her a moment before walking over and closing the door. "Want to tell me what really happened to you? Or are you still in denial about this house and the spirits in it?"

She didn't want to fight with him, even if she'd had the energy. "I found your Crying Woman," she said as she swung her legs over the edge of the bed and started to stand.

He moved quickly to grab her arm as she suddenly felt lightheaded and had to sit back down on the edge of the bed for a moment.

"What are you doing? You need to rest."

"No, I need to show you something." She moved to the door, opened it and looked out, half expecting to find Sierra or one of the others lurking there. The hallway was empty. "Come on," she said to her brother as she pulled the old skeleton key from her door and headed down the hall.

As he followed her to the north wing of the house, she motioned to him to be quiet. He rolled his eyes, but didn't argue.

Once at the broom closet door, she used the key to get inside. The panel slid back just as it had earlier. As she started to step through the opening, Landon grabbed her arm.

"You shouldn't go in there," he said. "Sierra doesn't want—"

"Inside here is where someone hit me and knocked me out," Alexa said. "I didn't faint out in the hallway and hit my head. Look at the dust on my clothes."

He released her and she stepped through, squeezed through the narrow space between the stairs and hallway wall and stopped at the spot where she'd found the speakers.

It took a moment for her eyes to adjust to the darkness. She could hear Landon next to her.

"What are we doing?" he asked.

She wished she'd thought to have him bring a flashlight, but she hadn't wanted the others knowing what they were up to. "Strike a match." She suspected he still had matches from the fire he'd built for Sierra in their room.

In the blackness, she could hear him rummaging in his pocket. A moment later came the scratch of the match head. She'd been right and was now all the more curious about the papers Sierra had burned.

The small burst of the light illuminated the interior wall. Alexa stared at the wall, telling herself she shouldn't have been surprised. The wiring and speakers were gone. Whoever had struck her had taken her proof.

She looked over at her brother as the match burned down. "It's gone. The wiring, the speakers, the Crying Woman deception. I didn't get a chance to find the rest of the device before I was struck by whoever was in here with me."

Just before the flame died, Alexa saw her brother's expression. He thought she was lying. Again.

Marshall was relieved when he got Alexa on the phone. "Are you all right? When I stopped by earlier, the woman who answered the door said you'd had an accident and couldn't come down."

"Was the woman blonde, bossy and seemed to be put out that she'd had to answer the door?" Alexa asked.

He let out a laugh, relieved that she sounded fine. "As a matter of fact, she was."

"That's Sierra Wellington Cross, my sister-in-law."

"So you're all right?"

"None the worse for wear."

Something in her voice told him she wasn't as fine as she was pretending to be. Her scream as she'd run across his pasture last night was too fresh in his mind. He couldn't shake the feeling that there was more to her bad dream than she was letting on. And now she'd had an accident? He was all the more anxious about her staying in that house.

"Have supper with me," he said impulsively.

"My sister-in-law has something planned for this evening. Can I take a rain check?" She forgot she wasn't going to see him again.

"Sure. Why don't you give me a call when you can get away," Marshall said and gave her his number. "Call any time. Even in the middle of the night if you have another bad dream."

She chuckled. "You don't mean that."

"I do. The truth is I'm worried about you being in that house, especially after I heard that you fainted and hit your head. That is what happened, isn't it?"

He heard a click on the line.

"I appreciate your concern," Alexa said. "We'll talk soon."

As he hung up, Marshall knew why her voice had changed and she'd quickly gotten off the line. Someone had picked up another line in the house and was listening in.

Alexa had heard the click as well. She'd heard the person on the line, felt them listening to her conversation. Sierra?

After returning to her bed on Landon's orders, she'd waited until she was sure he'd gone back downstairs with the others before she'd taken her key again and gone over to the north wing.

She'd tapped lightly at Sierra and Landon's bedroom door, then had let herself in, feeling like a thief in the night. But she had to know what Sierra had burned in the fireplace. It was probably nothing, and yet she had the feeling that Sierra didn't do anything without a good reason.

Burning papers instead of just throwing them away made Alexa suspicious. Using the poker, she carefully dug the unburned portions out of the ashes, shook them off and gave them a cursory glance before hightailing it back to her room.

Once there, she tried to make sense of what appeared to be financial documents. She couldn't and found herself wondering if she hadn't wasted her time retrieving them. There were a couple of names she could make out. She started to write them down when a tap at the door made her jump.

Sierra stuck her head in. "Supper's ready. Gigi cooked her famous chicken enchiladas. I hope you feel well enough to come down. You already missed her margarita pancakes. You can't miss the enchiladas."

Her stomach growled in answer as she covered the partially burned documents with a book she'd been reading. "I wouldn't dream of it."

"You do feel up to coming down, don't you? We're going to play charades after dinner in the main hall. Your brother is terrible at it so I want you on our team. Hurry down. Everyone is waiting," she said and closed the door.

Alexa groaned as she hurriedly wrote the two names from the document into her notebook that she always carried for reporting at the newspaper, put it back in her purse and picked up her wrap from the chair where she'd thrown it earlier. This drafty old house was starting to get to her, but she couldn't let on. They were all watching her, probably more closely than ever after today's incident.

On her way down the hall, she noticed the phone in a small alcove. It could have been Sierra who picked up the line and listened in. Alexa wouldn't have put it past her.

Hurrying down to the kitchen, she found Gigi making margaritas to go with dinner. Everyone seemed in great spirits. Except Landon. He didn't look up as Alexa took her place at the table amid all the lively conversation and laughter.

After they'd left the space behind the wall earlier, he'd accused her of making up what she'd seen rather than accepting that the Crying Woman was one of many spirits trapped in this house.

"If I can feel something in this house, then you sure as hell can," he'd said. "Do you want to know what Mother told me on her deathbed?"

She hadn't. Not that she could have stopped him, though, from telling her.

"She said if I ever needed you, you would quit lying about your gift and help me. Don't you see? She had seen the future. She knew about this place."

That was such a leap that Alexa had only stared at him speechless. "I am trying to help you," she said finally.

"Are you?"

She had silently cursed her mother for this as she'd watched her brother walk away. Landon would rather believe in the paranormal than what was right in front of him. Someone in this house was behind all of this and as Alexa accepted a margarita, she felt even more determined to find out who it could be.

She'd proven, at least to herself, that someone was behind the Crying Woman. But her brother was right. There were other things in this house. She needed to learn the history of this house and the people who had lived in it, because she suspected whoever was behind the Crying Woman already had.

Alexa couldn't wait to talk to Marshall. She was sure he would know the history of Wellington Manor or who to talk to about it. But there was no way she could get out of dinner or charades. She took a sip of her margarita. It tasted wonderful and it numbed her senses just enough that she didn't feel the house watching her—as well as the people in it.

Hoyt had called the sheriff the moment he'd entered the ranch house.

"You're sure it was Aggie?" was McCall's first question when she arrived twenty minutes later.

"It was her." Emma knew she could prove it by producing the note, but she wasn't ready to do that and it wasn't as if by having the note, the sheriff could find Aggie.

She knew it was crazy, but Aggie was trusting her and she couldn't betray that trust. Had she said that to Hoyt he would have had her head examined.

Everyone believed that Aggie wanted her dead. But Aggie'd had all kinds of chances to kill her when she'd abducted her—and hadn't. Aggie swore she was trying to save her and a part of Emma believed her.

The trouble was that no one believed Laura Chisholm was still alive. Even Emma, but especially Hoyt. But what if Laura was? Hoyt had admitted that Laura was horribly jealous in the short period of time they were married before she was believed to have drowned.

"Did she say something to you?" the sheriff asked Emma.

"No. By the time I ran out of the store and across the street she was gone."

McCall frowned. "Why did you run after her?"

"That's what I'd like to know," Hoyt said. Emma could tell he was scared and that made him all the more angry with her for taking a chance like that. "What if Aggie had had a gun?"

"I just saw her standing there and didn't think," Emma said. "She looked as if she wanted to say something to me."

"And yet she disappeared when you came out of the store?" the sheriff said.

Emma nodded. "I think she was scared off."

"I hope she was scared out of town," Hoyt said.

The sheriff shook her head. "I doubt that's the case. I'm surprised she would take such a chance to see you—or have you see her. That was reckless on her part."

Hoyt shot his wife a look. "That's what frightens me. You would think she'd have the good sense to skip the country. Who knows what the woman will do next?"

After the sheriff left, Hoyt finally went out to feed the horses and left Emma alone for a few moments, something that surprised her.

She was just about to make the call to Aggie when the back door opened and two of her stepsons came in. Emma realized that Hoyt had called them to watch over her until he got back from the barn.

After visiting for a few minutes, she excused herself and went upstairs to her bathroom. Closing the door, she pulled out her cell phone and the note from Aggie.

Reading it again, she debated what she was about to do. She did tend to be impulsive. But she'd learned as she'd gotten older to follow her own instincts.

She dialed the number and listened as the phone began to ring.

* * *

Everyone was a little tipsy by the time they'd played charades. Alexa enjoyed herself even though Sierra was disappointed her team didn't win.

"Sorry, I'm terrible at charades," she told her sister-in-law later that evening.

Sierra gave her a look that said she hadn't been trying or, even worse, had been cheating. The woman really didn't understand how Alexa's "powers" worked.

Everyone but Carolina and Alexa got up and wandered into the kitchen for a midnight snack. Carolina had been quiet all evening, seemingly lost in her own thoughts.

Now she moved over to sit next to Alexa on the couch. "Please," she said sounding close to tears. "Tell me my future." She held out her hand, palm up.

"I'm sorry, I don't—"

"Please." There was pleading in her gaze. "I have to *know*."

"Palm reading is just a parlor game," Alexa said, not unkindly, but she took the woman's hand, unable to ignore the pain she saw in her eyes. As she idly ran her thumb across Carolina's palm, she had planned to tell her that she saw a rosy future, but the words caught in her throat as she felt a jolt race up her arm.

She let go of Carolina's hand as if it were a deadly snake.

"What?" the young woman cried.

Alexa felt the weight of what she'd seen pressing against her chest. "It's nothing. Just a cramp in my fingers."

Carolina stared down at her palm. "It's bad, isn't it? I knew it was bad."

"I told you palm reading is nothing more than a parlor game," Alexa said, trying to reassure her. "No one can tell your future by looking at your palm."

She was angry with herself for not only scaring the woman, but also scaring herself. She realized the margaritas had weakened the barriers she'd built up and, while she'd sensed horror and dread, she couldn't have told Carolina what would happen in her future or when—only that it would be very bad.

"You are going to have everything you want out of life," she said, the lie almost choking her.

Carolina looked a little less stricken. "Really?"

"Absolutely." Alexa remembered what her mother had said when Landon had once asked, "What do you do when you are looking into a client's future and you see something bad?"

"I look for something good. I never lie," Tallulah Cross had said. "The last thing you want to do is lie." She had looked over at Alexa then, the warning clear.

"What will happen if you do lie?" Alexa had asked. She must have been all of ten years old at the time. Her brother a precocious five.

"You don't want to know," her mother had said.

Alexa had just lied. But then she'd been lying for twenty-three years, hadn't she?

Aggie Wells answered on the fourth ring. Emma had been about to hang up when Aggie picked up. She sounded so…normal, not at all like a delusional criminal who had law enforcement officers across the country looking for her.

"I'm glad you called," Aggie said. "I've been so worried about you."

"Aggie, you need to turn yourself in so you can—"

"Get locked up in the state mental hospital? Emma, you wouldn't have called me if you thought I was crazy."

Emma sighed. "How could Laura Chisholm be alive?"

"I don't know. I just know that she is and I can prove it. I have photographs of the woman."

"Why haven't you taken the information to the sheriff?" Emma asked.

"I can't trust that Laura won't find out and get away again. She's been like a chameleon since she allegedly died thirty years ago. That's why she's been so hard to track down."

Did Emma really believe any of this? "You found her?"

"She was only a few hours away from Whitehorse. She will be coming after you next, Emma."

Emma could well imagine what Hoyt or the sheriff might say about this. "How can you be sure she's Laura?"

"She's changed over the years, of course. Some of the changes I'm sure were so no one in Whitehorse would recognize her, but I have no doubt that Hoyt will be able to."

"You said you had proof," Emma said, thinking that even if the woman was Hoyt's first wife, it wouldn't prove that she killed his other wives or that she was after his fourth—her.

"Meet me and I will give you the photographs and all the information about Laura."

"Why don't you send it to me?"

"You know why. Hoyt might intercept it and call in the sheriff," Aggie said. "If Laura is scared away, she might not surface for a long time. Neither of us will ever be safe until she is caught."

"I don't understand how my getting the information—"

"Come on, Emma, of course you do. You and I have to trap her. She wants you. She's biding her time and will strike when you least expect it. But if we go after her—"

"You want to use me as bait?"

"Don't sound so shocked. I've come to know you, Emma. You're tough as nails. I'd want you on my side in any fight. I hope you realize that I'm good at what I do and I'm not some crazy woman. Obsessed, maybe. I want to solve this. If I get sent back to the state mental hospital, Laura will kill you and who knows what they'll do with me. I have to see this through. You can understand that, can't you?"

Emma thought of her ex and the chance she'd taken to make sure the bastard went to prison for what he'd done. She also thought about her life right now and Hoyt's. This had to end. Even if it only ended with Aggie being caught—and some woman who might look like Laura Chisholm being cleared.

"When?" she asked.

"You're going to have to come up with some way to get Hoyt off your tail, so to speak. You think you can do that tomorrow?"

"It won't be easy getting away from Hoyt," Emma said. "He wouldn't let me go into town by myself before I saw you. Now he will insist on going into the store with me."

"That's why I think we should meet on the ranch," Aggie said.

"How would you suggest we do that?"

"There is a trail behind the house that goes down to the river. It's not that far. All you have to do is figure out a way to get out of his sight for a few minutes. Once you're in the trees, he won't know where you've gone."

"And when I come back up from the river?" Emma asked.

"I'm afraid you are going to have to lie about where you've been and why."

"I don't like doing that." Especially when Hoyt was just trying to keep her safe.

"You haven't told him about the note I left you—or this call, have you," Aggie said. "You're doing this for him as well as for yourself."

Emma couldn't argue that. She still questioned why they had to meet in person and said as much.

"I have to know I can trust you," Aggie said. "Once you see the evidence I have, we'll take the next step."

The next step being the two of them taking this woman down? Emma knew she was taking a hell of a chance just meeting Aggie.

But, while she couldn't tell Hoyt or the sheriff this, she believed Aggie was trying to help her. She thought if she met with Aggie, she could convince her to turn herself in.

"Tomorrow afternoon," Aggie said. "Try to come after lunch. I know Hoyt likes to go out and check his horses after lunch."

Yes, Aggie knew a lot about them. The insurance company she used to work for said Aggie was the best investigator they'd ever had.

So wasn't it possible she could be right about Laura Chisholm being alive?

"I'll wait for you until two-thirty," Aggie said and hung up.

When Emma came out of the bathroom, Hoyt was waiting for her.

Chapter 7

Marshall looked up in surprise at the knock on his front door. He hadn't heard a vehicle nor was he expecting anyone this late.

When he opened the door he was even more surprised. "Not another bad dream, I hope," he said as he motioned Alexa in.

"I know it's late, but you still had a light on...."

"I couldn't sleep," he said as she stepped in. "How about you?" he asked, studying her. She was beautiful, so exotic and apparently wide-awake this time. But he still sensed a desperation in her like she'd had the first time she'd come to visit late at night.

"Couldn't sleep," she said, appearing uncomfortable. He guessed her showing up here had been impulsive and was something she was now regretting.

"Sit down. I'll get us a beer. I bought extra, hoping you'd stop by," he said and started toward the kitchen.

"None for me, thanks. But I would take a glass of water."

He returned a few moments later, not sure she would still be there. She was. He felt relieved even though she was still standing. She took the glass of water he offered her and finally sat down.

"Are you all right after your fall?" he asked.

"Marshall..."

It was the first time she'd used his name. He liked the way she said it and found himself looking at her bow-shaped lips. Just the thought of kissing her—

"Can I be honest with you?"

"Do you really even have to ask?" he said as he dropped into the chair across from her.

"My brother thinks Wellington Manor is haunted," she said.

"What makes you think it isn't?" He could see she was surprised by his response.

"I'm sorry, but you don't seem like a man who believes in ghosts," she said.

He smiled at that. "Since we're being honest, the first time I saw you, you could have made me a believer. I thought you were a ghost and—" He shook his head. "I still wasn't sure when I saw you come running across my pasture."

Alexa had glimpsed something cross Marshall's features and remembered the first time she'd seen *him*— and that odd sense of desire and darkness she'd felt.

"What was it you were going to say a moment ago, but changed your mind?" she asked.

He was taken aback by the question.

"I'm sorry but I saw the change in your expression. Was it something about the first time you saw me?"

Marshall studied her for a moment. "Not much misses your attention, does it?"

"I told you. I'm a reporter. You have to be able to read people. You remembered something a moment ago that bothered you, maybe even scared you."

He let out a chuckle but she could tell it was to hide the truth. He *had* seen something that had scared him the first time he'd laid eyes on her.

"You're going to think I'm nuts. I do."

"I might surprise you," she said. "Please. Tell me."

Marshall sighed, then met her gaze. "I saw something behind you that day. Some*one*."

"My brother?"

He shook his head. "It was a woman."

She felt the hair rise on the back of her neck. Goose bumps rippled across her flesh and it took all her willpower not to shudder. "What did this person look like?"

"This is where it gets crazy. It was a woman who looked exactly like you only…" He was the one to shudder. He laughed. "I'm sure it was probably nothing more than a shadow behind you."

"But you sensed evil."

Marshall opened his mouth to deny it. Saying it out loud would make it real. But when he looked into those amazing violet eyes of hers… "Yeah, that was the feeling I had. Something…dangerous. Or at least not of this world. Crazy, huh?"

He waited for her to tell him he'd merely been seeing things.

Instead, she chewed at her lower lip for a moment and when she lifted her glass to take a drink, he saw that her hand was shaking.

"Wait a minute. Are you telling me I really did see someone?"

She took a sip, then carefully put the glass down on the coffee table. "My mother."

He couldn't help his relief—or his embarrassment. "Your mother is here with you and your brother. I'm sorry. I can't imagine why I thought—"

"My mother's been dead for over a year."

The rest of his words froze in his throat. "Whoa. I don't know what to say."

She hesitated but only for a moment. As her gaze met his, she said, "My mother was a clairvoyant."

"A clairvoyant," he repeated.

"A fortune-teller, if you like."

"I know what a clairvoyant is."

"She specialized in reaching those who had passed over and she made a tidy sum doing it."

He heard anger in her tone. "You sound skeptical."

She shook her head. "Unfortunately, I think she might have been the real thing."

Marshall let that sink in for a moment. "That must have been interesting, growing up with a mother with that kind of…talent."

Alexa laughed. "You might say that. I was her precious daughter until I told her that I didn't have her gift. After that she centered her world around my brother."

"I'm sorry. So your brother has—"

"No." She shook her head. "He doesn't have her abilities and while I'm being honest, I didn't faint earlier today. Someone hit me."

"What?" He listened as she told him about the Crying Woman. "Why wouldn't your brother believe you?" he asked when she'd finished.

"Because he thinks I've been lying to him for years," she said and met his gaze. "My mother was convinced that I had her abilities."

"You mean that you're clairvoyant like her?"

She nodded.

"And you're not?"

She looked away and he felt his heart drop even though he'd already suspected this was what had her so terrified—not just whatever was going on over at that house.

"I'm not like her," Alexa said as she turned back to face him.

"But you're a little like her," he said carefully.

She looked as if she might try to deny it. Instead, tears filled her eyes.

He moved to sit on the couch next to her. "That's why you're so scared," he said as he reached over to take her hands in his. "The nightmares? Is that part of it?"

"I don't know. Maybe." She looked into his face. "This doesn't scare *you*?"

He laughed. "Only if you tell me that you know what I'm thinking."

She smiled through her tears. "I can't read your

mind." She looked down at his large hands cradling her own. "I can't see your future either. Or my own." She sounded relieved by that and maybe a little worried.

He grinned. "That's good. Then you don't know that I've been wanting to do this since the first time I saw you." He leaned toward her and gently kissed her full mouth. Desire raced through his veins, as hot as a summer day and just as wonderful. He drew back to look into those beautiful violet eyes of hers.

She was smiling. "Maybe I *can* see the future," she said.

Marshall hoped he did too. But he felt her draw back and could see she was almost as afraid of getting involved with him as she was of that house and whatever was going on over there.

"You've been so understanding," she said. "A lot of men—"

"I'm not like a lot of men."

"No, you aren't."

"What I mean is that I don't scare off easily. Tell me about this house you're staying in."

"That's the problem. My brother doesn't just think it's haunted. He believes it is trying to kill him."

Marshall saw it then. "He thinks you can save him."

"He's wrong." She'd said it too quickly. He watched her look away, but not before he'd seen the pain in her expression and something else. Guilt.

"So they both blamed you for not having this alleged gift? Or at least not admitting that you might have it."

She smiled at his insight. "That about covers it."

He didn't think so. He had a feeling there was a lot more going on, but he was thankful she had opened up to him and didn't want to push it. She'd tell him, he hoped, when she trusted him more.

"Someone wants you to believe the house is haunted, but why?" Marshall asked.

"That's what I have to find out. I need to know more about the Wellingtons. Can you help me?"

"I know someone you can talk to," he said. "We could go visit him tomorrow in town. Maybe have supper afterward?"

"Thank you." She touched his face, leaning in to kiss him. He kissed her again and she melted into his arms. If he had one wish, it would be that he never had to let her go.

"In the meantime," he said as the kiss ended and she rose to leave, "I don't like you staying over there."

"I can't leave. Not until I can get my brother to go as well. Maybe what we find out tomorrow will help."

He sure hoped so as he walked her to the door, because he feared what was waiting for her in that old mansion. Ghosts? Or someone who would do anything to keep the truth from coming out?

Alexa carefully opened the back door and slipped inside, glad she'd gone over to Marshall's tonight. She couldn't believe she'd confided in him. Or how relieved she was that she had.

She felt warm and happy and realized it was because he was right. He wasn't like other men. He hadn't panicked when she'd told him about her mother. Or when he'd seen what could only have been her mother standing behind her that first day.

Instead, she was the one who'd felt panic. She'd wondered how long it would be before her mother contacted her.

As if that wasn't enough to scare her off, someone wanted the people in this house, maybe especially Landon, to believe Wellington Manor was haunted. They'd been trying to run him off—and soon, she feared, herself as well.

But she was more afraid of what she'd been feeling. For Marshall Chisholm. And in this house. The sensations were growing stronger. She didn't want to admit that even to herself, though. But she knew it was part of the reason she kept fleeing to Marshall's farmhouse every night.

It wasn't just fear driving her out of Wellington Manor and sending her straight for Marshall Chisholm. She'd also needed the levelheaded cowboy more than he could know. When she'd gone up to bed tonight, she'd seen his lights on and, on impulse, had been drawn to the place, hoping that the light didn't go off before she reached it.

He and his house were a haven. She could sit in his old farmhouse with its warm essence and feel safe— and normal. She didn't feel anything in his house but peace. There hadn't been any violence inside those walls. There'd been hardship, as with any life that had lived within an old house, but there had also been an abundance of love.

While the house was definitely a draw, it was the man she'd needed to see. Desire stirred in her at the thought of him. She had always feared letting anyone get too close. But she'd never met a man quite like Marshall Chisholm. She sensed his strength, his integrity, his connection to the earth and living things.

All her senses told her this cowboy was a man she could trust—and that somehow they had become intricately linked. From the first time she'd seen him, Marshall Chisholm had gotten through the barriers she'd built around her.

With a start, Alexa realized something she hadn't first noticed when she'd stepped into Wellington Manor.

The hallway was dark.

She'd purposely left a small lamp on so she didn't crash into anything and wake the rest of the household. Someone had turned it out.

She reached out in the pitch blackness, found the small table by the back door and cautiously felt around for the lamp. The lamp wasn't there. Why would someone—

She felt a warm hand, let out a cry and stumbled back. The lamp came on, blinding her for an instant. "Been out for another nightly run in the pasture?"

Alexa tried to still her pounding pulse as Jayden set down the lamp and turned to her. "You startled me." She pressed her hands to her heart as she realized that Jayden had seen her leave the other night as well. Still, she told herself she had nothing to fear.

But the knot on her head from earlier was a painful reminder of what she had to fear in this house. Someone knew she had found the Crying Woman device. And that someone could very easily be Jayden.

"I should warn you that I'm not the only one in this house who knows about your late-night rendezvous," Jayden said. "I get why you'd run off in the middle of the night to meet a handsome cowboy. But I don't think your brother is as understanding as I am. He seems upset that you're spending so much time away from the house."

"What does my brother think of *your* late-night rendezvous down by the pond?" she asked before she could bite her tongue.

Jayden's eyes narrowed. "Touché. Apparently I'm not the only one who has been keeping an eye on what goes on around here. Is that why your brother invited you to come stay with us? To spy on us?"

"I'm not here to spy on anyone," she snapped. "I just don't want to see my brother hurt."

There was almost a sadness to his smile. "I'm afraid it's too late for that."

Before she could ask what he meant, Jayden turned and strode down the dark hallway.

Alexa stared after him, more convinced than ever that she needed to get her brother out of this house—and herself as well. The longer she stayed here, the harder it would be to keep lying to herself—let alone Landon—about what she was sensing among them.

She was relieved when she reached her room and quickly locked the door behind her. She desperately wanted to talk to her brother away from this house—and his wife. But that wasn't going to happen if Sierra had anything to do with it.

As she stepped toward her bed, she saw the tray with milk and cookies—and the note. She felt her heart soften when she recognized Landon's neat script.

Alexa,
I'm sorry. Tomorrow let's get away from here
and talk.
Love,
Landon

Relief and love for her brother made tears well in her eyes. If they could get away from Sierra and this house, maybe she could talk some sense into him. He was right about one thing. There was something in this house controlling him. But Alexa knew it was flesh and blood—not some avenging spirit.

She smiled as she sat down on the edge of the bed and picked up one of the cookies. Chocolate chip, her favorite. Landon remembered.

She took a bite. The cookie was delicious. When she was little, her father would have the housekeeper bake cookies for her in secret. Tallulah didn't like her eating sugar, especially right before she went to bed. She swore it was the cause of Alexa's nightmares. But her father called that poppycock and snuck cookies and milk in to her. They would share them and talk about their day. It was the best of her childhood memories.

Alexa wished she and Landon had shared the same father, since his had been little more than a sperm donor. She'd tried to make up for what he'd missed, not having a father, by baking chocolate chip cookies and sneaking them and milk in to her brother at night after their mother had gone to bed.

Touched by her brother's thoughtfulness, she finished the cookies and milk. But as she started to get ready for bed, she suddenly felt lightheaded. A terrible thought wove itself through her muddled conscious. *No.* She lunged for the phone on the nightstand. It was the last thing she remembered.

Chapter 8

The next morning Marshall drove to the Chisholm Cattle Company main ranch house. He was worried about his folks since hearing the news. He still couldn't believe that Aggie Wells had escaped. He was also feeling a little guilty about the amount of time he'd been taking off to work on his house—and most recently, to spend with Alexa.

Last night after Alexa had left, he'd gotten back on the computer and called up a list of psychics. It hadn't taken long to find Tallulah Cross. Alexa had played down just how famous her mother had been and how often her predictions had been right.

What had really bowled him over though was the photograph he'd found of Alexa's mother. The two could have been twins. He'd felt a chill in the warm room. The woman was the same one he swore he'd seen standing behind Alexa the first time he'd seen her.

Scrolling down, he'd found Tallulah Cross's obituary and seen that Alexa and Landon were mentioned. What would it have been like to have a clairvoyant for a mother? He and his brothers wouldn't have been able to get away with anything.

Instead, Marshall had spent his life without a mother. Emma was as close to a real mother as he'd had. He'd either been too young or his father's other wives had lasted such a short time, he couldn't remember them.

Hoyt had been both mother and father though, doing the best he could, which was damned good. When the boys had gotten older, he'd always seemed to be one step ahead of them. It wasn't until Marshall was grown that he realized the reason his father always had known what mischief he and his brothers had gotten into. His father had gotten into the same mischief when he was young.

"Hey, stranger," his brother Logan said as he came into the kitchen. He could smell blueberry muffins and made a beeline for them and a mug of coffee. Everyone was seated about the big kitchen table. His brothers were elbowing each other, snickering. "How're the new neighbors?"

He shot Tanner a look, wishing he hadn't confided in him. His brother held up his hands and looked confused as if he didn't have any idea what Marshall was upset about.

"How's the house coming along?" his father asked.

"Slowly," he said, feeling guilty that he hadn't worked on it much since meeting Alexa Cross. "I could use a few more days, if that won't put too much pressure on the rest of you."

There were moans and groans but his father said not to worry, take what time he needed.

"With his mind on *other* things, he's pretty worthless anyway," Tanner joked.

Marshall felt Emma's gaze on him. If anyone was clairvoyant, it was Emma McDougal Chisholm. Earlier, she'd seemed distracted with her own problems—Aggie Wells being on the loose again. He could tell that his father was anxious as well about Emma's safety.

As the rest of the family cleared out, Hoyt saying he would be in the barn but not to leave without saying goodbye, Emma said, "So who is she?"

Marshall started to play dumb, but knew he'd be wasting his time. "Her name's Alexa Cross. She's staying over at Wellington Manor."

Emma lifted a brow.

"Sierra Wellington married her brother, Landon. They're remodeling the old place, thinking of making it into a bed-and-breakfast."

"Tell me about this Alexa."

He smiled, unable not to. "She's amazing. She's gorgeous, smart…" He shook his head, realizing he could go on forever about her.

"So what's the problem?" Emma asked.

"There isn't—"

"Something's wrong. Tell me. That is why you're here this morning, isn't it?"

It amazed him how she could see through all of them, maybe especially Hoyt. "I was also worried about you."

"Thank you, I appreciate that," Emma said. "Now pour us another cup of coffee and tell me what's wrong."

"It's kind of complicated. Alexa's brother thinks the house is haunted. I'm not one to hold much stock in all that, but…"

"You've *seen* something?"

He nodded. "The first time I saw Alexa there was a woman standing behind her. Turns out it was her mother—who's been dead for a year."

Emma shivered in spite of her next words. "It must have been a trick of the light."

"Yeah, that's what I said, but it turns out her mother was a clairvoyant. I looked her up on the internet. She was a famous psychic."

"And her daughter?" Emma asked.

Yes, that was the question, wasn't it? "I can't be sure but I think she might be as well, though she doesn't like the idea and doesn't want to be clairvoyant. Something is going on with her and that house and her brother and maybe even her mother. I know that sounds crazy."

Emma shook her head.

"What?" he asked.

"It's you Chisholms. You all prefer women in trouble."

Alexa woke to daylight, a horrible nightmare following her up from the darkness. She sat up, shocked to find herself still fully dressed and on the floor. Next to her was the broken plate and glass that had held the cookies and milk. She must have knocked them off the tray as she fell.

She leaned against the bed, her head swimming, as she tried to remember what had happened. Had someone hit her again? The last thing she remembered was eating the cookies and milk that Landon had left her.

The thought froze in her mind. Landon's note. He hadn't mentioned the cookies and milk. Or had he?

Alexa got to her feet, found the note on the tray and reread it. Her head ached and she felt sick to her stomach. Landon *hadn't* mentioned the cookies and milk. He would have—had he been the one to leave them. But who else could have known about the ritual?

Sierra. Of course Landon would have told her.

Alexa had to sit down on the edge of the bed for a moment, her head spinning. *Her brother's wife had drugged her?* She was going to be sick! She made a mad dash for the bathroom, barely making it before she threw up.

Feeling a little better, she turned on the shower, stripped off her clothes and stepped under the hot spray. She still felt awful, but this was more heartsick. Her brother had no idea whom he'd married, *what* he'd married.

Why would Sierra drug her?

Had her intention been to scare Alexa off? Or had she hoped for a drug overdose that killed her?

She had just come out of the shower when she heard the tap on her door. Last night she'd had the good sense to lock the door but anyone with a skeleton key could open any room in this house.

"Alexa?" Gigi called. "I just wanted to come up and check on you. Landon was worried, but Sierra said to let you sleep."

Oh, she did, did she?

Alexa glanced at the clock. It was almost two in the afternoon! She'd slept all night and most of the day?

"I'm fine. I was just being lazy and I had a book I

wanted to finish," she improvised. "I'm getting ready to take a shower."

Gigi sounded relieved. "No problem. I'll let your brother know. When he called and I told him we hadn't seen you, he asked me to come check. He and Sierra are on their way back from town, but he'll be glad that you're relaxing. We were just about to eat a late lunch."

"Tell everyone to go ahead and eat without me. I'm not really hungry. I'll come down later and get something."

"All right."

Alexa waited until she heard Gigi's footfalls recede down the hall before she checked to make sure the hallway was empty. It was. She closed the door and locked it again.

The last thing she wanted was food. Her stomach was still roiling, especially after hearing that Sierra hadn't wanted Gigi to wake her. At least Landon had been concerned enough to send someone up, she thought, as she looked at the clock and realized Marshall would be picking her up soon.

She had felt guilty last night about researching Sierra's family. Now she was more determined than ever to find out everything she could about the Wellingtons.

As she started to get dressed, she noticed the book beside her bed had been moved. She quickly picked it up as she remembered the partially burned papers she'd put under it. They were gone.

Emma had been walking around on eggshells since almost getting caught yesterday on the phone with Aggie.

"I wondered where you'd gone," Hoyt had said when she'd opened the bathroom door and found him standing there. "The boys are leaving. I knew you'd want to say goodbye. Do you feel all right?"

She'd known she'd looked suspicious. "My stomach is a little upset."

He'd pulled her into his arms, making her feel guilty again. But her stomach had been upset, so she hadn't really lied.

She'd almost confessed everything, but she knew her husband. He would never let her meet Aggie, especially alone, if he knew what she was up to.

Now with her stepsons gone, she could sense Hoyt's impatience to get back to ranch work and his real life. She felt the same way.

"I think I'll make some cookies," she said. Baking was the only thing keeping her sane.

"What kind of cookies?" Hoyt asked, coming up behind her as she creamed the butter and sugar for the cookies in her large mixer.

"Your favorite, snickerdoodles."

He planted a kiss on her neck. She was grateful for the amazing intimacy they shared. But as she glanced at the clock, she knew she couldn't let him talk her into going upstairs for even a quickie. She needed to meet Aggie and the sooner the better.

"Any chance of leaving that for a little while?" he asked as he put his arms around her and snuggled closer.

Oh, she was tempted. But feared she might not be able to get away later. "I can't really leave these ingredients right now. Don't you need to check on that mare of yours again? I should have the first batch done by the time you get back."

She could tell he had other things on his mind than his horses and he didn't want to leave her alone, even though he'd only be out in the barn nearby. "What did the vet say when he came out and had a look at her?" she asked.

"He thought she had an infection in that one leg. He gave her something for it. Maybe I'd better go see how she's doing. I won't be long."

"Take your time. I'll yell if I need you."

He studied her for a long moment. "Maybe when I get back…"

She smiled as she leaned in to kiss him, then quickly turned around. "Let me finish my cookies."

"I don't know what I would do without you, Emma. It would kill me," he said behind her.

Guilt gnawed at her. She didn't dare turn around. "You won't ever have to find out."

"I hope not," he said.

Out of the corner of her eye, she saw him take his Stetson off the peg on the wall where he'd tossed it earlier. As he set it on his thick, graying blond hair, he said, "See you shortly."

The moment she heard the front door close behind him, Emma ripped off her apron and stepped to the doorway to make sure he hadn't forgotten something and was headed back.

Emma watched him striding toward the barn, thinking how blessed she was to have such a wonderful man. Guilt ate her up as she left the cookie dough and hurried out the back door, running down the trail to disappear into the woods.

Alexa had just finished getting dressed when she heard footfalls. At first she thought it was someone coming down the hall.

Then she realized they were coming from overhead. Someone was on the third floor. The footsteps
had stopped. Now whoever it was seemed to be moving
things around as if searching for something.

If everyone was down having breakfast, then who
was upstairs?

Grabbing her room key, she decided to find out.

The broom closet was locked—just as it had been
the other time. Alexa used her skeleton key from her
room to open it and quickly stepped inside, closing and
locking the door behind her.

She stood for a moment, listening. Hearing nothing beyond the panel door, she carefully slid it open,
stepped through and closed it behind her. She had to
feel her way to the stairs since she had no flashlight.
Once she started up them, though, she could see faint
light bleeding in through a space under the door at the
top of the stairs. She had her key ready, but found the
door to be unlocked.

Cautiously, she opened it. As the door swung open,
she saw that at least this part of the third floor was as
Sierra had described it.

The floor seemed full of old furniture and boxes. She
could hear someone moving around at the other end of
the room—directly over Alexa's room. The person appeared to still be looking for something.

Stepping behind one of the larger boxes, she eased
herself through the furniture, boxes and old trunks until
she was so close that she could hear the person breathing hard on the other side of a line of tall bureaus.

She tried to move one of the tallboys to peek through

to see who it was. The leg of the bureau scraped on the hardwood floor, making a squeaking sound.

The person on the other side froze. Alexa did the same for a moment, then realizing she'd been caught, stood and tried to push her way through.

But by the time she slipped between the tallboy and an old buffet, whoever had been rummaging around was gone, his or her footfalls quickly receding.

Alexa glanced around, curious what the person had been looking for. With a start, she saw two dark eyes staring at her from one of the boxes. As she stepped closer, she saw with a chill that someone had poked the eyes out of a doll with a sharp object that had left cut marks around the eye holes.

Unable to look away, as if at a car wreck, she reached for the doll. The moment her fingers touched it, she felt a tingle run up her arm and quickly jerked back from what flashed in her mind.

She'd seen a little girl in a pretty pink-and-white dress, a matching bow in her hair. There was blood on the girl's dress....

As she felt a small tug on the hem of her skirt, Alexa had to cover her mouth with her hand to keep from screaming. She jerked away, the fabric pulling tightly before swinging back against her legs.

She stood staring in the dim light at the empty space next to her. There was no little girl. It was all just— A ball rolled across the floor.

Alexa stumbled back against an old bureau. She had to grip the edge to keep from falling as the ball rolled past her. Her elbow caught on one of the boxes. It tumbled to the floor with a crash.

Old black-and-white photographs spilled out of it and across the floor.

Trying to get a grip on her panic, Alexa reached down to pick up the spilled photographs. One caught her eye. She lifted it from the floor and felt her heart stop.

The photo was an old one, the paper cracked and faded, but the image was a young woman, the resemblance to Sierra more than startling.

The woman was dressed in an old-fashioned dress, high-button boots, a fur stole around her slim shoulders. Her blond hair was piled high on her head, exposing a long, graceful neck and accenting her high cheekbones and stunning beauty. Around the woman's neck was an unusual necklace, the pendant hanging from a thick chain appearing to have something written on it.

Alexa squinted at the photo, trying to read the words.

"My great-great-grandmother," Sierra said, appearing out of nowhere.

Startled, Alexa dropped the photograph. It fell to the floor with a whisper of sound. "I'm sorry. I was—"

"I know what you were doing," Sierra said as she moved to pick up the spilled box of photos from the floor. There was coldness in her voice, anger. She glanced at the scrape in the floor where Alexa had moved the bureau aside, then at her sister-in-law. Her blue eyes could have been chipped from ice for all the warmth in them.

"You're digging into my family's history, trying to frighten my husband," she said, a warning in her tone.

"He was frightened before I got here."

Sierra cocked her head, as if listening to a voice Alexa couldn't hear. "You don't like me, do you?"

Alexa was taken aback by the bluntness of her question. "I'm concerned about your relationship with my brother."

"That doesn't answer my question."

"I want him to be happy."

"What makes you think he isn't happy?" Sierra idly picked up the photo of her great-great-grandmother and studied it as if looking at her own photo, searching it for a flaw in her beauty and finding none. "I'm his wife. He loves me."

Sierra placed the photograph carefully in the box on top of the others, then looked at Alexa almost as if she'd forgotten she was still in the room. "I think it might be time for you to leave. You really shouldn't be gone too long from your job. I'm sure if you tell Landon—"

"I'm not leaving until I find out what is going on in this house," Alexa said with surprising firmness.

It seemed to surprise Sierra as well. She let out a laugh. "So you aren't as meek as you pretend."

"When it comes to my brother—"

"Yes. Well, for his sake, I want you to leave. You don't want anything to happen to him, do you?"

Alexa was suddenly shaking inside. "That sounds like a threat."

Sierra laughed. "Why would I threaten Landon? I love him."

"Do you?"

Her sister-in-law's gaze narrowed. "I won't have you coming between me and my husband, that's all I'm saying. Don't make him choose between his love for you and his love for me, because you will lose."

With that, she turned and left.

Alexa stood, trembling with rage and fear, as she watched the young woman go.

Chapter 9

Everyone was gathered around the kitchen table when Alexa came downstairs. She saw that Landon had his arm around his wife. Sierra looked upset and Alexa guessed that she'd tattled on her to Landon.

"What's going on?" Alexa asked in the heavy silence she'd walked into.

"It's Carolina," Devlin said from the end of the table. "She's going back to California."

Alexa felt her heart drop. Was this because of that stupid palm reading last night?

"Look, it's all my fault," Jayden said. "I shouldn't have said anything about babies. I had no idea—"

"No, if anyone is to blame, it's me," Archer said, getting to his feet. "I knew how badly she wanted a baby and she knew I didn't want kids. We were bound to get to this point. It's been coming for a long time."

"You aren't going too, are you?" Sierra asked.

Archer nodded his head. "She's making arrangements, but the earliest flight she can get is the day after tomorrow."

Alexa was glad he wasn't going to leave Carolina alone, given what she'd seen when she'd taken the young woman's hand last night.

"I saved you some lunch," Landon said to his sister, letting go of Sierra to head to the stove.

She couldn't miss the way Sierra looked at her. A mixture of anger and jealousy. She wanted Landon all to herself. But how far did that need of hers go? All the way to murder?

"Thank you, but I have a date for supper later," Alexa said as she joined her brother at the stove.

Landon raised a brow. "With that *cowboy* again?"

She bristled at the way he said "cowboy." It sounded like something Sierra would say.

"At least taste this," her brother said shoving a spoonful of meatloaf toward her. "It tastes just like Mother used to make."

Meatloaf was one of the few things their mother did cook. "Yes, it does taste like hers." Her stomach roiled. She didn't need the meatloaf—or the reminder.

"He doesn't wait on me like that," Sierra said as she started to clean off the table.

"Sierra," Alexa said, loud enough for everyone to hear. "I wanted to thank you for the cookies and milk you left beside my bed last night."

"You left her cookies and milk?" Landon asked, surprise and pleasure in his tone as he stepped back over to the table.

"No," Sierra said and blinked her big baby blues. "It wasn't me."

"Oh?" Alexa said. "They were chocolate chip cookies. I thought Landon must have told you about a tradition we had as children."

Her brother was studying his wife, not quite as sure now. "You remember me telling you how Alexa would sneak me cookies? Mother hated us eating any sugar. Chocolate chip cookies were my favorite and Alexa's."

"You might have mentioned it," Sierra conceded, clearly flustered. "But I didn't leave her cookies and milk. I'm sorry I didn't think of it."

"Strange. I wonder who did?" Alexa said and glanced around the table at Archer, Gigi and Jayden. They all shook their heads.

"I have no idea who left them," Sierra snapped.

"Landon, did you mention our tradition to anyone else?" Alexa asked and saw him start to shake his head.

"*I* probably did," Sierra said quickly. "It was so sweet, I'm sure I shared it with someone, maybe Carolina." She turned to her husband. "It's my day to clean up the dishes. You should see if you can help Devlin."

"Actually," Alexa said. "Why don't you go see if Carolina's all right? Landon and I will do the dishes."

Sierra started to object, but Landon cut her off.

"It will give Alexa and me a chance to talk."

Sierra's face was a mask of fury, but she worked up a smile for Landon, gave him a quick kiss on the cheek and shot Alexa a hateful look before she flounced out, Archer, Gigi and Jayden leaving as well.

"You have a date and are definitely not doing dishes," Landon said after they were alone in the kitchen. "But I'd love it if you kept me company while I did them. I was worried about you when Gigi said you hadn't been downstairs all day. Are you all right?"

She was touched by his concern.

He turned to face her. "I think I know what this is about. Listen, I'm sorry, sis. I love you. It wasn't fair what I did to you, getting you here and then expecting you to—"

"It's all right," Alexa said, feeling awful. "I do want to help you, Landon, any way I can."

"I know." He gave her a hug and the two of them began to clear the table. It felt again like the way it had when they were kids. They'd been inseparable. Was that her problem with Sierra? Was she just jealous that she was no longer the most important person in Landon's life anymore?

"I'm concerned about what is going on in this house," Alexa said as they dumped the dishes in a tub of hot, soapy water.

She wasn't sure how to broach the subject with him, but he had to know. "Sierra probably mentioned that I was up on the third floor earlier."

"Sis, we told you how dangerous—"

"There was someone else up there going through boxes. I didn't get a look at the person, but whoever it was heard a noise and quickly left. Was everyone downstairs when you and Sierra returned?"

He frowned. "Everyone but Carolina. Archer told us that they'd had an argument and she was leaving."

Why, if that were true, would she have been going through boxes up on the third floor? Was it possible the argument had been a ruse?

"What difference does it make who was up there going through boxes? Maybe they were just curious. Or maybe what you heard wasn't even a person."

"Landon, there is something going on that has nothing to do with ghosts. You and the others haven't heard the Crying Woman again, have you? Someone wants you all to *believe* there are ghosts in this house. If we knew why, then maybe we would know why you keep having these *accidents*."

"I've been thinking about that," he said quietly, checking over his shoulder to make sure they were still alone. "A haunted bed-and-breakfast might bring in more people than one that isn't."

Relief swept over her. He *had* believed her and given it some thought. "You think Sierra might have been behind the Crying Woman."

"Or one of her friends. It isn't like any harm was done," he added quickly.

"When I found the device, someone hit me and left me lying out in the hallway, Landon," she said.

"They obviously panicked."

She wanted to shake him. "You suspected something or someone was responsible for your accidents when you called me to come out here. You wouldn't have done that if you hadn't been suspicious."

Before he could argue the point, she said, "My getting hit wasn't the only incident. Whoever left me the milk and cookies…they drugged them. I woke up on the floor."

He shook his head. "No. I can't imagine who would do something like that. It wasn't Sierra. You heard her—she swore it wasn't her."

Alexa said nothing as he laid the dish towel on the counter and sat down at the closest chair. Resting his elbows on the table, he put his head in his hands.

She took a chair next to him and put her hand on his shoulder. "It's not just you someone is trying to get rid of now. We have to find out why."

Alexa heard the doorbell and glanced at her watch. Her date. "I have to go," she said to her brother, squeezing his shoulder. "Just think about what I've said."

Landon nodded solemnly as the doorbell rang again. "I want to meet your date."

"Yes," Sierra said from the kitchen doorway. "We all do."

It was shady and cool in the cottonwoods along the Milk River. The river was narrow and deep where it cut through the Chisholm ranch, the water dark and surprisingly fast-moving along this section of the river.

Emma hadn't gone far when she saw Aggie step out of the trees and onto the path.

She felt her heart leap in her chest and, as she watched Aggie reach into the shoulder bag she carried, she feared she'd made a fatal mistake agreeing to this.

For one heart-stopping moment, Emma thought Aggie was about to pull a gun from her purse and slowed to a stop a few yards away, moving only when she realized how foolish she'd been as Aggie pulled out a large manila envelope.

"Are you all right?" Aggie asked, no doubt seeing her initial panic.

Emma nodded and joined the woman. "A little spooked."

Aggie laughed. "You have to trust me."

"I'm trying," she said as the woman laid the large envelope in her hands.

She opened the envelope and took out one of the surveillance photos. It had been shot from a distance with a telephoto lens, from the look of it.

The woman in the photo was in her early fifties, lean and pretty, with medium-length dark hair that accented her dark eyes.

"Well?" Aggie asked.

Emma had seen a photograph of Laura after she'd insisted that Hoyt must have one. He'd dug out a box of old photographs from the basement.

It took him a while, but he'd finally produced one of Laura. She'd been a beautiful redhead with long, luxurious hair and big, blue eyes.

"The hair and eye color is wrong," Emma said.

Aggie gave her an impatient look. "Hair dye and contacts. Do you really think she could have stayed hidden all these years if she had stayed a blue-eyed redhead? She would have stuck out like a sore thumb. But the way she looks now, I really doubt anyone in Whitehorse would recognize her. She wasn't from here and few would remember her, since she and Hoyt weren't married that long."

Laura Chisholm had been beautiful. No wonder Hoyt

had fallen for her. Emma felt a hard jab of jealousy. And she had been a redhead too.

"Look at her face," Aggie ordered. "The cheekbones, the shape of the eyes. Here." She reached into the envelope and brought out another photo. "It's a computerized age-progression photo of what Laura Chisholm would look like if she were still alive. I had a friend in law enforcement make it for me."

Emma was reminded that Aggie had a lot of friends. That was how she'd been able to avoid the mental hospital. She stared at the surveillance photo, then the computerized photo. The women could have been twins. "What is this woman's name?"

"She goes by Sharon Jones. Her address is in the envelope. She lives in Billings—just three hours away—and guess what? Sharon Jones didn't exist until four months ago—just about the time you married Hoyt."

Emma felt a chill at the thought that the person who might want her dead could be just three hours away. Or, just inches away, if she was wrong about Aggie, she reminded herself.

"Do you believe me now?" Aggie demanded.

"I have to admit, there is a remarkable resemblance," Emma said. "Aggie, you need to take this to the police in Billings," she continued, trying to hand the photos and envelopes back to her.

"I told you, no police. We're doing this together. It's your life that's at stake as well as mine. I don't trust the police not to blow this. If Laura disappears again, the next time you see her will be the day she kills you. Me, I'll be in the loony bin if the police don't get a confession out of her. But you and I—" Aggie suddenly broke off midsentence.

"You didn't tell anyone you were meeting me back here, did you?" Aggie demanded.

"No, I snuck out."

Aggie swore. "You called the sheriff."

"No." Emma turned and saw several deputies moving through the trees.

"You're going to get yourself killed!" Aggie cried, shoving the manila envelope with the photographs at her before turning to run.

"Stop!" A gunshot boomed.

Emma heard Aggie cry out as she stumbled and fell into the river. As she stared in shock, the deputies and sheriff came running up, followed moments later by Hoyt.

Emma could only stare at the spot where Aggie had gone under and hadn't come up again.

Marshall knew something was wrong the moment Alexa answered the door. He'd been smiling before that, but now whispered, "Are you okay?" She looked pale and her eyes weren't their usual brilliant violet.

"Why don't you come in," she said tightly. "Everyone wants to meet you."

Everyone? "Great," he said, tugging off his Stetson, then he wiped his feet and stepped into the mansion.

He'd known it would be impressive inside but still he was taken aback by how grandiose the interior had once been. Its looks had faded, but it was still beautiful. He took the opulence all in and let out a low whistle.

"High praise," Sierra said and stepped forward. "I'm Sierra Wellington. I'm glad you like my house."

"Wellington Cross," a man behind her corrected. He looked enough like Alexa that Marshall figured he was Landon even before he introduced himself.

The others were quickly introduced. Gigi, the former cheerleader, and no doubt, the most popular girl at school. Archer, the former jock. Devlin, the smug rich kid. Jayden, the odd man out. Only Carolina was missing.

He noticed that Alexa's brother looked uncomfortable and could understand now why Alexa felt the need to protect Landon. Marshall understood it even more after meeting Landon's wife. Under all that blond, blue-eyed, innocent exterior, Sierra was as cold as this house.

"So how many cattle do you have on your ranch?" Devlin asked.

"I couldn't say offhand," Marshall answered. It was impolite to ask a rancher how many cattle he ran. It was like asking someone how much he was worth.

"You probably have hired hands to do all the real work, right?" Archer asked.

"No, my brothers and I and our father work the ranch. We actually like getting our hands dirty," Marshall said.

"I apologize for them," Alexa said after they were seated in his pickup.

"You don't need to apologize for them," he said. "They aren't *your* friends."

"No," she agreed quickly.

"They're not your brother's either."

She glanced over at him. "You felt that as well?"

He nodded as he started the pickup and drove toward town.

"I keep telling myself they're young."

"Not that much younger than us. They're spoiled rich kids. I got the feeling your brother doesn't like them any more than you do."

"Does it show?"

He laughed. "No, you both hide it well. So that bunch is remodeling the mansion?" He couldn't help sounding skeptical.

"Apparently, though they work odd hours. They must work late at night since no one gets up early. I really don't know what they're doing."

He saw her frown. "Something else happen?"

She turned toward him, her expression softening. "Last night someone left me milk and cookies. I thought it was my brother because there was a note there from him and chocolate chip cookies and milk were a tradition when we were kids. They were drugged. I woke up on the floor—a couple of hours ago."

"Alexa," he said, unconsciously hitting the brakes as he reached over for her.

"I'm all right. They didn't give me enough drugs to kill me so I'm pretty sure they are just trying to scare me off."

He swore, terrified of what they might try next. He said as much to her as he saw Whitehorse in the distance, the tall cottonwoods marking the Milk River's trail past the small Montana town.

"That's why I have to know as much as possible about the Wellington family history. It doesn't make any sense why anyone would want me out of that house unless…"

"Unless?" he asked.

"My sister-in-law seems to be rather jealous of my relationship with my brother."

"So much so that she drugged you?"

"Possibly. I saw Jayden, the single man at the house, with one of the wives. It could have been Sierra, which would explain why she might want to get rid of my brother. That and his inheritance. And I have a feeling Sierra hasn't been honest about her past."

Yep, a viper's nest, Marshall thought as he pulled into the yard of an old house on the river on what locals called Millionaire Row. The houses were modest by most standards, two to three stories and wood framed. This one had a large shop next to it, where he figured they would find the owner.

"You sure you're up for this?" he asked as Alexa rubbed her temples.

She nodded, although he could see it hurt her head to do so.

Marshall led her toward the large metal shop building to meet a friend of his father's who had roots that ran back to before the railroad cut across this part of Montana.

"Hey, Little Chisholm," Dave called as they stepped into the cavernous building. He'd been calling all six of the brothers that since they were kids and his father used to bring them here on visits. He wiped his hands on a rag and stood from where he'd been working on a large lawn mower.

Marshall used to love to come over to Dave's shop

in the winter to sit by the woodstove and listen to his father and Dave talk hunting and fishing, the weather and what was going on locally. Dave usually knew everything going on. Marshall recalled many tall tales that got kicked around this building over the years.

"Dave, this is my friend Alexa Cross," he said by way of introduction. "She is interested in the Wellington family."

Dave, a wiry old man with a shock of white hair and intense blue eyes, smiled. "You one of them staying out there at the mansion?"

Alexa nodded, even though it hurt to do so. "Anything you can tell me would be greatly appreciated."

He studied her for a moment as if sizing her up, then invited them to sit in one of the mismatched chairs around a desk at the back. "You're not a relation, are you?" he asked as he walked over to an antique soda pop machine. "Coke or Dr. Pepper, those are your choices."

"No, I'm not a relative," Alexa said.

"I'll take a Coke," Marshall said and looked over at Alexa. She nodded. "Alexa will too."

"Wouldn't want to tell you anything if you were," Dave said with a shake of his head as he brought them each a Coke and a Dr. Pepper for himself. "Nasty business, those Wellingtons."

"So you knew the family?" Marshall asked.

Dave let out a chortle as he sat down behind his desk and leaned back in the chair. The desk was covered with papers, just as the shed was full of anything and everything a person could imagine. The heads of antelope, elk and deer lined the walls, along with old calendars and other memorabilia, including probably every metal license plate Dave and his family had ever owned.

"Now that was one scary family," Dave was saying. "I heard one of them had inherited the house. What's this one like?"

Marshall looked to Alexa. "How would you describe her?"

"Her?" Dave raised a brow.

"She is the great-great-granddaughter of the original builder," Alexa said.

"That would be Jedidiah Wellington. Growing up, I heard all kinds of stories about that old man. You've seen the house. He brought in German craftsmen to build it. Spent a small fortune. Craziest thing anyone had ever seen the way he designed it."

"Was it originally planned as a hotel?" Alexa asked.

Dave shook his head. "More like a lodge. He was going to bring in Europeans to hunt down in the Missouri Breaks and up into that wild country to the north of the Chisholm place."

"What happened to change his mind?" Marshall asked.

"His daughter hung herself in one of the rooms upstairs. She'd gotten pregnant by a local cowboy, had the baby and supposedly, because the man wouldn't marry her, killed herself."

"There were rumors that Jedidiah killed her in a rage for having a bastard child."

"What happened to the baby?" she asked with a shudder.

"The wife was raising it. Then one night she came into town, hysterical, said the baby had been kidnapped.

The infant was later found smothered to death in the basement. No one ever believed the baby had been taken, but they had no proof that someone in the house had done it. No kidnapper was ever caught. Figure the wife or Jedidiah killed it. The wife went mad after that, had to be locked up in one of the rooms. My grandfather said the wailing was unbearable. There'd been a small town there. But the railroad was coming through about then. They all moved away, wanting to get as far away from that kind of trouble as they could."

"That's horrible," Alexa said, thinking that it explained the Crying Woman device she'd found behind the wall. Someone at that house knew the Wellington's history, just as she had suspected. "She died in the house?"

"Yep. Sierra and Jedidiah had a son too," Dave said and stopped talking abruptly at the sound of Alexa's sudden intake of breath. "Something wrong?"

"No, I'm sorry. It's just that the woman who inherited the house, her name is Sierra," Alexa said, thinking of the old photograph and the resemblance to the current Sierra.

"Probably named after her great-great-grandmother," Dave said, as if he didn't see anything strange about that.

Named after a woman who went crazy in the house that Sierra Wellington Cross now wanted to live? Alexa took a drink of the icy cold soda pop in her hand, her hand shaking.

Dave got back into his rhythm again. "Jedidiah gave up on his plan to make it a hunting lodge, closed off a lot of the rooms, lived there with his son. Some family and servants came and went over that time. Rumors circulated about the horrible things that went on in that house. The son, I think his name was John, married. His young wife died during a hard winter. Froze to death just yards from the house. John said she'd gone out to check the chickens, but everyone believed she was trying to flee that house, fell and died in a snowdrift."

Dave took a sip of his soda pop. "She left behind a son who grew up and lived in the old place for a while. He was named after his grandfather, Jedidiah. Jed left, and no one saw him for years. By the time he came back, the rest of them were dead and buried."

Jed Wellington, Alexa realized, would have been Sierra's grandfather.

"Brought his wife and kids, a son and daughter. Daughter fell down an old well and died. Son left when he was old enough. He only came back a couple of times. I suspect the only reason was because of the scandal hanging over his head. Came back here to hide out."

"What scandal was that?" Marshall asked.

Dave took another drink, clearly relishing the story of the Wellingtons. "Money. Not sure of the specifics. I just know he stole a bunch of it from someone. Heard later that he killed himself."

Alexa stared at the old man as she realized he must be talking about Sierra's father. "What was this Wellington's name?"

"Went by J. A.Wellington. I had the newspaper clipping. Not sure what happened to it."

"What happened to the house?" Marshall asked.

"Some old-maid niece moved in with what family

was left. She was the last to die there. Hardly anyone had seen her for years."

Dave chuckled. "Did hear one great story about old Jed. Wrecked his car one night on the road out to his place. Swore to the sheriff and old doc that he was being chased by a phantom pickup—and it wasn't the first time either."

"A phantom pickup?" Marshall asked and chuckled. "Sounds to me like old Jed got into the sauce."

"Swore he hadn't had a thing to drink," Dave said. "After that there were occasionally stories about a pickup chasing teenagers out on that road late at night. Said the truck would almost run them off the road and then just up and disappear."

Alexa was still thinking about Sierra's father killing himself after some sort of scandal. She couldn't help but feel sympathy for her sister-in-law. She knew what it was like to grow up without a father.

"That family certainly met with a lot of tragedy," Marshall said, glancing over at her. She saw concern in his gaze and felt another heartstring sing. "Thanks for telling us everything, Dave."

"Yes. Thank you for the information," Alexa said as she got to her feet.

"A lot of hair-raising stories have come out of *that* house and the people who have lived there," Dave said. "Kids still tell tales about seeing things out there at night, including that old pickup trying to run them off the road. In their cases, though I'm sure alcohol was involved. Still, you couldn't get me to stay in that house for any amount of money."

"You believe in ghosts?" Alexa asked, surprised that he would.

"I believe in evil," Dave said as he chucked his empty soda can into a large trash container by the back door. "They say that when there is a violent death, the soul lingers. That's unholy ground out there. Someone should have burned that place down years ago. Take some dynamite to it."

"You all right?" Marshall asked as they left.

"I guess I'm not surprised." She'd sensed a dark past in the house, though she was shaken by what she'd learned. "Someone else in that house knows the history."

"The Crying Woman," he said. "You think it was meant to be the original Sierra Wellington."

She shivered at the thought that the *latest* Sierra might be behind all of this, since she would be the most likely to know the Wellington history.

But how could she use her family's tragedies? Why would she?

Chapter 10

Marshall had been wonderful at supper, but after everything she'd learned about her sister-in-law's family, Alexa hadn't been a very good date.

"I'm sorry I wasn't much fun tonight," she said as they left the restaurant.

"Hey, I just enjoy being with you," he said, smiling at her as he led her to his pickup. "I know you have a lot on your mind."

"I can't get my mind off the Wellington family's tragic history."

"Will you tell your brother about his wife's family?" Marshall asked as they left Whitehorse and headed north along the Milk River. It had gotten dark. The headlights of the pickup cut a swath of light through the blackness.

"I don't know. I doubt he'll see anything pertinent

about the information. He's blind when it comes to Sierra. He won't want to admit that she might be anything like her family. According to Sierra, she was raised by her single mother. Depending on when her father killed himself, she might not even be able to remember him."

"Your brother could have a point. How much of who we are can we blame on our genes? I never knew my biological father, barely remember my mother. I consider Hoyt Chisholm my father. He raised me with his values. I believe I'm the man I am because of him."

Alexa smiled over at him. She liked the man he was. But she could argue the part genetics played since she didn't just look like her mother. She had fought everything about her mother's life and yet here she was, her mother's daughter, cursed with at least some of her mother's gift. Wasn't it just as possible that a bad gene could be handed down? A criminal gene?

"Sierra certainly comes from an interesting gene pool," Alexa said. "I'd like to know more about her mother. Actually more about Sierra and her father."

"It probably wouldn't hurt to learn more about *everyone* living there right now, given what's happened to you," Marshall said.

He had a point. She wouldn't mind knowing more about all of the people in that house.

"What are you going to do if you can't talk your brother into leaving?"

"I don't know. Eventually I have to get back to work." Alexa looked out her side window. She had a job, an apartment, and she supposed that would be considered a life. But it had always felt temporary. Journalists moved around a lot, from paper to paper. She'd just assumed she would too until she could quit and write children's books. That was her dream.

"I'm sure you're anxious to get back," Marshall said.

She looked over at him. "Not that anxious, actually."

He smiled at her and started to reach for her hand when headlights suddenly flashed on behind them. Marshall let out a curse as a vehicle's headlights filled their truck cab with blinding light.

"What the hell?" he said.

Alexa saw what appeared to be an old pickup riding their bumper. "Is he trying to run you off the road?"

Just then the old truck slammed into the back of their pickup. Their truck fishtailed and the other truck fell back a little.

"Hang on," Marshall said and jammed his foot on the gas. His pickup took off down the narrow road, gravel flying.

As fast as they were going, the lights of the old pickup grew brighter and brighter behind them as the driver quickly caught up.

Alexa looked over at Marshall, then at the speedometer. They were going over a hundred. She knew there was a curve coming up. So did Marshall. She could see tension in his expression. His big hands gripped the wheel as they went down a hill and flew up another.

And suddenly the lights behind them went out. Alexa turned in her seat. The pickup was gone. It had just disappeared.

Marshall hit the brakes. The pickup skidded to a stop in the middle of the road just yards from the curve.

She could see he was shaken as he glanced back

in his rearview mirror, then over at her. "Tell me that wasn't the phantom truck Dave told us about."

All Alexa could do was stare back at the empty road as her heart rate slowly dropped back to normal.

Marshall knew there was no chance in hell that he was going to be able to sleep. He stood on the porch, the August night hot and without a breath of breeze. He couldn't help thinking about the old pickup that had tried to run them off the road. That coupled with what he'd learned about the Wellingtons was bound to give him nightmares. He couldn't even imagine what it would do to Alexa tonight.

He hated dropping her off at that house, knowing what they did. He wished she would come over but when he glanced out at Wellington Manor, he saw no lights on her side of the mansion.

The night should have soothed what ailed him. He loved this time of year, loved the smells as grains ripened and grasses turned golden. Standing here, he could hear the lowing of the cattle. On nights like this, he could feel that strong connection he had with this land, this place.

Unfortunately, that old pickup that had chased them nagged at him. While he might believe evil could be passed down from generation to generation and concede that some spirits just couldn't rest, he didn't believe in phantom pickups. The truck that had tried to run them off the road had been real. He'd heard the sound of metal meeting metal. There was nothing phantom about that truck—nor its driver—and tomorrow he'd prove it.

The heat pressed down on him. He glanced toward Wellington Manor again and caught the glimmer of the pond in the dark cottonwoods. What he needed was a swim. He hadn't gone swimming in the middle of the night since he was a kid and lately he'd been feeling like a kid again.

Alexa. She was responsible for the way he was feeling. He warned himself that she would be leaving soon. She'd have to get back to her job, as she'd said. But he remembered what he'd read about her in that interview. She wanted to write children's books. Couldn't you write children's books anywhere? Even in a remote part of Montana?

He shook his head at the fantasy his thoughts had taken and, grabbing a towel, headed for the pond to cool off.

Alexa had been grateful to slip into the house and find no one waiting up for her. She didn't know what she was going to tell her brother, but whatever she decided tomorrow would be soon enough.

She went straight to her room, unlocked the door and stepped in. Everything appeared to be as she had left it and yet she sensed that someone had been there. With all the locks the same in the house, anyone could come and go at will with a skeleton key, just as she had done.

It was late and she was exhausted after the day she'd had. She changed into a nightgown even though she doubted she would be able to sleep, her mind still whirling. What if everything that was happening was just as her brother had suspected? Something evil that emanated from this house? Some leftover evil from generations of evil?

Moving to the French doors, she stepped out on the

balcony to look toward Marshall's house. His house was dark. She marveled that he was able to put everything out of his mind and go right to bed.

Alexa started to step away from the window when she saw two figures in the trees beside the house. Jayden and a young blond woman. As they slipped into the house through a back door, Alexa recognized the woman Jayden had his arm around. Sierra.

She hurriedly stepped back. Her heart threatened to break. She didn't want to believe her sister-in-law would be cheating on Landon, especially since they'd only just married. But nothing was as it should be in this house.

Angry and upset, she threw herself on the bed and closed her eyes tight against the tears. She'd come here to help her brother, and now she would be the one to break his heart. Emotionally exhausted, she fell into a deep sleep.

"Alexa?"

She stirred.

"Alexa?"

Opening her eyes, she saw her mother standing next to her bed.

"You must save your brother," her mother said. "You know what you have to do."

Startled, Alexa jerked up in the bed, blinking wildly. For a moment, she was back in her childhood bedroom. But as she blinked again the bedroom at Wellington Manor came into focus. The room was empty. Her mother was gone.

If she had ever been there at all.

But her words still hung in the air and there was a familiar smell....

Alexa bolted from the bed. Her nightgown was drenched with sweat and she was breathing hard.

"It was just a nightmare," she whispered to herself as she stepped to the window, hoping for a breath of air.

That's when she saw him, his cowboy hat cocked back on his head. He wore nothing but jeans and boots, a towel draped over one shoulder as he sauntered toward the pond.

He disappeared behind the trees. A moment later she heard a splash.

The sound pulled her—just as the thought did of the cowboy in the cool water of the pond.

She grabbed her robe, drew it on and, taking her key, hurried out of her room. The hallway was empty. She tiptoed down the stairs and through the living room to slip out the front door.

For a moment, she stood on the step, hesitating. She'd already dragged Marshall into her nightmare. She knew what could happen if she continued down to the pond. Just the thought sent a shiver through her. She took a step, then another. As she walked through the deep shadows of the trees, she felt excitement stir within her—and desire. She began to run.

At the edge of the trees, she stopped. She could see him swimming through the dark water, droplets washing over his brown skin, his back and shoulders shimmering in the moonlight.

She'd never seen a more beautiful man.

Marshall took another stroke and opened his eyes. She was standing at the edge of the trees, a vision in white. It reminded him of the first time he'd seen her.

He watched, fascinated, as she stepped from the trees, her white robe sliding off her slim sun-browned shoulders. For a moment, she stood silhouetted in the moonlight making her nightgown transparent. He could see the lush curves of her breasts, the slim waist, the full hips.

As she waded out into the water, he saw the dark of her nipples, the points hard pebbles against the fabric.

His gaze locked with hers. Slowly she reached down and lifted the hem of her nightgown, raising it up and over her head. She tossed the gown back toward the dry shore, then dove into the water and swam out toward him.

Marshall realized he had been holding his breath. She was so breathtaking. The water felt like cool silk against his skin as he took a final stroke and drifted slowly toward her.

He drew up, treading water, as she moved into him and pressed her naked body against his. Her skin felt hot and silken. Water droplets jeweled on her lashes as she looked at him—her look hotter than her skin against his. His desire spiked as he pulled her closer.

"I saw you from my window," she whispered.

"I wished on that star up there that I would find you down here," he whispered back.

They kissed, sweet, gentle kisses that grew hotter. She wrapped her legs around his waist as he deepened the kiss and treaded water to keep them afloat.

Her full breasts were pressed against his bare chest, the hard nipples tantalizing. The porcelain feel of her skin against his stole his breath, revved his heartbeat. He'd never wanted a woman the way he wanted her.

He swam them toward shore where the trees were the thickest, the spot where she'd dropped her robe.

Carrying her from the water, he laid her down on the robe, the warm earth beneath her. For a long moment, he merely stared down into her beautiful eyes. He'd never made love like this, under the moonlight, his body still cool from the water, droplets falling from his hair onto her radiant flesh.

Alexa had never dared throw caution to the wind. And yet the moment she'd taken a step toward the pond—and this cowboy—she knew there would be no turning back. She'd never wanted a man enough to be so brazen until Marshall. She had opened herself up to him, but now it would be a total surrender.

He took her in his arms, his hands cradling her head as he kissed her lips, then kissed a trail of molten fire down her throat to her breasts.

Alexa sucked in a breath as his mouth captured one of her nipples. He teased it with his teeth, making her arch against him.

She reached for him, needing, wanting, pleading for him to take her. He slowly lowered himself onto her, and she felt the strength and weight of him.

She took him in, opening the last of herself to this cowboy.

Marshall lay on his back, staring up at the stars. He'd never felt such contentment. He could hear the soft lap of the pond as a fish broke the surface. In the shadows, several ducks honked softly to the flutter of wings and splashing water.

Beside him, Alexa breathed softly. He glanced over at her. She was smiling, also gazing up at the stars.

"A penny for your thoughts," he whispered.

"I've never felt like this before."

He laughed quietly and rolled onto his side to look at her. "Me either. I want to stay here forever."

She smiled ruefully. "If only we could."

A set of headlights scanned across the horizon as a vehicle pulled into Wellington Manor. Marshall and Alexa stayed hidden in the shadows of the trees down by the pond but could hear the sound of laughter and voices.

"Gigi and Devlin," Alexa said. "I hadn't realized they'd been gone when I came home."

He hadn't paid any attention to what cars were parked by the house either. He'd had too much on his mind to care.

"I should get back," she said, sitting up and reaching for her nightgown.

Marshall didn't want her to go—not back to the house, not back to Spokane. But he knew he couldn't stop her. Alexa had to finish what she'd come here to do—if she even knew what that was.

"I'm glad you came swimming with me," he whispered.

She smiled at him, touched his cheek with her cool fingers then rose to slip the nightgown over her.

He handed her the robe, now damp from where they had made love on it. She drew the fabric to her, touching it to her lips as her gaze locked with his.

"I wish I didn't have to go," she whispered.

He could only nod. There was so much he wanted

to say but he sensed the timing was all wrong. "Alexa, I... I've never felt like I do right now."

She kissed him. He pulled her closer for a moment, her kiss lingering on his lips. "I'll see you tomorrow."

And then she was gone, a white vision disappearing into the trees as she hurried toward Wellington Manor.

Marshall had the impulse to go after her, fear growing inside him that he wouldn't see her again because that house and the people in it would be the death of her.

Alexa slipped in through the front door and padded barefoot past the dark kitchen. Gigi and Devlin must have already gone upstairs. She breathed a sigh of relief as she headed for the stairs and froze as a door opened down the hall.

Sierra came out of Jayden's room and started toward her. Still cloaked in shadow, Alexa quickly stepped into an alcove beneath the stairs an instant before Sierra passed. She was dressed in her nightgown and robe, barefoot, her hair a mess.

Alexa wanted to confront her. But instead, she pressed her back against the wall as Sierra hurried up the stairs.

For a long time, Alexa stood, shaking inside. A part of her regretted not approaching her sister-in-law right there and then. But she knew that Sierra would turn this around somehow and the person who would suffer the most would be Landon.

It was going to break Landon's heart when she told him. But what was the alternative? Wait and let him find out on his own? Or have an accident that left Sierra a rich widow?

So Alexa stood there in the dark, giving Sierra enough time to return to her room. Her earlier contentment gone, she finally padded up the stairs. Alexa was almost to the top when she saw Jayden standing in the hall, watching her.

She didn't know how long he'd been there, but there was no doubt he knew she'd seen Sierra coming out of his room and he didn't look happy about it.

Chapter 11

Marshall awoke thinking about the pickup that had chased them and tried to run them off the road the night before. At breakfast at the ranch, he mentioned he'd seen the phantom truck.

His brothers laughed, but he asked anyway, "Logan, you said some friends of yours had been chased by it. When was that?"

"Probably fifteen years ago now."

"Did they describe the truck?" Marshall asked.

"You aren't serious, right?" Zane said.

"An old-model Chevy, stepside, two-toned. Is that what chased you?" Logan asked.

Marshall nodded as he rose from the table.

"I wouldn't go messing with somethin' you don't know about," Logan warned.

"That's just it. I think I do know what I'm messing

with," Marshall said. "The question now is only who's behind it?"

After leaving the ranch, he drove up the same road he and Alexa had taken the night before. He slowed at the point where he'd first seen the pickup appear behind him and turned his pickup around in the middle of the road to drive back over a small rise.

At the bottom were tracks in the dirt that led back into a stand of trees. From the trees, someone could have seen him and Alexa coming up the road, waited until they passed then pulled out and followed with their headlights off until they topped the rise and seemed to appear out of nowhere.

He drove to the point where the pickup had seemingly vanished. This time he knew what to look for and found where the pickup had left the road. The driver had done his best to cover the tracks, but Marshall was still able to follow them back into a stand of Russian olive trees around an old dump.

The pickup was hidden among a half-dozen other old vehicles that had been abandoned there. Most of the others were older. Stopping the truck, Marshall climbed out, wary of rattlesnakes in all this junk.

The phantom pickup was a 1956 Chevy 3100 stepside pickup, its two-toned paint long faded. As he opened the driver's side door, he saw that mice had nested in the floorboards and bench seat. But someone had brushed the nests from behind the steering wheel last night.

As he slid in, he made a note of how far back the seat had been pushed. The driver had been long legged, probably male. The other time the phantom truck had made its run had been because some teenagers had been snooping around Wellington Manor. Marshall didn't believe it was any coincidence that the driver of the truck had come after Alexa and him last night. Someone at that house knew she'd been snooping around. And probably suspected he was helping her.

As he climbed out of the old pickup, he wondered which of the males at the house had been driving this truck last night. There were four men at the house: Archer, Devlin, Jayden and Landon.

Marshall started to correct himself, to leave Alexa's brother off his suspect list, but unlike Alexa he didn't trust any of them—Landon included.

Someone had tried to scare them last night. Which meant that someone feared Alexa was getting too close to whatever secret they were trying to keep in that house.

From working in journalism, Alexa had made a lot of contacts over the years. It took only a few calls on her cell phone to get what she needed the next morning. She'd driven into Whitehorse and used her cell phone, afraid to talk on the Wellington Manor phone for fear someone would be listening on another line.

"I have the obit and the police report right here," a young journalist in Nevada told her.

"Police report?" Alexa said, glancing out the SUV window as a car went by. She couldn't help feeling paranoid, given everything that had happened.

"The suicide was investigated as a possible homicide," the reporter said. "The father, J. A. Wellington, died of a fatal gunshot wound to the head in their home outside of Las Vegas. He'd been a financial consultant.

Turned out it was all a scam. He'd bilked investors out of millions of dollars."

"Does it mention the wife and daughter?" she asked.

"The wife was cleared. Apparently she knew nothing about her husband's business and wasn't home at the time of the murder."

"What happened to them?" Alexa asked, thinking of a recent case like this where the family was left penniless.

"The wife and daughter left the state. We did a follow-up story five years later when the daughter was sixteen. The two were living down near Los Angeles in some dump. The wife was working as a waitress, but they were barely getting by. It was pretty sad. Apparently the husband knew the feds were on to him and killed himself. But what made the case interesting is that the money was never recovered."

At the age of eleven, Sierra Wellington had gone from filthy rich to flat broke. Alexa could only assume what that had done to Sierra.

Alexa felt her heart begin to pound. Was it possible she was secretly looking for the money in the house while pretending to remodel it for a bed-and-breakfast? "How is it possible that the money he stole never turned up?"

"Maybe he socked it away in another country or turned it into gold bars and buried it. Who knows?"

"But if that was the case, then why would he kill himself and not tell anyone where it was?" Alexa asked, thinking out loud.

"Maybe he *did* tell someone," the reporter said. "But

it wasn't the wife. The feds kept an eye on her. She died broke."

"What about the daughter?" Alexa asked, wondering if the feds were keeping an eye on her or if they thought she was too young at the time of her father's death to know anything about it.

"Last I heard she was in college on a hardship-case scholarship."

Marshall was glad to get Alexa's call. He'd tried the house and was told that she must have gone into town as her SUV was missing.

He could hear what sounded like arguing in the background and had barely hung up when Alexa had called. Marshall listened as she filled him in on what she'd found out about her sister-in-law.

"You think her father told Sierra where he hid the money?"

"Maybe. Maybe not," Alexa said. "But I wouldn't be surprised if she thinks it's in that house. It would explain a lot."

He agreed. "But wasn't it the old-maid relative who left her the house, not her father?"

"I'm not sure anyone left her the house. From what I've been able to find out, the house was tied up in the niece's estate. Sierra had petitioned for it as the last living Wellington and finally got the mansion. Apparently she'd been trying to get it for some time."

"It certainly sounds like she was anxious to have it," Marshall said. "But if she knew where the money was hidden, wouldn't she have already found it?"

"Maybe he didn't tell her where. Sierra told me that

the woman closed off most of the house, living only on the first floor in the servants' quarters. So if Sierra's father paid the niece a visit and hid the money, thinking he was going to get away with all of it, it could be anywhere. You could hide millions of dollars in that house and it might never be found."

"Still it seems crazy for her father to kill himself after all he went through to steal the money, and then not tell anyone where he hid it," Marshall said. "Sierra was eleven at the time, right? Maybe he didn't tell her for fear she couldn't keep the secret."

"Maybe," Alexa replied.

When she said no more, he told her about the pickup he'd found hidden at the old dump. "Someone was trying to scare us off. They don't like you snooping around. I'm worried what they will do next."

"So far all they've done is try to scare me," Alexa said. "I just hate that I've dragged you into this."

As if she could keep him out, he thought, and said as much. "I hope you don't regret last night."

Her laugh filled him with pleasure. "I could never regret last night."

"Me either. Listen, there's been some trouble at the ranch. I have to go by there and make sure my stepmother is all right. Call me later?"

"The group at the house were talking about going into town tonight to listen to some country-western band. Even Carolina has agreed to go along. I'm not sure if she has changed her mind about leaving here or if she just needs to get out of this house for a while since she can't seem to get a flight out yet," Alexa said.

"If they do, I plan to see what they've been working on in this house."

"Count me in. Just promise me you won't do it alone."

She laughed again. "I'm brave, but not that brave. The truth is this place gives me the creeps."

Marshall figured it was a lot more than that. If there was even a chance that Alexa had her mother's gift, then she had to be terrified of what she might see in that house.

Alexa thought about what Marshall had said. She was convinced that Sierra's father could have told the girl about the money. If he knew his daughter, he wouldn't have been worried about her being able to keep a secret. Sierra, Alexa believed, was like her father. She wouldn't have talked for fear someone might take the money from her or she might have to share it.

It was that last thought that sent an icy dagger straight to her heart. She had just assumed that Sierra had married Landon for his money, which still might be true.

But if she found the millions, she wouldn't need him anymore—and from the little Alexa had seen of Sierra, she knew the woman wouldn't want to share. Not that Landon would let Sierra keep the money if he knew where it had come from.

She was even more worried about her brother but dreaded telling him everything she'd learned. The truth was, she feared he wouldn't believe her. So far, all she had was conjecture. Nothing she learned proved that his life was in danger. Or even that Sierra was having an affair with Jayden.

But if she could find where someone in this house had been searching for the missing millions...

First though, she had to find out everything she could about the people now staying in that house. At the county library, Alexa got on the internet and began her search. There wasn't a lot to find on the occupants of Wellington Manor because they were young and hadn't done much with their lives yet.

But thanks to the internet, she was able to gather what was there easily. She started with the men. Devlin Landers had been the star of his debate team in high school and in college had majored in prelaw. He had married Gigi Brown after graduation. Gigi had been the head cheerleader in high school and a mediocre student in college, who'd majored in art history.

Archer Durand had been a football star in high school, played a little in college until he was injured then seemed to be more interested in the social life at his frat house. He'd majored in mass communication and had married Carolina Bates his senior year, her junior year.

Alexa frowned. Why did that name sound so familiar? She shook her head and typed in Carolina Bates. She had been a good student, graduating at the top of her class and had gone to college on a scholarship, majoring in criminal law.

She typed in Jayden Farrell. A half-dozen names came up, none of them matching the one staying at Wellington Manor. As far as she could tell, Jayden Farrell didn't exist—or he'd lied about who he was.

It struck her that Sierra might not be the only person looking for the millions her father had stolen.

By the time Alexa reached the house, the driveway was empty. She opened the door and called out, "Anyone here?"

No answer. But just to be safe, she walked down to Jayden's room and knocked. When there was no answer, she tried the knob. Locked. Using her key, she opened his door.

The room was almost too neat. He'd apparently brought little with him to Montana. She did a quick search, then, feeling the hair stand on the back of her neck, she spun around, half expecting to find him standing behind her.

There was no one there, but it had spooked her enough that she left his room and went to the phone.

"They've all gone into town," she said when Marshall answered. "Want to come over and see if we're right about what they've been doing over here?"

"I'll be right over."

True to his word, Marshall cut across the pasture and was there minutes later. She quickly filled him in on what she'd learned during her internet search.

"Jayden caught me coming home the other night. I'd left a light on and he'd turned it out and waited for me."

"You think he was trying to scare you?"

"Actually, I got the feeling he was trying to *warn* me. If anyone knows what's going on in this house, it's Jayden. And when I tried to find out more about him, I came up blank. I think he lied about who he is. I'm wondering how many people are looking for the money in this house?"

"They all could be working together," Marshall said.

Alexa didn't want to believe that, since it would be

harder for Landon not to be a part of it and she refused to think he knew anything about what was going on.

She led the way upstairs, and using the skeleton key from her room, began opening doors along the second floor. In each of the rooms, they could see places in the plaster-and-lath walls had been repaired.

"Are you thinking what I am?" Marshall asked.

"Someone has been looking in the walls, then repairing them when they haven't found what they were looking for?"

He nodded.

They found the same types of patch jobs in all the rooms and along the hallway. On the third floor, they wandered through the furniture and boxes. Everywhere behind them were places where someone had been searching, no doubt for the millions J. A. Wellington had stolen.

"It looks like they have run out of places to search," Marshall said after they'd found more patch jobs throughout the first floor as well.

"Except for the basement."

The door to the basement, they found, was padlocked. Marshall shot her a look. "Why would they padlock this door but no others?"

"Because they haven't finished searching down there. Can you open it?"

"Not without someone knowing we did."

She didn't care. "Open it."

From the tool bucket he found in a corner in the kitchen, he pulled out a hacksaw and went to work on the lock. A few moments later, she heard the lock snap open.

The door swung in to expose a dark stairway to an even darker basement.

Marshall handed her one of the flashlights he'd taken from the tool bucket, then pulled out the one he'd brought from home before leading the way down the stairs.

"I had to meet Aggie and put an end to this," Emma said, tired of all the questions and recriminations. "I made a decision. Maybe it was wrong—"

"Maybe?" Hoyt snapped. He had taken off his Stetson and now raked both hands through his hair in exasperation. Across the kitchen table, Sheriff McCall Crawford looked just as upset.

"I had to see what Aggie had found," Emma said as she motioned to the contents of the envelope that had been dumped out on her kitchen table.

"I saw your expression when you looked at the photographs," she said to her husband. "There's a chance the woman Aggie found is Laura, isn't there?"

He glared at her from across the table.

"You should have told me about the note and your plan to meet Aggie," the sheriff said.

"Aggie couldn't bring this to you," Emma replied to McCall. "She was afraid you wouldn't listen to her."

"What was the plan after she gave you this information?" McCall asked.

Emma made a point of not looking at her husband as she said, "Aggie and I were going to confront her."

Hoyt made a furious sound, shoved himself to his feet and walked out of the room for a few moments.

"Aggie was afraid that if this woman—"

"Sharon Jones."

"Right, if she thought law enforcement was on to her, she would disappear and then Aggie couldn't prove that she wasn't crazy—and I wouldn't know when Laura was going to strike."

"Laura is dead," Hoyt snapped as he came back into the room.

Emma shot him a look. "Is she? Can you definitely say that this woman is not Laura?"

"Yes. Because I saw her drown."

"You said the boating trip was Laura's idea," Emma said patiently. "Why would a woman who allegedly hated water and couldn't swim well want to go on a boat trip on Fort Peck Reservoir, especially when she was planning to divorce you?"

"I have no idea but she did."

"Exactly. And you said yourself that she was horribly jealous. If you even looked at another woman—"

"Emma," he said, dropping down in front of her and taking her hands in his. "Honey, you have to stop this. You are getting as nuts as that damned insurance investigator."

The memory of Aggie's cry after the shot was fired and her fall into the river sent a stab of pain through Emma.

"I believe Aggie." She looked to the sheriff. "Have your deputies found her yet?"

McCall shook her head. "We're dragging the river now."

Emma nodded, wondering if they would find her body. Laura Chisholm's body had never been found in Fort Peck Reservoir.

"What about Sharon Jones?" she asked the sheriff.

"I've contacted the Billings police. They're going to pick her up for questioning."

"Can you get DNA or fingerprints or something to prove who she is?" Emma asked.

"We'll take it one step at a time once she is picked up," McCall said.

Emma nodded, hoping Aggie wasn't right about what would happen.

The basement door opened on a room with a low ceiling crisscrossed with plumbing pipes.

Marshall shone the flashlight beam around the room, found a switch and several overhead bulbs blinked on.

The basement smelled musty and damp. Alexa hugged herself, trying to ignore the cold as well as whatever else had been down here. Impressions of dark events rushed over her. She closed her eyes for a moment, fighting off the house's past.

"Are you all right?" Marshall asked.

She nodded and opened her eyes.

"You don't have to do this."

"Yes, I do."

He gave her an encouraging smile. "Then let's see what's here."

As he shone the flashlight down one corridor after another, it reminded her of a subway tunnel. The chill, the smells, the clank of the old pipes.

"Which way?" Marshall asked.

"Look at the floor," Alexa said, after remembering the third floor and the trail through the dust. It wasn't as dusty down here, but there were scuff marks on the concrete—and mud. They followed them down one of the corridors.

Alexa had never been claustrophobic—until now. The low-hanging, large, corroded pipes seemed to press down on her. The basement was a maze of narrow aisles that ran between whatever machinery had originally provided heat and possibly electricity to the mansion. She found herself ducking her head even though, as tall as Marshall was, he didn't need to duck.

The trail ended in a dead end. Alexa knelt down to pick up a piece of dried mud from a boot sole. It had been dropped just inches from where the wall ended.

"This wall isn't concrete like the others," Marshall noted.

"There's a way through here," she said and began to search for a panel or switch that would open the wall.

Marshall found it, a small handle that looked as if it turned off water to the plumbing overhead. Instead, when he pulled it, a panel slid back into the wall with a groan.

He shot her a look as he shone his flashlight beam into the darkness beyond the wall.

Alexa saw another long corridor, this a tunnel, narrow and cramped. The smell coming out of it turned her stomach. The last place she wanted to go was down there.

"Why don't you stay here," Marshall suggested, no doubt seeing her revulsion.

It was tempting. But the option was waiting here for him. "Let's go," she said, happy to let him lead the way.

Marshall blocked the door open with an old, heavy

gear wheel he found in the corner and they started down the tunnel.

Alexa could hear what sounded like mice scurrying ahead of them. But it was what else she felt that had her trembling. Something horrible had happened down here. Her skin crawled, rippling with gooseflesh, as she fought to keep out the images that flashed inside her head.

They hadn't gone far when they came to something that brought Marshall up short. She heard him let out a curse, then turn to try to shield her from it.

But she'd already felt the horror and leaned past him to look. Even knowing what it was, she hadn't been prepared for the cage.

It had been built back into the earth like a root cellar, only this small hole had been fitted with bars to keep something inside.

Or someone. She shuddered and turned away. Marshall put his arm around her and pulled her into his chest. Like her, he must be thinking about the great-great-grandmother who'd gone crazy after the death of her daughter and granddaughter. Dave had said the basement was where the granddaughter's body had been found.

"It was the screaming," Alexa said. "He put her down here so he didn't have to hear it." She felt Marshall shudder, but he didn't pull away. Instead he drew her closer, smoothing her hair with his hand. "Have you seen enough?"

She shook her head. "We have to know what is at the end of this tunnel. If they've found the money."

"I would imagine that if they had, they would be long gone," Marshall said.

Maybe. Or maybe they would hide the money again until they could leave without causing any suspicion, Alex thought, thinking of Jayden, who'd already announced he would be leaving soon now that summer was almost over.

Marshall let go of her to shine the flashlight beam down the tunnel. The mud trail continued into the darkness ahead, the tunnel growing narrower, the air colder and danker.

Alexa saw him glance at his watch. They had to move quickly now. Time was running out. She didn't dare think about what could happen if they were caught down here.

Chapter 12

Marshall led the way as the tunnel grew more cramped. He'd never minded small places but this tunnel gave him the creeps. He kept seeing that cage back there in the wall. Alexa had known what it was for. He didn't even want to consider how she'd known.

Whatever was going on in this house, someone wanted to keep it a secret. Bad enough to kill?

He didn't want to find out.

Alexa was scared. He could see it in her face, but as he'd learned about her, she was strong and determined. That strength wouldn't let her turn back. Not yet.

"Let's move a little faster," he said, not wanting to alarm her and yet at the same time growing more anxious with each step.

They moved quickly down the tunnel until they reached a spot where someone had been digging in the wall. Bricks had been removed and stacked to one side. The hole was large—and empty.

"Is it a large enough hole to hold millions of dollars?" Alexa asked as her flashlight beam bore into the empty space.

"Depends on what he'd put the money in before he hid it," Marshall said and noted other holes in the brick walls. "It's hard to say if they found something of interest or not."

"But was it the same person who's been searching the rest of the house? Or someone else?" Alexa sighed. "I wonder what they did with the loot if they found it?"

"Squirreled it away somewhere until they can make their exit."

She nodded. "Let's get out of here."

Marshall shone his flashlight to where the tunnel ended just yards away in a set of stairs. "An exit?"

Stepping to the stairs, he looked up at what appeared to be a door. He shot Alexa a look, then tried the handle.

The door opened onto another set of stairs. Alexa could smell fresh air and bolted up the steps, but quickly stopped when she saw that the exit was covered with what appeared to be a heavy wooden gate.

"Let me," Marshall said, stepping past her. He handed her his flashlight and pushed on the gate. She'd expected it to be heavy, but the gate swung open with relative ease, exposing starlight in the dark canopy overhead and the feathery dark leaves of a cottonwood branch etched against the night sky.

She smelled the water at the pond even before she saw the moonlight glimmering off the smooth surface.

"It's a secret way in and out of the house," she said, stating the obvious. Is this how the lovers she'd seen the first time had been coming and going?

The gate was hidden behind some large rocks and bushes. She wondered who knew about this.

"We should retrace our steps and cover our tracks as best we can," Marshall said. But even as he spoke, Alexa saw car lights top the nearby hill and head this way.

"It's too late," she said. "We can't possibly get back before they enter the house and there is only one way up out of the basement—at least that we know of. They're going to find the broken padlock anyway."

Marshall let out a curse under his breath. "It's one thing for them to know that you were down in the basement. I left the tunnel open."

"It doesn't matter," Alexa said as the cars turned into the drive, the headlights sweeping toward them. "It's time I tell my brother everything."

They ducked down behind the rocks and bushes as the two vehicles came down the lane, stopping in front of the mansion.

They stayed like that until the others had gone inside.

"What if your brother already knows?"

She shot Marshall a shocked look.

"I don't want to upset you, but what if he got you here not to chase away the ghosts, but use your…instincts to tell him where the money was hidden? Or who already found it."

Alexa couldn't help her anger or her disappointment. "You don't know my brother."

"No, I don't. But I hate to see you get hurt. I'm afraid of what will happen when you tell him what you know."

* * *

Alexa walked up through the trees from the pond, taking her time in case she was being watched from one of the many windows.

She was furious with Marshall for even suggesting that her brother could be after the stolen money and even more furious with herself because she hadn't gone to her brother with the truth sooner.

Her excuse had been that she hated the thought of breaking her brother's heart. But the truth was, she was afraid. Afraid of his reaction. She feared Sierra might be right. If push came to shove, Landon would side with his wife—no matter how much evidence there was against Sierra.

Cursing her own doubts about her brother, she still feared for his safety. Whoever had found the money might decide to step up his or her timeline. If Sierra was involved, Alexa feared that the ultimate plan was to get rid of Landon—and her as well, now that she'd become embroiled in this.

What if she couldn't convince her brother to leave this house—and Sierra?

As she opened the front door, Gigi turned from the fire. Archer was throwing more wood on the blaze, the two of them complaining about the cold Montana summer night.

Just then, Devlin came out of the kitchen, carrying a tray with a bottle of wine and a half-dozen glasses.

"Oh, good, there you are," Landon said, appearing right behind her. "We were just about to have a nightcap. I was hoping you would join us."

Alexa felt her stomach knot. After being drugged

once she wasn't about to consume anything in this house that she didn't see someone else drink first.

She looked into her brother's face. This was the most relaxed she'd seen him since she arrived. She felt herself weaken. No way did Landon know what was going on in this house. And yet how could he not suspect?

As she let her gaze travel around the living room, her eyes rested on Jayden. Who better than to sneak down to the basement at night than the single man? The man who insisted on staying in the servants' quarters of the house on the main floor instead of in one of the grander rooms upstairs.

Her heart began to pound. What about the woman he'd met down by the pond? She suspected they had used the tunnel exit to meet. So at least one other person in this house had to know about the digging in the tunnel walls. Sierra? Or one of the other women?

"Join us," Sierra said. She appeared to have already had more than a little something to drink.

Alexa had no choice. "Thank you," she said as she watched Devlin pour the wine. Alexa took the glass she was offered, but simply held it between her hands as she moved over to the fire.

As she pretended to study the wine in the firelight, she secretly watched each of the people in the room, waiting for someone to take the first drink of the wine.

"None for me," Jayden said as Devlin tried to hand him a glass.

Alexa noticed that Devlin didn't take any either.

"To the future," Landon said, coming over to the fire to join Alexa. He lightly touched his wine glass to hers and raised his to his lips, stopping when she didn't do the same.

"Is something wrong?" he asked.

"No." She smiled, her heart hammering in her chest. How could she suspect her brother of anything, let alone drugging her? She raised her glass to her lips.

The glass slipped from her fingers, crashed on the fireplace hearth and shattered, sending red wine into the air to land like blood splatters on the floor.

Sierra let out a cry. "My great-great-grandmother's crystal!"

"I'm so sorry," Alexa said as she quickly hurried into the kitchen to get something to clean up the mess.

"It's no big deal," Landon said to her retreating back.

"What do you mean, 'no big deal'?" Sierra demanded. "Do you have any idea how much that glass was worth?"

"I'll buy you one that costs twice as much," Landon snapped.

The living room fell into a heavy, tense silence.

"I'm going to call it a night," Jayden said. The others agreed.

By the time Alexa returned to the living room, only Landon and Sierra remained. Landon had picked up the larger pieces of glass.

Sierra was standing with her back to the room, and from the way she was standing, she was clearly still furious. "You really know how to ruin a party," she said to Alexa.

"Sierra," Landon hissed under his breath.

"Well, she does."

"It was an accident," Landon said. "There is no harm done."

Sierra pouted but said nothing as Alexa and Landon cleaned up the mess.

"I'll be happy to replace the glass," Alexa said to her sister-in-law.

"That isn't necessary," Landon said.

"It wouldn't be the same anyway," Sierra said.

"I suggest you not use the glasses if they mean that much to you," Landon said through gritted teeth. "I'm going to bed. Can I see you up?" he asked his sister.

Sierra started to protest but Landon cut her off. "I haven't had hardly any time with my sister."

"That's because we are all trying to get this house ready for paying guests," Sierra snapped. "Not to mention your sister has been spending all her time with that cowboy."

Landon shot his wife a look that made her clamp her lips shut, then he and Alexa turned and left.

As they started up the stairs, Alexa looked back. Sierra hadn't touched her wine. The others had left their glasses untouched on the coffee table. She and Landon were almost to the top of the stairs when they heard a crash. Alexa looked back to see that Sierra had thrown the nearly empty wine bottle against the stone fireplace.

Landon's jaw tightened, but he didn't look back.

"I know what you're going to say," Landon said once they were in Alexa's room, the door closed.

A light breeze played at the curtains at the open French doors, the air cool, stars glittering in the huge velvet sky.

Alexa hadn't realized how late it was. Her eyelids felt like sandpaper and she felt tired all over. "I doubt that," she said and plopped down onto the loveseat, too exhausted to stand any longer.

"Sierra is young and headstrong and…" He met his sister's gaze. "Spoiled."

Alexa kept silent. Her brother was intelligent. He had to see that it was more than that.

"What is it you want me to say?" she asked finally.

He chuckled. "Tell me I didn't make a mistake."

She looked up at him and sadly shook her head. "I love you so much."

"I know."

"I just want you to be happy."

"I know," he said as he lowered himself to the chair opposite the loveseat. "I realize now I had a lot of reasons for inviting you here, all of them selfish."

"You were right. There is something going on in this house," Alexa said. "But it isn't the spirits you're worried about, is it?"

"Sometimes I wake up in the middle of the night and Sierra is gone from our bed," he said slowly. "When I ask her about it, she says she has trouble sleeping and likes wandering through the house at night because it's quiet."

"Do you believe her?" Alexa asked.

"I want to." He rubbed the back of his neck, looking as exhausted as she felt. "I haven't wanted to tell Sierra, but I don't want to run a bed-and-breakfast."

It surprised Alexa that he was finally being honest with her. "Why haven't you told her?"

He shook his head. "She seems so set on this.... I don't want to break her heart."

Too bad Sierra didn't feel the same way about him. "You're afraid if it came down to an ultimatum, she would choose the house."

He nodded, then let out a humorless laugh. "Says a lot about my faith in my wife."

"Says more about her feelings for..." Alexa was going to say "you." But quickly changed it to "this house."

"It's all she has," Landon said. "She's never had anything that she can call her own since she was a girl."

"She has you."

He smiled at that.

"Has she talked to you about her past? Her father?"

"I know he killed himself."

"Did you know that he also bilked a lot of money out of his investors?" She saw her brother start to defend the man. "The feds were about to arrest him when he killed himself."

Landon sighed and sank back into his chair. "That explains a lot, huh."

"The money was never recovered."

He looked up in surprise and she nodded.

"I believe he hid it in this house, and I'm not the only one who believes that. Someone has been looking for it. I think they might have found it."

Landon stared at her. "Sierra?"

"Maybe. It's millions of dollars. Are you sure she ever really planned to open a bed-and-breakfast? Or was it just a way to look for the money without anyone suspecting?"

He shook his head. "If Sierra found the money, why wouldn't she…" His voice trailed off as he realized why his wife wouldn't have told him. "What am I going to do, Alexa?"

"I can't tell you what to do, but I think you need to talk to her, tell her how you feel." She almost added, "Find out where she really goes at night," but bit her tongue. "You need to resolve this. Once you're honest with her, maybe she'll be honest with you and you'll know what to do."

He rose to his feet to leave.

"But Landon, be careful. I'm worried about these accidents you've been having."

A sadness washed over his features. "I wondered if she'd married me for my money. Yes, sis, it did cross my mind. But if she now has millions…"

"Or someone else in this house does." She could see he hadn't thought of that.

"You be careful too," he said, suddenly looking worried.

"We both need to get out of here," Alexa said. "Maybe we should go—" She was going to say "tonight" but he cut her off with a shake of his head.

"Tomorrow."

She couldn't hide her relief. "Tomorrow." As he left, she prayed tomorrow would be soon enough.

Marshall mentally kicked himself all the way back to his house. He shouldn't have accused Alexa's brother, knowing how protective she was of him.

He went over their last words to each other with

every step he took on the way across the pasture toward home.

"You're that sure he isn't involved in whatever this is?" he'd asked. He could see that she hadn't wanted to believe it, but she had a blind side to her when it came to her brother.

"Why would he get me here if that was true?"

He had hated to ask, but he'd felt he had to. "You say your brother inherited a lot of money. I assume you did too." He took her silence for a yes. "Who inherits if you die?"

He had seen the fear that leaped to her eyes for just an instant.

"My brother wouldn't—"

"But his wife would?"

She had looked at him, opened her mouth and closed it again then left him standing there as she headed back to that damned house.

He'd wanted to go after her, drag her into his arms and kiss some sense into her. But he'd known how well that would have gone over. He wanted desperately to keep her safe, but one of the reasons he loved her was that she never took the easy way out.

Loved her. The thought made him stumble and almost fall just yards from his house.

He swore. He'd always considered himself a reasonable man. Falling in love at the bat of an eye wasn't reasonable. Falling in love with a total stranger... Maybe worse, a woman whom he knew saw things he never wanted to know about.

He shook his head. As much as he wanted to deny it, he'd fallen in love with that woman.

Turning, he looked back at the house and knew he was no longer a reasonable man. He'd fallen in love with this woman in the bat of an eye and it scared the hell out of him.

The question now was, what was he going to do about it?

Alexa just wanted to fall into the bed and sleep until noon. Tomorrow she would pack and leave—as soon as she was sure Landon was leaving as well.

But tonight, she just wanted to close her eyes in dreamless sleep.

Unfortunately, her mind had something else to say about that. She kept thinking of the tunnel, the cage, the missing bricks where someone had been looking for something—and Marshall.

She hated that she'd left things so badly with him. She hated worse admitting that what he'd said had scared her, because she'd feared he might be right. She'd seen how Landon was around Sierra. How he had over-looked whatever his wife had been up to in the middle of the night. And how he hadn't told his wife how he really felt about this house's future.

Not that Alexa believed for a moment that Sierra had any intention of making Wellington Manor a bed-and-breakfast. All of Sierra's love for this house was noth-ing more than a ruse. Once she retrieved her father's stolen money, she would be out of here in a heartbeat. Not even her great-great-grandmother's crystal could keep that girl in this house. Again.

Unable to sleep, Alexa got up, pulled on her robe and opened her bedroom door. The hallway was empty.

There wasn't a sound other than the sounds old houses always made.

Taking her key, she locked her room, thinking how foolish that was, given that anyone with a skeleton key could get in any room in this house.

Pocketing her key, she headed downstairs to the kitchen. She needed something to help her sleep. No milk and cookies, thank you.

In the kitchen, she found a loaf of half-eaten bread, cut herself a slice then found peanut butter, her favorite, and huckleberry jam. She made herself a peanut-butter sandwich and washed it down with a glass of orange juice from the fridge.

Tomorrow she would apologize to Marshall. That and the sandwich made her feel better. Alexa thought that she might be able to sleep now. As she quietly left the kitchen and started for the stairs, she looked down the hallway to the servants' quarters—and saw Sierra coming out of Jayden's room.

Just then the old clock on the mantel struck two in the morning, making her jump. She ducked back under the stairs, plastering herself against the wall.

She could hear Sierra coming down the hallway. She prayed that her sister-in-law would go up the stairs, but of course Sierra would do just the opposite.

Sierra walked right past her and into the kitchen. Alexa let out the breath she'd been holding as she heard her sister-in-law getting something from the refrigerator.

Curious where Sierra was headed next, Alexa moved into the space under the stairs so she was better hidden.

A few minutes later, Sierra came out of the kitchen

with two bottles of beer. She padded back down the hallway. At Jayden's door, she didn't knock but simply opened it and, glancing back toward the living room, stepped inside and closed the door after her.

Alexa felt sick to her stomach. She knew Sierra must have been the woman she saw with Jayden, first arguing, then in his arms. She'd seen her coming out of his room the other time, Sierra's hair a mess, in her robe. How much more evidence did she need?

Landon needed to know the truth. It would make it much easier for him to leave Sierra, to leave this house.

But as much as Alexa wanted her brother away from Sierra and this house, she couldn't bring herself to tell him tonight. She suspected he now realized that Sierra had probably been lying to him about a lot of things. Alexa had to let him handle this his own way.

So why didn't he go looking for his wife on those nights when he woke to find her gone? Because he knew what he'd discover and he wasn't ready to face it yet.

Alexa waited until she was sure Sierra wouldn't be coming back out of Jayden's room, before hurrying back up the stairs to her room.

She unlocked the door, stepped in and locked the door behind her. For a moment she merely studied the room. It didn't appear anyone had been in here since she'd left.

Walking over to the bureau against the wall, she moved to the end of it and then, putting her weight into it, shoved the bureau across the floor.

She didn't care about the noise it made, figuring no one would hear anyway, given that everyone was in their own wings.

Once she had it blocking the door, she stripped off her robe and tumbled into the bed. She fell into a deep sleep—until she was awakened by her greatest fear. Her mother was standing by her bed.

Alexa woke with a start, half expecting to see her mother standing beside her bed. It had been just a dream, she told herself, and yet she shuddered at the memory as she looked around the room and realized it was still dark outside. Glancing at the clock, she saw that she'd only been asleep for less than an hour.

But something had brought her out of a deep sleep so abruptly that she found herself sitting up in the bed, her heart pounding. The nightmare? No.

A name.

She blinked. Bates. She remembered why it had seemed so familiar. It was one of the two names she'd seen on the burned papers she'd retrieved from Sierra's fireplace.

At the time, the papers had appeared to be financial documents. But that hadn't meant anything to Alexa because she hadn't known about J. A. Wellington bilking all those investors out of their money.

One of those investors had been named Bates.

She grabbed for her phone, found the number of the reporter she'd spoken with and quickly called him.

After apologizing for the early hour, she said, "I need to know if there is a Bates on the list of investors that Wellington cheated."

"Just a minute." He came back on the line a few moments later. "Bates. Yep. Harold and Carol Bates."

Carolina's parents, she recalled from Carolina's wedding announcement. The father had been deceased.

Alexa's heart pounded. "Can you tell me if any of these names are on the list?" She read off the names of the other occupants of the house.

"Sorry."

She frowned, remembering the other name on the burned sheet of paper from the fire. "What about a Welch?"

"I don't see a Welch."

She wasn't sure whether she should be relieved or not that none of the other people in the house appeared to have ties to J. A. Wellington. "There isn't a Farrell?"

"Nope." He'd already told her, but she'd had to ask again.

"Isn't it possible J. A. spent all the money?"

He laughed. "Trust me, he didn't spend it or the feds would have known."

She thought of Carolina's parents. "These people who lost their money were already wealthy, right?"

"Nope. They were middle-class and lower-income people who couldn't afford to lose their life's savings. He destroyed a lot of families."

"If that is true, how was he able to accumulate millions?"

"Apparently he was good at investing their money, showing them large enough returns to keep them from withdrawing their funds. Look, I don't know where you're going with this, but if there is a story here…"

"Don't worry, I'll make sure you get it," she said, thanked him and hung up.

She had to see Carolina. The only way to put a stop

to all this was to expose what was going on. It was too much of a coincidence that Carolina just happened to be the daughter of parents who had been cheated by Wellington.

Carolina either suspected the ill-gotten money was here or thought Sierra's interest in the house meant she knew where her father had hidden it.

The question was, did Sierra know that Carolina's family was one of the ones bilked by her father? Las Vegas was large enough that Sierra might not have known Carolina.

It explained what Carolina was doing here, but what if she wasn't the only one in the house after the money? What about her husband, Gigi and Devlin, and Jayden? And why, if Sierra was after the money for herself, had she invited these people to the house?

Alexa realized that Carolina might be after more than the money—she could be set on revenge.

She quickly dressed, desperately needing to talk to Carolina. But as she started down the hall, she heard voices downstairs. The moment she walked into the kitchen, she realized something had happened. Everyone but Carolina was sitting around the table with long faces.

"What's going on?" she asked and thought for a moment they weren't going to tell her.

"Carolina and Archer had another fight," Landon said. "Carolina's catching a ride to Billings today instead of waiting for a flight out."

She saw then that Archer was dabbing at his bleeding nose with a napkin. "The bitch hit me."

"Don't talk about Carolina like that," Gigi snapped. "She's upset."

"*I'm* upset," Archer snapped back. His face was also scratched. "But I'm sick of her acting like I'm a big disappointment to her."

"Where is she?" Alexa asked.

"Up in our room, but I wouldn't go up there if I were you," Archer said. "She said she wanted to be left alone."

Alexa just bet she did. Carolina had found the perfect way to make her exit with the money and without anyone suspecting what she was up to.

Taking the stairs two at a time, she hurried down the hall toward Carolina and Archer's room. She was almost to the door when she heard the raised voices.

"How did you get in here?" Carolina said, sounding surprised and angry, and Alexa realized with a start, fear. "I want to be left alone."

She heard something heavy hit the floor with a crash, muffling the other person's voice.

"Are you crazy? Don't come near me." There was panic in Carolina's voice. "Stay back!"

Alexa remembered what she'd seen in Carolina's future and grabbed the doorknob. Locked. She struggled to get her key from her pocket as she heard something else hit the floor then Carolina's scream. She fumbled the key into the lock and turned it. The lock clicked and as she started to turn the knob, she heard another bloodcurdling scream from Carolina and the horrible sound of glass shattering.

She shoved the door and it swung in as Carolina's

scream ended in a thud beyond the gaping hole where the window had been.

The room was empty. Where had the person Carolina had been arguing with gone?

Alexa rushed to the window to stare down into the darkness. She could make out a crumpled shape far below. She started to turn, to run downstairs to get help, even though she knew Carolina was beyond help.

But before she could move, she heard a panel slide open in the wall and was grabbed from behind, a wet cloth clamped down over her mouth and nose. No! The room began to dim and then the lights went out. As she slumped to the floor, her last thought was of Marshall.

Chapter 13

Marshall sat out on his porch, drinking a cold beer, staring at the Wellington mansion with all its lights on, thinking about Alexa. Worrying about her.

He hated the way he'd left things. He told himself the worst he could do was go over there this late at night and tell her how he felt about her.

He reminded himself that she wasn't even speaking to him. Not to mention she had enough problems at the moment. Given what they'd learned about the Wellingtons, he wasn't sure that bad blood had been passed down. If so, then the latest Sierra Wellington could be more dangerous than even Alexa suspected.

Alexa needed him. Right. Even after being drugged and hit on the head and knocked out, it hadn't scared Alexa off.

Yep, all the woman needed was for him to storm over

there and tell her that he was in love with her. In love with a woman who lived in another state, who may or may not see dead people and who didn't have a clue how he felt and probably didn't feel the same way about him.

She'd made it pretty clear she didn't want to see him again.

The light was still on in Alexa's room.

He took another sip of his beer. Clearly she couldn't sleep any better than he could on this hot August night.

He waited, half hoping she'd have a nightmare and come running across the pasture. He ached to kiss her, to hold her in his arms, to make love to her again.

Well, he wasn't going over there, he told himself as he finished his beer and got to his feet. If she wanted to see him, she knew where he lived.

He stared at the lights on over at the mansion, then at his watch and swore. Like hell he wasn't going over there. She might kick him out, but first she was going to hear what he had to say. He loved her, by damn, and it was time he told her.

Slapping his Stetson on his head, he headed across the pasture. He hadn't gone far when he heard a terrifying scream, followed only a few minutes later by gunfire.

He'd reached the rocks and bushes that covered the secret entry to the basement when he saw Jayden come stumbling out the front door of the house, a gun in his hand. Ducking down, he opened the door and slipped inside. His only thought was finding Alexa.

The stench was unbearable. Worse, Alexa woke to find not only that she was trapped in the tunnel cage, but also she wasn't alone.

She could feel something unearthly huddled in the dark, back corner, an old woman, her breathing ragged, her mental anguish palpable.

Alexa's captor had left a flashlight lying on the floor of the tunnel, its beam turned toward the opposite wall. There was just enough light to see where she was, but beyond that faint beam was nothing but pockets of darkness.

Don't turn around. Don't—

She screamed as she felt the woman grasp her ankle. Alexa tried frantically to pull away as the woman clawed at her, pulling herself to her feet and turning Alexa to face her.

Alexa squeezed her eyes shut, willing herself not to open them, not wanting to look into the tortured eyes of the first Sierra Wellington. A scream rose in her throat but died off as she heard the sound of footfalls coming down the tunnel. She didn't dare open her eyes, afraid that it was a trick of either the spirits in this house—or her own imagination.

"Alexa?"

Marshall. Her eyes flew open. She blinked. She was alone in the cage and Marshall had found a piece of pipe and was breaking the lock. Moments later she was in his arms.

"What the hell is going on over here?" he demanded. "I heard gunshots."

"Someone killed Carolina, then they grabbed me...." Gunshots? "We have to find my brother." The words were barely out before they both turned at the sound of someone coming toward them from the house side of the tunnel.

* * *

Marshall wished he had more of a weapon than the piece of pipe he'd used to open the cage door. He grabbed a flashlight from the floor, the batteries low, the beam faint. He turned it off as he pulled Alexa behind him.

"It's just me," came a voice, then a flashlight blinked on a half-dozen yards down the tunnel.

"Devlin," Alexa said.

"Alexa?" Devlin asked as Marshall turned on the flashlight again and Devlin moved toward them. "Thank God it's you and not Sierra. What are you doing down here?"

"You don't know?" Alexa asked.

He shook his head, grimacing as he glanced toward the cage. "Someone put you in there? What is going on? All hell has broken loose upstairs. Did you know Carolina killed herself?"

"Or someone in this house killed her," Alexa said. "Have you seen my brother?"

"No." Devlin looked confused. "But Sierra is looking for you and she has a gun."

"My brother." She tried to push past Marshall to run toward the entrance to the house, but he held her back.

"Listen," he said. They all fell silent, he and Devlin turning off their flashlights as they heard someone come down into the tunnel. A light shone at the other end, illuminating Sierra. She had a flashlight in one hand, a gun in the other.

"Landon?" she called. "Alexa? Anyone down here?"

Marshall held Alexa against him. He could feel her

holding her breath, just as he was. Devlin must have been doing the same.

Sierra stood there for a long moment, then turned and retreated back up the stairs to the main floor. They waited until they heard the door close before any of them made a sound.

"We have to get out of here," Devlin said.

"No, I have to find my brother," Alexa argued.

"Sierra doesn't know where he is," Marshall assured her. "He must have gotten out of the house."

"Marshall's right," Devlin agreed. "You can't help him if you run into Sierra and she kills you. Come on. Once we get out of here, we can call for help." He pointed his flashlight toward the exit by the pond. "Get Alexa out. I'll be right behind you."

Alexa caught movement behind them. Devlin had pulled a gun, striking Marshall in the head. Marshall let out a groan of pain and fell at her feet.

"What are you doing?" she cried and dropped beside the cowboy.

Devlin jerked her to her feet, jabbing her with the barrel of the gun. "Unless you want me to shoot him, shut up and come with me."

She looked into his eyes in the light from Marshall's dropped flashlight and knew Devlin was more than capable of murder. "You're the one who locked me in that cage."

"I'm going to do worse if you don't come with me now."

She touched Marshall's cheek. He was still breathing. Then she rose and let Devlin drag her out of the tunnel.

She feared her brother might still be in the house, maybe even looking for her, or that Devlin had already taken care of him. And where were the others? But she didn't argue as they climbed up out of the tunnel and into the faint moonlight.

Breathing in the fresh air, filling her lungs, she tried to dispel her fear as well as the smell and memory of the cage and the old woman in there.

She looked toward the house and saw that all the lights were on. Someone was beside the house and she could hear what sounded like heart-wrenching sobs. Archer. He was kneeling on the ground under the window where Carolina had fallen. He was holding her body, rocking and wailing.

The sound sent a sliver of ice down her spine.

Devlin was standing in the moonlight, a gun in his hand, a strange look on his face.

"You're working with Sierra?" Alexa asked in confusion.

Devlin scoffed. "Sierra is a *Wellington*." There was contempt in his tone. "Her father destroyed mine."

"Yours?" His name hadn't been on the list of those people who'd been bilked by J. A. Wellington. "I don't understand. I thought your father owned a vineyard."

"That's my stepfather. He adopted me after he bought my father's vineyard for pennies on the dollar—and got my mother in the deal as well. My father is a drunk who spends most of his time in prison, and all because J. A. Wellington swindled him just like he did Carolina's father."

"You and Carolina?" Alexa said.

Devlin smiled. "It was so easy to get close to Sierra. She didn't have any idea who we were."

"So this is all about the money," Alexa said.

"That and justice. I was more into the money. Carolina…" He shrugged.

Alexa saw it now and let out a small gasp. "You killed her."

"Sierra said you were psychic, that you knew things." Devlin frowned and took a step back, the gun in his hand not quite as steady. "I told Carolina we had to get rid of you right away. But she talked me into waiting. She wanted to know her future." He suddenly looked alarmed. "You saw that she was going to die, didn't you? That's why she was freaking."

"You killed her because you wanted the money all to yourself?" Alexa asked.

"You know that's not why. This is all your fault," Devlin said, anger making his perfect features look inhuman. "You made her think the money was cursed and that if either of us took it…" He shook his head. "She wanted to burn the place down, the money with it."

"But you had already found the money. No," she said as she realized why Devlin had abducted her. "*Carolina* found the money. She moved it and then wouldn't tell you where. You think I can tell you where she hid it."

He looked surprised and nervous. "You're good."

"And Sierra?" Alexa asked. "She was looking for the money too."

Devlin snorted. "I thought her old man had told her where it was, but I guess not." He raised the gun until the barrel was pointed at her face. "But now you are going to tell me where it's hidden."

"Why don't I tell you your future instead," Alexa said, stalling. She had no idea where the money was hidden. It hadn't taken any psychic talent to see through Devlin.

"I know my future," he said with a quick shake of his head. "I'm going to be filthy rich. I'm never going to have to ask my stepfather for another dime."

"You're not going to kill me because then you will never know where the money is hidden."

For a moment Devlin looked uncertain, but then he smiled. "You're right. I'm not going to kill you. I'm going to go back in and kill your boyfriend and then your brother. Yes, I know where he is. I left him bound and gagged in another part of the basement."

Alexa felt only a moment's relief.

"So what's it going to be?" he demanded.

"Take him to the money." With a start, Alexa saw her mother materialize behind him.

"What?" Devlin demanded. "Are you trying to freak me out or something?"

She knew she had gone pale. She tried to still her trembling as she stared at the apparition of her mother behind him.

"Tell him where the money is," her mother said, and yet the sound didn't come from her lips but seemed to come from inside Alexa's own head.

She closed her eyes, shaking her head, not wanting to hear her mother's voice, not wanting to see her mother. Only crazy people saw the dead, talked to the dead.

"Crazy people and some clairvoyants," her mother said. "Tell him you will take him to the money."

Alexa hadn't realized that she'd spoken.

"Who are you talking to?" Devlin demanded, looking worried.

"My mother."

"I thought your mother was—" He glanced over his shoulder. "If you think you can scare me—"

"She told me to take you to the money."

He glanced around, nervous and unsure. "She knows where it is?"

"She said she will lead me to it."

Alexa could tell he desperately wanted to believe what she was saying was true. But like a lot of people, he didn't believe in ghosts. Or at least he didn't want to.

"This had better not be a trick," he warned.

"Lead him down to the pond," her mother said.

They hadn't gone but a few steps when Alexa saw Marshall moving through the darkness of the cottonwoods. He had the piece of pipe. Marshall had the piece of pipe he'd used to free her. She was never so happy to see anyone in her life.

Marshall came out of the trees quickly, moving with a swiftness and sureness of a man on a mission.

Devlin never knew what hit him.

Marshall dragged her into his arms. "Alexa, I love you. I don't care that this is probably the worse possible time to tell you how I feel but—"

Suddenly they were surrounded by agents of the U.S. Department of the Treasury.

Epilogue

The rest of the night was a blur. It wasn't until the next morning, sitting in Marshall's warm kitchen having a cup of coffee that Alexa finally felt it was over.

Last night, after the federal agents had released them, Marshall had brought her back here. They'd made love in his bed upstairs. She'd told him she loved him.

"I still can't believe Jayden is with the Department of the Treasury," Marshall said as he took a chair across from her. Jayden had been wounded by Devlin, but was going to live. Devlin had been taken into custody.

"Last night when I saw Sierra with that gun… I guess we all thought the worst of her when she was only trying to find Landon and save him from Devlin."

Marshall nodded. "So Jayden and Sierra weren't having an affair?"

"Apparently not," she said and took a sip of her coffee. Sunlight streamed in the windows, warming her more than the coffee. "Sierra was working with the feds by coming back to the house and pretending to open a bed-and-breakfast."

"And Landon didn't know?"

Alexa shook her head. "Sierra said she wasn't allowed to tell him anything. Apparently when Devlin and Carolina befriended her, the feds had already been watching the whole bunch of them. It had been easy to let Devlin and Carolina think it was their idea to come to Montana to help renovate the house for a bed-and-breakfast."

"So all the spouses were in the dark?"

"I guess so, though I suspect at least Archer must have known what was going on," she said. "I think that's what he and Carolina argued about that night before Devlin killed her and got out of the room through one of the secret passages only to come back for me."

"How is Landon taking all this?"

"I don't know. I only got to see him for a few minutes after the agents brought him up out of the basement, where Devlin had left him. I think he is probably in as much shock as the rest of us."

Marshall reached across the table and took her hand. "A lot happened last night."

She met his gaze, recalling with a start that he'd seen her mother standing behind her that day he rode by on his horse. "You saw her last night, didn't you?"

He nodded. "Only this time, I knew that feeling of evil I'd felt wasn't coming from her."

"No," Alexa agreed. She had faced her greatest fear

in that house—seeing her mother again. She'd also quit denying that she hadn't inherited her mother's gift. "She helped save us last night."

Marshall nodded. "By leading you and Devlin down to the pond, I was able to follow in the trees."

Alexa looked into this man's bottomless dark eyes and felt more peace than she had ever known. He knew all her secrets and yet he was still here. He'd saved her life last night and he'd told her that he loved her. But where did they go from here? Or did they?

At a knock at the door, she heard her brother call out her name.

Landon looked the worse for wear this morning. Like her, she doubted he'd had much sleep. He came in and took the coffee Marshall offered him then Marshall left the two of them to talk in the living room.

"Are you all right?" Alexa asked her brother. He seemed older somehow, not the young man she'd always felt she needed to protect.

"I've been better."

"And Sierra?"

He shook his head.

"I still can't believe Devlin set the place on fire," Alexa said. She could still smell the smoke in the air. She'd avoided looking at what remained of Wellington Manor and so had Marshall. Neither of them had been sorry to see the place burn.

"That's Sierra's story anyway," Landon said.

"You can't think she set the fire? I thought she really cared about the house and the things in it," Alexa said, remembering the scene with the wine glass she'd broken.

"Who knows what Sierra cared about and how much was all an act?" Landon said. "I can forgive her for not telling me what was really going on. But there are other things…. I didn't want to admit that I rushed into the marriage. Now I realize that Sierra needed a husband in order to come back to Wellington Manor."

"But wasn't that the feds pushing her to make those hasty decisions?"

Landon laughed softly. "Let's be honest. Sierra married me for my inheritance just in case she couldn't find her father's money he stole. As for Jayden, sure she was meeting with him some of those nights, but a lot of them she was looking for that money, hoping she found it first. I think we both know what she would have done with it."

"Have the agents found the money yet?"

"Carolina had called them and told them she'd buried it by the pond. Jayden didn't get the word until Carolina had already been killed. When he moved in to arrest Devlin, that's when he was shot and Sierra took his gun, fearing Devlin would be coming after her next."

"When I saw her in the basement, she was looking for you and me."

He smiled. "She was responsible for my accidents. I'm just lucky she didn't kill me, that way she could have at least had my money, and possibly her father's as well."

"I'm sorry."

"I've already told Sierra that I'm filing for a divorce. You'll be happy that I'm going back to college. The one thing I am certain of is that the woman I fell in love with doesn't exist. I'm just sorry I put you in such a terrible position. I could have gotten you killed and all because I was so sure—"

"You were right. I am like Mother."

He stared at her in surprise.

"I have no control over it, still am afraid of it and not sure I want to use it, but I'm no longer denying its presence. I'm sorry I lied to you."

"Mother would be so happy if she knew."

"She knows."

"And Marshall?" her brother asked.

She nodded and smiled. "I'm in love with him. I'm not sure where it's going...."

"I'm happy for you, sis."

The moment Emma saw the sheriff's expression she knew. "Come in," she said, stepping back and letting McCall enter.

"The woman Aggie believed was Laura Chisholm got away, didn't she?" Emma asked as she led the sheriff into the kitchen, where Hoyt was sitting at the table, having a cup of coffee and some homemade blueberry crumble cake.

"She was gone when the police got there," McCall said after declining both coffee and coffee cake. "She'd cleaned out the place so she must have found out that Aggie was making inquiries about her."

Emma sighed. "So it wouldn't have made any difference even if Aggie and I had gone to Billings."

Hoyt sent her a look that said he would never have let her go anywhere. He'd become suspicious after overhearing Emma on the phone and had called the sheriff, suspecting what Emma was up to. The man knew her too well.

Maybe if she hadn't said she was going to bake his favorite cookies…

Well, it was too late to start second-guessing her mistakes.

"What about Aggie?" she asked the sheriff.

"We're still dragging the river for her body."

No luck. That didn't surprise Emma. She would bet that Aggie Wells might have more in common with Laura Chisholm than anyone knew. Laura had said she was afraid of water. Emma suspected Aggie swam like a fish—even injured.

"If Aggie contacts you again—" the sheriff began.

"I'm to call you at once," Emma said, cutting her off.

"Yep, but that was what you were supposed to do this last time," Hoyt said.

The sheriff and Hoyt both looked at her as if they knew Emma would do whatever she decided to do and to hell with the consequences.

"I'll try to keep better track of her," Hoyt told the sheriff.

"For how long?" Emma demanded. "You have a ranch to run and now both Aggie and some woman who may or may not be your first, jealous, murderous wife, back from the grave, are out there. With one, if not both of them, wanting me dead."

"The boys can run the ranch just fine without me," Hoyt said.

"Well, I can tell you right now, I won't have you watching over me like I'm one of your horses. I won't be corralled." With that Emma stormed out of the room, only to have Hoyt follow her up to their bedroom and take her in his arms.

"You have to forgive me," Hoyt said as he pulled her close.

"Forgive you for what?" Emma asked, all her earlier anger evaporating the moment he held her.

"You blame me for what happened to Aggie. But Emma, if you had come to me and told me you were going to meet her—"

"You would have stopped me."

He fell silent. "You're my wife. I want to protect you."

"You Chisholm men. You all love a woman in trouble. But Hoyt Chisholm, you fell in love with a strong, independent woman—just like four of your sons have done."

"I know. What do you want me to do, Emma? I can't take the chance that there is someone out there who wants you dead and that if I'm not around…"

"Yes?"

He sighed. "I know you can take care of yourself. That is one of the many things I love about you. But we're talking about a killer, Emma."

"A killer who might never strike again."

"Or one who might strike tomorrow."

"Then I'll be ready tomorrow," Emma said. "And if I need you, I'll holler. It's time for you to be the rancher I married. I love nothing more than seeing you on a horse, doing what you love."

He smiled at her. "I've never met a woman like you."

"I know."

* * *

After Landon left, Marshall came down to find Alexa standing at the window, staring out across the pasture at the smoldering remains of Wellington Manor. He was glad that soon, when he looked out this window, he would no longer see anything but the Montana horizon.

"Are you all right?" he asked as he put his arms around her to pull her close. He breathed in her freshly showered scent and told himself he couldn't bear the thought that she might go back to Spokane and he'd never see her again.

"I'm fine. Landon's divorcing Sierra but he seems stronger now. I'm not worried about him anymore. I guess it's finally over."

"That's funny because I was just thinking that some things were just beginning," he said as he turned her in his arms to look into her beautiful face. "I guess I should ask you, though, since I forget that you can see the future."

She smiled at him. "Not if I'm too close to it. Like I am with you."

"So then you don't know what's going to happen now?"

She laughed. "You're going to kiss me?"

He looked into her violet eyes and saw desire and love burning brightly. He could see the two of them living in this house, raising children who would one day ride across this land, their land, with the two of them, their lives blessed through all the love he and Alexa had to share.

"Or did you have something else in mind?" she asked.

He laughed. "Apparently I'm able to see the future better than you can."

"Oh?"

He nodded. "Want me to tell you about it?"

She shook her head. "No, I want you to surprise me."

And he did.

* * * * *

Nicole Helm grew up with her nose in a book and the dream of one day becoming a writer. Luckily, after a few failed career choices, she gets to follow that dream—writing down-to-earth contemporary romance and romantic suspense. From farmers to cowboys, Midwest to *the* West, Nicole writes stories about people finding themselves and finding love in the process. She lives in Missouri with her husband and two sons and dreams of someday owning a barn.

Books by Nicole Helm

Harlequin Intrigue

A Badlands Cops Novel

South Dakota Showdown
Covert Complication
Backcountry Escape
Isolated Threat
Badlands Beware
Close Range Christmas

Carsons & Delaneys

Wyoming Cowboy Justice
Wyoming Cowboy Protection
Wyoming Christmas Ransom

Stone Cold Texas Ranger
Stone Cold Undercover Agent
Stone Cold Christmas Ranger

Visit the Author Profile page at Harlequin.com for more titles.

STONE COLD
CHRISTMAS RANGER

Nicole Helm

To late-night train whistles when everyone else is asleep and the Janette Oke books that introduced me to romance.

Chapter 1

Bennet Stevens had learned how to smile politely and charmingly at people he couldn't stand before he'd learned to walk. Growing up in a family chock-full of lawyers and politicians, and many of the Texas rich and powerful, he'd been bred to be a charming, cunning tool.

His decision to go into police work had surprised, and perhaps not excited, his parents, but they weren't the type of people to stand in someone's way.

Everything was far more circumspect than that, and after five years as a Texas Ranger, easily moving up the ranks beyond his counterparts, Bennet was starting to wonder if *that's* how his parents were attempting to smoke him out.

Make everything too damn easy.

He was as tired of easy here at the Texas Rangers

headquarters in Austin as he was of political parties at his parents' home where he was supposed to flirt with debutantes and impress stuffed suits with tales of his bravery and valor.

Which was why he was beyond determined to break one of the coldest cases his Texas Ranger unit had. The timing couldn't be more perfect, with his partner in the Unsolved Crimes Investigation Unit taking some extended time off giving Bennet the opportunity to solve a case on his own.

He glanced over at said partner, Ranger Vaughn Cooper, who was leaning against the corner of their shared office, talking on his cell in low tones.

No amount of low tones could hide the fact taciturn Ranger Cooper was talking to his very pregnant wife. Bennet could only shake his head at how the mighty had fallen, and hard.

Vaughn said his goodbyes and shoved his phone into his pocket before he turned his attention to Bennet, assessing gaze and hard expression back in place. "Captain won't go for it," Vaughn said, nodding at the file on Bennet's desk.

"He might if you back me up."

Vaughn crossed his arms over his chest, and if Bennet hadn't worked with Vaughn for almost four years, he might have been intimidated or worried. But that steely-eyed glare meant Vaughn was considering it.

"I know you want more…"

"But?" Bennet supplied, forcing himself to grin as if this didn't mean everything. When people knew what it meant, they crushed it if they could. Another Stevens lesson imparted early and often.

"I'm not sure this case is the way to go. It's been sitting here for years."

"I believe that's the point of our department. Besides that, I've already found a new lead," Bennet said, never letting the easy smile leave his face.

Vaughn's eyebrows rose in surprise. "You have?"

"There was a murder around the same time as this case that the FBI linked to the Jimenez drug cartel. That victim's wounds were the same as the victim's wounds in our Jane Doe case. If Captain lets me take on this case, I want to find a connection."

Vaughn blew out a breath and nodded. "You have the FBI file?"

Bennet turned his laptop screen so Vaughn could read. Vaughn's expression changed, just a fraction, and for only a second, but Bennet caught it. And jumped. "What? What did you see?"

Vaughn sighed heavily. "I didn't *see* anything. It's just… Jimenez."

"What about it?"

"Alyssa Jimenez."

"I know that name." Bennet racked his brain for how, because it hadn't been in any of the files he'd been poring over lately. "The Stallion. Oh, she was with Gabby." Vaughn's sister-in-law had been the kidnapping victim of a madman who called himself The Stallion. Vaughn had worked the case to free Gabby and the handful of other girls she'd been in captivity with.

Including Alyssa Jimenez. "Wait. Are you telling me *she* has something to do with the Jimenez drug family?"

"I don't know that she does. But based on what I do know, I wouldn't be surprised."

"But you haven't followed up?" Bennet asked incredulously.

"Natalie and Gabby took her in after Gabby's release. They've adopted her like a sister, and I have yet to see anything that points to her being involved with any of the many members of the Jimenez drug cartel family."

"But you think she is," Bennet pressed, because Vaughn wouldn't have brought it up if he didn't.

"Alyssa is…different. It wouldn't surprise me if she had connections to this family. She's built something of an underground bounty hunter business, and the contacts she has?" Vaughn shook his head. "I promised Gabby and Nat I wouldn't interfere unless it was directly part of my job."

"You? You, Mr. By-the-Book, promised not to investigate something?"

"She hasn't done anything wrong, and believe me, I've watched. *If* she's connected to that family, it's only biological. Not criminal. She's been through a lot."

"Wait. Wait. Isn't she the one who fought the FBI when they raided The Stallion's compound to release the women?"

Vaughn stood to his full height, disapproval written all over his face, but Bennet wouldn't let it stop him. Vaughn's family leave started tomorrow, and he couldn't stand in Bennet's way for weeks.

"She didn't fight them off. She just didn't exactly drop her weapon when they demanded her to do so. There is a difference. Now, Bennet, I need you to understand something."

Bennet held himself very still, especially since Vaughn rarely called him by his first name. They were partners, but Vaughn was older, more experienced, and Bennet had always looked up to him like something of a mentor.

"Do not let your need to do something big compromise your job, which is to do something *right*."

The lecture grated even though Bennet knew it was a good one, a fair one. But he didn't particularly want to be good or fair right now. He wanted to *do* something. He wanted a challenge. He wanted to feel less like this fake facade.

He would do all that by doing that something right, damn it. "I want her contact information."

"I didn't say I'd back you up. I didn't say—"

"I want her contact information," Bennet repeated, and this time he didn't smile or hide the edge in his voice. "I have found a lead that no one else has found, and I will rightfully and lawfully follow up on it once Captain Dean gives me the go-ahead. Now, you can either give it to me and smooth the way and let this be easy—for me *and* for her—or you can stand in my way and force me to drag her in here."

Vaughn's expression was icy, but Bennet couldn't worry about that. Not for this. So, he continued.

"You're out for a month to spend with your wife and your upcoming new addition. Take it. Enjoy it. And while you're gone, let me do my job the way I see fit."

Bennet couldn't read Vaughn's silence, but he supposed it didn't matter. Bennet had said his piece, and he'd made it very clear. He would not be dissuaded.

"If you get Captain Dean's go-ahead, I'll give you Gabby's contact information. It'll be the best way to get ahold of Alyssa."

When Bennet frowned, Vaughn's mouth curved into the closest it ever got to a smile on duty.

"Best of luck getting anything out of Gabby Torres."

Bennet forced himself to smile. "I can handle your sister-in-law." And he could handle this case, and the potential to crack it wide open. Starting with Alyssa Jimenez.

Alyssa never knew what to do when Gabby went into full protective mode. While Alyssa had grown up with five intimidating older brothers, they had protected her by throwing her in a room and locking the door, by teaching her to use any weapon she could get her hands on. They had protected her by hiding her.

Not ranting and raving about some half-cocked Texas Ranger wanting to talk to her.

Not that Alyssa needed Gabby's protection, but it was still interesting to watch.

"The *nerve* of that guy, thinking he can question you about something that doesn't even have anything to do with you!"

Alyssa sat with her elbows resting on her knees in a folding chair in the corner of her very odd little office. It was a foreclosed gas station in a crappy part of Austin, and Alyssa hadn't made any bones about making it look different from what it was. Shelves still stood in aisles, coolers stood empty and not running along the back wall. The only thing she'd done was add some seating—mostly stuff she'd found in the alley—and a desk that had a crack down the middle.

Her clientele didn't mind, and they knew where to

find her without her having to advertise and attract potential…legal issues.

The only time the office space bothered Alyssa was when Gabby insisted on showing up. Even though Alyssa knew Gabby could take care of herself—she'd recently graduated from the police academy, and she'd survived eight years as a prisoner of The Stallion to Alyssa's two—Alyssa hated bringing people she cared about into this underworld.

"Alyssa. Are you listening?"

Alyssa shrugged. "Not really. You seem to be doing an excellent job of yelling all by yourself."

Gabby scowled at her, and it was moments like these Alyssa didn't know what to do with. Where it felt like she had a sister, a family. People who cared about her. It made her want to cry, and it made her want to…

She didn't know. So, she ignored it. "I can talk to some Texas Ranger. I talk to all sorts of people all the time." Criminals. Law enforcement. Men who worked for her brothers, men who worked for the FBI, including Gabby's fiancé. Alyssa knew how to talk to anyone.

Maybe, just maybe, it made her a little nervous someone so close to Natalie and Gabby had possibly discovered her connection to one of the biggest cartels operating in the state of Texas, but she could handle it.

"Crap," Gabby muttered, looking at her phone. "Nat went into labor."

"Well, hurry up and get to the hospital."

"Come with me."

"No."

"Alyssa, you're ours now. Really."

"I know," Alyssa replied, even though it had been

almost two years since escaping The Stallion and she still wasn't used to being considered part of the family. "But all that pushing and yelling and weird baby crap? I'm going to have to pass. I'll come visit when it's all over, so keep me posted. Besides, I have some work to catch up on. My trip to Amarillo took longer than I expected."

She'd brought a rapist to justice. Though she'd brought him in for a far more minor charge, the woman who'd come to her for help could rest assured her attacker was in jail.

It wasn't legal to act as bounty hunter without a license, but growing up in the shadow of a drug cartel family, Alyssa didn't exactly care about legal. She cared about righting some wrongs.

Some of that pride and certainty must have showed in her expression because Gabby sighed. "All right, I won't fight you on it. Get your work done and then, regardless of baby appearance, at least stop by the hospital tonight?"

"Fine."

Gabby pulled her into a quick hug, another gesture Alyssa had spent two years not knowing what to do with. But the Torres sisters had pulled her in and insisted she was part of their family.

It mattered, and Alyssa would do whatever she could to make sure she made them proud. She couldn't be a police officer like Gabby, or a trained hypnotist assisting the Texas Rangers like Natalie, but she could do this.

"See you tonight," Gabby said, heading for the door.

"Yes, ma'am."

Gabby left, and Alyssa sighed. Maybe she should

have gone. Natalie had had a difficult pregnancy, enough so that her husband was taking almost an entire month off work to be home with her and the baby the first few weeks. And, no matter how uncomfortable Alyssa still was with the whole childbirth thing, they were her family.

Her good, upstanding chosen family. *Who don't know who you really are.*

Alyssa turned to her work. There was some paperwork to forge to collect her fee for the last guy she'd brought in, and then she had to check her makeshift mailbox to see if any more tips had been left for her. She worked by word of mouth, mostly for people who couldn't pay, hence the forging paperwork so she could pretend to be a licensed bounty hunter and collect enough of a fee to live off of.

Her front door screeched open, as the hinges weren't aligned or well oiled. She glanced over expecting to find a woman from the neighborhood, as those were usually her only word-of-mouth visitors.

Instead, a man stepped through the door, and for a few seconds Alyssa couldn't act, she could only stare. He was tall and broad, dressed in pressed khakis and a perfectly tailored button-down shirt, a Texas Ranger badge hooked to his belt. He wore a cowboy hat and a gun like he'd been born with them.

Alyssa's heart beat twice its normal rhythm, something unrecognizable fluttering in her chest. His dark hair was thick and wavy, and not buzzed short like most Texas Rangers she'd come into contact with. His eyes were a startling blue, and his mouth—

Wait. Why was she staring at his mouth?

The man's brows drew together as he looked around the room. He cleared his throat. "I'm sorry, are you... You are Alyssa Jimenez, aren't you?"

"And you must be the Texas Ranger Gabby's trying to hide me from," Alyssa offered drily. "How *did* you find me?"

"I followed Gabby."

She laughed, couldn't help it. She'd expected him to lie or have some high-tech way for having found her not-publicly-listed office. But he'd told her the truth. "Awfully sneaky and underhanded for a Ranger."

His mouth curved, and the fluttering was back tenfold. He had a movie-star smile, all charm and white teeth, and while Alyssa had seen men like that in her life, she'd never, ever had that kind of smile directed at *her*.

"You must know Ranger Cooper, antithesis of all that is sneaky and underhanded. We aren't all like that."

Something about all that fluttering turned into a spiral, one that arrowed down her chest and into her belly. She felt oddly shaky, and Alyssa had long ago learned how to ward off shaky. She'd grown up in isolation as part of a criminal family. Then she'd been kidnapped for two years, locked away in little more than a bunker.

She was not a weakling. She was never scared. The scariest parts of her life were over, but something about this man sent her as off-kilter as she'd ever been.

It wasn't fear for her life or the need to fight off an attacker, but she didn't know *what* it was, and that was the scariest thing of all.

"Why are you here?" she asked, edging behind her cracked desk. She had a knife strapped to her ankle, but she'd prefer the Glock she'd shoved in the drawer when Gabby had stormed in an hour earlier.

She wouldn't use either on him, but she didn't want him to think she was going to do whatever he wanted either. He might be a Texas Ranger, but he couldn't waltz in here and get whatever he wanted. Especially if what he wanted was information about Jimenez.

"I have some questions for you, Ms. Jimenez, that's all."

"Then why is everyone trying so hard to keep you from meeting me?" Alyssa returned, sliding her hand into the drawer.

The Ranger's eyes flicked to the movement, and she didn't miss the way his hand slowly rose to the holster of *his* weapon. She paused her movement completely, but she didn't retract her hand.

"Maybe they're afraid of what I'll find out."

She raised her gaze from his gun to those shocking blue eyes. His expression was flat and grim, so very *police*. Worst of all, it sent a shiver of fear through her.

There were so very many things he could find out.

Chapter 2

Bennet didn't know what to make out of Alyssa's closed-down gas station of an office. Could anyone call this an office? It looked like nothing more than an abandoned building, except maybe she'd swept the floors a little. But the windows were grimy, the lights dim, and most of the debris of a convenience store were still scattered about.

Then there was this pretty force of a woman standing in the midst of all of it as though it were a sleek, modern office building in downtown Austin.

She wore jeans and a leather jacket over a T-shirt. The boots on her feet looked like they might weigh as much as her. Her dark hair was pulled back, and her dark eyes flashed with suspicion.

Something about her poked at him, deep in his gut. He tried to convince himself he must have dealt with her before, criminally, but he was too practical to convince himself of a lie. Whatever that poke was, it wasn't work related.

But he was here to work. To finally do something worthwhile. With no help from any outside forces.

She didn't take her hand off what he assumed to be a weapon in the drawer of her desk—though it was hidden from his view—so he kept his hand on his. Alyssa might be a friend of people he knew, but that didn't mean he trusted her.

"I guess what you find out depends on what you're looking for, Ranger..." She looked expectantly at him.

Though she was clearly suspicious, defensive even, she didn't appear nervous or scared, so he went ahead and took his hand off the butt of his weapon. He held out his hand between them. "Bennet Stevens. And I don't know why your friends are being so protective of you. All I'm after is a little information about a case I'm working on. If you have no connection to it, I'll happily walk away and not bother you again."

Nothing in her expression changed. She watched him and his outstretched hand warily. She was doing some sort of mental calculation, and Bennet figured he could wait that out and keep his hand outstretched for as long as it took.

"What kind of case?"

"A murder."

She laughed, and something in his gut tightened, a completely unwelcome sensation. She had a sexy laugh, and it was the last thing he had any business noticing.

"I can assure you I have nothing to do with any murders," Alyssa said, still ignoring his outstretched hand.

"Then what do you have to do with?" he asked, giving up on the handshake.

She cocked her head at him. "I'm pretty sure you said that if I didn't have anything to do with your case, you'd leave me alone. Well, you know where the door is."

He glanced at the door even though there was no way he was retreating anytime soon. His initial plan had been to come in here and be friendly and subtle, ease into things.

It was clear Alyssa wasn't going to respond to subtle or friendly. Which meant he had to go with the straight-forward tactic, even if it ended up offending his friends.

He held up his hands, palms toward her, a clear sign he wouldn't be reaching for his weapon as he slowly withdrew two papers from his shirt's front pocket.

He unfolded the papers and handed the top one to her. "Is that you?"

It was a picture of a young girl, surrounded by five dangerous-looking men. Men who were confirmed to be part of the Jimenez drug cartel.

Bennet had no doubt the girl in the picture was Alyssa. Though she did look different as an adult, there were too many similarities. Chief among them the stony expression on her face.

She looked at the picture for an abnormally long time in utter silence.

"Ms. Jimenez?"

She looked up at him, and there wasn't just stony stoicism or cynicism in her expression anymore, there was something a lot closer to hatred. She dropped the picture on her ramshackle desk.

"I really doubt I need to answer that question since

you're here. You've decided it's me whether I confirm it or not. You clearly know who those men are, decided I'm connected to them. I doubt you'll believe me, but let me head you off at the pass. I have not contacted anyone with the last name Jimenez since I was *kidnapped* at the age of twenty."

He wouldn't let that soften him. "Then I guess it's fitting that the case I'm looking into is sixteen years old."

Confusion drew her eyebrows together. "You want to question me about a crime that happened when I was eight?"

"Yes."

She made a scoffing noise disguised as a laugh. "All right, Ranger Hotshot. Hit me."

"Sixteen years ago, a Jane Doe was found murdered. She's never been identified, but I found some similarities between her case and a case connected to the Jimenez family. *Your* family. I'd like to bring some closure to this cold case, and I think you can help."

"I was eight. Whatever my brothers were doing, I had no part in."

"Brothers?"

She didn't move, didn't say anything, but Bennet nearly smiled. She'd slipped up and given him more information than he'd had. He'd known Alyssa was connected, but he hadn't known how close.

Yeah, she was going to be exactly what he needed. "I'd like you to look at the picture of the Jane Doe and let me know if you remember ever seeing her with your *brothers*. It's not an incredibly graphic picture, but it can be disconcerting for some people to view pictures of dead bodies."

Alyssa rolled her eyes and snatched up the picture. "I work as a bounty hunter. I think I can stand the sight of a…" But she trailed off and paled. She sank into the folding chair so hard it broke and she fell to the ground.

Bennet was at her side not quite in time to keep her ass from hitting the floor. "Are you okay?"

She was shaking, seemed not to have noticed she'd broken a chair and was sitting in its debris, the picture fisted in her hand.

"Alyssa?"

When she finally brought her gaze to his, those brown eyes were wide and wet and she was clearly in shock.

"Where'd you get this?" she demanded in a whisper, her hands shaking. Hell, her whole body was shaking. Her brown eyes bored into his. "This is a lie. This has to be a lie." Her voice cracked.

"You know her?" he asked, gently rubbing a hand up and down her forearm, trying to offer *something* to help her stop shaking so hard.

Alyssa looked back down at the picture that shook in her hands. "That's my mother."

The tears were sharp and burning, but Alyssa did everything she could to keep them from falling. She forced herself to look away from the picture and shoved it back at the Texas Ranger, whatever his name was.

It wasn't true. It couldn't be true. Her mother had *left* her. She'd been seduced away by some rival of her father's. *That* was the story.

Not murder.

It didn't make sense. None of it made any sense.

She tried to get ahold of her labored breathing, but no matter how much she told herself to breathe slowly in and out, she could only gasp and pant, that picture of her mother's lifeless face seared into her brain forever.

Murder.

She realized the Ranger had stopped rubbing her arm in that oddly comforting gesture and instead curled long, strong fingers around both her elbows.

"Come on," he said gently, pulling her to her feet.

Since the debris of the rickety chair that had broken underneath her weight was starting to dig into her butt, she let him do it. Once she was standing somewhere close to steady on her feet, he didn't release her. No, that strong grip stayed right where it was on her elbows.

It was centering somehow, that firm, warm pressure. A reminder she existed in the here and now, not in one of the different prisons her life had been.

She blinked up at the Texas Ranger holding her steady. There was something like compassion in his blue eyes, maybe even regret. His full lips were down-turned, slight grooves bracketing his mouth.

He was something like pretty, and she'd rather have those cheekbones and that square jaw burned into her brain than the image of her dead mother.

"If I'd had any idea, Alyssa…" he said, his voice gravel and his tone overly familiar.

She pulled herself out of his grasp, pulled into herself, like she'd learned how to do time and time again as the inconsequential daughter of a criminal, as a useless kidnapping victim.

She'd spent the last two years trying to build a life

for herself where she might matter, where she might do some *good*.

This moment forced her back into all the ways she'd never mattered. What other lies she'd accepted as truth might be waiting for her?

She closed her eyes against the onslaught of pain. And fear.

"My brothers didn't murder my mother, Ranger Stevens," Alyssa managed, though her voice was rusty. "I know they're not exactly heroes, but they never would have killed my mother."

"Okay." He was quiet for a few humming seconds. "Maybe you'd like to help me find out who did."

She didn't move, didn't emote. She'd worked with law enforcement before, but she was careful about it. They usually didn't know her name or her friends. They definitely didn't know her connection to the Jimenez family.

This man knew all of that and had to look like Superman in a cowboy hat on top of it. The last thing she should consider was working with him.

Except her mother was dead. Murdered. A Jane Doe for well over a decade, and as much as she couldn't believe her brothers had anything to do with her mother's murder—*murder*—she couldn't believe they didn't know. There was no way Miranda Jimenez had stayed a Jane Doe without her family purposefully making sure she did.

Alyssa swallowed. Making sure her mother had stayed a Jane Doe, all the while making sure Alyssa didn't know about it. Her brothers had always claimed they were protecting her by keeping things from her, and it was hard to doubt. They *had* meant well. If they hadn't, she'd have been dead or auctioned off to some faithful servant of her father's before she'd ever been kidnapped.

Ranger Stevens released her, and she felt cold without that warm, sturdy grip. Cold and alone. *Well, that's what you are. What you'll always have to be.*

"Take some time. Come to grips with this new information, and when you're ready to work with me, give me a call." He pulled his wallet out of his back pocket and handed her a card from it.

She took the card. That big star emblem of the Rangers seemed to stare at her. It looked so official, so *heroic*, that symbol. Right next to it, his name, *Bennet E. Stevens. Ranger.*

She glanced back up at him, and was more than a little irritated she saw kindness in his expression. She didn't want kindness or compassion. She didn't know what to do with those things, and she already got them in spades from Gabby and Natalie and even to an extent from their law enforcement significant others.

Everyone felt sorry for Alyssa Jimenez, but no one knew who she really was. Except this man.

"Do you have a phone number I can reach you at?" he prompted when she didn't say anything.

She didn't want to give him her number. She didn't want to give him anything. She wanted to rewind the last half hour and go with Gabby to the hospital. She would have avoided this whole thing.

Not forever, though. She was too practical to think it would have lasted forever.

"Fine," she muttered, because, as much as she knew

she'd end up working with this guy, the promise of solving her mother's murder was too great, too important, and she didn't want to give him too much leverage. She'd make him think she was reticent, doing *him* a favor when she finally agreed.

She grabbed a pen and scrap of paper from her desk and scrawled her number on it. He took it, sliding it into his pocket along with the pictures he'd retrieved. She'd wanted to keep them, but she had to keep it cool. She'd get them eventually.

"I'll be in touch, Alyssa," he said with a tip of his hat. He paused for a second, hesitating. "I am sorry for your loss," he said gravely, before turning and exiting her office.

She let out a shaky sigh. The worst thing was believing that kind of crap. Why would he be sorry? He didn't know her or her mother. It was a lame, placating statement.

It soothed somehow, idiot that she was. She shook her head and collected her belongings. She'd stop by the hospital to check on Natalie and Gabby, and then she'd go home and try to sleep. She'd give it a day, maybe two, then she'd call Ranger Too-Hot-For-Her-Own-Good.

She locked up and exited out the back, pulling her helmet on before starting her motorcycle. It was her most expensive possession, and she treated it like a baby. Nothing in the world gave her the freedom that motorcycle did.

She rode out of the alley and onto the street that would lead her to the highway and the hospital. Within two minutes, she knew she was being followed.

Her first inclination was that it was Ranger Stevens

keeping tabs on her, but the jacked-up piece-of-crap car following her was no Texas Ranger vehicle.

She scowled and narrowed her eyes. Of course, anyone could be following her, but after the Ranger's visit and information, Alyssa had the sneaking suspicion it was all related.

Maybe her brothers had ignored her existence since she'd been kidnapped and then released, but that didn't mean they couldn't find her if they wanted to.

If they were after her now, they wouldn't give up until they got her. But that didn't mean she had to go down easy. Certainly not after they'd abandoned her.

She took a sharp turn onto a side street, then weaved in and out of traffic the way the car couldn't. She took a few more sharp turns, earning honks and angry middle fingers from other drivers, but eventually she found herself in a dark, small alley. She killed her engine and stood there straddling her bike, breathing heavily.

Did her brothers know Ranger Stevens was investigating their mother's death? Did they have something to hide?

She squeezed her eyes shut, finding her even breathing. They couldn't have killed their mother. They couldn't have. Alyssa couldn't bring herself to believe it.

Her phone rang and she swore, expecting it to be news about Natalie's baby. Instead, it was a number she didn't recognize. Her brothers?

She hit Accept cautiously, and adopted her best take-no-crap tone. "What?"

"You're being tailed."

She scowled at Ranger Steven's voice. "I'm well aware. I lost them."

"Yeah, well, I'm tailing them now."

"Idiot," she muttered. How had this man stepped into her life for fifteen minutes and scrambled everything up?

"What?" Ranger Stevens spluttered.

Alyssa had to think fast. To move. Oh, damn the man for getting in the way of things. "Listen, I'm coming back out. I want you to let them follow me. And when they take me, I need you to not get in the way." Her brothers had never come for her, and she'd stopped expecting them, but if they were coming for her now… she was ready.

As long as she could get rid of the Texas Ranger trying to protect her.

Chapter 3

Bennet wanted to argue, but he had to keep too much of his attention on following the men who'd been following Alyssa to try to outtalk this girl.

Let them take her? "Are you crazy?"

"We both know it's someone from my family, or sent by them anyway. If I let them take me, I get information."

"And end up like your mother." Which was probably too blunt when she'd only just found out about her mother, but he couldn't keep compassion in place when she was talking about getting herself abducted.

He heard a motorcycle engine roar past him, and swore when Alyssa waved at him.

He tossed his phone into the passenger seat and followed. It was reckless and possibly stupid not to call for backup. But while Captain Dean had given him the go-ahead to take on this case, Bennet wasn't ready to bring in other people yet. He needed more information. He needed to know what he was dealing with.

The fact of the matter was he had no idea what he was dealing with when it came to Alyssa Jimenez.

She cut in front of the car that had originally been following her. He watched the streetlights streak across her quickly moving form, and she waved at those guys too.

She *was* crazy.

While Bennet had been worried in the beginning that the tail's goal had been to hurt Alyssa, it was clear they were after something else. If they wanted to hurt her, they could run her off the road and drive away. No one would know the difference except him, and Bennet didn't think they knew *they* had a tail.

It was clear they wanted Alyssa. Whole. She had wanted him to let them take her, so it seemed she knew she wasn't in imminent danger from these people, as well.

Was she working with them? Was he the fool here?

Except when she finally quit driving, he could only stare from his place farther down the street. She'd led them to the public parking of the Texas Rangers headquarters.

What on earth was this woman up to?

She parked in the middle of the mostly empty parking lot—employees parked in the back and public visitors rarely arrived at night. The car that had been following her stopped at the parking lot entrance. Clearly her followers didn't know what to do with this.

Bennet made a turn, keeping the parking lot in view

from his rearview window. When the car didn't follow, the occupants instead kept their attention on Alyssa, he knew they hadn't seen him following them.

He made a quick sharp turn into the back lot and then drove along the building, parking as close as he could to where Alyssa was without being seen. He got out of his car and unholstered his weapon. He crept along the building, keeping himself in the shadows, watching as the car still idled in the entrance while Alyssa sat defiantly on her motorcycle in the middle of the parking lot, parking lights haloing her.

That uncomfortable thing from before tightened in his gut at the way the light glinted off her dark hair when she pulled off her helmet. Something a little lower than his gut reacted far too much at the "screw you" in the curve of her mouth. She looked like some fierce warrior, some underground-gang queen. He should not be attracted to that even for a second.

Apparently some parts of his anatomy weren't as interested in law and order as his brain was.

"What are you guys? Chicken?" Alyssa called out.

Bennet nearly groaned. She would have to be the kind of woman who'd provoke them.

"How about this—you send a message to my brothers. You tell them if they want me, they can come get me themselves. No cut-rate, brainless thug is going to take me anywhere I don't want to go."

The engine revved, and Bennet moved closer. He wasn't going to let these men take his only lead on this case. Even if she was trying to get herself killed.

But in the end, the car merely backed out and screeched away.

Leaving him and Alyssa in a mostly empty parking lot.

She turned to face him as if she'd known he was there all along. "I bet that got their attention, huh?" she said. She didn't walk toward him, so he walked to her.

"Yes. How smart. Piss off your criminal brothers you claim to have nothing to do with so they come after you."

"Yes, exactly."

"I thought you wanted me to let them take you." Which he never would have done.

"I was going to, but then I saw what cut-rate weaklings they sent after me. Afraid of a little Texas Ranger parking lot." She made a scoffing sound. "The only way to really get some answers is to get inside again, but guys like that? Dopes with guns? Yeah, I'm not risking my life with them. My brothers can come get me themselves if it's that important to them."

"You're not going back inside that family."

She raised an eyebrow at him. "Since when did you become my keeper?"

"Since I'm the reason you think you need to go back there. We'll investigate this from the outside. You don't need to be on the inside." He'd sacrifice a lot to actually accomplish something, but not someone else's life.

"Shows what you know. Not a damn thing. I've been gone a long time, but I still know how the Jimenez family works. I can get the answers we need."

"*We* need?"

She looked at her motorcycle, helmet still dangling from her fingertips. He'd watched her shake and tremble apart after seeing her mother's picture, but she was nothing but strength and certainty now.

Again, Bennet couldn't help but wonder if he was the sucker here, if he was being pulled into something that would end up making a fool out of him. But he'd come too far to back out. Gotten the okay on this case, gotten to Alyssa. He had to keep moving forward.

"My brothers didn't murder our mom," she said, raising her gaze to his. Strong and sure. "I know they didn't. I'm going to prove it. To you. And when you find out who really did it, you can bring them to justice."

Her voice shook at the end, though her shoulders-back, chin-up stance didn't change.

He couldn't trust her. She was related to one of the biggest drug cartels in the state. And while Gabby and Natalie had befriended her, and Vaughn thought she hadn't had contact with her brothers in years, this felt awfully coincidental.

She must have seen the direction of his thoughts. "You don't have to trust me, Ranger Stevens. You just have to stay out of my way."

"I'm afraid I can't do that." No matter what it took, he had knocked over whatever domino was creating these events. He was part of it, and whether he trusted her or not, he had some responsibility for bringing her into this.

"They must have my office bugged," Alyssa said, scowling. "The timing is too coincidental, too weird. It's been two years since the kidnapping rescue, and they've left me alone. They had to have heard you questioning me. So, they know. You have to stay out of my way so we can know what's *really* going on."

"How can you think they had nothing to do with it if they're stepping in now when they supposedly know what I'm after?"

"They didn't kill our mother, but cartel business is tricky. Complicated. Their never identifying her when she was Jane Doe, it could be purposeful or they feel like they can't now or... I don't know, but I have to find out. I'm going in. You can't stop me, and God knows you can't stop them."

He didn't agree with that. He could put a security detail on her, keep her safe and away from her brothers for the foreseeable future. Even if the Rangers pulled support, he had enough of his own money to make it so.

But it'd be awfully hard to make it so when she was so determined, and it'd make it harder to get the information he needed. It would make it almost impossible to solve this case.

He studied her, looking at him so defiantly, as if she was the one in charge here. As if she could stand up to him, toe-to-toe, over and over again. Some odd thing shuddered through him, a gut feeling he didn't want to pay attention to.

He'd made his decision, so there was only one way to settle this. "If you're going in, then I'm going in with you."

And this Texas Ranger thought *she* was crazy.

"You think you're going to come with me. You think in *any* world my brothers would allow a Texas Ranger into their home or office or whatever without, oh, say killing you and making sure no one ever found out about it?"

"Except you."

Unfortunately, he had a point. Also unfortunately, her last name might keep her safe for the most part when it came to the Jimenez family, but she knew without a shadow of a doubt, if she outright betrayed her family, she'd be killed.

Like your mother.

She couldn't get over it, so she just kept pushing the reality out of her mind as much as she could. Still, it lingered in whispers. *Murdered. Murdered. Murdered.* How on earth could Mom have been murdered? It didn't make any sense.

Except she left. Betrayed your father. Maybe it makes all the sense in the world.

She couldn't. She just couldn't. She couldn't focus on possibility. She had to focus on truth.

"I can handle this," Ranger Stevens said resolutely.

"No. You can handle being a Texas Ranger. You can handle being a cop. You can't handle being inside a drug cartel. Even if they let you, you'd want to arrest everyone. And trust me, that wouldn't go well for you."

"They didn't hurt you. They ran away."

"Of course they didn't hurt me. Even if I'm not involved in the business, I'm the daughter of a cartel kingpin. I'm the sister of the people who run it. They hurt me, they're dead. It's a matter of honor, but that doesn't mean that protection extends to you." Or to her, if she betrayed Jimenez.

"So we'll have to find a way for them to think it's a matter of honor not to kill me."

"How on earth do you suggest we do that?"

"I have a few ideas, but I'm not discussing them here in this parking lot." He gestured toward the Texas Rangers building.

Alyssa laughed. "I'm not going in there. My brothers are going to think I'm working with you on a lot more than Mom's…" she cleared her throat of the lump "…murder."

"You know it isn't just me at stake here. Natalie and Gabby. Their families. They're a part of your life, and now—"

She took a threatening step toward him—or it might have been threatening, if he wasn't about six inches taller than her and twice as wide. "You don't think I know that? You don't think I have made my life very separate so they would never get pulled into this if I had to be?"

"I don't know you at all, Alyssa. I don't know what your plans are."

"My plan is to live a normal life. That's all I want." She realized, too late, she'd yelled it, shaking all over again. Normal had seemed almost within reach lately, and then this Texas Ranger had walked into her office and everything had changed.

She was Alyssa Jimenez again. Not bounty hunter and friend, not even kidnapping victim, or the inconsequential relative of very consequential people. She was in danger and in trouble, and she couldn't do anything about it.

He reached out, and she hated that something like a simple touch on her arm could just *soothe*. She'd never understood it, but Gabby would hug her back in that bunker, and even out here in the open, and everything would feel okay. This guy, this stranger of a Texas Ranger, touched her, and it felt like she could handle whatever came if he was touching her.

It was insanity.

"If they bugged your office, it's likely they've bugged your house."

Alyssa thought of her little apartment above Gabby and Jaime's garage. Was it bugged? Was the whole house bugged? Had she brought all of her family's problems into the house they'd been kind enough to open up to her?

Guilt swamped her, pain. Tears threatened, but she wouldn't be that weak. She'd fix this. She had to fix this.

"Come home with me."

She jerked her head up to look at Ranger Stevens and carefully pulled herself out of his grasp. Everything in her rebelled at the idea of going home with him. His house. His life. Him.

"I have a big house. Multiple rooms. You can have your own bathroom, your own space. We can get some sleep, and in the morning we can talk knowing that no one has bugged my place."

"They know who you are now. If they bugged my place, they know your name. They know what you're after."

He seemed to consider that with more weight than she thought he would. "All right. I have somewhere else we can go. It might require a little bending of the truth."

Alyssa frowned at him. "What kind of bending of the truth?"

"We'll just need to pretend this isn't related to my job. That you're not so much a professional acquaintance but a, ah, personal one."

"Where the hell are you taking me?" she demanded, touching her bike to remind herself she was free. He couldn't take her anywhere unless she agreed.

And if you go home, would you be putting Gabby and Jaime in jeopardy?

"My parents have a guesthouse. I use it on occasion when necessary. I can say I'm having my house painted or remodeled or something and they'll believe it, if they're even home. But if I'm bringing you with me, they're going to need to think..." He cleared his throat.

Alyssa's mouth went slack as it dawned on her what he was suggesting. "You want me to pretend to be involved with you like...sleeping-over involved?" Her voice squeaked and her entire face heated. Her whole body heated. She'd never been sleeping-over involved with anyone, and she was pretty sure that was a really lame way of putting it, but she didn't know how else to say it.

She didn't know how to wrap her head around what he was suggesting.

"My parents aren't invasive exactly. Actually, they're incredibly invasive, but like I said, it's unlikely they're there. They have some of the best security in Austin, so we'll be safe, or at least forewarned. Should one of the staff mention I had a woman over, then they'll assume it's personal and we'll just go with it."

"Your parents have a guesthouse and staff?"

"Your father runs a drug cartel?" he returned in the same put-off tone.

She wanted to laugh even though it wasn't funny in the least little bit. "No one's going to believe I'm involved with...*you*."

Something in his expression changed, a softening followed by an all-too-charming smile that had her heart beating hard against her chest.

"Am I that hideous?" he asked, clearly knowing full well he was *not*.

"You know what I mean. I look like a street urchin," she said, waving a hand down her front. "You look like..." She waved her hand ineffectually at him.

He cocked his head. "I look like what?" he asked, and there was something a little darker in his tone. Dangerous. But cops weren't dangerous. Not like that.

"I don't know," she muttered, knowing she had to be blushing so profusely even the bad lighting couldn't hide it. "A guy who has servants and guesthouses and crap."

"They'll believe it because there's no reason not to. Street-urchin chic or no, my parents wouldn't doubt me. They might assume I'm trying to give them an aneurism, but they won't suspect anything."

Alyssa looked at her bike. She could hop on, flip him off and zoom away. Zoom away from everything she'd built in the past two years, zoom away from everything that had held her prisoner for the first twenty-two.

But she hadn't left Austin on her release from her kidnapper, and she had people to protect now. She couldn't leave Gabby and Natalie in the middle of this, even if they were both married to men or living with men who would try to protect them.

She studied Ranger Stevens and knew she had to make a choice. Fight, and trust this man. Or run, and ruin them all.

It wasn't a hard choice in the slightest. "All right. I'll go."

Chapter 4

Bennet drove from the Texas Ranger offices to his parents' sprawling estate outside Austin. It wasn't the first time he'd been self-conscious about his parents' wealth. Most of the cops and Rangers he knew were not the sons and daughters of the Texas elite.

Nevertheless, this was the life he'd been born into, and Alyssa hadn't been born into a much different one. Just on opposite sides of the law, but if her father was the Jimenez kingpin, then she'd had her share of wealth.

She followed him, the roar of her motorcycle cutting through the quiet of the wealthy neighborhood enough to make him wince. There would be phone calls. There would be a lot of things. But the most important thing was they were going somewhere that couldn't have been infiltrated.

He drove up the sprawling drive after entering the

code for the gate and hoped against hope his father was in DC and his mother was at a function or, well, anywhere but here. Because while they might ignore his presence, maybe, they would never ignore the presence of the motorcycle.

Parking at the top of the drive, he got out of his running car and punched the code into the garage door so it opened.

"*This* is a guesthouse?" Alyssa called out over the sound of her motorcycle.

Bennet nodded as the garage door went up. He walked back to his car and motioned for her to park inside the garage. Maybe if the evidence was hidden, and it was late enough, it was possible no one would notice the disturbance. A man could dream.

Alyssa walked her motorcycle into the garage and killed the engine. She pulled off her helmet. It seemed no matter how often her hair tumbled out like that, his idiotic body had a reaction. He really needed to get a handle on that.

"Follow me," he said, probably too tersely. But he felt terse and uncomfortable. He felt a lot of things he didn't want to think about.

He slid the key he always kept on his ring into the lock of the door from the garage to the mudroom. He didn't look back to see how she reacted to the rather ostentatious guesthouse as they walked through it. It wasn't his.

He led her into the living room. "Feel free to use anything in the house. The fridge probably won't be stocked, but the pantry is. The staff keeps everything clean and fresh for visitors, so—"

"You keep saying 'staff,' but I have a feeling what you mean is servants."

He gave her a doleful look. "I'll show you to a bedroom and bathroom you can use. I suggest we get some sleep and reevaluate in the morning."

"Reevaluate what?"

"How we're going to handle getting me into see your brothers with you."

"There's no way. There's *no* way. They'll kill you on sight knowing you're a Texas Ranger. They have all this time while we're 'reevaluating' to plan to kill you and make it look like an accident, make you just disappear." She snapped her fingers. "It will be suicide. I don't think you get that."

"I told you I had some ideas."

"Like what?"

"Like what we're doing right here."

She threw her arms up in the air, clearly frustrated with him. "What are we doing right here?

"If your brothers think that we…" He cleared his throat, uncomfortable with his own idea, with telling it to her, with *enacting* it. But it made sense. It was the only thing that made sense. No matter how much he didn't want to do it. "If your brothers think we are romantically involved, there's a chance they wouldn't touch me. If I were important to you."

Alyssa blinked at him for a full minute. "First of all," she said eventually, "even if that was remotely true, if they have my office bugged, they know we just met. It was part of that conversation."

"We'll say it was a lure."

"You can't be this stupid. You can't be."

That offhanded insult poked at a million things he'd never admit to. "I assure you, Ms. Jimenez, I know what I'm doing," he said, crossing his arms over his chest and giving her a look that had intimidated drug dealers and rapists and even murderers.

Alyssa rolled her eyes. "Spare me the 'Ms. Jimenez' crap. It makes far more sense for me to go there on my own and handle things my own way. You can trust me when I say I want to get to the bottom of my mother's murder more than you do. I have no reason not to bring you whatever information I find so my mother's murderer can be brought to justice."

"I think you're bright enough to realize all of this is so much more than a murder case. The things your brothers are involved in aren't that easy. It's not something I can trust a civilian to go into and bring me back the information I need to prosecute. I need to go in there with you. I need to investigate this myself."

She shook her head in disgust, but she didn't argue further. Which was a plus.

"How far are you willing to go?" she demanded.

"As far as I need to. This case is my number one priority. I won't rest until it's solved."

She sighed while looking around the living room. "I can't sit anywhere in here. I'll stain all this white just by looking at it."

He rolled his eyes and took her by the elbow, leading her to a chair. It *was* white, and it was very possible she'd get motorcycle grease or something on it, but it would be taken care of. Stains in the Stevens world were always taken care of.

He pushed her into the chair. She sat with an audible

thump. "What about this? You tell them I'm a double agent. That I want to be a dirty cop."

"They wouldn't believe that."

"Why not?"

"Because you are the antithesis of a dirty cop. You look like Superman had a baby with Captain America and every other do-gooder superhero to ever exist. No one would believe you want to be a dirty cop."

"Have you ever had any contact with a dirty cop?"

"Well, no."

He took a seat on the couch, leaning forward and resting his elbows on his knees. He never took his eyes off her—this was too important. "It has nothing to do with what you look like and everything to do with how desperate you are. How powerful you want to feel. Cops go dirty because... Well, there are a lot of reasons, but it's not about how you look or where you're from. It's about ego, among other things."

"Okay, it's about ego, which I'll give you you've got, but that doesn't mean they're going to believe any of it."

"It doesn't mean they won't."

"You're not going to give up on this, are you?"

"We can do it the easy way or the hard way. The easy way is where you work with me. The hard way is where you work against me. Either way, I'm doing it."

She sighed gustily, but he could see in the set of her shoulders she was relenting. Giving in. One way or another, she was going to give in.

"Fine. But we're not doing it your way. If we're doing it together, when it comes to my brothers, we do it *my* way. I tell them I'm using you to get information. I don't know if they'll buy it hook, line and sinker, but it's better than all your ideas."

"Gee, thank you."

"I'm afraid you're going to have to leave your ego at the door, Mr. Texas Ranger."

"I'll see what I can do."

Alyssa rubbed her temples. She had to be exhausted and stressed and emotionally wrung out from the things she'd found out today.

"Let's go to bed. We'll work out the details in the morning."

She sighed and pushed herself out of the chair. "Fine. Lead me to my castle."

"You're awfully melodramatic for a street urchin."

"I'm not the one living in this place."

"I don't live in this place," he muttered, standing, as well.

"You also don't live in an apartment above a garage."

"Is that where you live?" Which was neither here nor there, knowing where she lived or anything about her current life. All that mattered was her connection to the Jimenez family.

"Yes. I live in an apartment above the garage of my friends' house. My friends who are now in danger because of me, because of this." She let out a long sigh and faced him, her expression grave, her eyes reflecting some of the fear she'd kept impressively hidden thus far. "I need them safe, Ranger Stevens."

"I may not know Gabby very well, but I've worked with Jaime on occasion, and Vaughn has been my partner for a long time. I care about your friends. They're *my* friends, too. Nothing's going to happen to them."

"My, you are a confident one."

But no matter how sarcastically she'd said it, he could see a slight relaxation in her. His confidence gave her comfort. "Confidence is everything."

"Except when you have nothing."

Bennet didn't know what to say to that, so he led her down a hallway to the bedrooms. The farthest one from his. It would be the best room for her, not just for keeping her far away from him. He wasn't that weak to need a barrier, or so he'd tell himself.

"That door back there leads to a private bathroom. Feel free to use it and anything in it. I'll see you in the morning."

"Hey, have you heard anything from Vaughn about Nat?"

Bennet looked down at his phone. "I don't have any messages."

"I don't know what to tell them. They'll expect me to visit, and…" She shook her head, looking young and vulnerable for the first time since she'd seen the picture of her mother.

He wanted to help. He wanted to soothe. Which was just his *nature*. He was a guy who wanted to help. It had nothing to do with soft brown eyes and a pretty mouth.

"You're a bounty hunter, right? Well, an unauthorized and illegal one, anyway."

She frowned at him. "Yes. I have my reasons."

"Criminals always do." But he grinned, hoping the joke, the teasing, would lighten her up, take that vulnerable cast of her mouth away. "Tell them you had an important case, and you'll be back as soon as possible. You're not going back to your place, so it's not like they'll have any reason to believe you're in town."

"I don't like lying to them."

"It's not my favorite either, but—"

"I know. It'll keep them safe, and that is the most important thing to me."

"It's important to me, too. Never doubt that."

She nodded, hugging herself and looking around the room. "You know this kind of insane show of wealth is usually the sign of a small dick, right?"

He choked on his own spit. That had not been at all what he'd expected her to say, but from her grin he could tell that's exactly why she'd said it.

"I suppose that's something you'd have to take up with my father, since this is neither my show of wealth, nor is that a complaint I've ever received."

Two twin blotches of pink showed up on her cheeks, and Bennet knew it was time to close the door and walk away before there were any more jokes about...that.

"Are you sure your parents won't get wind of this?"

"Unless it furthers their political agenda, my parents won't be sticking their nose anywhere near it. They'll stay out of it and safe."

"Political agenda?"

"Oh, didn't you put it together?" he asked casually, because he knew much like her small-dick comment had caught *him* off guard, this little tidbit would catch *her* off guard.

"Put what together?"

"My father is Gary L. Stevens, US senator and former presidential candidate. My mother is Lynette Stevens, pioneer lawyer and Texas state senator. You may have heard of them."

She stared slack-jawed at him, and he couldn't ignore the pleasure he got out of leaving her in shock. So he flashed a grin, his politicians' son grin.

"Good night, Alyssa."

And Bennet left her room, closing the door behind him.

Alyssa tossed and turned. Between trying to come to full grips with the fact that Bennet Stevens was the son of two wealthy and influential politicians, and Gabby being mad about her taking a job before coming to see the baby, she couldn't get her mind to stop running in circles.

She hated when someone was mad at her and had every right to be. She hated disappointing Gabby and Nat. But this was keeping them safe, and she had to remember that.

And more than all of that, the thing she kept trying to pretend wasn't true.

Her mother had been murdered. She knew Ranger Stevens suspected her brothers. No matter what horrible things they were capable of, though—and they were enormously capable—Alyssa rejected the idea they could be behind the murder of her mother. *Their* mother.

Maybe she could see it if her father was still in his right mind, but he had succumbed to some kind of dementia before she'd even been kidnapped. He was nothing but a titular figure now, one her brothers kept as a weapon of their own.

Once it was finally a reasonable hour to get up, Alyssa crawled out of the too-comfortable bed and looked at herself in the gigantic mirror. She looked like a bedraggled sewer animal in the midst of all this pristine white.

It was such a glaring contrast. Though she'd grown up surrounded by a certain amount of wealth, it had all been the dark-and-dirty kind. She'd lived in a sketchy guarded-to-the-hilt home for most of her life, and then been kidnapped into a glorified bunker.

But what did contrasts matter when she was simply out for the truth? She tiptoed down the hallway, wondering where Ranger Stevens had secreted himself off to last night. What would he look like sleep-rumpled in one of those big white beds?

She was seriously losing it. Clearly she needed something to eat to clear her head. She headed for the kitchen, but stopped short at the entrance when she saw Ranger Stevens was already sitting there in a little breakfast nook surrounded by windows.

"Good morning," he offered, as if it wasn't five in the morning and as if this wasn't weird as all get out.

"Morning," she replied.

On the glossy black table in front of him, he had a laptop open. He was wearing sweatpants and a T-shirt, and while the button-down shirt he'd been wearing last night hadn't exactly hidden the fact this man was no pencil pusher, this was a whole other experience.

He had muscles. Actual biceps. Whether it was on purpose or not, the sleeves of his T-shirt hugged them perfectly and made her realize, again, how unbearably hot this man was. And how unbearably unfair that was.

"There's coffee already brewed. Mugs are in the cabinet above it. As for breakfast, feel free to poke around and find what you'd like."

"Not much of a breakfast eater," she lied. She didn't know why she lied. She just felt off-kilter and weird and didn't want to be here.

"I'd try to eat something. Got a lot of work to do today."

"Don't you have to go to, like, actual work?"

"My actual work is investigating this case."

"If my brothers get ahold of you and you don't report for work, what's going to happen then?"

He looked at her over his laptop with that hard, implacable Texas Ranger look she thought maybe he practiced in the mirror. Because it was effective, both in shutting her up and making those weird lower-belly flutters intensify.

"I'll handle my work responsibilities," he said, his voice deep and certain.

Alyssa rolled her eyes in an effort to appear wholly unaffected. She walked over to the coffeepot. She didn't drink coffee, but she figured she might as well start. That's what adults did after all. They drank coffee and handled their work responsibilities.

"Sugar is right next to the pot. No cream, but milk is in the fridge."

"I drink it black," she lied. She tried to take a sophisticated sip, but ended up burning her tongue and grimacing at the horrible, horrible taste.

"You take it black, huh?" And there was that dangerous curve to his mouth, humor and something like intent all curled into it. She wanted to trace it with her fingers.

So, she scowled instead. "Let's worry less about how I take my coffee and more about what we're going to do."

"First things first, we're going to go back to your office and check for a bug. We need to know exactly what your brothers know about me and what I'm looking for."

She wasn't in love with him deciding what they were going to do without at least a conversation, but unfortunately he was right. They needed to know for sure what was going on.

"Once we've figured that out, we'll move on to trying to lure your brothers out."

"I'm guessing my leading their cronies to Texas Rangers headquarters and yelling probably did it."

"Probably, but we need to make sure. We also need to make sure it seems like we don't want to be caught."

She studied him then because there was something not quite right about all this.

"This is official Ranger business, right?"

He focused on the computer. "What do you mean 'official'?"

"This isn't on the up-and-up, is it?"

His mouth firmed and his jaw went hard and uncompromising. He was so damn hot, and she kind of wanted to lick him. She didn't know what to do with that. She'd never wanted to lick anyone before.

"I've been okayed to investigate this case," he ground out. "It's possible we'll have to do some things that aren't entirely by the book. I might not tell my superiors every single thing I'm doing, but this is one of those cases where you have to bend the rules a little bit."

"Doesn't bending the rules invalidate the investigation?"

"Depends on the situation. Do you want to find the answers to your mother's murder or not?"

Which she supposed was all that really mattered. She wanted to find the answers to her mother's murder. Everything else was secondary. "Okay. Well, let's go, then."

His mouth quirked, his hard, uncompromising expression softening. "Aren't you going to finish your coffee?"

She glanced at the mug, and she knew he was testing her. Teasing her maybe. She fluttered her eyelashes at him. "You make shitty coffee."

He barked out a laugh, and she was all too pleased he was laughing at something she'd said. All too pleased he would tease her. Pay attention to her in any way.

It was stupid to be into him. So she'd ignore that part of herself right now. Ignore the flutters and the being pleased.

A door opened somewhere, and Bennet visibly cringed when a voice rang out.

"Bennet? Are you here?"

It was a woman's voice. Did he have a girlfriend? Something ugly bloomed in her chest, but Bennet offered some sort of half grimace, half smile. "Well, Alyssa, let's see what kind of actress you are."

He pushed away from the table, and an older woman entered the room. He held out his arms.

"Mother. How are you?"

"Surprised to find you here." She brushed her lips across the air next to Bennet's cheek.

Alyssa pushed herself into the little corner of the countertop, but Bennet wasn't going to let her be ignored. He turned his mother to face her.

"Allow me to introduce you to someone," he said easily, charmingly, clearly a very good actor. The woman's blue gaze landed on Alyssa.

"This is Alyssa... Clark," Bennet offered. "Alyssa, this is my mother, Lynette Stevens."

"Alyssa Clark," Mrs. Stevens repeated blandly.

Alyssa didn't have to be a mind reader to know Mrs. Stevens did not approve. She might have squirmed if it didn't piss her off a little. Sure, she looked like a drowned sewer rat and was the daughter of a drug kingpin rather than Texas royalty, but she wasn't a bad person. Exactly.

Alyssa smiled as sweetly as she could manage. "It's so good to meet you, Ms. Stevens. I've heard *so* much about you," she said, adopting her most cultured, overly upper-class Texas drawl.

Mrs. Bennet's expression didn't change, but Alyssa was adept at reading the cold fury of people. And Mrs. Stevens had some cold fury going on in there.

"I didn't realize you were seeing anyone at the moment, Bennet," Mrs. Stevens murmured, the fury of her gaze never leaving Alyssa.

"I don't tell you everything, as you well know."

"Yes, well. I just came by to see what all the noise complaints were about. If I'd known you were busy, I wouldn't have bothered you."

"It was no bother, but I do have to get ready for work."

"And what's Ms. Clark going to do while you work?"

"Oh, I have my own work to do," Alyssa said. She smiled as blandly and coldly as Bennet's mother.

"Yes, well. I'll leave you both alone then. Try to avoid any more noise disturbances if you please, and if you're around this evening, bring your young lady to dinner at the main house."

"I'll see if our schedules can accommodate it and let Kinsey know," Bennet replied, and Alyssa had not seen this side of him. Cool and blank, a false mask of charm over everything. This was not Ranger Stevens, and she didn't think it was Bennet either.

"Wonderful. I hope to see you then." She gave Alyssa one last glance and then swept out of the kitchen as quickly as she'd appeared.

Alyssa looked curiously at Bennet. "That's how you talk to your mother?"

"I'm afraid so."

"Why did she hate me so much?"

"You're not on her approved list of women I'm allowed to see."

"She doesn't have a list."

Bennet raised an eyebrow. "It's laminated."

Alyssa laughed, even though she had a terrible feeling he wasn't joking. "So, she wants you to get married and have lots of little perfect Superman babies?"

"It's a political game for her."

"What is?"

"Life."

Which seemed suddenly not funny at all but just kind of sad. For her. For Bennet. Which was foolish. She'd grown up in a drug cartel. What could be sad about Bennet's picture-perfect political family?

"Why'd you give her a fake name when you introduced me?"

"Because her private investigators will be on you in five seconds. If you've ever stripped, inhaled, handed out fliers for minimum-wage increases, I will know it within the hour. But a fake name will slow her down."

"She checks out all your girlfriends?"

"All the ones I let her know about. Which is why I don't usually let her know. Which I imagine is why she's here at five in the morning and overly suspicious. But you don't have to worry."

"Because you didn't give her my real name?"

"Because I think you can eat my mother for lunch."

Alyssa glanced at the way the woman had gone. She didn't think so. She might be a rough-and-tumble bounty hunter, but Mrs. Stevens had a cold fury underneath that spoke to being a lot tougher than she looked.

Still, Alyssa didn't mind Bennet thinking she could take his mother on.

"Let's head over to your office."

Alyssa nodded and followed along, but Bennet's mother haunted her for the rest of the day.

Chapter 5

"I can't find a damn thing," Bennet muttered. They'd spent over two hours searching Alyssa's office from top to bottom. Meticulously. They'd taken her desk apart, pulled at loose flooring, poked at soft drywall.

It was possible they'd overlooked something, but Bennet didn't have a clue as to what. Surely, surely the office had been bugged. How else would anyone have known to follow Alyssa last night?

He tried to push the frustration away, since it wouldn't get him any further in this case—and he'd already come further than he'd expected to in twenty-four hours—but something about knowing who the Jane Doe was, and who cared about her, made it seem all the more imperative to unravel this mystery.

Alyssa tossed some debris into a corner. "This is pointless. It could be anywhere. In anything."

"We've been through everywhere and everything. Maybe there was no bug."

"Then why would they have followed me last night?" She looked out her smudgy windows, frowning. Her profile reminded him of last night, when she'd stood in the middle of that parking lot and all but dared two thugs to harm her.

He shifted, trying to ignore the uncomfortable way his body reacted to that memory. "Maybe it's something else. Something seemingly unrelated. Had you ever seen those guys before?"

"No… Wait. Wait." She rushed over to her desk, pulling a crate off the floor.

"We already went through that."

She waved a hand. "Did you get the license plate off that car last night?"

"License plate. Make. Model. Picture on my phone."

"Pull it up."

He pulled out his phone and pulled up the information and placed it on the most level side of the desk. She pulled a little notebook from a seemingly endless supply of them and began rifling through it.

She found a page, read it, then glanced at his phone screen and swore. She shoved the notebook toward him, poking her finger at a few lines of chicken scratch. "I have seen those guys—well, their car. It was following me when I was on my last skip in Amarillo. Kept getting in my way. I thought it was friends of the skip trying to stop me, but…" She shook her head, forehead furrowed in confusion. "It is the same car. Same plate."

"So, your brothers have sent someone after you before, which means your office might not be bugged."

"But why? Why now?" She shoved her fingers into her hair, pulling some of the strands out of the band they were in. "Two years. I…" She trailed off, shaking her head, grappling with something bigger than this case.

She hardened her jaw, tossing the notebook back into her crate of notebooks. She stalked around the desk, shoving his phone back at him, something like fury in her gaze. A fury that definitely did not come from this alone.

"Okay, what's next?"

Bennet stilled. Next? Hell if he knew. He'd expected to find a bug and then go from there. He hadn't expected this twist.

"You're the Ranger. You have a plan. Don't you?"

"Why don't we take a deep breath and—"

"You *don't* have a plan."

"Alyssa—"

"You're probably not even really a Texas Ranger. Your mommy and daddy gave you a badge and everyone plays along. Pretends you aren't some idiotic—"

"Have a seat," he barked, gratified when she jumped a little.

"You don't order me around," she replied, lifting that chin, leveling him with that furious glare. It was only the fact there was some panicky undercurrent to it that he didn't bark out another order.

But he did advance, no matter how defiantly she kept his gaze. He stared her right down, getting up in her personal space until they were practically touching. "I said, have a seat," he growled.

Her screw-you expression didn't change, but she did blink and, after a few tense seconds, where he was thinking far too much about the shape of her mouth and not nearly enough about the threat he was trying to enact, she glanced behind her and pulled one of the folding chairs toward her.

She sat carefully, scowling at him all the way.

"I understand this is emotionally taxing for you, Alyssa." She scoffed, but he kept talking. "You will not lash out at me if you'd like me to allow you to—"

"Allow me, my a—"

She tried to stand up, but he took her by the shoulders and firmly pressed her back into the seat. "You're an asset, but don't forget you are working with me because I consider you one. Should you stop being one, I will no longer require your assistance."

"Perhaps," she said, speaking in the same way she had this morning when his mother had been around, mimicking a smooth, soft drawl, "I no longer require your assistance, Ranger Stevens." She shoved his hands off her shoulders with a flourish.

Which irritated him about as much as her words and her fake drawl and everything else about today that wasn't adding up.

So, he took her by the face, which was a mistake, his big palms against her soft cheeks. He felt her little inhale of breath, could see all too easily the way her pupils dilated as he bent over her.

He could feel the way her cheeks heated, the little puffs of breath coming out of her mouth, and there was an insane, blinding moment where he forgot what he was doing, why he was here. All he could think was that if he pressed his mouth to hers he'd know if she tasted as sharp as she always sounded.

He released her face and stepped back, shoving his hands into his pockets. "Getting pissed off at each other solves nothing. We need to arrange a meeting with your brothers somehow. Ferret out what they know." He paced, trying to focus on the information he had rather than the way the strands of her hair had felt trailing against the back of his hand. "Did your skip have something to do with them?"

"No," Alyssa said quietly. "At least, I don't think so."

"But he could have?"

She frowned in concentration. "I think I would have found a connection somewhere, something that rang familiar, but…"

"But what?" he demanded, no patience for her inward thinking that she wasn't sharing.

"I didn't know much about cartel business. I was kept very separated and very isolated from their world. My brothers always acted like I was in imminent danger. They told me if I ever went somewhere alone, there'd be a target on my chest. They were protecting me, they always said."

She seemed to doubt it now, in retrospect, and he couldn't help but wonder if they'd been so protective, so diligent in keeping her separate, then how had she been kidnapped? He hesitated to point that out, then berated himself for it.

He had an investigation to figure out. He could not be ignoring pertinent questions to spare her feelings. "How were you kidnapped?" he asked, gently. Softly. Certainly not in a tone befitting a Texas Ranger.

She hugged herself in that way she seemed to do only

when she was really rattled, gaze sliding away from his. "I don't know," she whispered.

Something about that whisper, the vulnerable note, made the desperation wind inside him like a sharp, heavy rock, and he knew then and there he'd find out. He'd find out just how she'd come to be kidnapped, regardless of his case.

And if that was stupid and foolish, well, so be it.

Alyssa didn't want to talk about the kidnapping. She didn't want Bennet to talk to her in that gentle way that had to be a lie. Gentleness spoke to care, and all she was to him was a means to an end.

"What do you mean, you don't know?" he asked, and all of that fury and those hard edges from before when she'd insulted him and he'd ordered her to sit down were gone, softened into this...*concern*.

Which was too tempting, too alluring. She wanted to tell him everything, when she'd never told or wanted to tell anyone anything. Even Gabby knew only bits and pieces, because Alyssa didn't like to bring that pinched, pained look to her friend's face. Gabby had been a prisoner for eight years. Nearly all of her twenties. It wasn't right. It wasn't fair.

But life never had been, Alyssa supposed. Which meant she had to tell Bennet the facts. She wouldn't let emotion get wrapped up in it. She'd just tell him what had happened, and if this had something to do with that...

She closed her eyes, trying to breathe, trying to work this all out in a way that made her want to act instead of cry.

"Take your time," Bennet said softly, giving her arm a quick squeeze, nothing like the way he'd grabbed her face and had those blue eyes boring into her, dropping to look at her mouth as though…

She snapped at him to keep her thoughts from traveling too far in that way-wrong direction. "Don't tell me what to do."

His mouth firmed, some of that softness going away, thank God.

"All I know about the kidnapping is one minute I was asleep in my bed, the next moment I woke up in the back of a van with a hood on my head. I was taken inside some giant warehouse, and there wasn't one person I recognized. A guy examined me, The Stallion, and I got taken to one of his little lairs."

"You would've had to have been drugged," Bennet said, focusing on the details of the kidnapping rather than the emotional scars as if he could read her mind and what she wanted.

"It's the only explanation," Alyssa replied. "I just don't know…how. My brothers kept me locked away. *They* brought me my food. *They* protected me all those years. Before my mother disappeared. Before…" Well, she didn't feel right about letting Bennet in on their biggest family secret—that Dad wasn't in his right mind, or even in his right body. He was a shell in a locked-up room, just like she'd been.

"There's no way *they* could have arranged it?" Bennet asked, with something like regret on his face.

Or maybe that was projection, since she regretted this conversation, regretted and hated the doubts plaguing her. "Why would they protect me for twenty years, keep me safe and from harm, then with no warning hand me over to some crazy guy?" *Who only ever kept me as locked up as my brothers did.*

"I don't know," Bennet said carefully. "But if they protected you so well for twenty years, I don't understand why all the sudden you were kidnapped."

She swallowed at the lump in her throat and did everything she could to appear unaffected. "Well, neither do I."

"Come to think of it, the other night, they followed you. Not me. Alyssa, maybe this doesn't have anything to do with me and what I talked to you about, and everything to do with you."

She forced herself to breathe even though panic threatened to freeze her lungs. Why would it have to do with her? Why had they left her alone for *two* years? Why would they come *now*?

"I could be wrong," Bennet said, and he studied her with those soft eyes that made her want to punch him.

That's not really what you want to do with him.

She shook her head trying to focus, trying to *think*. "We need a next step," she said more to herself than him. "We need to get this over with so that I can enjoy Christmas with my…" She almost said "family." She'd let Gabby and Natalie become her family because her brothers hadn't come for her.

They'd left her. Abandoned her. And now they were back, lurking around the corners of her life.

Bennet reached out to touch her again, but before he could say anything, her door violently screeched open.

Two men in ski masks stepped inside, one with a very large gun, and when Bennet reached for his gun,

they fired off a warning shot all too close to Bennet for
Alyssa's comfort.

"On the ground," one of the men growled. Bennet
didn't move, his face impassive, his hand on the butt of
his weapon, though he didn't move another inch.

Alyssa knew she should move off her chair, should
follow instructions, but Bennet's stoicism kept her calm,
as did the way the man without the gun tapped long fingers against his thigh.

"I said get on the ground," the gunman said in that
fake raspy voice.

Alyssa slowly stood, staring at the shape of the man's
mouth, the breadth of his shoulders. The way he held
that gun.

"Jose," Alyssa said, making sure it was clear she
knew it was him, not just suspected. She glanced at the
man without the gun, the brother closest in age to her.
"Oscar. It's been a while."

Both men froze. Jose glanced at Oscar, still training
the gun on Bennet. "How did she know it was us?" Jose
demanded in a sad attempt at a whisper.

"I told CJ she wasn't stupid," Oscar muttered in disgust.

Alyssa swallowed at the odd lump in her throat,
blinked at the stinging in her eyes. Four years. Four
years ago her entire life had been torn from her, and
now here was half of her entire life, the brothers who'd
kept the closest tabs on her, in ski masks and with a gun.

Men she'd trusted her entire childhood to keep her
safe. At least she'd always thought that's what they'd
been doing. Had she been so wrong? So naive and stupid?

Two years she'd been imprisoned with that madman,

The Stallion, and had slowly gone crazy realizing she'd *always* been imprisoned, for her entire life, but she'd waited. Waited to be rescued. To be found by the men she'd loved and trusted.

But she hadn't been rescued by them. She'd been rescued by the FBI. And for two years her brothers hadn't done a damn thing to contact her. They'd left her for dead.

Now, *now* they'd crashed back into her life and were just *standing* there discussing whether CJ was right about her intelligence level.

Furious, and more than a little emotional, Alyssa stomped over to them and their sad little whispered argument. Jose's eyes widened, but he kept the gun trained on Bennet, who was standing calmly and placidly near where she'd been sitting.

She ignored Jose for the time being, and instead stood toe-to-toe with Oscar, her closest brother, her sweet and kind and caring closest brother, and slapped him across the face as hard as she could.

"What did you do that for?" Oscar howled, cradling his smacked cheek.

She tried to yell all the reasons why she'd hit him, but what she really wanted to do was cry, so she couldn't manage a yell, or anything more than a squeak.

She moved to slap Jose, too, for good measure, for mixing her up and making her want to cry, but before she could do anything, three more men stormed into the office.

Two with masks and guns just like Jose's went straight for Bennet. They jerked his arms behind his back and had him pressed to a wall, face-first, in seconds flat.

The other man stared straight at her, maskless, dark eyes cold and furious.

"I knew I couldn't trust you two," he muttered, glancing disgustedly at Jose and Oscar. "It's broad daylight. What the hell are you taking your time for? Eric, Benji, get the Ranger in the van. *Now.*"

"What about Alyssa?" Oscar asked, still cradling his cheek.

CJ, her eldest bother, the leader of the cartel, looked her over as if she was some kind of cargo. "Alyssa comes with me."

If she had any sense in her head, she'd let CJ take her. Her oldest brother had always been cold, remote and mostly ruthless, and it didn't make sense to cross him when she and Bennet had been planning on being taken anyway.

But slapping Oscar had only unleashed more fury rather than soothed any of it. She wanted to hit all of them. She wanted to beat them until they bled. She wanted answers, and hell if she was going to be calm or patient in the getting of them.

"Let him go," Alyssa said calmly and evenly, coolly even, matching CJ's cold stare with one of her own.

CJ leaned down, so close their noses almost touched. "Are you warming that Texas Ranger's bed, Alyssa? I didn't think we raised you to be a whore."

Those words, that tone, lit a fire to something inside her that had been simmering for all of these four years. She'd never acknowledged it, this blistering hurt and rage.

They'd abandoned her, to be kidnapped, to be let go. They'd given up any claim to her in four years of silence.

Now they had Bennet pressed to a wall with a gun to his head, and she wasn't stupid enough to think her brothers were *that* much stronger and smarter than him. No, Bennet was standing there *letting* them press him up against the wall.

For her.

No. No, for the *case*.

But it didn't matter, because she wasn't giving her brothers this kind of power. They'd run her life for years, but those years were over.

In a move she'd practiced for as long as she'd known how to walk, she pulled the gun out of her coat so swiftly, she had it shoved to CJ's gut before he'd even blinked an eye.

His mouth hardened, but he made no other reaction. "Am I supposed to believe you'd shoot me, my sweet Lyssie girl?"

She could almost believe he cared when he used that voice, that old nickname, but four years of separation had given her too many questions, too many doubts. "If you don't think I have the guts to shoot you right here, right now, then you don't know the woman you raised."

"You'd shoot your own brother? Whatever happened to loyalty?"

"Loyalty? You dare speak the word *loyalty* to me?" Alyssa shoved the gun against him harder, and he winced. "Family was supposed to be the only thing that mattered to you. Family was the rallying cry in *protecting* me. But I wasn't protected. I got kidnapped.

I've been free from that for two years, and where have you been?"

"It's complicated," CJ growled.

"It's not. You weren't there, and now I don't need you." She looked down at the gun in her hand, surprised to find herself steady. When she looked back up at CJ, she smiled. "But I may spare your life."

CJ scoffed. "Jose, give me that gun."

"I'll shoot him if you move, Jose. And what would the world do without CJ Jimenez in it to pull its strings?"

"What do you want?" CJ asked, feigning boredom, but Alyssa could see a faint line of concern on his forehead.

She fiddled with the safety of her gun, just to show him she wasn't messing around. "Our mother was murdered, and I want to know why."

CJ's mouth curved and his gaze moved to Bennet, who somehow looked calm and model-like pressed to her grimy office wall. "I think your Ranger has a few more answers about these things than he lets on."

Alyssa didn't jerk, didn't react, though inwardly her stomach tightened into a painful cramp. Had Bennet been lying to her? Someone was. It could be him. But CJ was her impending doom right now, and she had to take care of him first.

"Drop the guns, let the Ranger go, or I shoot CJ. I'll count to ten."

She watched as her brothers all stood wide-eyed and frozen as she counted down. Finally, CJ inclined his head. "Let the Ranger go," he grumbled.

"And drop the guns. Now."

The two brothers holding Bennet let go, slowly putting their guns on the ground along with Jose. Bennet didn't scurry away, didn't scowl, didn't outwardly react in any way. He simply picked the guns up and used the straps to sling them onto his shoulder.

"I want you all lined up in front of the door," Alyssa said, pushing CJ back toward the door with the gun.

They scrambled to do her bidding, and Alyssa couldn't ignore the thrill it gave her. She was in charge. *She* had outwitted them. *She* was going to get what *she* wanted for once. For damn once.

And there they were. All five of them. The men she'd loved and trusted for her entire life.

She'd spent the past two years fearing they didn't love her. Being so afraid she didn't matter or that they thought she was tainted in some way. But none of that fear or sadness was inside her right now. All she felt was rage. Rage that they'd abandoned her. After giving her very few skills with which to survive—only violence and suspicion.

Bennet came to stand behind her, and she expected him to tell her what to do. She didn't know what, but she expected *something*. He hadn't uttered a word this entire altercation.

He still didn't. He just stood there. Behind her. A calming, supportive force. Because it was her turn. *Her* turn to be in charge of her life.

"I want all the information you have on my kidnapping and our mother's murder. And if I think you're lying, I'll pick you off one by one."

"And I'll help," Bennet added cheerfully, holding one of the guns in his hands, sights set on CJ.

Chapter 6

For a few moments Bennet could only stand behind Alyssa and stare. He hadn't known she had a gun on her. How could he have missed that, and what kind of Ranger did it make him that he had?

But that moderate shame was no match for the other feeling that assailed him. Awe. She'd fended off an attack from all five of her brothers. Who did that? They were the leaders of a *cartel*, three of them had guns, and yet she'd gotten them to drop their weapons, all without his having to lift a finger.

He'd been content to let her brothers think they had the upper hand, eager for them to pull him into their world so he could find his answers.

But Alyssa had a gun on them and point-blank asked for those answers, and so he'd stood behind her and backed her up. It was the only thing to do.

"Why don't you ask your Ranger, Lyss?" the clear leader of the group said, dark eyes zeroed in on him.

Alyssa didn't flick so much as a glance back at him, but he saw the way her shoulders tensed, the way CJ insinuating Bennet knew something he wasn't telling her bothered her.

"If I knew anything about either, I wouldn't be here," Bennet replied coolly.

CJ cocked his head, and even if Bennet didn't know about her brothers and their documented work in cartel dealings, he'd know this man was dangerous. Powerful.

But this man had cowered to Alyssa, and that was something to use.

"When are you going to run for office like Mommy and Daddy, Ranger boy?" CJ asked.

Something prickled at the back of Bennet's neck, that telltale gut feeling something was seriously wrong, but he didn't have enough to bluff his way through this one. So, he had to go with the truth. "I'm not a politician."

"Hmm." CJ considered Bennet as if two guns weren't pointed at him. "And I suppose the name Sal Cochrane means nothing to you."

Bennet racked his brain, every memory, every case, every person he'd ever met, but he came up blank.

"Salvador Dominguez, then?"

Bennet was very careful to keep the recognition off his face. The Dominguez cartel was newer and less powerful than the Jimenez one, but it had been gaining in power of late. But who the hell was Sal Cochrane?

CJ kept studying him, but Bennet didn't know what the man was looking for. What the man thought Bennet knew.

"Politics is dirty business, Ranger Stevens," CJ said, putting extra emphasis on his last name, and there was that scalp prickle again. Foreboding.

"I suppose it is, but like I said, I'm not a politician. That's my parents."

"I guess we'll see," CJ murmured.

"Who the hell are you here for, CJ?" Alyssa demanded. "Me or him?"

CJ's mouth curved in what Bennet assumed was supposed to be a smile. "If I wanted either of you, I'd have you."

Which sent a cold chill down Bennet's spine, because he was beginning to realize this was all a little too easy. For five men involved in a drug cartel with an insane amount of weaponry, one woman—sister or not, remarkable or not—they hadn't actually been bested.

This was all an act. Bennet kept his gun aimed at CJ, but he started looking around. There was a back entrance, but he'd not just locked it when they'd entered through it, he'd barred the door. They at least couldn't be ambushed without warning that way.

Alyssa shoved the gun in CJ's gut again, with enough force that CJ coughed out a breath. "Why was I kidnapped?" she demanded. "You're not leaving here without telling me. How the hell did someone drug me and get me out of the house?"

CJ's mouth firmed, and the one who'd come inside without a gun stared at his feet. Whatever the reason, these men all knew it, which meant they were probably part of it.

Which, unfortunately, Bennet knew would hurt Alyssa immeasurably. She'd seen them as her protectors all this time, and not coming after her had been a betrayal—even if Bennet thought she was better off without them—but this?

"You never came for me," Alyssa replied, and on the surface her voice was calm, collected, but there was something vibrating underneath, something Bennet figured she was trying to hide. Emotion. Hurt. "And now you're here spouting threats at *him*. What is this?"

"Still dying to be the center of attention after all these years, Lyssie?"

Bennet opened his mouth to say something, anything to put the man in his place, but that's when he saw a flicker of light outside the grimy windows, and when the glass exploded seconds later, he couldn't be sure what was coming through, but he knew it wasn't good.

And far too close to Alyssa. He lunged for her, knocking her onto the ground and underneath him. He couldn't make out whatever words of protest she was making, because something exploded.

He could feel heat, bits of debris painfully pelting his back and Alyssa breathing underneath him.

She was swearing, pushing at him, but breathing. In and out. Bennet was almost afraid to see what had caused the explosion, afraid to see what casualties there might be, but he could still feel the heat on his back, which meant the place was on fire.

He pushed off her and onto his feet, offering his hand to help her up, but she scrambled past him unaided.

"Where'd they go?" She stared at the door and the flames licking around it. None of her brothers or her brothers' bodies were anywhere to be seen. There was only a line of flame slowly spreading down the length of the front wall.

She whirled on him. "Where'd they go?"

"Alyssa…"

"You let them get away. You…" She slapped her palms to his chest and pushed. Hard, and while in normal circumstances it wouldn't have hurt him in the least, a searing pain shot through his shoulder and back at his body's movement.

He hissed out a breath, and some of her desperate fury was replaced by confusion, and maybe concern. She tried to move past him, but he moved with her, keeping his back hidden.

"We need to get out of here," he said, sucking in a smoky breath before reaching his arm out to take hers. To usher her out the back way. The fire wasn't huge, but they needed to get out before the smoke got worse, and they really needed to leave before anyone saw them.

He nudged her in front of him, pushing her down the hall no matter how often she scowled over her shoulder at him. He pulled the heavy rack he'd pushed in front of the back door earlier away, no matter how his back screamed, then pushed her out the door and into the alley where they'd parked his car.

He wasn't sure how he was going to drive like this, but they had to get out of here before they were seen. If he had to explain this to the Rangers, other law enforcement would be brought in, and he wasn't ready for that yet. Not when he knew so little.

Not when CJ Jimenez had dropped hints about his parents.

No, he had to figure out what this whole thing

was about before anyone else got involved. If his parents were connected to something… He could hardly stomach the thought, but he wouldn't protect them. He couldn't. Not at the cost of everything he'd sworn himself to.

But he had to be sure first.

"Oh my God. You're bleeding," Alyssa gasped when he passed her to head for the driver's side.

Bennet paused and glanced down his back as best he could. "It's just some glass," he muttered.

"We have to get you to a hospital."

"No," he said, leveling her with his most serious glare. "We have to get the hell out of here."

"Bennet, there are *shards* of glass sticking out of your back. How do you suggest we get the hell out of here?"

He looked down at the keys in his hand and then shrugged, wincing in pain. He tossed her his keys, trying not to show how the move hurt him. "You're driving."

Alyssa drove Bennet's fancy car through the streets of Austin, back to his parents' guesthouse, glancing occasionally in the rearview mirror to the back seat, where Bennet was pretzeled into a position where his back wouldn't hit anything.

It looked awful, and Alyssa was half-tempted to drive him to the hospital against his will.

But none of this made sense. Not her brothers' appearance, not their disappearance and not Bennet's refusal to stick around and deal with it as an official law enforcement agent. He'd called 911 and given the pertinent information, but not his name.

Luckily she didn't really care if her office burned to the ground. She still had her gun and her motorcycle, which were the most important possessions she owned. The paperwork she kept in the office was helpful, but not necessary. The few important documents she had, she kept in a safe-deposit box at the bank. Losing the office meant nothing.

Losing out on answers meant everything.

She glanced at Bennet again as she drove the long, winding drive to his parents' guesthouse after he'd ground out the code to the gate and she'd punched it in.

She supposed that man meant a little bit. He'd certainly jumped between her and harm. She could be the one with shards of glass sticking out of her if he hadn't acted so quickly.

As much as she might want to blame Bennet for letting her brothers get away, she wasn't stupid. Everything that had happened—from her knowing Jose and Oscar on sight even with masks, to the firebomb that allowed the Jimenez brothers to escape—had all been part of a plan.

CJ hadn't given her any information he hadn't wanted to, and while he'd given her nothing, he'd planted all sorts of new doubts about Bennet in her head.

She parked the car at the garage door and pulled the keys from the ignition. "Let me guess, you have a magic doctor on staff who's going to stitch all that up?"

"No, I'm afraid that's going to have to fall to you. Hope you're not squeamish." On a grunt, he shoved the door open. Wincing and breathing a little too heavily, he maneuvered himself out of the car without any help.

Alyssa scrambled to do just that—help. No matter

what insinuations CJ had made, this man had stepped between her and an explosion. His first instinct had been to protect her, which was not an instinct apparently any of her brothers shared. And even before all that, Bennet had given her something no man in her entire life had ever given her: power.

He'd let her hold a gun on her brothers and question them without stepping in, without riding roughshod. He'd given her space, and he'd protected her.

Maybe he knew more than he'd let on, but she wasn't about to let CJ manipulate her into doing what *he* wanted. No, she was going to make up her own mind. Slowly. Carefully. Once she had all the evidence laid out before her.

She followed Bennet inside, through the vast white rooms and plush hallways and into a bathroom that was about the size of her entire above-the-garage apartment.

He bent over, hissing out a breath as he pulled a white box out from under the sink. He dropped it on the beautiful countertop. "First aid kit. I doubt there will be anything to pull the glass out with, though."

Alyssa unzipped her jacket and turned slightly away from Bennet. Once her front was shielded from his view, she pulled her Swiss Army knife out of her bra before turning around and holding it up. "I've got tweezers."

His mouth curved, and his little exhale of breath was something close to a laugh. "Of course you do." He reached behind him and tugged at his collar, but winced and dropped it. "Help me get this off," he ground out, turning his back to her again.

The shirt was ruined—torn, bloody—and if she focused on that she would maybe not focus on the fact he'd just asked her to help him take his shirt off.

"I, uh, should maybe get some of the glass out first." Which was the truth, not some excuse to keep from having to touch his naked back.

"Go for it."

"Right." She blew out a breath and ignored how her hand shook as she pulled the tweezer tool out of her Swiss Army knife.

She had to splay her hand across the least torn-up shoulder blade to try to find her balance and leverage. Some of the tenseness in his shoulder relaxed at her touch, and she didn't know what to make of that. That or the too-hard beating of her heart.

She took a deep breath and focused on the largest piece of glass sticking out of Bennet's back. She bit her lip and used the tweezers to pull it out. Bennet didn't move, didn't make a sound. She placed the stomach-curdling piece of bloody glass on the sink, wincing a little at the thought of the blood staining the countertop.

"Well, I think it might look worse than it actually is," Alyssa offered hopefully, shuffling awkwardly closer to get the next piece of glass.

"Great," Bennet muttered.

"This would be easier with you lying on a bed."

He glanced at her over his shoulder, something about the wide-eyed look and slight curve of his mouth causing her face to heat.

"J-just for…leverage."

His mouth curved even more. "Leverage," he repeated, far too amused.

She scowled at him. "You want this glass out of you or not?"

"The bed it is. You want to take my shirt off first?"

She pretended to study his back if only so she didn't have to meet his gaze. "All right," she said, refusing to let any of her uncertainty come out in her voice.

She flexed her fingers, willing away the slight tremor in them before touching the hem of his T-shirt. She could do this. Take some glass out of his back, take off a shirt. It was all just...business.

Sort of.

She swallowed and pulled the shirt away from Bennet's back, then lifted the fabric. "You're, uh, going to have to bend over or pull it or something."

He reached back with only a minimal sucked-in breath and pulled the shirt off, leaving his back completely bare. And broad. And strong. And bloody.

"Oh." His injuries weren't anywhere near serious, but it looked so ugly. Glass and blood and scratches. She touched her finger to an unmarred spot, feeling oddly protective, hurt by this silly little attack on him.

"Not looking so great now?"

She pulled her hand away, something like guilt washing over her. "You'll live."

He made a considering noise then gestured toward a second door. "To the bed, then?" And somehow this man with bits of glass shards in his back was grinning at her. Charmingly.

She'd faced down her brothers, a madman of a kidnapper and all his goons, a parcel of FBI agents in an attempt to garner some power, admittedly foolish in retrospect. She'd faced all those people down without a qualm, but it was always the quiet moments she didn't know what to do with.

Gabby and Natalie's kindness. A charming smile from an all-too-handsome Texas Ranger. It made her feel young and stupid.

She grabbed the first aid kit and lifted her chin at him. "I'll follow you."

He walked out the door and into a huge bedroom, all white and black just like every other room in his bizarre place. Where was the color? The charm? The—

Bennet got on the bed, lying stomach down on the pristine white blankets. He crossed his hands under his head and rested his temple on the back of one hand, studying her.

She looked away and placed the kit on the nightstand and focused on getting out and opening bandages and not staring at a Texas Ranger all sprawled out half-naked on his bed after saving her from…well, minor injury.

"I do have an investigation to start if we could hurry this damn thing up."

"Right." Except he was lying there, and she wasn't sure why she thought this would give her more leverage. Oh, she could reach all places on his back easier, but she'd have to lean over him. Brush against him. Hell, it'd be easiest if she could just straddle his legs and go at it that way.

She was *not* going to go at it that way. But she did have to do it. So, enough of being a silly little girl. Maybe she was a sheltered virgin in the oddest sense of the word, but she had a job to do. Bennet had helped her out, and now it was her turn to help him.

So, she focused on the glass shards and pulling out all she could see. She focused on using the antibiotic ointment on the cuts and bandaging them up. And if she noticed that his skin was soft, or that his muscles rippled appealingly any time he moved, well... So what? Adult women did that sort of thing, didn't they? Noticed attractive men.

"There might still be debris in there," Alyssa said, bandaging up the last of the cuts. "I only got out what I could see."

"It'll be good enough," he replied, pushing himself into a sitting position on the bed.

"You should go to the hospital. Some of those bigger cuts might need stitches."

He shook his head.

"Why aren't you reporting this?" There was a reason, and she was a little afraid she knew what it was.

His jaw firmed, but he didn't look away. That blue gaze pinned her in place. "First off, they'd put me on medical leave for a day or two and give someone else the case. Second of all..."

"Your parents?"

"That was your brother's insinuation."

"And you believe him?"

Bennet looked away for a moment. "I don't know. It could be a trick. It could be true. It could be a lot of things, but I want to be the one to figure it out."

"I should go."

He looked back at her, brow furrowing. "Go where?"

"Home. No one was bugging my place, and my brothers didn't hurt me or take me, which means they aren't going to. There's no reason for me to stay here."

He scooted to the edge of the bed and took her hands with his before she could think to step away. "Alyssa, that doesn't mean you're not in danger," he said seriously.

"I've been in danger before. I can handle myself."

He studied her, and she couldn't read his expression or guess what he was looking for, but when she tried to tug her hands away, he only held on tighter.

"I know your brothers insinuated that I know something about your mother, about anything, but I don't. You have to believe that."

"I do." Maybe she shouldn't, but why would he have come to her with her mother's picture as a Jane Doe if he knew anything?

"If either of my parents is involved in some kind of crime, I will not hesitate to turn them in, Alyssa. I took an oath. For what it's worth, my parents took an oath, and if they are not representing their constituents in a lawful fashion, then it's out of my hands."

She blinked at the vehemence in his tone. "O-okay."

"So you don't need to worry."

"What do you think I'm worried about?"

"You're trying to leave. You must be worried about something."

"I'm… You don't need me, Bennet. You got your Jane Doe name, and there's no point trying to get drawn into my brothers' world now. They know too much." She was useless to him. *Just like you're useless to everyone else.*

Again she tugged her hands, but Bennet held her in his grasp.

"Until we know how this all connects, until we can be certain you're safe, you're under my protection."

Tears pricked her eyes unexpectedly. Protection. She was so tired of being under someone else's protection. And yet, today Bennet had let her fight her own battle within that protection. He hadn't abandoned her or allowed her to be hurt like everyone else had.

"And you're right, we can't go into your brothers' world now, but we have a much bigger challenge ahead of us," he said gravely.

We. *We.* As if they were a team, working together, protecting each other. "We do?" she managed to ask past the lump in her throat.

"I have to bring you into mine."

Chapter 7

Bennet didn't bother to find a new shirt, and he didn't bother to try to figure out what Alyssa's silence meant. They had work to do.

"Did you recognize either of the names your brother mentioned?"

Alyssa blew out a breath. "Sal Cochrane not so much."

"And Salvador Dominguez?"

Her expression shuttered, and he supposed it was answer enough, though it didn't sit well with him that she knew.

"I've been a bounty hunter—"

"Illegal bounty hunter," he interrupted, because he liked the way she scowled at him when he did. "You don't only know Dominguez from the past two years. Don't insult me with a lie at this point."

She had the decency to look a little shamed. "I don't know Salvador Dominguez, but I have heard of him."

"From your brothers?"

She shook her head almost imperceptibly.

"Then from who?" he demanded, as irritated with her hesitation as he was with the burning sensation in his back.

"My father, but…" Alyssa rubbed her hands together, clearly working out something in her head without letting him in on pertinent information.

"But what?"

"He wasn't… He isn't… When he told me about Dominguez, none of it made any sense. And when I told CJ, he…"

"He what?"

Her gaze flew to his. "Oh my God. He made me think Dad was crazy. He convinced me Dad had lost his mind but… But Dad said Salvador Dominguez had our mother. That she hadn't left, that someone had double-crossed him and *I* would be next and… Bennet, they convinced me Dad was crazy, but maybe he wasn't."

"Why tell us? And what does it have to do with Sal Cochrane?"

She shook her head, eyebrows drawn together, hands clasped. "I don't know. I don't know." She paced, fury taking over her features. "I hate that we have to find out when that's just what he wants us to do."

"Maybe it's some kind of warning. Some kind of way to help you, and if we find out—"

She laughed. Bitterly. "I might be able to convince myself of that if it had been any of my other brothers, but CJ has been in charge too long to have any decency left in him. Whatever reason he has for showing up, for letting me go, for dropping those little breadcrumbs, it is for the cartel's well-being and that alone."

She wrapped her arms around herself, and he curled his hands into fists so he didn't reach out. They could probably stand a little less touching, a little less close quarters, and a lot less his being an idiot and trying to make her blush.

How this unbelievably strong fighter of a woman could *blush* at the remotest sexual thing was beyond him, and he liked it far too much.

But *sexual* was not something he could afford to be thinking about. No matter how gently she'd tended his wounds, or how brave she was, or how much he wanted to protect her.

"Does The Stallion have anything to do with the cartels?" she asked, still hugging her arms around herself.

"The Stallion has been in prison for two years," he reminded her as gently as he could.

"Before that, I mean. It all has to connect, don't you think? Not just now, either. This is sixteen years in the making, if it connects to my mother."

Bennet sighed. He didn't know. It seemed there were a million connections and he didn't have a clue about any of them. It was more than possible a rival cartel could have killed Alyssa's mother, but that didn't explain why she'd been left a Jane Doe.

There were too many unanswered questions, and what clues he had came from criminals with their own agendas. If he thought he'd been frustrated at the prospect of a Jane Doe, it had nothing on *this* frustration.

But this was what he wanted. A challenge. To do something good for once. All on his own.

"Bennet," a voice boomed from the entryway.

Bennet swore. The last thing he wanted to do right now was go toe-to-toe with his father.

"I assume that's not the staff," Alyssa offered drily.

"It's my father."

"Do your parents know how to knock?"

"Not if it doesn't suit them." Bennet glanced at the door. It was no use to hide Alyssa when Mother would have already told Father about her, but he didn't want to waste time trading fake niceties or old-hat arguments with his father.

He took a step toward Alyssa. There was one possible way to get his father out of here quickly. And he was already shirtless.

"I need you to go along with something, all right?"

"With what? Being Alyssa Clark? I did this morning. I don't see why…"

She trailed off when he slid his arms around her, her eyes widening as she looked up at him.

"W-what are you doing?"

"We need time, and if my father comes in here he won't be sweeping out anytime soon. Not like my mother. He'll want to stay and chat and charm and who knows what all. We don't have time for that, so we're going to pretend we are otherwise engaged."

"Bennet?" the voice boomed again, closer.

"Otherwise. Engaged," Alyssa repeated breathlessly, and though she leaned away from him she didn't jerk away or try to escape.

So, he pulled her close and lowered his mouth close to hers. "It's only pretend. Like…undercover work."

Her eyelashes fluttered and her breath came in short bursts, and he had no business wondering if the attraction he felt wasn't one-sided. If she might feel some of that in return. If she might…

"Bennet?" This time followed by a knock on the bedroom door as the knob turned.

Bennet pressed his mouth to Alyssa's, but all she did was stand there. Frozen and wide-eyed and not at all pretending. She didn't slap him either, but she didn't relax or even feign a kiss back.

"You have to kiss me back," he whispered across her mouth.

"B-but I don't know how."

Hell.

Bennet was kissing her. His mouth was on her mouth, and no matter that he held her sturdily against him, that he'd called it pretend, she didn't know what the hell to do with her mouth or her arms or with anything.

His father was stepping inside the room and—Bennet's fingers tangled in her hair, angling her whole head so that his mouth slid more easily across hers. Sweetly. Gently. It was warm and…nice. Nice enough to relax into, to soften. She very nearly sighed.

So, this was kissing. Well, she supposed having her body pressed up against the large, hard body of a man while his soft, firm mouth angled over hers had its appeal. It made her whole body feel warm and heavy, it made every place her body touched his seem to sparkle to life, and to taste another person—

A throat cleared, and Alyssa jerked. She didn't know how she'd lost so much track of where she was or what…

She could only blink up at Bennet, but his expression was blank, his jaw hard and his gaze not on her.

"Sorry to interrupt," an unfamiliar voice drawled, sounding very much not sorry.

Alyssa finally gathered enough sense to step away from Bennet and look at their intruder. Which made Alyssa blink all over again.

"*Are* you sorry to interrupt, Father?" Bennet asked, his voice cool and unaffected. "Because a gentleman would perhaps just step back out."

Mr. Stevens smiled widely and looked so much like his son Alyssa could only stare.

"Gary L. Stevens," he said in that charming drawl, holding out a hand to her. And Alyssa would have to give him credit. He might have worse timing than Bennet's mother, but he was certainly kinder.

"I would really prefer it if you weren't introducing yourself to women in my bedroom when we are in the middle of something."

"So traditional," Mr. Stevens said with a wink to Alyssa.

"What are you doing here? I am busy," Bennet said through gritted teeth.

"Your mother sent me on a fact-finding mission, and you know how she gets. I wasn't about to return empty-handed. You must be Alyssa. Clark, was it?"

Alyssa nodded mutely. Where Mrs. Stevens had put her back up with her cold disapproval, she didn't know what to do with Mr. Stevens's easy friendliness. Much like she didn't know what to do with Bennet's fake kisses that apparently affected him not at all.

"I know it's incredibly rude of me, Ms. Clark, but I need just a few moments in private with my son or I'll never get any peace at home."

Bennet opened his mouth, presumably to argue, but Alyssa didn't think that would do anyone any good. She adopted her smooth, fake drawl and smiled sweetly at Mr. Stevens. "Of course." She glanced at Bennet, reminded herself she was playing a part. And the part was that of possible floozy girlfriend.

She patted his bare chest and attempted to look pouty and alluring even though she had no idea how to look that. "You might want to put a shirt on, honey."

Especially if he was going to keep the injuries hidden from his father.

Alyssa walked out the door, pulling it almost closed behind her, but she left a crack. When no one finished closing it, she took a few steps down the hall, then stood exactly where she was, gratified when she could hear everything being said.

"Her last name isn't Clark," Mr. Stevens offered with no preamble.

"You think I don't know that?"

Mr. Stevens sighed heavily. "Your mother is having a conniption."

"Then everything's normal, I assume."

"She wants a name."

"She won't get it from me."

"If the girl has nothing to hide, let your mother run her little background checks. And if she does have something to hide, well, you know your mother won't go exposing her. It would only look poorly on us."

"Regardless of what's in her background, I don't want you two poking around in it or coming after her. She is none of your business. If Mother can't get that through her head after all this time, I don't know what to tell you."

"And yet you're here, under our roof."

Alyssa edged closer to the door, trying to see through the crack in the door. She could see a sliver of Bennet— who'd pulled on a sweatshirt at some point—but she couldn't see his father. She couldn't help but be curious about what Mr. Stevens's reaction might be to that cold fury in Bennet's expression. And, more, she couldn't understand Bennet's relationship with his parents.

She knew her family was warped beyond belief, and she knew that her brothers fought, sometimes furiously, over cartel business, but she'd assumed that was the life of criminals. Not the life of someone like Bennet and his parents.

"What do you know about Sal Cochrane?" Bennet asked with no finesse, no easing into it. Alyssa frowned. Couldn't he be smoother than all that?

"Is that a friendly question, son, or an official one?" Mr. Stevens returned easily.

"Is that a political evasion or you just being difficult?"

After another long sigh, Mr. Stevens answered. "He's one of your mother's silent donors, I believe. Never met the man myself, so that's about all I know. You're not going to bring your mother into trouble."

Which was not a question. Even Alyssa knew that from her eavesdropping spot in the hall.

"If she isn't already in any."

"Bennet, we've never stood in your way when it came to police work or joining the Rangers. We've never—"

"I'm not going after Mother," Bennet interrupted, clearly irritated by his father's line of conversation. He stepped out of her slim view through the crack in the door. "Sal Cochrane is who I'm after, and it's only for information, so if you have any information, I'd appreciate it. Officially."

"I'll see what I can do." Mr. Stevens stepped into view. "In return for that young woman's last name."

Bennet made a scoffing noise, and Mr. Stevens turned his head, in a seemingly casual move. But as Alyssa didn't have time to move out of the way, she doubted there was anything casual about it.

He'd either known she was there or suspected it, and she wasn't stupid enough to believe Mr. Stevens hadn't caught her spying. Crap.

Still, better to give the illusion she didn't know she'd been caught. She hurried as silently as possible down the hall and to the bedroom she'd slept in last night. She desperately wanted to listen to the rest of that conversation, to see if Bennet would trade her name for the information he wanted, but as she stepped into the blindingly white room, she realized she had bigger fish to fry.

"What are you doing here? How did you get in?"

Oscar smiled sheepishly. "Hi, sis."

"You…you can't be here." It would be bad enough if Bennet saw him, but if Mr. Stevens saw him, too? Alyssa didn't have a clue as to what might happen, but she knew it wouldn't be good. At the very least her brother would be arrested, and while he might be deserving of that...

Oscar had snuck her checkers and Baby-Sitters Club books. He'd given her sweets and taken her on walks when none of her other brothers would. He'd treated her like a girl, a sister, not just a possession. A statue to protect.

She couldn't let anything happen to Oscar. Not like this. She grabbed him by the arm and tried to pull him toward the door, but he jerked out of her grasp.

"I don't have time, but I had to warn you. Don't try to figure this out. Don't get involved. Stay low, get your Ranger to stay low, and you'll be fine. But if you let CJ drag you into this, you will get hurt."

"Drag me into what?"

"I'm risking my life here, Alyssa. That's all I can say."

"Os—"

But before she could even get the words out of her mouth, he was climbing out the window Alyssa hadn't realized was open. She might have followed him, she might have grabbed him again, but she could hear footsteps in the hall and she couldn't risk being discovered.

"Alyssa!" Oscar hissed from outside.

She pushed the curtains back and looked at her brother standing in the perfectly manicured yard of the Stevenses' guesthouse, a figure all in black, the faint scar across his cheek he'd never told her how he'd gotten.

"Don't tell your Ranger I was here. Please." And then he was gone, running silently around the corner of the house.

"Well, I hope you know how to clean up," Bennet said, and Alyssa whirled away from the window. Probably the only thing saving her from being caught was the fact Bennet's attention was on a card in his hand.

"Clean up?" she echoed stupidly, her heart hammering a hundred times in overdrive.

He looked up at her, that charming smile so easily camouflaging his true emotions.

"We're going to a ball, Cinderella."

Chapter 8

Bennet sat at the kitchen table, casually eating his dinner, while Alyssa continued to rant. And rant. And rant, rant, rant. It was almost amusing, really, considering he'd watched this woman fly down a highway on a motorcycle waving at very bad men, watched this woman hold a gun on her brothers, and yet those weren't the things that caused her to come unglued.

No, she was losing it at the prospect of going to one of his parents' idiotic Christmas balls or galas or whatever they were calling this one.

"I'm not going."

"Yes, you are."

"I don't work for you, Bennet."

"No, but you're working with me."

"Are you always this infuriatingly unruffled?"

He shrugged, grinning at her. "When it suits." He

hadn't been unruffled this afternoon. Not with his father, and certainly not with Alyssa and the kiss.

The *fake* kiss. That had made him far more irritable with his father than he should have been. Too direct. Too…everything.

"Maybe we shouldn't," Alyssa said, and when he looked up at her, she had her back to him while she pretended to make herself a sandwich. Pretended because she'd been doing so for the last twenty minutes without finishing.

"Maybe we shouldn't what?"

He watched her shoulders lift and fall as though she was inhaling deeply, steeling herself for something. She turned, and though she looked at him, he got the distinct impression she was staring at his nose instead of meeting his actual gaze.

"Maybe we shouldn't work together. Work…period. If my mother's death was cartel business, what does it matter?"

Bennet stood slowly. "It's an unsolved murder case, that's what it matters." He narrowed his eyes at her. Suddenly she was fidgety, and backing off, and that was very much not the Alyssa Jimenez he'd come to know in a short few days.

So maybe you don't know her at all.

"You said yourself that CJ *wants* us to find this all out, and I'm worried about playing into that trap." She hugged her arms around her even as she kept looking at him defiantly. But something had rattled her, and Bennet wasn't about to let her get away with it.

"Why?"

"What do you mean *why*? Did it escape your notice my brother is a dangerous man?"

"Who didn't hurt you when he had the chance."

"That doesn't mean he won't ever hurt me or…"

"Or what?"

"Or you, idiot," she snapped. "He wants us to go looking for this information, but what will happen if we find it? Why can't he find it himself? It's stupid to go after it. It's like helping him."

Bennet took a few steps toward her, and no matter that what she said held some truth, this was all a sudden change from how she'd been earlier. A woman didn't change her mind like this without provocation. "Alyssa. What happened?"

"Noth—"

He curled his fingers around her shoulders and cut her off. "Do not lie to me again. What happened?"

She swallowed, but she didn't lose that defiant tilt to her chin. "It isn't safe to go after this, and I don't want to go to your dumb ball."

"Is that all this is, Princess? Don't want to wear a dress?"

"It isn't funny."

"Then what is it?"

"Dangerous! And not just to us, or to my family, but to your parents. CJ wants to bring them into this. All of us. Why are we falling for it?"

"And why are you suddenly skittish?" Something inside him went past irritation to worry, but that only served to irritate him. He had no business worrying about her state of mind. He had a case to solve.

She gave him a push, stalking past him, though she didn't leave the kitchen, just started pacing across it.

"Alyssa, we'll get nowhere if you lie to me."

Her breathing hitched, and a little sob escaped, and no matter how clearly she tried to fight back the tears, they slipped down her cheeks.

"I don't know who to trust. Who to believe," she said in a squeaky voice, tears tracking down her jaw.

Bennet knew he should keep his hands to himself, but he'd known a lot of things in his life that feeling had taken over, and this was no different. He stepped toward her and brushed the tears off her cheeks. "I know what that's like, and I know I can't make you believe or trust me, but I haven't let you down yet, have I?"

She shook her head.

"I grew up in a world of lies and deception, where it mattered more what people thought than what people did. 'Oh, Mr. So-and-So beats his wife, but the checks he writes for the campaign are quite large, so we'll look the other way.' I hated it, always, so I sought out the exact opposite of that world. Not truth, not honesty, but—"

"Justice," she finished for him in a whisper.

He blinked at her, but he shouldn't have been shocked she understood. She'd grown up in a cartel, and since her kidnapping release had built a bounty hunter business. It might not be legal, but it was a search for justice.

Just like him.

He should stop touching her face, and he would. In a minute or two. "Yeah, I guess you know something about that, don't you?"

"Oscar was here," she said in a whisper.

His hands dropped from her wet face. "What?"

"While you were talking to your father. He…he was in my room. He told me not to listen to CJ. That it was dangerous."

Bennet wanted to yell at her, demand to know why she'd kept it from him for *hours*. Demand everything, but he'd seen that look on her face in so many victims he'd come across in his work.

Fear, and—worse, so much worse—a kind of grim acceptance that pain and suffering were just around the corner.

So, he swallowed down his anger, flexed his fingers from the fists they wanted to curl into. He breathed evenly, doing his best to unclench his jaw. "And you believe him?"

"Oscar was always the nicest of all of them. The one with a heart, if you can believe it. There'd be no nefarious reason to warn me off. No self serving ones. He was trying to warn me so CJ didn't hurt me. Didn't hurt both of us. He told me not to tell you, Bennet. He's afraid, too. If CJ found out…" She closed her eyes as if she couldn't bear to think about it.

"I know they're your brothers, but I need you on my team, Alyssa. I need your eyes, and I need your brain and memories. I need you to be in this with me so we can find out what happened to your mother, and to you. Justice. For both of you. But you have to trust me, and if Oscar contacts you again, I have to know you'll tell me. I have to be able to trust you. It is necessary."

She used the back of her hand to wipe off her cheek.

"Is there anything else you're keeping from me?"

She looked up at the ceiling as if she was shuffling through all her memories of what she might have kept from him. She eventually shook her head. "No. You've been with me every moment except that one."

"And last night."

"I was sleeping last night," she said, her tear-stained cheeks turning an appealing shade of pink.

There was something seriously warped with him. He should still be angry. He should be nervous and worried and thinking about Sal Cochrane.

But all he could think about was that kiss. *Fake kiss. Fake.*

"Why'd you say you don't know how to kiss?"

Her cheeks darkened into a shade closer to red, but she met his gaze, attempting and failing at looking regal. "Because I *don't*. My brothers didn't exactly let me out of the compound to *date*, and then I was, you know, kidnapped by a psycho who wouldn't touch me because my belly button wasn't symmetrical."

"Your belly button wasn't… What?"

But she was bulldozing on. "So, I haven't exactly been kissed or anything else, thank you very much."

"You've been free two years." Which he shouldn't have pointed out, nor should he continue this line of conversation, or step even closer.

But he did. Stepped closer and continued.

Her eyes were wide and dark and on him like she couldn't quite force herself to look away. "I… I… I've been building a business," she said, her voice something like a squeak. "And a f-family of sorts, and I… Guys aren't really impressed when you can kick their ass."

His mouth curved. "I don't think you could kick my ass, but you can try if you'd like."

"Bennet," she said so seriously he held his breath,

afraid to speak and ruin the moment when her eyes held his and she looked like she was going to confess the world.

Or move in for a real kiss.

"I can't go to a ball," she said in that same serious, grave tone. "Look at me."

His breath whooshed out and he cursed himself for an idiot. She was not going to kiss him, and he should hardly want her to. She was innocent on every level and involved with the most important case of his life.

He needed to get himself together. Focus. Channel a little all-business Vaughn Cooper. "Admittedly your current look is a little bedraggled, but I can fix that."

"*You* can fix that?"

"Well, my staff can make you blend right in."

She folded her arms over her chest and scowled at him skeptically, but he noticed she stopped arguing.

"The ball will be attended by a variety of my mother's political supporters and donors, which means the possibility of Sal Cochrane being there is high. I need you there, on the off chance you recognize him or something about him. I'll need an extra set of eyes who knows at least enough about the Jimenez and Dominguez cartels to notice something that might connect. You're integral, Alyssa."

She seemed to consider that very hard and then finally rolled her eyes. "Fine."

Bennet grinned. "Who knows, you might even enjoy it."

When Alyssa woke the next morning, it was with her cheek stuck to a variety of printouts Bennet had given her last night to pore over. She yawned, peeling the paper off her face. She'd dozed off before finishing the read-through.

But lists of people she'd never heard of and the kind of money they handed over to Bennet's parents for political crap was not exactly tantalizing reading. She'd much prefer criminal records or something with a little pizazz.

She stretched out on the big bed and sighed. Oh, a girl could get used to this kind of luxury. She'd had nice things growing up, even if she had been kept mostly locked up and away, but between two years with The Stallion and two years on her own, luxury had been sorely missing from her life.

But this was a luxury borne of the investigation into her mother's murder. Which caused her to think about last night. A few too many things about last night, but mostly Bennet saying she deserved justice, too.

She was afraid of how much that disarmed her. How much all those little touches that seemed to come so easy to him—an elbow touch, wiping tears off her cheeks—kept throwing her off balance, changing something.

Alyssa blew out a breath. She had to find some kind of power against him. Something to shield herself from all that charm and random acts of sweetness or saying things that felt like soul-deep truths.

Justice. For both of you.

Her life had been unfair, and she knew dwelling on that would send her spiraling into the same awful mental space she'd been in when she'd been kidnapped by The Stallion, but justice had been a foreign concept.

The fact it no longer was, the fact someone wanted to fight for her own justice was... Overwhelming. Scary.

Irresistible. And she'd never had to resist anything before. There'd been nothing to resist. She'd only ever wanted freedom, and she'd been given it at twenty-two and somehow created her own little box to exist in.

But all her boxes were colliding, and she didn't know what to do with that. Unfortunately, staying in his comfortable bed was not an option. Something had to be done, and...

She stared hard at the ceiling above her. Bennet had said he needed her. Her help. Her brain. No one had ever needed her before. Gabby had been the first person in her whole life to ask her for help, but Gabby had always been the clear leader in the kidnapping house. Alyssa had followed, had helped, but Gabby hadn't needed her. Not really.

Bennet used the word *need*. Repeatedly. It filled her with hope and fear and a million other things she didn't know what to do with, but the possible only positive of living in basic captivity was that she'd learned to deal with just about anything.

All you could do was keep going.

She slid out of bed and went to pull on her jeans, but noticed that just inside the door was a stool with a pile of neatly folded clothes. She frowned, uncomfortable that she'd slept through someone putting something in her room.

She peered at the stack and noticed a note on top.

Amazing what staff can do. Should fit well enough.

She scowled at the note and then the stack of clothes. Arrogant man. Still, it *would* be nice to put on some clean clothes. Of course, it reminded her she still hadn't visited Natalie in the hospital. They were probably going home today.

Alyssa shook her head as she got dressed. She had to do what she had to do, and with Oscar clearly knowing where she was and how to get inside without tipping any security off, Alyssa had to be careful. She couldn't bring Natalie and Gabby into this.

So, she grabbed her phone and texted her most sincere apologies to both women. She'd make it up to them, explain everything, she just had to make sure she was out of danger first.

And if you're never out of danger?

A question for another day. She headed for the kitchen, where she had no doubt she'd find Bennet hunched over his computer.

"You're terribly predictable, Ranger Stevens," she offered in greeting, heading for the coffee. She was going to get used to the stuff if it killed her. "How's your back?"

"Sal Cochrane does not exist," Bennet said, ignoring her question.

"What?"

"I have been through every lawful search I can make on that name, every spelling, everything. There is no Sal Cochrane in Austin, Texas. And expanding the search doesn't give me any leads either."

"Maybe he doesn't live in Texas."

"Maybe, but why would someone who doesn't live in Texas donate anything to my mother's campaign? She's a state senator."

"Well, that's if we're working under the assumption

Sal Cochrane is on the up-and-up." She felt bad bringing it up, because it implicated his icy mother, but still. It was true. "I could ask Jaime for help. He might have access to some different searches than you guys do, or maybe the name has been involved in an FBI investigation or two."

His face blanked. "We're not bringing in the FBI."

"Not even just for information?"

"It's never just information with the FBI, Alyssa."

Which was maybe true, but it didn't help them any. She wanted to argue with him, but she'd figured enough out about Bennet that arguing only made him dig his heels in deeper. She could always contact Jaime herself, ask for any information he could give without the FBI getting involved, but she didn't think lying to Bennet would go over well. Especially after she'd kept the Oscar thing from him, no matter how briefly.

"I emailed my father's assistant for a list of Mom's campaign donors, along with the guest list of the ball. Maybe that'll give us something to go on."

"Why did you email your father's assistant for information about your mother's campaign donors?"

Bennet smiled wryly. "Because if my mother got wind of my asking her assistant for anything, the barrage of questions I would be piled under would make a criminal interrogation look like a walk in the park. Dad already knows I'm nosing around, so it made sense to go through his people."

"And he won't tell your mother?"

"I believe he'd also like to avoid the interrogation." Something on his computer pinged. "There it is." He gestured for her to come next to him where she could see the screen, too.

He opened one of the email attachments, and they both started scanning it.

"There," Alyssa said, pointing at the name. "S. Cochrane."

"S. Cochrane. SCD Enterprises LLC," Bennet muttered. "That sounds like a front company if I ever heard one."

"A front for what?"

"Anything. Money laundering. Drugs."

"A cartel?"

He sucked in a breath, let it out. "It could be."

Which meant his mother might be connected to cartel business. "Bennet—"

"I don't suppose those names mean anything to you or what you know about your family's business."

"I wouldn't know anything about actual business. I sometimes overheard names or connections, but nothing official like this."

"All right, well, I'll start doing some searching on this LLC and we'll see what I find, but first..." He pulled up the other document, the guest list for the Stevens Christmas Gala.

"He's on the guest list." Bennet nodded firmly. "That's good. That's very good."

Alyssa studied him. He was all tense muscles and clenched jaw and steely gaze today. No charming smiles, no little insinuations over how close they were standing. He wanted to pretend this was all business, but it wasn't. It was family, too.

"If you did turn this over to the FBI, you wouldn't have to be the one who—"

His cutting blue gaze stopped her dead.

"If my mother is knowingly involved in something illegal," he began firmly and forcefully, "then it is my duty and my right to bring her to justice."

"It isn't always that easy."

He stood abruptly from the table. "For me, it is." He stalked over to the coffeepot and Alyssa glanced at the guest list. For a second, it felt as though her heart had stopped.

"Bennet?"

"Please don't try to argue—"

"My father is on the guest list."

Chapter 9

Bennet stared at the name he hadn't paid any attention to. Carlos Jimenez.

"My parents did not invite a known drug cartel kingpin to our Christmas gala. The press would crucify them both. This is insanity." In no world would his parents invite *Carlos Jimenez* to their Christmas gala. Good lord.

"Bennet..."

"It's a mistake of some kind. A different Carlos Jimenez. Some horrible prank by a political opponent."

"Bennet."

He glanced at her then instead of the completely insane name on his computer screen. She was pale, hugging herself, wide-eyed.

"What is it? You're not going to have to see him. It can't be true."

"I know it isn't true. Bennet, my father... He isn't

well. Mentally or physically. CJ runs everything now. He couldn't possibly come even if he wanted to."

Bennet tried to process that, *understand* it. The FBI, the Rangers and probably half of the Austin police department were trying to find Carlos Jimenez, and he wasn't *well*.

"This is bad. This is wrong and bad and..." She looked up at him, looking as scared as he'd ever seen her. Which, per usual when it came to Alyssa, didn't make any damn sense.

"It's got to be some other Carlos Jimenez. That's a common enough name. It's just a coincidence."

"It's not a coincidence. It's a warning. It's... Something is very, very wrong here. There aren't coincidences right now."

"We'll go to the gala and find out ourselves. Whatever's wrong, whatever's weird, we have the upper hand."

"How?"

"We're on the right side."

She laughed bitterly. "Oh, you are Superman, without the invincibility. Right is not an upper hand. Nothing is an upper hand with all this. CJ is screwing with us, and maybe not just CJ. We don't know who all is involved, and this... Something is very, very wrong, Bennet."

"Yes, we have some question marks, but that's the point. We have to find out, and if we do it right, we will. We'll find out and we'll bring them down."

"Or they kill us, Bennet. Because they can."

She was exhausting. Every time he thought he'd gotten through to her she backed away. Got scared.

"How do you ever track down a skip with this kind of attitude?"

"I'm not tracking down a skip. I'm trying to keep myself and the people I care about *safe*. I'd been safe for two whole years until you showed up."

"So, you're blaming me?"

She raked her hands through her hair. "No!"

"Do you want to stop?" he demanded.

"I…"

"Because we can stop. We can name the Jane Doe, call the case cold, leave it all alone. The end. There are plenty of other cold cases I can work on. Your brother and whoever else was involved in your mother's murder and *your* kidnapping can go along doing whatever they're doing. Justice can just die here, if that's what you really want."

"Oh, screw you," she muttered, and stalked out of the kitchen.

Which he'd take as a no, that's not what she wanted. She wanted justice just as much as he did. More, maybe. She was scared, clearly, though it surprised him. She'd described an awful childhood, a terrible ordeal being kidnapped for *years*, was an illegal bounty hunter for Pete's sake, and yet she was running scared. Constantly.

Something didn't add up, and he didn't like that. She'd promised him she'd told him everything, and he needed to be able to trust her. How could he do that—

An odd noise broke through the silence. Bennet frowned and listened. Silence. Well, maybe Alyssa had just stomped or punched a wall or something. She *was* quite pissed.

Something else, a squeak or a groan or… The back

of his neck prickled with foreboding, and maybe he was overreacting, but in the current state of things it didn't hurt to check out a little overreaction.

He moved down the hall silently, listening for any more sounds. Silence, silence, then something that sounded like a bump. Alyssa was probably just stomping around her room, but...

Bennet curled his fingers around the butt of his gun in the holster on his hip as he approached Alyssa's room. She'd probably laugh at him, but maybe she'd stop being so scared if she laughed at him.

He eased the door open, and Alyssa was standing by the window.

"Oh, good. I thought I—"

The distinct sound of a safety clicking off and the cold press of metal to his temple pissed him off. Not nearly as much as the drop of blood trailing down Alyssa's cheek from her temple.

"Keep your head forward and drop any weapons and kick them behind you," the man with the gun whispered. "You try anything, I kill you both."

"Oh, come on now. You're not going to hurt your sister."

"You think I'm Jimenez? Insulting."

The gun dug harder into Bennet's temple, and he'd admit there was a little fear now. Was this really not one of her brothers? That couldn't be good, but it *did* mean they were moving in the right direction.

"Drop the weapons."

Bennet forced himself to remain calm, to carefully pull his weapon from its holster. Jumping out of the way or swinging the gun at this man was too dangerous. He would fire off a shot one way or another, and it could hit Alyssa.

So, Bennet had to worry about disarming him before he worried about weapons. He set the gun on the ground, gently nudged it behind him as he held up one finger at his side where the man couldn't see him, then held up two, adding his best questioning eyebrow, hoping Alyssa understood his code.

She lifted her bound hands to the wound this man must have inflicted on her, and would pay for. Bloodily. But as she dropped her hand, she held up one single finger.

One he could take.

"On your knees," the man demanded, jabbing the gun harder against his head again.

"Just don't shoot," Bennet said, trying to inflict his voice with some fear, even though the last thing he was was afraid. He was furious.

"No use fighting, idiot. I'm taking her, and if you try to stop me, you will die. Maybe not today, but soon, and painfully, and in a way no one will ever find your body. Do we understand each other?"

"Perfectly," Bennet replied, and before he'd even gotten the word out he struck, landing a tight-fisted blow to the man's throat.

The gun went off at almost the exact time Alyssa launched herself across the room and against her assailant. The man fell and Bennet flung himself on top of the assailant, who'd fallen to the ground at Alyssa's attack, ignoring the pinpricks of pain in his back from yesterday's wounds. The attacker fought viciously, kicking and nearly landing an unmanning blow before Bennet had him pinned to the ground. But pinning him meant he didn't have any limbs left to inflict a blow.

He glanced up at Alyssa. "Break his nose."

"Gladly." And with perfect form, even with her hands bound together, Alyssa jabbed her elbow into the man's nose with a sickening crack and a satisfying spurt of blood.

The man screamed in pain, and Bennet used the distraction to shift enough so he could roll the man onto his stomach, using his knee to hold him down while he jerked the man's arms behind his back roughly.

"I think he has more zip ties in his pocket," Alyssa said, nodding behind her back.

This man had broken into his home, restrained and hurt Alyssa, and he had *more* zip ties in his pocket. Bennet dug his knee harder into the man's back. "Kneel on his hands."

"Oh… I… Okay." Alyssa shuffled one way and then the other before lowering into a kneeling position on the back of their assailant.

"Really dig your knees into his wrists so he can't move, and I'll grab the zip ties."

The man groaned in agony, and Bennet flashed a grin. "Good girl." With absolutely no finesse, he roughly searched the man's pockets until he found the zip ties. He gave Alyssa a boost back to her feet then as roughly and tightly as he could, he connected the ties around the man's wrists and ankles.

Bennet stood and watched as the man writhed and groaned. Bennet was tempted to kick him for good measure, but Alyssa still had her hands bound and he wanted to get her freed as soon as possible.

"Where's your knife?"

She cleared her throat. "Well, it's where it always is."

"Which pocket?"

"Um… Well…"

"Where, Alyssa?"

She met his gaze, something indecipherable on her face. "My bra." She bent her elbows, clearly trying to maneuver her fingers into her shirt, but she couldn't bend her elbows or twist her fingers enough to fish it out.

Bennet forced himself to look away from her attempts. "I'll just go get the, uh, kitchen scissors."

Alyssa rolled her eyes. "And leave him here? Just pull it out of my bra, for heaven's sake."

Bennet laughed, couldn't help himself. "And here I thought this job couldn't surprise me any more."

Alyssa's temple throbbed from where it had hit the bed after the strange man had pushed her down after she'd stepped inside her room. She had no idea where he'd come from, since she'd kept the window locked ever since Oscar had snuck in that way.

She was furious, just righteously livid, that this man had caught her so off guard he'd managed to knock her down and tie her hands. When he'd heard Bennet's approach, he'd jerked her to her feet and told her to stand by the window without saying a word.

She would have told him to take a flying leap, but she hadn't wanted to risk Bennet's life, and she'd trusted that Bennet could get them out of this, and he had. Not just gotten them out of it, but let her break her attacker's nose.

It felt good. It felt like teamwork.

Now Bennet Stevens, Texas Ranger, one hundred tons too charming for his own good, was retrieving the knife from her bra like he was afraid of a pair of breasts. *Her* breasts in particular.

"Don't act like you've never gotten to know your way around a woman's underwear before," she muttered, irritated that no matter how nonchalant she tried to act, her skin felt prickly and tight and all too desperate to know what Bennet's fingertips might feel like across her skin.

He let out a sigh, and then his hand was moving inside her shirt. He paused briefly and cleared his throat. "Um…right or left?"

It was her turn to laugh because, dear Lord this was the most ridiculous situation she'd ever found herself in. "Right."

His fingers brushed the outline of her bra, tracing the seam, touching her skin with the rough, blunt tips of his finger. Oh, God. She was dizzy. Which was possibly the head injury, or the fact he was touching the wrong breast.

"I—I meant *my* r-right," she managed to squeak out. "Not your right."

"That would have been helpful to know before feeling up the other one."

Cheeks on fire, Alyssa did her best to scowl. "You'll live." She knew without a shadow of a doubt she should keep her gaze on the floor, or look up at the ceiling, or even at the bad guy writhing around on the floor, but her gaze drifted to Bennet's.

Who was smiling, all lazy, Texas charm. "Yes, I do

believe I will live," he murmured, pulling the Swiss Army knife out of her bra and shirt. "Now, hold out your wrists so I can cut those off."

"What are we going to do with him?"

Bennet stared icily at their attacker. "We're going to leave him here for the time being."

"Here?"

Bennet carefully pulled the knife against the plastic of the zip ties until they snapped, freeing her hands. Then he bent over and retrieved the man's gun and handed it to her. "Keep this on him. He so much as moves a muscle, you have my permission to shoot. I'll be right back."

"Bennet—"

But he was already gone, striding out of the room and picking up his gun he'd been forced to put down on the way out.

"You'll be a dead woman by week's end," the man hissed.

Alyssa kicked his shin. Hard. Then waited for him to finish howling before she spoke. "But I'm not one yet." He would have had her if not for Bennet, and that was humiliating, but Bennet had been there, and Alyssa was no longer running scared.

No, from here on out every clue that led them closer would only firm her resolve. Someone wanted to murder her like they'd murdered her mother? Well, it would take a damn army. No amount of brothers or her father's name could change that.

Bennet returned with a pair of handcuffs and a roll of duct tape. Whistling something that sounded an awful lot like "We Wish You a Merry Christmas," he handcuffed one of the man's bound hands to the foot of the bed. Then, still whistling, he ripped off a length of duct tape and fastened it over the man's mouth.

Without another word, he stood and took Alyssa's arm and led her out of the room. Once in the hallway, any smiles or humor or whistling stopped. Bennet's face went hard and, if Alyssa wasn't totally bad at reading him, furious.

"Wh-what are we going to do?" she asked, because no matter how she tried to free her arm from his grasp, it was like iron. Leading her through the house and to the door to the garage.

"We're going to get you over to my parents' house. They have much heavier security over there."

"What about him?"

"Once I get you settled, I'm going to call the police and report an attempted burglary, of course."

"You're going to lie to the police?"

He stopped her before they walked out the door, taking her by both elbows and pulling her close. "He was one minute away from kidnapping you, and possibly killing you. This isn't just your brothers anymore, and your safety is paramount. I will do whatever it takes to keep you safe while we solve the case, including lying to the local police. Now, can I count on you to do the same?"

"But—"

"But what if my parents are in on it?" he finished for her, clearly irritated by her line of thought.

Still, she nodded.

"Mother will be at her lunch meeting. Dad is at some charity thing until three. Once I get this situated, you are not leaving my sight until we figure this out, and we won't be going anywhere unarmed."

"I'm always armed."

"More than a Swiss Army knife in your bra."

"So, you're going to follow me to the bathroom? Sleep with me?" Which was possibly not the right wording of her question.

"If I have to," he replied unperturbed, beginning to pull her again. Through the garage and out into the open, one hand on her elbow and the other on his holstered gun. He moved quickly and efficiently, scanning every inch of the landscape as they moved from guesthouse to main house.

"He had to have gotten here somehow. Do you think someone else is out there?"

"Maybe," Bennet said in that cold, detached Texas Ranger tone. "If someone else is, they can't be too close with a vehicle. They'd never get past the gates. But we need to hurry on the chance someone is out there, and make sure they don't come looking for our friend."

Bennet keyed a code into the main house's garage door. Practically silently, it glided open and Bennet moved them inside, closing the garage door behind them.

They stepped into what was some sort of finished basement cellar-type thing—stainless steel deep freezer, matching fridge, a pantry full of canned goods and alcohol and all kinds of nonperishables.

Bennet led her up a staircase, and they stepped out in a kitchen where two people were sitting at a table sipping tea.

Bennet nodded at them. "Mrs. Downy. Kinsey. Can

you make sure no staff enter my room for the next few hours?"

The older-looking woman nodded. "Of course."

Then Alyssa was being led out of the kitchen, down another hall, through another room she couldn't ascertain the use for. Then they were clearly in the main entryway because a giant chandelier glittered above them.

It was like a movie. There was a grand staircase in the middle, all gleaming polished woods decorated with garland and red bows. On the other side of the staircase she could catch a glimpse of what had to be a gigantic tree decorated completely in gold.

But Bennet didn't give her any time to soak it in. He was pulling her up the stairs and down a long hall and into another giant room. This one wasn't white, though. It was a kind of forest green and some kind of tan color. Very woodsy and masculine.

"This is *your* room."

"Well, it was when I lived here. Now you're going to sit tight," he instructed, going through and checking all the windows even though they were on the second story. "Don't leave. Don't move, and on the off chance someone comes in this room, you shoot," he ordered, pointing at the gun he'd handed her earlier.

Alyssa frowned at the weapon she held. "What if it's someone from your parents' staff?"

"You heard me leave instructions for no one to enter. So, if someone does, you can almost be certain it's nefarious."

And clearly she wasn't as smart as she'd always fancied herself to be because she finally understood what was happening. "So, I'm just supposed to sit here in this room? Locked up."

Bennet didn't even pause, already striding for the door. "It's for your own protection, Alyssa."

"That's what they said, too."

He stopped and turned, frowning at her in that way she might have been intimidated by if she wasn't so irrationally hurt by all this.

"It isn't fair to compare me to your brothers."

"Isn't it?" she returned, shrugging as if she didn't have a care in the world.

"I don't have time for this," he muttered, raking a hand through his hair, but he didn't walk out. "I can't have you call the police because then you have to explain why you're in my parents' guesthouse. It's too complicated. You can't go milling around the house because I don't know who in this house we can trust. I actually don't know who we can trust, period, and neither do you. This is temporary while I deal with the police, and I need you on board."

"You need me to sit down and shut up."

"Hey, I let you break that guy's nose. Never accuse me of not using your unique talents." He smiled, but she couldn't bring herself to smile back. This was all too familiar, all too…much. She couldn't stand the idea that she'd felt like Bennet's partner there for a little bit, and now he was going to lock her away, too.

"Alyssa, I can't imagine what this might feel like from your perspective, but try to think about it from mine, okay? I'll be back." And then he was gone and the door was locked. End of discussion.

Alyssa sat down on the bed, fury and hurt pumping

through her. But the worst part was knowing he was right and that she had to, once again, sit in a locked room and twiddle her thumbs.

Chapter 10

Bennet dealt with the police, half his mind elsewhere. He wanted the squad car gone before either of his parents returned home, and he wanted to get back to Alyssa ASAP.

Everything had gotten completely out of hand, and he was half-tempted to send the whole of the Texas Rangers after CJ Jimenez.

But it wouldn't solve his case, and it wouldn't help Alyssa.

Luckily, being a Ranger himself helped speed up the Austin police investigation, and by the time Bennet was allowed to go, they even had a suspected partner in crime and vehicle for the getaway car.

He didn't know who'd sent the men, though, and that was a problem. All of this was an increasingly complicated problem. Bennet grabbed his laptop, his extra sidearm, all the clothes he'd gotten for Alyssa and shoved everything into a bag.

He didn't like the idea of staying at the main house whether his parents were involved in this mess or not, but he couldn't think of a safer place for them right now. Security was tight, and if one of his parents turned out to be his enemy, he'd keep them close and smoke them out.

That was something he couldn't allow himself to think too deeply on. Whatever happened, whatever *justice* was, he'd deal with the emotional fallout when it was over.

He entered through the garage again. When he got to the kitchen, Kinsey was still there, though she was no longer sipping tea with Mrs. Downy, who was in charge of the kitchen. Kinsey was sitting at the table, alone, a computer in front of her.

She'd run this house like a military institution since Bennet could remember, so when she gestured for him to approach, Bennet could only obey.

"Shall I tell your mother you and a guest will be staying with us?"

"You haven't yet?"

Kinsey's mouth curved just a fraction, but Bennet had known the severe woman most of his life. Which meant he knew that smile was a feat indeed, just like when he was a teenager and she'd finally allowed him to call her Kinsey instead of Ms. Kinsey.

"The girl was bleeding. Police cars. I don't want to be the one to break all that to your mother."

"Then don't."

"Someone will."

"*I* will." At least that way he could control the information, gauge his mother's reaction. Did she know? Was she part of this? He hated having doubts about his own parents. No matter how little he got along with them, they were still his family. He loved them.

And it was looking more and more likely one of them had cartel ties.

Kinsey pushed a small box toward him. "Clean her up first."

Damn. He'd been so worked up about getting the attacker and police taken care of, he'd forgotten all about Alyssa's head wound.

"She's pretty," Kinsey commented as Bennet took the box.

"She's work," he replied firmly.

Kinsey made a noncommittal sound that Bennet didn't have time to argue with. He strode through the house and to his room. He knocked, offering his name.

The door unlocked and opened a crack, the barrel of the gun the only thing appearing in the crack.

"Alyssa."

"Just making sure." The door opened the rest of the way, and she was smirking, gun still in her hand. It should not arouse him in the least.

"Uh-huh."

Alyssa set the gun down on the nightstand once he'd entered and closed and locked the door behind him.

"So, what happened?"

"They arrested the guy for breaking and entering and attempted burglary. They think they have a lead on the car that was waiting for him outside the gates. Did you recognize our guy?"

She shook her head. "I tried to pay attention to anything that might have been familiar or connect to anything, but he was nobody I've ever met."

"What about this man?" Bennet asked, pulling out his phone and bringing up the pictures he'd had the Austin officer send him. "He's our suspect for being the driver of the getaway car."

Alyssa frowned, leaning closer to the screen. "He looks familiar. He… He used to work for my father."

"Used to?"

"Yeah. Eli… I don't know last names, or even if that's his real name, but his name was Eli and he worked my father, but he defected." She looked up at him. "I'm sure of it."

"What exactly does *defected* mean?"

"I'm not sure of the exact cartel meaning. I used to think it was going to the cops, but it's what my brothers said about my mom. She defected. To a cartel rival. And if we put it together with what my father told me about Dominguez having my mother… Maybe that's the connection."

"Except we don't know what Dominguez has to do with any of this."

Alyssa swallowed, and though she was trying to look tough, to act tough, he could see the worry in her eyes. "He wants me, though. For whatever reason, he's after me."

"Why now? You've been free for two years. If he wanted you as revenge, he's had years to do it."

"There has to be an inciting incident we don't know about."

"That started recently, but before I came to your office, if your brothers' men were following you on your last job."

"But… I don't know what it would be."

"We'll start looking into cartel cases and see if we can't find some recent dustup we might make a connection to."

"And if we can't?"

Bennet didn't know what to say to that. He was tempted to make a joke about crossing bridges once they were burning behind them, but she didn't look like she'd laugh. Or smile. Or do anything except maybe break.

He couldn't bear the thought of breaking her.

"I don't want to be a prisoner anymore, Bennet. Not one of my family, or a madman, or whatever the hell is going on here. I don't want to be locked up and shoved away. I won't live like that, even if it puts me in danger. I'd rather be dead."

"You're not going to end up dead. Not on my watch."

"What do you care? I shouldn't be anyone to you."

It was such a vulnerable statement, clearly speaking to all those hurts she'd somehow survived. Trust broken over and over again.

He didn't know what it was like to be a prisoner, not in any sense of the word. Even in the world his parents had created he'd broken mostly free. Maybe they'd greased some palms for him that he'd wished they hadn't, but it was hardly kidnapping or betrayal.

But somehow, despite his complete lack of experience in the matter, he could feel that pain of hers, and he wanted to soothe it. He wanted to be as honest as she was being when he should be cagey or stone-faced or whatever would best benefit this case.

But as gung-ho as he'd been just days ago about solving *this* case, the oldest cold case on file at the Texas Rangers, it had irrevocably become about something else. About her.

"What do I care?" He shook his head. "You hold your own. You make me laugh at the wrongest of times. You're smart, and we understand each other. Justice. We understand that. Not everyone does. Maybe you shouldn't be anyone to me, but you are."

He stepped forward and more than anything else he'd ever wanted in his whole life, he wanted to press his mouth to hers. Not in some ploy to convince his father to leave, or just because he wondered what it might be like. No, he wanted to kiss her because she was her and he thought somehow their mouths fitting together would make everything all right.

But it wouldn't. So, he held up the first aid box Kinsey had given him. "Now, it's my turn to bandage you up."

Alyssa hated poring over paperwork. It was boring. As much as she often had to do some investigating when she was hunting down a skip, she at least got to do stuff. Call people. Go places. Plan.

This was all looking for some magical clue, one that could be absolutely anything. She glanced at Bennet, who was sitting on the window seat, legs stretched out in front of him and crossed at the ankles, focus lasered on the computer screen in front of him. He didn't lean against the wall, likely because of his cuts, but he still looked...powerful and smart and a million other things she should ignore.

Anytime he found something he thought might be important or relevant, he printed it out and made her read it.

She wanted to be useful, but she also wanted to make a move. She'd already learned that being kidnapped with someone wasn't all that much different from being kidnapped alone. In The Stallion's house, there'd been three other girls with her, but it hadn't changed the fact she'd been alone and shut in.

"You can go to bed if you're tired," Bennet offered, never taking his gaze off the screen.

"I'm not tired," Alyssa muttered, poking at the tray of food an older woman had brought up a few hours ago. "I'm bored."

"You'd make a terrible policeman."

"Why do you think I'm a bounty hunter?"

He glanced over at her, mouth curved at one side. "Illegal bounty hunter."

She flashed him a grin. "Even better. Don't have to worry about following any pesky laws."

"How's your head?"

"How's your back?"

"Fine. How's your head?" he repeated, clearly unamused by her unwillingness to answer the question.

"You should see the other guy."

"I believe I did. Impressive indeed. Seriously, though?"

"It's fine." If fine was painful throbbing. "Didn't even lose consciousness."

"Look, we'll have to sleep in shifts, so you might as well try to grab a few hours."

"Why do we have to sleep in shifts?"

"Well, for starters I'm not going to sleep on the floor."

She cocked her head. She'd sort of assumed she'd sleep on that cushy window seat he was on. He was too tall to fit, but she'd be able to stretch out just fine. It was a little interesting he hadn't thought of that, though. He'd gone straight to the only option being him sleeping on the floor.

Apparently with her was not an option. *You know it's not.* And it shouldn't be something she was imagining. She needed to focus on reality. "You don't think we're safe."

"I don't *know* if we're safe. For the time being, one of us is always on guard. We sleep in shifts. And, while one is sleeping, the other one is working. Until we get to the bottom of it."

Alyssa flopped back on the bed, frowning. "And how am I supposed to sleep with all the lights blazing?"

Without Bennet even moving from the window seat, the lights flicked off.

"Your computer—"

He made a move with his arm without even looking and suddenly he was pulling a curtain from behind him to enclose the little window seat alcove. The room was completely dark.

"Good night, Alyssa," he said from behind the curtain.

Since it was dark and he was behind a curtain, she indulged in the childish impulse to stick her tongue out at him.

"It's too quiet in here," she grumbled.

"No, it isn't, because you keep whining."

She scowled and shifted deeper into the unbelievably soft sheets. She wasn't tired in the least, but she
also wasn't *whining*. She was going insane. The walls
were closing in, and at least complaining kept them at
bay for a while.

How could she sleep when she was locked up again?
Oh, this was by far the nicest room she'd been locked in,
but amenities didn't matter when you were essentially a
prisoner. Hands tied from *doing* anything because they
didn't know what the hell was going on.

She scowled over at the curtain Bennet was behind.
The irritating thing was she understood why they had
to do all this. She just hated it. Hated feeling locked up
and ineffective. She wanted to do something. Even if it
meant smashing her elbow into some assailant's nose.

At least that had been action. At least that had *felt*
good. She wanted something that felt good instead of
dark and oppressive. Instead of like her life would only
ever be some terrible, lonely prison.

But she wasn't exactly alone right now, curtain or no
curtain. Her mind drifted to her kiss with Bennet. *Fake
kiss.* Except no matter how the pretense had been fake,
the kiss hadn't been. His mouth had been on hers, and
more than once his hands had been on her.

Sometimes he looked at her and she was almost certain that whatever she'd felt in the midst of that fake
kiss—attraction and need and the desperate curiosity
of what more he could do with that all-too-charming
mouth of his—he felt it, too.

She didn't know *why* he'd be attracted to someone like her, and she realized she probably wasn't the
world's leading expert in men and attraction, but she

also wasn't stupid. He'd gently bandaged her head, but on occasion his gaze had drifted to her mouth.

That meant something. She'd spent the past two years in the orbit of Gabby and Jaime, who couldn't seem to keep their hands off each other no matter how committed they got. So, she may not have experience with attraction or lust or anything, but she did know what it looked like.

She'd really like to know what it *felt* like. She'd spent the past two years building something of a free life, but she hadn't dated or flirted or even put herself out there in any way, shape or form because she'd been waiting for something to come to her.

Like all her life she'd waited for freedom. What a waste all that waiting was.

"Bennet?" she asked into the quiet of the room.

"What?"

"How many women have you kissed?"

He made a sound, something like a cough or rough inhale. "I… How is that relevant to anything?"

"I didn't say I was going to ask you a *relevant* question. I'm just asking you *a* question."

He cleared his throat. "I… I don't know. I don't have a running tally."

"Oh? That many." And on some level she wanted to know everything about them. Why he'd kissed them. How far it had gone. What he'd felt.

And on some level she wanted to elbow every woman in the nose just as she'd done to the man who'd attacked her.

"It isn't about how many, it's just… I'd have to do the math and… Why are you asking me this?"

"Well, you know, I've only kissed you."

There was a moment of heavy silence. "That wasn't a kiss," he said, his voice something closer to a growl.

"Oh? What was it then?"

"A...charade."

"A *charade*," she repeated, because even though it had been an act, a fake, *charade* seemed such an oddly proper word.

"That's what I said."

"But I was just thinking if I'm going to die—"

He jerked the curtain open, the harsh computer light glinting off the angry expression on his face. "You're not going to die."

"You can't *promise* I'm not going to die, and God knows someday I will. So. You know. I should probably know what it's like."

"What what's like?"

"Sex."

He didn't move, didn't speak, and she was almost certain he didn't even breathe. Which was kind of funny, all in all. That it just took the mention of sex to catch Ranger Stevens off guard.

And since he was off guard, she slid out of bed and walked over to him. He watched her approach warily, but he didn't ward her off, and he didn't tell her to stop. She walked all the way until her knees were all but touching the window seat. She looked down at him.

He held her gaze, but he still didn't say anything. Everything she knew about Bennet suggested he'd be the kind of man who'd make the first move, and yet he just *sat* there. Not making *any* move.

"It would be something of a no-no, wouldn't it?" she

asked, her voice a little breathless with something like nerves but not quite that. Adrenaline, maybe. *Anticipation.* "Because I'm involved in this case."

"First of all, please never say the phrase 'no-no' again. Second of all, yes. It would be incredibly wrong. On every level."

"Come on. Not *every* level."

"Okay, nine out of ten levels," he returned, and she could tell he was trying very hard not to be amused.

"So, maybe we explore that one-out-of-ten level," Alyssa offered hopefully, covertly moving to take the computer off his lap. Except as she glanced at the screen she noticed something oddly familiar. Something she hadn't seen in years.

"What is this a picture of?" she asked breathlessly, this time not nerves or anticipation or anything other than the excitement they might find a lead.

"What... What?" Bennet asked, clearly not making the leap to work quite as quickly as she had.

"The picture you have on the screen," she said, pointing at it as she leaned in closer. "What's it of?"

"Uh... I... The FBI believes the man on the right is Salvador Dominguez. It's the only known picture of him law enforcement has as far as I know."

"And the man next to him?"

"No one's identified him. It's too shadowy, he's looking away from the camera and there're no markings to give any clues."

"But there is an earring."

Bennet squinted at the screen. "I suppose."

"It's one of my brothers."

His head jerked toward hers. "How do you know that?"

"The earring. It's a *J* with dragon horns. It was my father's. Now, that definitely isn't my father. This guy is too tall, too broad. But it's one of my brothers, I can almost guarantee it. My father wouldn't have given that earring to anyone else. When was this photo taken?"

"Last month."

"So, one of my brothers is photographed talking with the head of a rival cartel a month ago."

Bennet blew out a breath. "Well, it looks like we might have our inciting incident, doesn't it?"

"I don't know what *I* have to do with it, though."

"Your brothers love you. To bad men trying to hurt each other, love is a weapon. A weakness."

She glanced at Bennet, feeling unaccountably sad for some reason. "That isn't just to bad men trying to hurt each other, Bennet. Love is always a weapon."

"It doesn't have to be," he replied steadfastly, his blue eyes an odd shade in the light of the laptop screen.

Her chest felt tight, and her heart felt too much like it was being squeezed. She'd wanted to feel something, but not this. Not anything to do with love, especially when it came to her brothers. *If* they loved her, that love had only ever been used as a weapon, no matter what Bennet thought.

"Well, I guess we've got something to go on now," she said, straightening and wrapping her arms around herself. She felt sad and alone and suddenly she wouldn't mind just going to bed and being locked away. "I'll take my sleeping shift, then."

Before she realized what he was doing, Bennet had

his hand fisted in her shirt and jerked her down so that she had to grab his shoulders or risk just falling into his lap.

Then his mouth was on hers. Gentle, and something that kind of made her want to cry because there'd been so little of it in her life. Softness. His lips caressed hers, his tongue slowly tracing the outline of her bottom lip, and all she could do was soak it up.

She felt like melted wax and a firework ready to burst all at the same time, and underneath her hands his shoulders were just these steady rocks to lean on.

He pulled away, though his hand was still fisted in her shirt, and his breath wafted across her still-wet lips.

"*That* was a kiss," he murmured. He released her and grabbed the curtain. "Now go to sleep," he ordered, and snapped the curtain closed between them.

Chapter 11

Bennet woke with a start and then a groan of pain. He'd dozed off on the stupid window seat and now his neck and shoulders were paying the price, the cuts on his back throbbing. He rubbed his eyes, realizing through the gauzy fabric of the curtains that covered the window, daylight shone far brighter than he'd have liked.

He should have been up hours ago. He should have never fallen asleep. Sleep was wasting precious time they didn't have to unravel all of these confusing clues.

He fumbled for the curtain that separated the window seat from the room and managed to shove it open.

Alyssa was sitting in the bed, cross-legged with his laptop perched on her thighs. There was a tray of fresh fruit and bagels and a coffeepot on the bed next to her.

"How'd you get that?"

"Ms. Kinsey brought up the food and coffee—much

better than yours, FYI. The laptop? I took it while you snored away. Very unattractive, I might add."

Bennet grunted irritably, remembering exactly why he'd allowed himself to doze off on the window seat.

The thought of waking up Alyssa, asleep in his bed, warm and soft and more alluring than she had any right to be, had been a little too much to bear at two in the morning. He'd been afraid that if he'd even simply nudged her shoulder he'd want to touch all of her.

And that was most wholeheartedly a *no-no*. Which made kissing her last night inexcusable and irrational and something he had no business considering in the light of the morning.

"Coffee?" she asked sweetly.

"Are you always this obnoxious in the morning?"

"Morning is the absolute best time of day."

He grabbed the coffeepot and one of the mugs and poured. "You're evil."

She laughed, and no matter how much he hated mornings or the awful, digging pain in his neck and the fact his back felt like it was on fire, he liked hearing her laugh. He liked a few too many things about Alyssa Jimenez, drug kingpin's daughter.

Yeah, that was never going to fly in any of his lives— Texas Ranger, politicians' son. The conclusion of this case would be the conclusion of their time together.

You can't promise I'm not going to die, and God knows someday I will. So. You know. I should probably know what it's like.

Those words kept bouncing around in his brain, completely unwelcome. Someday she *would* know what it was like, but it wouldn't be with him. For all the reasons he'd gone through a million times over.

"Find anything?" he asked, easing onto the other side of the bed, enough space and a tray of food between them, to keep his head on the case.

Maybe.

"Well, I found that no matter how hard or zoomed in I look at the picture, I can't tell which of my brothers is in that picture. I have committed Salvador Dominguez's face to memory, though, and I can't help but thinking he's behind yesterday."

"Agreed."

"How did you connect my mother to me when she was a Jane Doe?"

"Happenstance. I was searching old case files and happened to notice a similarity in a murder that was committed by a known member of the Jimenez cartel. The victim in that murder had the exact same wounds and was buried in the exact same way not too far from where…"

She'd looked away, but he understood that thinking of her mother's wounds and where her body was found was too much even for Alyssa.

"What I didn't know when I came to see you was that my Jane Doe *was* a Jimenez."

"Who was the man convicted of the other murder?"

"Dom Coch… Holy hell. Dom Cochrane. Spelled differently, but that's too much of a coincidence to the name your brother gave us."

"I don't remember anyone named Dom, but I wouldn't have known everyone, I guess."

Bennet gestured for her to hand over the laptop. She

did so, and he logged into the Ranger system while he sipped his coffee. "I'm going to do some searches for Dom Cochrane and see what pops up."

Alyssa took one of the bagels off the tray between them and spread cream cheese across the top. She frowned at it while Bennet typed the name into the database.

Something was bothering her, and she wasn't saying what. He didn't like knowing she was keeping something from him, even if it was feelings rather than information. He wanted to know everything. About the case. About her.

Which was the absolute last thing he needed right now. He tried to focus on the results of his search, but Alyssa licked a smudge of cream cheese off her thumb. Which he shouldn't watch. Or think about.

Either she felt his gaze or just happened to look over, but somehow their gazes met as her thumb disappeared into her mouth. Everything inside him tightened and ached, and would it really be *that* bad to indulge in something this potent? He'd still solve the case, and maybe it was morally ambiguous to get involved with someone connected to one of his cases, but hell, Vaughn had done it, and he was the most morally upstanding person Bennet had ever met.

A sharp knock sounded at the door, and they both nearly jumped a foot, the tray tipping over and spilling the remaining bagels onto the bed.

"Who is it?" Bennet growled.

"Kinsey."

He shoved the computer off his lap and strode over

to the door, doing everything he could to take his mind off the completely untimely erection.

He opened the door a crack. "Yes?"

Kinsey looked vaguely amused, but her message was brief.

"Ms. Delaney is here with the dresses. Shall I send her up here?"

"That would be perfect. Thank you."

Kinsey nodded and Bennet shut the door. He had half a mind to bang his head against it. Instead, he turned back to the bed to find Alyssa staring at him, her eyebrows drawn together.

"You really grew up like this?"

"Like what?"

"Servants? Everything at your beck and call. Dresses... Wait." She sat up straighter on the bed. "What did she say about *dresses*?"

Bennet tried not to smile, but half his mouth curved of its own accord. "You'll need something for the ball."

"But..."

"We can't exactly go to the *mall* after you've been attacked, so I asked Kinsey what we could do. She suggested calling one of my mother's personal shoppers with your size and have them make a house call."

"B-but... I can't afford..."

"Alyssa, honestly."

"I don't want you paying for stuff," she said stubbornly.

"Except I'm the one *forcing* you to go to this gala, and you'll need to fit in if we have hope of getting any information. Which means jeans and a T-shirt aren't going to cut it, and neither is…well, no offense, darling, but anything you'd pick out on your own."

She scowled at him, which was good. Better her to be angry with him than anything else.

"And, just so you can settle into the idea before Friday night, I'll also be hiring a hair and makeup person to do all that stuff women do."

"What stuff?"

"Hell if I know, but the person I hire will, and that's all that matters. Now, you can pick whatever dress you'd like. Cost is no option."

"Oh, well, then why don't you shower me with jewels, too," she returned sarcastically.

"Don't tempt me."

She opened her mouth, likely to say something scathing, but another knock sounded at the door.

Bennet opened it, smiling at Tawny Delaney, whom he'd met on occasion at events such as the Christmas gala. Her father was in oil and a dedicated donor to his father's many political endeavors.

Tawny also *might* have been on the list of women he'd kissed, and he couldn't help but be glad Alyssa didn't have any such list.

"Ben. It's so good to see you again," Tawny said, smiling up at him.

"Thank you for coming," he returned, ushering her in. A man with a rolling rack of what Bennet could only assume were dresses began to push the rack inside, but Bennet slapped a palm to the rack.

"I'll take it from here, sir. You can wait down in the foyer, if you'd be so kind."

"Ben?"

"Sorry. Can't be too careful right now."

"Oh. Well. That's fine," Tawny replied, though she looked a little nervous. "Where's our client?"

Bennet gestured to the bed, where Alyssa was sprawled out, defiantly so, scowling. Bennet wanted to laugh even though it was ridiculous.

"Oh, well." Tawny cleared her throat, her smile looking so forced Bennet winced. "Won't this be fun?"

"Yes, it will. Won't it, Alyssa?" he said, giving her a meaningful look he hoped she realized meant *get your butt off the bed*.

"Sure it will, *Ben*," Alyssa said, emphasis on the shortened name, still lounging on the rumpled covers.

It was more than likely he was going to end up paying very dearly for this.

Alyssa watched as Tawny the tall, put-together blonde started taking the covers off the dresses on the rack. She chattered on about jewel tones and coloring, and all Alyssa could think was she would never in a million years look like this woman.

There would always be a little drowned sewer rat in her. A girl who'd grown up locked in a room with only men for companions. Even when her mother had been alive and around she hadn't spent much time *around*. The kids were supposed to play with each other while the adults did the serious business of running a cartel.

"Where should we do the trying on?" Tawny asked brightly.

"There's a bathroom through that door there," Bennet offered.

"Perfect." Tawny turned her attention to Alyssa,

all bright smiles and comforting drawl. "We'll start with three. More than three and it gets overwhelming." She plucked three dresses off the rack and rested them across her arm before marching for the bathroom. "These are my top choices based on your coloring and build."

She stepped inside the bathroom and waited for Alyssa to hesitantly enter before she closed the door shut and hung the dresses on the shower curtain.

"My, the Stevenses do know how to build a house, don't they?" Tawny said conversationally. She handed Alyssa a blindingly gold dress. "Let's start with this one."

Alyssa recoiled. Visibly. "No."

Tawny blinked, and for a fraction of a second Alyssa felt kind of crappy for her antagonistic behavior. It wasn't this woman's fault she was everything Alyssa wasn't and never could be.

"It's a beautiful dress," Alyssa offered, shoving her hands into her pockets. "It's too loud for this. I need to blend in."

Tawny smiled indulgently. "Isn't it every woman's fantasy to stand out?"

The question landed a little hard, right in the heart. Stand out? All standing out had ever gotten her was locked up, and somehow she still wanted that moment. A moment when the attention was on her for something *good* for once.

But, this wasn't that moment. "This is more a business venture than a personal, womanly venture."

"Okay, well, let's try the black, then." She held out a black dress with a fluffy thing of green hanging off it.

Alyssa wanted to refuse this one, too, but it was no use. She did have to fit in, and fitting in meant some fancy dress the likes of which she'd never even dreamed about wearing it was so foreign to all the lives she'd lived.

She took it and waited for Miss Texas Perfect to leave, but Tawny just waited expectantly.

"Oh, well, I'm supposed to stay with the dresses," Tawny explained. "Part of the job. I do it all the time." Sensing Alyssa's continued hesitation, Tawny nodded. "How about I turn my back?"

"Sure," Alyssa muttered. Maybe it was stupid, but the last thing she wanted was Tawny seeing her subpar underwear. Tawny probably had a matching set. All silk or lace or something beautiful and expensive.

And what would you ever do with something like that?

Hoping to get it over with as quickly as possible, Alyssa shucked her clothes and roughly pulled on the dress. It was black, somehow fit like a glove, and though she'd probably *never* feel comfortable in a dress, it wasn't scratchy or uncomfortable or anything.

"So, how do you know Ben?" the woman asked conversationally, trailing her perfectly manicured pink nails across the decorative towels hanging off a rack next to the sink.

"Uh. Work," Alyssa muttered, tugging the zipper in the back up as far as she could.

"Oh. Are you a Ranger?" Tawny asked, as if it was somehow possible her scrawny self could be a Ranger.

Alyssa couldn't help but smile. "No. Just…helping out."

"It must be dangerous if you're working with the Rangers. Aren't you scared?"

"Sometimes, but I know how to protect myself."

Tawny sighed. "No wonder Ben likes you. He's one of the few men I've ever met who wasn't impressed or enthralled by weakness."

Alyssa didn't know *what* to say to that, so she smoothed her hands down the dress. "Uh, I'm done."

Tawny turned and clapped her hands together. "Oh, isn't that perfect!"

Alyssa had her doubts about perfect, but Tawny was immediately fussing, pulling the zipper up the rest of the way, tying the green ribbon around her waist into a beautiful bow Alyssa would never be able to replicate.

Tawny nudged her over to the full-length mirror, forcing Alyssa to look at her reflection.

"You'll want to sweep your hair back, and have someone do your makeup, obviously," Tawny said, pulling Alyssa's hair back herself, artfully brushing some hair to hide the bandage on her forehead. "Maybe a tasteful necklace. Diamonds or rubies. Nothing ostentatious. You'll fit right in without standing too far out."

Even with no makeup and someone else holding her hair back, Alyssa didn't recognize herself. It was like someone had put a fancy filter over the girl she'd always been.

"Do you want Ben's opinion?"

Even though she'd warmed to the woman a little bit, Alyssa still *hated* her calling Bennet Ben. "No. I think I'd like it to be a surprise."

The woman smiled somewhat wistfully. "He isn't an easy man to surprise, but this might do the trick."

"Do you know him well?"

Tawny's smile didn't change. "Sometimes I wonder if anyone knows him well. And for the record, I call him Ben because it irritates him and that's about the only time he'll pay me any mind."

"Oh."

"But you don't seem to have that trouble."

Alyssa turned away from the mirror. This woman was confusing, and Alyssa didn't have any idea how to talk to her. She seemed...well, perfect for Bennet's world of icy mothers and charming fathers and smooth, Southern drawls.

And somehow this tall blonde with class and elegance for miles seemed to be under the impression Bennet liked Alyssa. And that wasn't weird, just something to sigh over.

Alyssa moved back to her regular clothes, and Tawny dutifully turned her back again. "W-why do you think he likes me?" Alyssa couldn't help but ask, pulling the zipper down. "This is all work."

"You're in his bedroom, sweetheart. He might be calling it work, but men are apt to say lots of things to get a woman into their bedroom."

It all sounded so worldly and adult, and Alyssa felt like a child again. A child playing at being an adult.

Except she was twenty-four. And she'd survived what might kill most people. She was not some little girl. She was just a little inexperienced.

But Bennet had kissed her last night. Of his own accord, with no pretending it had been meant to throw anyone off. It had been a *real* kiss. He'd said so himself.

So, it was time. Time to get rid of the inexperience,

and if she ended up doing that before they unraveled their myriad of mysteries, well, so be it.

She had a life to live, after all, and she was tired of it being thwarted.

Chapter 12

Once Tawny left with the dresses, Bennet made himself scarce. He knew Alyssa wasn't happy with him for running some mysterious errands, but he also knew she was losing her mind locked up in that room. So, he set about a safe way to give her a little excursion.

It wasn't necessary, and it would take time away from the case he was trying to solve, but…

Hell. He hated that wild look in her eyes like she was reliving all the ways she'd been a prisoner in her life. He hated the way she paced that room like it was some kind of cage. And, worst of all, he liked way too much the way she'd sometimes stare at him, considering, assessing. The same look she'd had in her eyes last night when she'd approached him before seeing the picture on his computer and recognized one of her brothers.

One of her brothers. Possibly fraternizing with a rival

cartel. A lead, something to go on. What he should be focused on instead of Alyssa's state of mind.

But no matter how he chastised himself for his lack of focus, he still secured his parents' screening room, checking every nook and cranny, locking it down in a way that eased his worries. It was still just another locked room, but it wasn't the room he currently had her locked in.

He had no idea if she'd appreciate it, but it was worth a shot. And she could pick a movie and some snacks and he could still focus on finding a connection between Sal/Dom Cochrane, Salvador Dominguez and one of Alyssa's brothers.

So, he was hardly ignoring his duties or his case. And if he'd told Captain Dean he was taking a vacation until after Christmas even though he was working on this case 24/7, it was only to keep Alyssa safe. It wasn't lying to his superior. It was protecting a vulnerable piece of the case.

He'd work on believing that. He left the movie room, locked sufficiently, and went to collect Alyssa for their little…night in. Not theirs. Hers. It was like a gift.

Certainly not like a date.

He forced that thought out of his head and walked up the stairs, hand on the butt of his weapon, scanning every corner for anything suspicious.

It was strange to walk through his parents' house feeling like danger could be lurking anywhere. He'd grown up in this house and there had been a lot of feelings it had prompted. Suffocating, cold, frustration, disgust. But never fear.

It made him sick to his stomach to think too hard

about his mother being involved in this, but if Sal Cochrane was connected to Dom Cochrane, and they were both connected to Salvador Dominguez...

Ambition had made worse monsters out of people. He just hated to believe it of his mother even with as strained a relationship as they had.

But he would find the truth regardless. Justice. One way or another.

He walked down the hall to his room, something uncomfortable jittering in his gut, and it wasn't the fear of danger or worry over his mother's involvement.

It was anticipation and nerves. No one had ever affected him quite like Alyssa did, and he wasn't altogether certain he liked it, but he seemed incapable of resisting it.

He knocked, three hard raps. "It's Bennet."

The door edged open, just a crack. She didn't open it farther, so he pushed in himself.

He made a noise, one he couldn't have described to save his life. Everything just kind of whooshed out of him.

She was standing there in one of his button-down dress shirts. And that was all. Her long legs bare from midthigh on down to her toes. She'd left the top of the shirt unbuttoned far enough he could see the enticing tops of her breasts.

"This is your shirt, right?" she asked, her expression unreadable.

"Uh, yup. That's...my shirt." He glanced around the room and found her jeans and pointed at them. "You should put some pants on."

She cocked her head, toying with the top buttoned button of his shirt. If she undid it...

"Why?"

He'd completely lost his train of thought. "Why what?"

"Why should I put pants on?"

"Oh, right." He cleared his throat, trying to speak past the dryness there. "I have a surprise for you."

She took a few steps toward him, still toying with that button, and no matter how strictly he ordered himself to look away, he simply couldn't. She looked impossibly soft, even knowing how tough and strong she could be.

She reached out, pressing her palm against his chest, looking up at him from underneath her lashes. "Let's do my surprise first."

He should not ask for details on that. He should not be deterred. He should... Hell.

He managed to clear his throat and put his hand over hers, gently pulling it off his chest. "I have a feeling your surprise isn't very...appropriate."

"No, it's very, very inappropriate." She grinned up at him, and he shouldn't smile back, but he couldn't help it.

"Alyssa..."

"Don't say no to the virgin throwing herself at you. That'd scar her for life."

He reached out and touched the edge of the bandage on her head. She hadn't complained about it once. "Nothing I could do would scar you for life."

She stepped closer. This time instead of pressing her palm to his chest, she stood on her toes and wound her arms around his neck. She was all soft curves against him, the fragrance of his own damn soap on her skin and in her hair.

"I want you, Bennet. And you want me, too… I think."

"I do."

"Okay, well, you may have gotten most of the things you've wanted in life, but I've gotten very few. So, it's my turn to get something, have something, I want."

"I thought you wanted to get out of here."

"This'll do." Then her mouth was on his, and what could he do but pull her closer, sink into that kiss. He slid his hands down the sexy curve of her back, exploring her mouth with his tongue. When his hands slid over her ass, he realized she was not, in fact, wearing any underwear.

"Hell."

She laughed against his mouth, pressing her body more firmly against his. "I figured if the shirt didn't work, full-on naked would do the trick."

"You do the trick all on your own," he murmured, lifting her up.

She clung tighter, smiling against his mouth as he maneuvered her onto the bed. He should resist. He knew he should resist, but she smiled up at him from beneath his body, and who had that kind of willpower? He'd wanted her since she'd reached for the gun in her desk all those days ago, and it had only intensified each second of getting to know her.

She was beautiful and seemed so sure, but he knew she'd been sheltered. She was untouched.

Except she wanted him, and she might be innocent, there might even be hidden fragile pieces of her, but

Alyssa Jimenez knew what she wanted, and who was he to keep it from her?

"After all this is done, I can't promise—"

"I didn't ask you to promise anything, Ben."

He scowled. "Don't call me that."

Her mouth curved. "Why do you hate it so much?"

"It isn't my name."

"Hmm," she murmured, tracing his hairline with her index fingers. "It's half of your name. Why don't you like it?"

Bennet sighed. He had *no* idea why they were talking about this when they could be doing far more interesting things that she'd initiated, but he also knew she wouldn't just let it go. "It was my grandfather's name. Well, Bennet was, but he went by Ben. Everyone loved him."

"It doesn't sound like you did."

"He used to hit me."

Everything on Alyssa's face morphed into shocked outrage. "What do you mean hit you?"

"It's the Stevens way. Beat you into proper behavior."

"And your parents *agreed* with that?"

"They didn't practice it themselves, but they didn't stop it either. You can hardly be shocked by that. You grew up in a cartel. You must have seen far worse things."

"I was sheltered from the good and the bad, I suppose." She studied his face then wiggled beneath him. "Let's focus on the good right now, huh?"

"Yes, I like the sound of that. Why don't you unbutton the rest of that shirt?"

She smiled up at him as she brought her fingers to

the buttons that were still buttoned. She pushed one button free, and then the next, and next until they were all free and he could pull the fabric apart and reveal her body completely.

She was petite, all bronze skin and slight curves. Everything inside him tensed and hardened.

"You're beautiful." And his, somehow. She was his.

Alyssa didn't quite know how to handle Bennet's words. Whether it was that sad little story about his grandfather, or telling her she was beautiful with such awe she almost believed it.

So, she pulled his head down and kissed him, because she knew what to do with her mouth then. Absorb the warmth of him, trace his lips with her tongue until he groaned and invaded her mouth with his.

She pressed her naked body to the rough fabric of his jeans and then pulled at the hem of his shirt, wanting to feel *him* against her. Skin and skin and hearts beating erratically against each other.

He pulled the shirt up and off his body, discarding it on the floor before his mouth returned to hers. But only briefly. Then it was moving down her jaw, her neck, feather-light brushes, the occasional brush of his tongue.

His palm slid up her stomach and rib cage until he was cupping her breast, kissing down her chest until his tongue touched her nipple. Her body would have jerked off the bed if Bennet hadn't been above her, a solid, warm wall of muscle.

She felt as though she was pulsing with something. Need probably, because the more his tongue played with her nipple the more restless she became—needing to move, needing to press against him, needing more. More, so much more.

But he seemed content to kiss and lick her everywhere but where she needed him most.

Nothing in the whole world had ever felt like this. Not the sight of the sun after two years of confinement. Not the closure on someone's face when she put a dangerous skip away. Nothing. Nothing had this kind of physical and emotional charge to it.

"Let me go get a condom," he said in a raspy voice that sizzled over her skin.

"You have condoms?" she asked dazedly.

"Sure. Rangers are like Boy Scouts. Always prepared."

"I hope Boy Scouts aren't prepared in *that* way," she called after him when he disappeared into the bathroom. When he reappeared, she grinned at him. "Wait. Please tell me you were a Boy Scout."

"Of course I was. Made it all the way up to Eagle Scout. You have no idea the things I can do with my hands." He grinned.

She spread out on his bed. "Show me."

He tossed the condom on the bed then undid his belt, eyes never leaving hers. Goose bumps rose on her skin at that steady, brazen gaze. He thought she was beautiful. He wanted her as much as she wanted him.

And still that need coiled deeper, no matter that she didn't think it could. She could barely sit still as he pushed his jeans and boxers off in one quick push, and then he was standing there naked.

He was just always so impressive. Tall and strong and broad. Long and hard and something close to intimidating. But no matter how nerves hammered in her chest, she didn't even think of backing out or changing her mind.

Not because she only wanted something good or to cross some adult rite of passage off the list, but because she wanted him. Only him.

He slid onto the bed, over her again, spreading her legs apart with his knees. His fingers trailed up her calves, over her knees, her thighs.

She should do something, too, but all she could seem to do was lie there and breathe, watching his blue eyes intent on the most intimate part of her. He stroked her there and she whimpered, much to her own chagrin.

But his fingers *were* like magic. Sparking, spiraling the pleasure of magic as they entered and stroked, found places inside her that had her panting, writhing, pleading. She'd never felt this out of control, this desperate for something, except freedom.

But she didn't want freedom now. Not from Bennet. She wanted more of him. More of him inside her, on top of her.

"Please," she whispered, so close to some unknown cliff she didn't understand but knew she wanted to fall over. Over and over again.

He paused for a second, grabbing the condom and pulling it out of its package. She watched as he rolled the condom on his thick erection, and Alyssa couldn't quite fight the little kernel of panic that settled in her chest. "Bennet."

His blue eyes met hers, sure and steady as he positioned himself at her entrance. "Shh. It's all right. I'll take care of you."

She relaxed. "I know." It'd probably be easier if she could stop believing in people, but everyone who'd come into her life since she'd left that bunker had proved to her that her brothers' betrayal was their shortcoming. Not hers.

She could feel the tip of him slowly take the place of where his fingers had been. She was still pulsing with that lost orgasm, and as he slowly pushed inside she tried to chase that almost pleasure as much as she tried to ignore the uncomfortable tightness.

Everything was too big and too much, and yet everything she'd wanted was right there. Bennet inside her, Bennet on top of her, Bennet. Hers.

He moved, and there was a dull pain mixed in with that pleasure, but it was diluted enough she could enjoy that pleasure. Chase that joy that needed release. He moved slowly, his body hard against hers, and it made her feel safe. Protected.

All without being locked in or hidden away. He was bringing her to life even as he made sure nothing bad happened to her.

"Alyssa," he said, sounding pained, and that's when she realized a few tears had escaped her cheeks.

"It's not bad crying," she managed, because it wasn't. It was a release like any other. Too many emotions and feelings built up and leaking out.

"Good." He kissed a tear, his hand curling around her hip, angling himself differently, and this time when he slid deep, she gasped.

So, he did it again. And she forgot about that odd fullness and focused instead on the way he pulsed through her, uncoiled that heavy tight knot deep in her belly. This time she moved with him, and something seemed to explode inside her, waving through her, an intense, pulsing pleasure she wanted to bask in forever.

And still he moved inside her, making it all last longer, spiral harder, brighter. Until he was pushing deep, groaning and holding her tight to him.

She was so crushed to him she couldn't even wrap her arms around him like she wanted to. She wanted to hold on and never let go.

Someday you'll have to let go.

She closed her eyes against that thought, listening to the heavy beating of his heart. This was just like any other captivity. You only had the time you had. She'd enjoy it while she had it.

"Don't sleep on the window seat tonight," she said into his chest.

His mouth brushed across her temple. "I won't."

Chapter 13

Bennet knew they were falling into too much of a routine, and yet he couldn't seem to help himself. What man in his right mind could?

They explored each other at night, researched all angles of the case during the day and sometimes distracted themselves with more sex then, too.

They hadn't gotten anywhere, and it should irk him more than it did. But it was hard to be irked about anything with Alyssa in his bed.

Even now, when they were both dressed, focused on reading through different things to do with Dom Cochrane's case. It felt…right. Right to be working in the company of someone he could quickly talk into getting naked.

Which seemed like a hell of an idea right now, since

they'd have to start getting ready for the gala soon. He slid the laptop off his lap and rolled onto his side.

Alyssa was engrossed in the papers she'd been rifling through, her eyebrows drawn together, her bottom lip pulled between her teeth.

The feeling in his chest scared him more than a little. He'd told her he couldn't make her any promises a few days ago, but every time he looked at her he wanted to make a million. He wanted to make sure she was always with him.

There was something warped in that probably, but no matter how often he told himself he was being an idiot, he wanted her beyond measure. In bed and out. Now and later. She just seemed to belong here, at his side.

So, he tugged one of the papers out of her hand, but she slapped his hand away. "Wait."

"My charm can't be wearing off *this* quickly."

"No, I think I've got something. Bennet, what if..." She arranged some papers he'd printed off for her. The picture of Salvador Dominguez and one of her brothers. The paperwork on Dom Cochrane's murder case.

She spread them all out, pointing at the pictures of Dom and Salvador. "What if Sal Cochrane, Dom Cochrane and Salvador Dominguez are all the same person, just different aliases? They've got the same nose. Same mouth. Salvador is older, obviously, but it has been sixteen years."

"Salvador has a clear scar on his chin."

"He could have gotten it in the time between pictures."

Bennet rubbed a hand against his jaw. "And if that's true, a man who worked for your father got out of jail, started a new identity and built a cartel to rival your father's. And is now a donor to my mother's campaign."

Alyssa blew out a breath. "What reason would she have?"

"I don't know. Getting donations has never been a problem for the Stevenses, but perhaps things have gone south and I don't know about it."

"Maybe they're not the same person."

"He was convicted. Dom was convicted of murder, a murder that was probably ordered or sanctioned by your father. Yeah?"

Alyssa nodded, studying the pictures, so he did, too. Dom Cochrane and Salvador Dominguez certainly did look alike if you looked hard enough.

"Typically a cartel doesn't let that happen. They don't want one of their own talking to lawyers. They don't want to risk connections."

"I guess that's true, but he was the one stupid enough to get caught."

When he raised an eyebrow at her, she shrugged. "That's how they'd think about it. He got caught, and we never have. I love my brothers, Bennet, because... Well, a lot of complicated reasons, but I'm under no illusion they're good men or have never killed anyone. It's the life."

"Why were you sheltered from it?"

"I'm a girl." She shrugged again. "It's the only reason I ever got. Even before my mother left or whatever it is that happened, the way they'd talk about her... They thought she was weak, and maybe she was. She never spent much time with me."

"So, what was she doing if she wasn't spending

time with her daughter and was too weak to be part of things?"

"I don't know."

Bennet studied the pictures again. "Let's work off the theory they're all the same man. Dom Cochrane had orders from your father to kill someone as part of cartel business. Dom gets caught, tried, sent to prison. Who would Dom be most angry with?"

"My father, but like I said, my father hasn't been well for years. Years upon years. CJ runs the show."

"So, maybe he transfers the revenge. It's personal enough, and the cartel family is actual family. It all works together."

"Except one of my brothers meeting with him."

"You still don't know which one?"

"It would make the most sense if it was CJ. He's the head of things, and it would make sense if Dad passed that earring on to him, but… It doesn't look like CJ to me. Something about the hand."

"What about it?"

"CJ is always angry. Fists clenched or on a weapon. My other brothers are always armed, except Oscar." She paused, her finger touching the hand of the man in the picture. "It can't be Oscar," she whispered, shaking her head. "But everything points to Oscar."

"Are you certain?"

"No. But he taps his fingers on his legs when he's nervous. Did you see him do it at my office? He's always done it. This man's fingers are on his leg, as if he's tapping them out of sight of Dominguez."

She looked up at him, her expression sad and a little lost. "Oscar was the sweet one, sweet to me. I can't believe he'd double-cross the family. It's not in him. Not like the others."

"So, maybe it's not him."

Alyssa swallowed and nodded, looking back at the picture of Dominguez. "How did we turn out okay? I mean, assuming your parents are part of this. How did we…"

"You know, I learned something from dear old Grandpa Ben."

She frowned and reached out and touched his cheek. "I don't like your making light of that."

"You can't beat who someone is out of them or beat who you are into them. I'm not saying it doesn't shape them or leave a mark, but it never does exactly what the bad wants it to do." He took her hand and kissed her palm. "We are who we are because that's what we are."

"So, we'll still be what we are after this is all over?"

Which wasn't as simple a question as he'd like. She was the daughter of a drug cartel kingpin, and whether his mother was involved in all this or not, he was the son of a US senator and, more, he was a Texas Ranger. It would be complicated. It would be…

She withdrew her hand from his, and he wished he had the words to make it right. To say they could be.

"Your hair lady is going to be here soon."

"My nothing. *Your* hair lady. *Your* dress. *Your* party."

"I'll pass on wearing a dress tonight, but we need to go over the plan one more time," he said, ignoring her irritation, really ignoring her hurt. They didn't have time for that. Not right this second. Afterward when he could work it all out, he'd figure them out, too, but they had to do this first.

Alyssa rolled her eyes. "Never leave each other's side. Be on the lookout for Dominguez and anyone he talks to. File as much away as we can, and if we have the opportunity to follow him we do, as long as we're together. That about cover it?"

"Trust no one."

"Except you."

"We'll trust each other."

A knock sounded at the door, and Alyssa sighed heavily.

"Who is it?" Bennet called.

"Ms. Delaney is here," Kinsey returned.

Bennet got off the bed and headed for the door to let Tawny in.

"Wait. Tawny's doing my hair and makeup?"

"When I asked her for referrals for someone, she suggested herself. I figured that'd work out, keep fewer new people from traipsing in and out."

"If I look ridiculous after this, I'm blaming you," Alyssa muttered.

"Be very hard on me. I probably deserve it," he replied, grinning at her as he opened the door.

Alyssa felt like hyperventilating. Tawny had done her hair and makeup, chattering on and on about statement colors, and had put diamonds around her neck, and all Alyssa could think was this was all wrong.

Tawny should be going to this party, talking to debutantes and rich politicians and whatever. Alyssa should be in a little apartment above her friends' garage in her jeans and T-shirt, considering her next bounty-hunting case.

But Alyssa was in some expensive gown, her hair

swept back in ways she never would have dreamed it could be curled and coiffed. She was wearing lipstick of all things, and anytime she caught a glimpse of herself in the mirror, she wanted to rip off the weird little gold hairpiece Tawny had pinned into her hair and run screaming in the opposite direction.

But Bennet was counting on her, and no matter how he'd hesitated when she'd mentioned *after* earlier, she couldn't let him down. He'd given her too much, even if they were coming to the end of that particular line.

"Now, I know you don't want to draw too much attention, but I brought two possible pairs of shoes. One is the sensible choice, and one is the little flash-of-fun choice." Tawny pulled out two pairs of heels from her bag.

Heels. Tall, tall, impossible-looking heels.

"I've never walked in heels before."

"Never walked in… Honey, where *did* you come from?"

Now that was a question.

"They aren't any different from regular shoes. Mostly," Tawny offered brightly.

"I don't believe that for a second."

Tawny laughed. "Okay, it requires some balance and some…well, beauty is pain and whatnot." She handed Alyssa the less flashy pair. "Here, these are shorter."

Alyssa slid her feet into the heels and tried not to wince as she stood.

"Just balance on your heels and it'll be all good. Besides, Ben will catch you if you fall."

"Did he ever tell you why he doesn't like that?" Alyssa asked, failing at the breezy, conversational tone Tawny always used.

"Like what?"

"Shortening his name to Ben."

Tawny cocked her head. "No. Why?"

Alyssa knew she shouldn't say anything. It was none of her business. But, well, Bennet was always protecting *her*. Maybe it was time for her to do the same for him. "Maybe you just shouldn't."

Tawny stood there and didn't say anything for the longest time. Eventually, she nodded. "All right. Well, you're all finished. I'll leave you to make a grand entrance." Tawny collected all her things and opened the door with a wink.

"Hey, um, I know you're getting paid for this and all, but thanks. I appreciate it."

Tawny smiled that big, pretty smile Alyssa knew even with years of practice she wouldn't be able to duplicate. "You're very welcome, Alyssa. Good luck to you." She slid outside, and Alyssa knew she had to follow. No matter how desperately she wanted to avoid *any* gala, but especially *this* gala, it was a job. One she had to do well.

Which meant she had to ditch the heels. She kicked them off and grabbed her tennis shoes. The dress was long enough it would cover the faux pas, she hoped. And if not, well, hell, she'd at least have the ability to run if she needed to, and the dress was already enough of a detriment.

A knock sounded on the bathroom door. "Are you coming?" Bennet demanded. "Tawny said you were done."

Alyssa took a deep breath and took a few halting steps toward the door. All the nerves were just worry over what they might find out tonight and what danger they might be in. It had nothing to do with Bennet seeing her in this getup.

"Don't say anything stupid," she called through the door.

"Well, thank you for that wonderful vote of confidence. Now, would you get the hell out here so we can—" He stopped abruptly as she stepped into the bedroom.

Then he didn't say anything at all. He didn't even move. He just stared at her. Expressionless.

Alyssa fidgeted. "I know I said don't say anything stupid, but you could say *something*."

"You..." He reached out and touched the cascade of golden circle things Tawny had fastened into her upswept hair. "You look like some kind of goddess."

"That counts as stupid."

"That counts as a compliment," he returned, leaning in.

She shoved him back. "You cannot ruin my makeup. I don't know how to fix it. Besides, you said we needed to get going."

"I think I changed my mind." His hands landed on her hips, and no matter how she pushed him away, his mouth brushed her neck.

And, okay, maybe she didn't push all that hard. It was entirely possible she just sighed and leaned into him while his mouth did unfathomable things to her neck.

She didn't want to go out there. She didn't want to face strangers or even try to solve a mystery or catch any bad guys. She wanted to stay right here, because once they did all that solving and catching, she wasn't so sure right here would exist anymore.

Since that caused an annoying lump in her throat, she gave him a little nudge. "We have to go."

He sighed heavily against her neck, but he pulled away. He looked her in the eye, Mr. Texas Ranger all over his face.

"We're going to go over this one more time—"

"Bennet."

"We don't separate unless absolutely necessary. You have your cell phone, your knife and your gun on you at all times." He swept his gaze over her. "Where the hell did you put the gun?"

She grinned, lifting the long skirt up to her hip, where a thigh holster held her Glock. "I mean, God help me if I need it quickly, but at least it's there."

"And the knife is in your bra?"

"Always."

He grinned. "A very, very unique goddess." He cocked his head as his gaze followed her dress hem back down to the floor. "Are you wearing tennis shoes?"

"Don't you dare tell Tawny. She'll kill me."

Bennet chuckled as they moved toward the door, but any humor left them both. What lay ahead of them was risky, and potentially dangerous, most especially for her since her attacker a few days ago had said she'd be dead within the week.

But that only made her more determined. She'd been through one horrible thing in her life already with the kidnapping, and no pissant minion who botched the simplest kidnapping attempt was going to make her cower in fear.

Dead within the week? Not without a fight.

Bennet stopped abruptly with his hand on the knob. He turned to face her, staring at her intently, and Alyssa didn't know what he was looking for, what there was to say in this moment.

"No unnecessary risks," he said eventually.

"What if it leads to the answer?"

He released the knob and curled his fingers around her upper arm. Hard. "No unnecessary risks. Promise me." No jokes, no charming smiles. This wasn't even that Texas Ranger stoicism thing he had down so well. It was dark and dangerous.

But she wasn't about to promise things he wouldn't. "You first."

His mouth flattened into a grim line, and the tight grip he had on her arm didn't loosen.

"No unnecessary risks is a two-way street, Bennet. Either we both take them, or neither of us do."

It took him another few seconds of whatever inner arguing he was doing to speak. "Fine. Neither."

Which was not the answer she had expected in the least. "But… We have to figure this out. It's your important case. It's my mother's murder. You can't honestly think we should play it safe."

"Yes, that's what I honestly think," he replied grimly.

"Why? When we've worked so—"

He took her other arm, giving her a little shake. "You mean more to me than whatever this is," he said, so darkly, so seriously, Alyssa could hardly catch her breath.

He blinked, his grip loosening, as if he was a little

surprised at his own vehemence. "So, we play it safe. Got it?"

She could only stare at him. Mean more to him? When had she ever meant more to someone? When had her safety ever been paramount to an end result? Oh, her brothers had kept her safe for twenty years, but for the cartel. She'd been a burden and a duty, not something someone cared about. She'd maybe never thought of it that way, but she understood it now.

Understood it because she'd never felt like a burden to Bennet. She felt…important. Central.

"Alyssa."

She nodded stupidly. "I got it." She swallowed down all the tremulous emotion in her throat. "No risks."

He released her from his grip, holding out his elbow with one arm and opening the door with his other hand. "Then, let's go."

She slipped her arm through his, still looking up at the hard planes of his face. Clean-shaven and so dashing-looking in his suit. And she meant something to him. Something enough that he'd rather her be safe than solve this case that had been so important to him just days ago.

It was a big deal, no matter what she tried to tell herself. It was a big deal he'd think that, say that, prioritize keeping her safe over solving this case.

He led her to the staircase, and she had to focus on the steps instead of his handsome face. Even though everyone in the house would be attending the party, it was still decorated to the hilt. Christmas lights and evergreen garlands sparkled over the curving banister of the grand staircase.

The floor gleamed, clean and expensive. Even the wood trim seemed to glow in the twinkle of the Christmas lights. The Christmas tree shone bright white from the living room, and it was like walking through a magazine or a castle or anything but anywhere she belonged.

She'd never fit into this sparkling world of wealth and appearances. No matter how many dresses Bennet bought for her or how often Tawny did her makeup. She was a Jimenez. Criminal by association no matter whom she might help bring down.

Bennet could never accept that. She might mean something to him, but once this case was over, the only way they could go was in opposite directions.

So, there was no use getting her hopes up and, more, no use keeping her promise.

Chapter 14

Bennet scanned the crowd for a flash of anyone who might resemble the photograph he had of Salvador Dominguez. He scanned the crowd for any of Alyssa's brothers. He scanned the crowd over and over again.

But all he ever saw were legions of his parents' friends and donors and Texas elite. From the looks of it, Alyssa was just as frustrated about it as he was.

"Let's dance."

Alyssa grimaced. "You think I know how to dance?"

"It's just swaying to a beat." He used the arm that had been situated around her waist the whole evening to lead her to the small cluster of people dancing to slow, jazzy Christmas music. Once on a corner of the dance floor under sparkling lights and all the sparkling jewels on bodies all around them, he drew her close.

She put one hand on his arm and the other she clearly

had no idea what to do with. He took it in his, placing it on his shoulder. He eased her into a simple side-to-side step.

"Why do you know how to dance?" she grumbled. "They teach that at Texas Ranger school?"

"Cotillion."

She wrinkled her nose. "What the hell is that?"

He laughed, drawing her even closer. "If I explained it, it would only horrify you."

"That I believe." Her gaze did another scan of the room before returning to his. "Is he not coming? Is he hiding?" she whispered.

"I don't know."

"This is crazy-making, all these questions. All this waiting. Why doesn't he grow a pair and make a move?"

Bennet wanted to laugh, but the thought of any one of the numerous potential "bad guys" out there making a move filled him with dread. They'd already been too close to Alyssa being hurt.

But all he could do was sway to the music, holding her close and watching the room diligently. Maybe whoever it was—Sal or Dom Cochrane, Salvador Dominguez or one of Alyssa's brothers—wouldn't dare try anything as long as he was by her side.

Well, if that were the case, he wouldn't leave it. And no matter how much she'd chafe at the idea, it didn't bother him in the least.

A moody version of "I'll Be Home for Christmas" started playing, and Alyssa rested her cheek against his chest, and he could all but feel the sadness waving off her.

He wanted to promise he'd get her back to her old

life by Christmas next week, but how could he possibly promise that? No matter how many little clues they managed to put together, they were still as in the dark about the end game as they'd ever been.

"It'll be all right," he murmured, rubbing a hand down her back and up again.

She sniffled a little. "What if they don't forgive me?"

"Who?"

"Gabby and Natalie. I haven't visited the baby. I've been ignoring their calls. If I miss Christmas… What if they don't forgive me? It's not like we're related by blood or anything. They don't owe me anything, and then I'd be alone. Again."

"You won't be alone." No matter how many qualms he had about what might happen *after*, he couldn't imagine his life anymore without Alyssa in it. Didn't want to.

She'd stiffened in his arms, and she didn't raise her head. He could all but feel the questions in her, but she didn't voice any of them.

"Besides, they'll forgive you. Even if you're not blood related, they're family, and you'll be able to explain this all to them afterward. They'll understand. They know how these kinds of things work. Not only are they both involved with law enforcement, but they've both been in danger before. They know what it's like."

She finally pulled her head back and looked up at him. "Did you really mean—"

There was a tap on Bennet's shoulder and a loud, booming voice. "May I cut in?"

Bennet glanced back at his father, who had his best politician's smile plastered on his face. Bennet tried to fight the scowl that wanted to take over his mouth.

"You've been hiding your date all night, Bennet," Dad said jovially, clapping him on the back a little hard. "Let one of us old hats have a turn."

"It looks like your mother's free," Alyssa said, nodding toward Mom walking away from the cluster she'd been talking with earlier. "Why don't you go dance with her?"

He should. He should do some digging about Sal Cochrane here where things would be so busy and booze-filled Mom was likely to forget his questioning in the morning. And Alyssa wasn't just a grown woman, but a capable, *armed* grown woman who could handle his father for a quick dance. Even if Dad said something asinine.

He wanted to finish their conversation. He wanted to assure her he meant *everything*. And he downright hated the thought of leaving her, stupid as it was.

But what could happen to her if she was dancing with Dad? It wasn't like whoever they were waiting for was going to pop out and snatch her away when she was dancing with a US senator, for God's sake.

"All right," Bennet said, smiling tightly and probably not at all convincingly. "Just return her to me after the song, huh?"

Dad rolled his eyes, taking Alyssa's hand off Bennet's shoulder and clutching it in his own.

"Such a caveman I raised, Alyssa. I hope this boy has a few more manners than that." Dad slid his arm around Alyssa's waist and started leading her away.

Bennet stood at the corner of the dance floor like a fool. Dad was either trying to piss him off or... Well, no, probably just trying to irritate him. Bennet shouldn't let him win.

He forced himself to walk over to his mother, tried to make the scowl on his face soften into something bordering on pleasant.

"Are you having fun?" Mom asked.

"The time of my life," Bennet replied drily, causing his mother to chuckle.

"You look quite cozy with that girl."

Bennet merely grunted. Once the case was figured out he'd fight Mom on this battle, but not before. For now, he'd be as discreet and noncommittal as possible.

"You know, there were a few names on the guest list I didn't recognize," he offered, failing hard at casual.

"Worried about security, dear?"

"Something like that. I don't remember you ever mentioning Sal Cochrane before."

Mother's eyebrows drew together. "Cochrane. That name doesn't ring any bells."

"He's a donor of yours."

Mom chuckled. "No. Honey, trust me. I know all my donors. I make sure of it."

Bennet frowned. Mom could be lying, he supposed, but he knew his mother fairly well. He knew her politician charm and the way lies could fall out of her mouth with the utmost authenticity, but she was rarely flippant about lying.

He pulled out his phone and brought up the email from Dad's assistant with the donor list and handed it to her. "It says Sal Cochrane right here."

Mom took the phone and squinted at the screen before scrolling. "Mariah must have made some kind of mistake. This isn't my donor list."

"You're certain?"

Mom nodded, scrolling more "Julie Dyer is on it. Trust me, she wouldn't give me a cent if her life depended on it. That's your father's donor list." She handed the phone back to him, and Bennet nearly dropped it.

If this was Dad's list, then Dad was the connection.

And he was dancing with Alyssa.

The whole not-knowing-how-to-dance thing was a little less concerning when she was dancing with Bennet. Dancing with his father, no matter that there was far more distance between their bodies, made her inordinately tense.

"This is a nice…party. Gala. Thing." Alyssa wanted the floor to swallow her whole. She sounded like an idiot.

"My wife just loves her…party gala things," Mr. Stevens replied with a wink.

Alyssa took a deep breath and tried to relax. Mr. Stevens was nice. A little slick, but nice nonetheless. None of Mrs. Stevens's ice.

"Are you all right, dear? You're looking a little peaked. Why don't we step out onto the balcony? Get a little fresh air."

"No, I'm all right."

But Mr. Stevens was tugging her through the swaying throng of dance-floor people and across the room.

Alyssa wasn't quite sure what was going on, but something didn't sit right. She glanced over at where

Bennet had been. His head was bent over his phone as he talked to his mother.

Mr. Stevens all but pulled her onto the balcony, and she was about to scream, jerk her hand away, anything, but there were people on the balcony, even a waiter carrying around trays of champagne with little red fruit floating in the top, sprigs of what looked like holly decorating the bottom of the glass.

It could hardly be that sinister if there were plenty of people around. It could hardly be that sinister considering Mr. Stevens looked downright jolly.

Mr. Stevens took two champagne flutes as a waiter passed, handing her one. She took it even though she had no plans to drink it.

"Now, you've made quite an impression on my son, and that is a hard thing to do. God knows he'll keep you away from my wife and me as long as that's the case, so I wanted to corner you a bit. I hope you don't mind."

"Well, um, no. I guess not," she managed. It was stupid to want to impress him, please him, but no matter how strained Bennet's relationship might be with his parents, he did love them. And no matter how she told herself there was no future for her and Bennet... She couldn't quite bring herself to blow up that tiniest inkling of a chance.

"Tell me about yourself, Alyssa." He took a sip of his champagne, looking like some ritzy watch or cologne ad.

"Oh, well, there's not a whole lot to tell."

"Where'd you grow up? What do you do? How'd you meet my son?"

Alyssa opened her mouth, hoping some kind of lie

would just fall out, but it didn't. Nothing did. Not even a squeak.

"Are they really that difficult of questions, Ms. Jimenez?"

Alyssa froze. He knew her name, and something about that slick smile that had never quite settled right with her now suddenly seemed sinister.

But he was as relaxed as ever, watching her as he sipped champagne and waited for her to answer.

"Cat got your tongue? Have a few drinks. Might loosen things up for you."

Alyssa swallowed, trying to think straight and not panic. "What exactly is it that you want from me?"

"I'm just concerned about my son, Alyssa. Surely you understand what kind of good, upstanding man Bennet is. He has such a clear sense of right and wrong. I'd hate for him to get wrapped up in the wrong kind of people and get himself hurt."

"Your son can take care of himself," she returned, trying to figure out an exit strategy that wouldn't draw attention. But the people on the balcony were dwindling, and the waiter had disappeared.

Pretty soon she'd be out here alone with Mr. Stevens, and she didn't think that would be very good at all.

"Are you so sure about that?" He said it so casually, so offhandedly, it shouldn't mean anything. It couldn't mean anything, but Alyssa couldn't help but read it as a threat.

This was all wrong. All wrong.

"I should get back," she muttered, taking a retreating step backward.

Mr. Stevens's hand shot out and clamped onto her

wrist in less than the blink of an eye. "Now, now, Ms. Jimenez. Surely you don't need to rush off just yet."

"Let go of me," Alyssa said between gritted teeth. She tugged at her arm, but he held fast, something in his expression hardening.

Alyssa wanted to panic, but she fought it off. She just had to break his grasp and run inside and to Bennet. She could always grab one of her weapons with her free hand, but she didn't think waving a knife or gun at a US senator for some veiled threats was going to go over very well.

She heard the click of a door and jumped, jerking her gaze to the doors that led to the balcony. The now-empty balcony, one door shut and, if that clicking sound was any indication, locked.

But there was still one open. She just had to break his grasp and get through it.

She pulled hard, but Mr. Stevens only jerked her toward him.

"What is this?" she demanded.

"This, Ms. Jimenez, is business. Now, I suggest you stop trying to put up a fight. I'd hate to bruise that pretty face of yours, and I'd hate to have to get my son involved. Bennet's an excellent policeman, but we both know he'd put himself in harm's way before he let you be put in it."

"You would hurt your own son?" she asked incredulously.

"Oh, Ms. Jimenez, I'll do whatever I have to."

Before he finished the sentence, Alyssa pivoted and elbowed Mr. Stevens as hard as she could in the chest.

He stumbled back, releasing her grasp, and she ran for the open door.

But a man stepped through, closing it behind him. Alyssa stopped short at the sight of her youngest brother blocking her exit.

"Oscar, what are you doing?" She took a few more steps toward him, reaching out to him. Even if Oscar was working with Mr. Stevens, he wouldn't hurt her. "Oscar, you have to help me," she whispered, looking at him imploringly. "Let me through. Please."

"Sorry, Lyss," Oscar said, sounding truly regretful.

Before she could beg, or push him out of the way, pain exploded in her head. And then there was nothing but darkness.

Chapter 15

"You're sure he came this way?" Bennet demanded of the shaking waiter who was leading him down a back hallway out of the hotel.

"Y-yes, sir."

"Then where the hell is he?" Dad and Alyssa hadn't been anywhere in the ballroom. No hallways, no bathrooms. Bennet had tactlessly started asking questions, all the glitzy attendees of the ball looking like he was crazy, but the waiter had spoken up and said he'd seen Dad.

But there was no sign of him or Alyssa. There was nothing but an empty stretch of hallway. Bennet felt sick to his stomach. He didn't want to believe this of his father, but they'd been there one second, and gone the next.

Gone. Just gone. In the few minutes he'd discussed

donors with his mother, they were suddenly nowhere to be found.

He scrubbed his hands over his face and focused on the waiter. "And you didn't see the woman either?"

"No. No woman. Nobody really. I mean. Except Mr. Stevens. Who went this way." The waiter swallowed with a loud gulp.

Something about the way the kid looked away and took in an unsteady breath poked at Bennet. He took a threatening step toward the shaking, sweating waiter. "Are you lying to me?" he demanded, getting in the guy's face.

"N-no, sir. Mr. Stevens… He told me… I mean…"

Bennet grasped the man's shirt in his fist and gave him a hard shake. "You are talking to a Texas Ranger in the middle of a life-or-death investigation, so if you want to keep your nose intact and your ass out of jail, you better start telling the truth."

The waiter started crying.

"Look, I don't know what he threatened you with, if anything, but if someone dies because you kept it to yourself, you're an accessory, and I will do everything in my power to punish you to the fullest extent of the law."

The waiter started crying even harder. "I don't know, man. I was just following orders. All he told me was to tell you he went this way, but I don't know where he went."

Bennet swore. A distraction. "What else do you know?" he demanded, giving the guy another hard shake.

"I don't know. I don't know," the man sobbed. "There

was someone with him. A guy named Oscar. But that's all I know."

Bennet released the man and swore, barely acknowledging the waiter crumpling to the floor. He had to calm down and think. *Think*. What the hell could his father possibly be doing?

Oscar. Alyssa was so sure her youngest brother was the nice one, but Bennet couldn't let that console him right now. There were too many variables, and since he knew Alyssa would under no circumstances disappear of her own volition, they were all really shitty variables.

He didn't even know where to start. He had no idea what he was dealing with. All he knew was she was gone, and she wouldn't have done that to him.

Which meant he had to focus. He had to be the Texas Ranger he'd been trained to be. He had to find Mom. Based on the conversation he'd had with her earlier, he didn't think she was involved, but she would know all the places Dad could go.

He left the waiter sobbing on the floor and strode back toward the ballroom, but before he made it down the length of the back hallway, Mom pushed through some doors.

"Bennet. There you are. You've made something of a scene. What's going on?"

"I'll tell you what's going on. Your husband has kidnapped my…" What the hell was she? He didn't know. "I need a list of all the property you and Dad own jointly or separately. Emailed to my work address ASAP." He pushed past her. He'd start at the main house. It was a long shot, but maybe there'd be some clue in Dad's office or…

"Bennet, you don't honestly think—"

"You're right. I don't think, I know. I know what he did, what he's done." He turned to face her. "Mom, if you really have nothing to do with any of this, I'd suggest getting your lawyers together."

"What on earth are you even talking about? Bennet? Bennet! I don't have any earthly clue—"

"My, my. What is all this commotion?"

Bennet turned incredulously to find his father pushing through the doors, then standing there, brushing at his sleeve as if there was some minuscule piece of lint. Pristine and politician perfect in his suit as if everything was fine. Normal.

Bennet lunged, missing only because two of Dad's plainclothes security guards stepped in and grabbed him, holding him back. "Where is she?" he demanded, shoving against the guards.

Dad had the gall to look incredulous and quizzical. "Where is who?"

"You were the last one with her. Now I want to know what you've done with her."

"You mean Alyssa? Oh, she said something about going to the bathroom and—"

"Bullshit," Bennet spat. "You don't think I've put it all together? You and Dominguez and Jimenez. I've got more evidence than you can possibly imagine, and if you think kidnapping her—"

"You aren't making any sense, son. Should I perhaps put in a call to Captain Dean? I have to say I have been worried about your mental state as of late."

Bennet laughed. As if the threat of his job would get through this haze of fury and fear. "Come after me, Dad. Throw it all at me. I will destroy you," Bennet said and then, with a well-placed elbow, escaped the security guard's pathetic hold and pushed past his father and back into the ballroom.

It was teeming with people, many who gave him odd looks, and there was just too much of a world out there. He couldn't do this on his own.

He hadn't wanted to bring in anyone else this whole time because it was his case to solve, but Alyssa's safety trumped all of it. He would find her, and if anyone had hurt her he'd kill them himself.

He pulled his phone out of his pocket, jogging through the ballroom to the exit to the parking lot. He searched his email for an old correspondence with Jaime Alessandro over The Stallion case, found the phone number he needed and called.

"Hello?" Alessandro answered, clearly skeptical at the unknown number.

"Agent Alessandro, this is Bennet Stevens with the Texas Rangers."

"Ah, yes, I've been hearing your name quite a bit around these parts. Not exactly kindly."

Which might have been funny in any other situation. "I need your help. Alyssa needs your help."

There wasn't a second of hesitation. "I'm all ears."

When Alyssa came to, head throbbing painfully, stomach roiling, she was in a basement of some kind. She took a deep breath in and out to fight the nausea and the panic at the realization she was tied to a chair, her hands behind her back, her ankles each to a leg of the chair, and then another cord around her thighs and the seat of the chair.

But she could see, and she could breathe. Important things to focus on. If she panicked, nothing good could happen. If she panicked, she *would* end up dead.

Of course, how she was still alive was a mystery. Surely a US senator wasn't going to leave loose ends lying around. *If* she escaped his life would be over.

And what will Bennet think of that?

She had to close her eyes against the painful thought of Bennet. He would not be taking any of this well. But he would save her. He would. He knew the last person she'd been with was his father.

And he's going to choose saving you over bringing his father down?

She couldn't think like that. Besides, Mr. Stevens had said it himself. Bennet had a clear sense of right and wrong. Even if he wanted to protect his father, his conscience wouldn't allow him to do it at her expense.

She hoped.

She was still in her dress, but she could tell the gun she'd had strapped to her thigh was gone. She could feel the outline of her knife against her breast, and that was good. If she could get untied, she had a chance.

Something sounded behind her, a squeak and groan. A door opening maybe. She tried to turn her head, but the way her arms were tied behind her back limited how much she could look back.

Footsteps approached, and Alyssa did everything in her power to breathe normally. To stay focused and calm no matter who appeared.

"You're awake. Good," Oscar offered cheerfully.

Alyssa could only stare at her brother as he stepped in front of her. He'd knocked her out, and by all accounts was the one who'd tied her up here, and he was acting as if it was all normal.

"You hit me."

"You didn't listen," he returned as if they were arguing semantics, not whether or not he'd knocked her out in the middle of a party.

"What is going on?" she said, her breathing coming too fast, the panic rising too hard. "Oscar, please, explain this to me." She might have tried to hold back the tears, but she had to hope they would get through to her brother. Her sweet brother. How could he be doing this to her?

"You should have listened to me, Lyss." Oscar paced the concrete room, tapping his fingers on his leg. "I'm running out of options here. Why'd you have to keep pushing? I could have kept you out of this if you'd only listened."

"Kept me out of *what*?"

"He wants you."

"Who? Stevens?"

Oscar laughed. "Please. Gary Stevens is nothing more than a pawn. A distraction to get you here. Dominguez is who you should be afraid of. He wants revenge, and it has to be you. Stevens only helped because Dominguez owns him."

"And Dominguez owns you?"

Again Oscar laughed. "No one owns me, Lyss. Dominguez and I are like partners."

"Why are you working for Dominguez?"

Oscar scoffed. "You have to ask that question? CJ

wouldn't even let me carry a gun, or run a raid by myself. He thought I was stupid and weak. Well, he'll see who's stupid and weak now."

"Oscar. He's our brother. I'm your sister. Whatever is going on—"

"He killed our mother, you know. CJ. Our own brother. He killed her. And then he gave you over to The Stallion, all so The Stallion wouldn't encroach on cartel business."

Even though it confirmed too many suspicions, Alyssa could only shake her head, the tears falling faster now. "No."

"He did, Alyssa. On Dad's order he killed our mother. And when The Stallion threatened us and all we built, he offered you."

She couldn't get a full breath. She couldn't…

"Dominguez might not be blood, but he's honorable. He'd never ask me to kill you."

"But he had you kidnap me."

Oscar shrugged, as if that was neither here nor there.

"I'll die anyway. His men who tried to kidnap me last week said he wants me dead."

"But I won't be the one to do it. He'd never ask that of me."

Alyssa had no rebuttal for that. None at all. He didn't care if she died, as long as he didn't have to do it.

"He might not kill you, Lyss. If you can prove some worth, he might just keep you."

"Prove some… Have you lost your mind? Have you lost your heart? What happened to you?" Alyssa demanded, trying so very hard not to sob.

Oscar refused to meet her gaze, and the sound from

before echoed in the concrete room. A door opening. Oscar straightened as footsteps approached.

"Good work, Oscar. I knew I could count on you," a booming voice said.

Oscar beamed and Alyssa thought she was going to throw up as a new man stepped into view. Definitely the man from the picture they had of Salvador Dominguez. Tall and lanky, his graying black hair pulled back in a ponytail, the faint scar on his chin. His dark eyes glittered with something that looked eerily close to joy.

"And here she is." He shook his head as if she was some long-lost friend he was so happy to see. "You look just like your mother." He reached out to touch her cheek and Alyssa flinched, trying to back away from the touch but held too still by the ropes.

"Well, where are my manners? Introductions are necessary, of course. Salvador Dominguez, at your service." He made a strange little bow. "I know we haven't met yet, but I know so many of your family. Oscar here, of course. And I used to work for your father before he became something of an imbecile."

He smiled widely, and Alyssa tried to keep herself still, to not react at all.

Salvador cocked his head. "You don't seem surprised by that information. My, my, maybe you and your Ranger were more thorough than I gave you credit for. Good thing we moved when we did, Oscar." Salvador clapped Oscar on the back as he continued to smile at Alyssa. "Your brother is quite the prodigy. I've been very impressed."

Alyssa wished she could wipe the tears off her cheeks and put on some unemotional, screw-you manner. As it was, she couldn't imagine how foolish she looked tearstained, makeup streaked, hair falling out of all Tawny's ruthless pinning.

"A quiet one. How unlike the Jimenez clan. Even your mother was quite the chatterbox. Of course, I loved to listen to her chatter. You see, I loved her. What a beauty she was, and so…passionate." He reached out and touched her face again, the skim of his index finger down her cheek causing her to shudder as her stomach roiled more viciously.

Salvador leaned in close, so close she could feel his heavy breath on her neck. "I bet your Texas Ranger would say the same about you."

Alyssa wished she could throw up on him, but no matter how nauseated she felt, all she could do was sit there and try not to cry no matter how disgusting his breath felt across her bare skin.

"Don't worry, little girl, I would never test out that theory…in front of your brother," he whispered.

Alyssa worked on her best withering glare. "I don't know what you want, but—"

"Oh, that's simple," he said downright jovially, stepping back and straightening to his full height. "Your family let me rot in jail for years, and while I did, they killed the woman I loved." He waved his arms dramatically as he spoke. "So now, I'm going to kill you."

Alyssa didn't gasp. She didn't allow herself to. She simply stared at her brother imploringly, no matter how he avoided her gaze, until Salvador stepped between them.

"Eyes up here, beautiful."

"You won't kill me," she said, even if she wasn't certain she believed it. She wasn't going down without a fight. Without some backbone.

"Well, maybe not *now*. We might need to have a few *conversations* first, but then you will definitely die. On camera. For all of the Jimenezes to see."

Chapter 16

Bennet and Jaime had split up the list of properties Mom had emailed him and were checking them out one by one. Austin PD was currently questioning his father and had put out an APB for Alyssa. To Bennet's surprise, Mom had snapped into her own kind of action, scouring Dad's financial records for any transactions that might give them a hint.

But still nothing was *happening*, and even as Bennet searched another of his father's Austin properties, he knew it was damn pointless. He was fighting a losing battle, and he didn't know what else to do.

His phone chimed, and he brought it to his ear. "Stevens."

"Gabby found something," Jaime said with no preamble.

"Gabby?"

"I figure if you can do a few things off the record, so can I. She's a better analyst than half my men anyway," Jaime muttered. "I had her look through the files on a raid the FBI did on a house a few months ago. We'd gathered information Salvador Dominguez was doing business there, but the raid found absolutely nothing."

"Well, that doesn't exactly sound promising," Bennet replied, heading back to his car after another property was completely empty.

"It doesn't. Until we tracked down the owner of the house. Originally we hit nothing but dead ends and fake LLCs, but Gabby discovered a tie to your father."

"Address," Bennet barked, starting his car.

"Austin, luckily. I'll text it to you and meet you there."

Bennet hit End and backed out of the parking lot and added the texted address into his GPS. It was all the way on the other side of the city, but the link to both Dominguez and his father was too much to ignore.

He flew through town, then slowed down as he approached the address, looking for an inconspicuous place to park his vehicle.

It was a nondescript-looking house in the middle of a very middle-class neighborhood. Dark had descended, but most of the houses in the neighborhood had lights of some kind on. Except this one. Dark shrouded it so much Bennet could barely make out anything, especially with a privacy fence extending around the front yard as well as the back. Bennet parked his car three houses down and got out of the car, trying to canvas the best way to approach.

If Alyssa was here, there had to be some kind of security in place. Not just alarms, but cameras surely, and if there'd been an FBI raid here a few months ago that had found nothing, surely they were not dealing with amateurs.

He wouldn't let that make him feel sick, because the most important thing wasn't anything except getting Alyssa out, and he'd do whatever it took. Whatever it took, enough that he had to pray she was here, and safe.

He glanced down the road as another car approached. It stopped five doors down and on the opposite side of the street. The headlights stayed on as Jaime got out casually, scanning the neighborhood in the exact way Bennet had. He nodded to Bennet and turned off the lights of his car, shrouding him back in darkness.

What had Bennet's hand resting on the butt of his weapon was another car three houses up from the current house parking as conspicuously. Of course, the minute the driver stepped out of the car and into the light of the streetlamp, Bennet could only stare.

"Is that Vaughn?" Jaime asked as he came up to Bennet's side.

"It is," Bennet replied, watching as his partner approached. "What are you doing here?"

Vaughn studied the privacy fence in front of them. "Gabby told Natalie all the details, and I was instructed to help or be excommunicated or something, and I'm not keen on arguing with a woman and a newborn. Three law enforcement officers are better than one. At least when they're the three of us."

"Then I don't have to brief you?"

"Alyssa is missing. We're likely dealing with the Dominguez and Jimenez cartels in some capacity. We have no idea who or what is in that house. That about cover it?"

"About," Bennet muttered, eyeing the privacy fence again. "The fence is weird, and I assume if this really is some kind of cartel headquarters or meeting place or whatever, it's got cameras everywhere."

"Likely," Jaime replied. "Gabby found me possible floor plans, though," he said, holding out his phone. "This was on the developer's website, and it looks about right. Now, we don't know what kind of modifications the owners might have made over the years, but it gives us an idea."

They each took a turn looking at the floor plan and committing what they could to memory.

"We don't know what kind of arsenal they have," Bennet said. He didn't mind risking himself, but he couldn't put these two men at risk like this. He needed their help, he knew that, but he couldn't risk their lives like this. "I want you two to stay back."

Vaughn scoffed and Jaime shook his head.

"Look, they could be watching for us. They could be armed. You really want to get your head blown off? You're supposed to get married soon," he said, pointing at Jaime. "And you just had a kid."

"We've both done raids, Bennet," Vaughn said. "We know the risks, and the best practices. I've got a vest on. You?"

Jaime and Bennet nodded.

"So, we do what we'd do in any other situation. We're careful, but this is still our job. If something goes bad, it's the risk we took when we took those badges. And I think Natalie and Gabby would understand since they consider Alyssa their sister."

"Fine. We do this together, but I take the risks, you understand? I screwed this up, and I let her out of my sight. This is on me." Bennet knew Vaughn wanted to argue, but they didn't have time. "We'll split up to check the perimeter and see if there are any vulnerabilities in the fence. Vaughn, you stay here and watch for any comings and goings. Stay in the dark so no neighbors get worried and call the cops. Jaime, you take the east side. If they have a monitoring system, they won't know you as any different from a neighbor walking down the street. I'll start on this side, and we'll meet in the back. Understood?"

Vaughn had stiffened, and Bennet knew his partner well enough to know Vaughn didn't particularly care to take orders from him. But, Vaughn didn't argue. He and Jaime both nodded.

Which was all Bennet needed to take off. He walked down the fence that hid the side of the house, running his hands up and down the surface, trying to find a weakness. He'd brought a few tools when he'd started out in case he'd have to do some not-quite-lawful breaking and entering. If he could find a decent crack or opening, he could possibly pry a section open and sneak in undetected.

He had to believe they had the element of surprise on their side. They wouldn't expect him to figure out their hiding spot, at least not this quickly, but that didn't mean they weren't being diligent.

Bennet made it down the entire side of the house,

and when he turned the corner, the shadow of Jaime was turning the one across from him.

Bennet was half-tempted to just blow a hole in the damn fence, but that'd probably draw unwanted attention, and he might as well go through the front if he was going to go down that route.

But there was something of a joint at the corner of the fence here. Where the side had been one long sheet of whatever material the fence was made out of, where they connected at the corner had something of a space. Oh, the materials butted up against each other and were clearly screwed together tightly, but Bennet had to believe with enough force he could pry it open.

Jaime crossed to him. "You're going to need a crowbar or something like it."

"Luckily, I came prepared to do a little breaking and entering." He'd had no trouble jamming the crowbar into his pocket. It had torn the fabric of the pocket, but the curved part of the tool had hooked onto his waistband well enough to keep it secured.

"Good thinking," Jaime said, looking around the back. The house behind them had inside lights on, but none in the back to cast a light on them. Jaime positioned himself in front of Bennet so that if anyone did look out, they hopefully wouldn't notice a man crowbarring open a fence.

Of course, they might notice the tall, broad man just standing there, but Bennet couldn't worry about that. He shoved the sharp edge of the crowbar into the small space between joint and fence and worked to pull it apart.

It took longer than he wanted, but eventually the

fence began to give, and once he'd separated the parts, he used his body weight to bend the joint enough he could step through and into the pitch-black of the back-yard.

"I'm going in. Get Vaughn."

"And if they pick you off?"

"You know not to come this way, and you call in every law enforcement agency to handle the situation."

"We could do that right now, you know."

Bennet looked at the dark shadow of the house. "I can't risk her safety like that. If she's in there, if we let SWAT or some other high-handed assholes handle this, you know as well as I do she has less of a chance."

"Normally I'd argue with you."

"But you won't, will you?"

"No. I care about Alyssa, and apparently so do you. So, we'll do this our way first."

Bennet was already stepping through the space he'd made in the fence. He stayed close to the side fence, using it as a guide to bring him closer to the house.

There were no lights on, and with the moonlight hitting the upper half of the house, he could make out that there were no windows. Not one.

Interesting. He couldn't make out the bottom half of the house, but he could feel his way. He started at one edge and moved his body across the siding of the house until he felt the indentation of a door.

He paused, listening to the quiet of night. Nothing moved, no shots rang out, and if there *were* cameras on this side of the house, he didn't know how they'd be able to see anything.

He had a chance. He crouched next to the doorknob

he'd felt out. He pulled out the tiny penlight from his pocket, followed by the lock-picking kit he'd shoved into his jacket pocket.

He heard Vaughn and Jaime quietly approach and went to work. If his picking the lock drew attention, ideally Jaime and Vaughn would have a chance to surprise anyone who came out.

He didn't care about his own safety right now. He'd gladly die if it meant they got Alyssa out of here in one piece.

Still, he pulled the gun out of his holster and placed it next to his feet while he worked. He'd die for Alyssa in a heartbeat, but he wouldn't die without a fight.

Salvador had left her and Oscar alone while he "readied his supplies," and Alyssa racked her brain for anything she could say to get through to her brother.

"They'll only kill you, too."

Oscar looked at her as though she were a fool. "I'm Dominguez's right-hand man. Not only will he protect me, but hundreds of men who work for us will, as well. CJ can't touch me. I'm nearly as powerful as him, and with Stevens in our pocket, it's only a matter of time before we use every law enforcement agency in Texas to take down the Jimenez cartel."

"Dad would be so disappointed in you."

"Dad doesn't know what century it is, Alyssa. He's completely gone."

"So, you're going to let this man rape and murder me?"

Oscar's throat worked for a few seconds before he turned away from her. He pressed his forehead to the concrete wall of the basement. "You don't understand, Lyss. I have to do this. I don't have a choice. Can't you understand the position CJ put me in?"

Alyssa opened her mouth to yell at him that she didn't care about CJ or Jimenez or anything, she just wanted to live, damn it, but the doorknob on the door across from her seemed to...make a noise.

Considering Oscar and Dominguez had appeared from behind her, she could only assume this door led somewhere else. Maybe even outside?

Then the doorknob downright jiggled. She jerked her head to look at Oscar, but he didn't seem to notice, either in alarm or to go open it for anyone. Not with his head pressed to the wall.

Alyssa's heart leaped in hope. Maybe it was foolish to hope, but Bennet wouldn't give up. He'd do whatever it took. She knew he would, and if it was a chance...

"Can't you do one favor for me, Oscar?" she breathed, trying to sound sad and terrified instead of elated. "One last favor before you let me die?"

"It's not up to me, Alyssa," he said, sounding sad and resigned as he thunked his head against the concrete of the basement wall. Over and over. "I don't have a choice. You forgive me, don't you? You will. I think you will. Once you understand."

"Can't you bring me milk and cookies? One last time?" Even though it was a fake request, it caused a lump to rise in her throat, but she had to speak loudly enough that the increased shaking of the knob didn't get his attention. "Please, Oscar, I'll forgive you if you show me this one kindness."

Oscar turned slowly, and Alyssa forced herself to

hold his gaze instead of looking at the jiggling knob. She had to keep his attention on her, or on the wall, but nowhere near that door.

"You will? Really?"

"I promise. I'll do whatever you want of me, if you just… Bring me milk and cookies like you used to."

Oscar swallowed and nodded slowly, then more quickly. "Okay. Okay, I mean, I doubt we've got milk and cookies, but I'll find a snack. A good one. He'll have to let me do that. A show of respect. It's a show of respect," he said, and leaned down to kiss her cheek.

She tried not to flinch, tried to smile tremulously as she squeezed her eyes shut, hoping a tear would fall over.

"A delicious snack coming right up," Oscar whispered, heading behind her where she couldn't see. She could only hope he'd have to leave the room they were in. She could only hope whoever was on the other side of that door was someone who could save her. Who would.

She heard the door open and close behind her and then prayed, fervently, for the shaking knob to do more than just shake.

"Please, please for the love of God," she whispered, watching the door and wishing with everything she had it would open and Bennet would be on the other side.

When that happened almost exactly as she imagined it, she nearly couldn't believe it. But the door opened with a click, slowly inching open, before Bennet appeared.

She nearly cried out with joy, swallowing it down at the last minute. Tears erupted, but she swallowed down the sobs. For a brief second Bennet kneeled there looking around the edge of the door as if shocked to see her, but then he was all action and movement before she could even register it.

He was at her feet, pulling the knife out of her bra before she could manage a word.

"Tell me everything you know," he whispered, the command calm and clear and helping to keep her focused.

"There're two men that I know of," she whispered as he began to cut all her ties quickly and efficiently. "Dominguez and Oscar. But I woke up right here so I don't know what's up there. Oscar's getting me a snack. Dominguez is getting what he needs to kill—"

The telltale sound of the door behind her squeaking open had her stopping, icy fear gripping her. They'd kill Bennet and then her and—

But the last of the ties fell off and Bennet shoved the knife into her hand as he pulled his gun. A shot fired and Alyssa cried out because she knew Bennet couldn't have fired yet. His gun clattered to the ground, and he stumbled back.

Alyssa clutched the knife in her hand, turning to see Salvador standing there, gun in each hand pointed at both of them. She tried to step in front of Bennet, but he was already on his feet, pushing her back behind *him*.

"Are all Rangers this stupid?" Salvador demanded, pointing both guns at Bennet. Bennet stood there, shirt ripped and blood dripping from where the bullet must have grazed. He was standing, though, looking defiant and pissed as ever, so Alyssa had to believe he was okay. She had to.

"Are all common criminals this stupid?" Bennet returned conversationally.

Salvador's laugh was low and horrible. Alyssa shuddered, trying to think. A knife didn't trump a gun, but maybe she could throw it? Maybe she could lure him close enough to...

"Oscar. Tie up the Ranger. He's going to be our audience, I think. Yes, I think he'll enjoy what I have planned for our little lady."

Bennet whistled, high and quick. Salvador frowned, and then a shot was fired from somewhere behind her and Bennet.

One of Salvador's guns clattered to the ground on a howl of outrage, red blooming near his elbow. "Oscar," he screamed. "Shoot them!"

"I... I left my gun in the kitchen," Oscar whispered, wide-eyed and terrified.

"You have three seconds to drop the weapon, Dominguez," a man from behind them ordered. Alyssa looked back, and her knees nearly gave out. Vaughn and Jaime were standing at the door, weapons trained on Salvador and Oscar.

Jaime began to count off. "Three, two—"

But Salvador grinned. Everything else after that awful, soul-freezing grin went too fast. The next thing Alyssa fully understood was Bennet on top of her and the sounds of at least two gunshots being fired.

"Bennet?" she managed, barely able to breathe between his crushing weight and the hard, cold concrete ground.

He groaned, and panic clutched her throat. She tried

to get out his name again, but her throat felt paralyzed. *She* felt paralyzed.

"Vest," he finally wheezed, pushing off her.

"Vest?" she returned dumbly, but he was getting off her. He was standing up. He had to be okay. She rolled onto her back as he straightened to full height, looking a little too pale for her comfort. But he held out his hand as if she was supposed to take it.

She could only stare. Surely, he'd been shot, but he was standing there trying to help her up.

"You're one lucky bastard," Vaughn muttered, standing behind Bennet and studying his back. "That bullet isn't even an inch away from the edge."

Bennet merely grunted, now not waiting for her to find the wherewithal to grab his hand. He bent over and took her hand and tugged her onto her feet.

"Are you hurt?" he asked, his fingers curling around her shoulders as he studied her intently.

"You've been shot. Twice," she returned, staring at his gorgeous face, a little afraid this was all a dream.

"Yeah, and I'm still standing. Now, are you hurt?" he repeated, more forcefully this time.

"No. I mean, Oscar knocked me out, but—"

Bennet whirled around, but whatever he'd been about to do, Vaughn stepped in front of him.

"Let's let the law handle the rest of this."

That's when Alyssa finally felt like things were real. This had all happened. She looked over at Jaime, who stood above the two men who'd kidnapped her. Jaime was talking on his cell, Salvador laid out in a pile of blood, but his hands were cuffed behind his back as he lay there facedown, so it was possible he was still alive.

Oscar was in a sitting position, rocking back and forth, his hands also cuffed behind his back. Everything seemed to fade away at that moment except her brother.

Her brother who had knocked her out. Who had been a part of a plan to rape and kill her. Who had considered that *fine* because he wouldn't be the one doing it. All for revenge. All because CJ wouldn't respect him.

Alyssa pushed past Bennet. Whatever Vaughn and Bennet said to her, she didn't hear any of it. She stormed over to Oscar, who was looking up at her with tears in his eyes.

"I'm so sorry, Lyss. So sorry. Can't you forg—"

Alyssa didn't want to listen to another syllable, so she bent over and elbowed him in the nose as hard as she'd elbowed the man who'd tried to abduct her last week.

Oscar cried out, blood spurting from his nose.

"I *hate* you," she spat at him, a few tears spilling over her own cheeks. "And I'll never forgive you, you weak, soulless bastard." She turned away from him then, and Bennet was right there. Bleeding and beautiful.

"You saved me." It was all she could think to say, standing in this basement, surrounded by injured men and lawmen and this man. This wonderful man who had saved her from the worst thing she'd ever faced, and that was saying something.

His throat worked for a few seconds before he spoke. "I never should have let you out of my sight."

"But—"

Suddenly men were pouring through the door. Police and FBI, all talking and ordering things, radios squawking, paramedics jogging.

And somehow she was being led out of the basement, away from Bennet, too many questions being asked of her, too many hands prodding at her when all she wanted to do was cry in the comforting circle of Bennet's arms.

But he was still in that basement, not looking at her, and Alyssa realized she might have been saved, but nothing much had changed. He was still a Ranger, and she was still a Jimenez.

Nothing could change that.

Chapter 17

Bennet was doing everything in his power not to shove the paramedic working on his arm. He didn't particularly feel like having his wounds tended to right now.

Nor did he feel like answering anyone's endless questions, not when Alyssa had been taken out of the basement that was now crawling with all manner of law enforcement.

"We're going to have to transport you, Ranger Stevens. Even a minor bullet wound is a bullet wound."

Bennet tried to make his face do anything other than scowl, but it was a lost cause. He didn't want to go to a damn hospital. He wanted to sit down and go through everything that had happened. Not with FBI or other Rangers or anyone. Just Alyssa.

Who had been led away and hadn't reappeared.

"I'll go see if the second ambulance is here, if you'll wait."

Bennet nodded, staring at the chair Alyssa had been tied to when he'd gotten inside. Tied up. *This* close to dying. Because of him and all the mistakes he'd made along the way.

Jaime reappeared from wherever he'd been outside. Bennet glanced up at the man who'd helped him. Bennet didn't know much what to say. What could be said when you'd made this kind of a mess of things?

"Paramedics checked Alyssa out, and she was cleared to go home. Vaughn is taking her back to his house. Gabby's there, and she'll take good care of her."

Bennet nodded. "They're going to make me go to the hospital."

"Bullet wounds will do that to you. I'll let Alyssa know once she's had some rest. Don't want her rushing off to the hospital."

Bennet laughed bitterly. "I'm the reason she was put in this position. I wouldn't worry about it."

"Come on, Bennet. We've both been doing this too long to talk like that."

"I let my guard down. I trusted the wrong people. She could have been killed."

"But she wasn't. You know those seconds matter. The end result matters. Justice matters in the end."

"It's different," Bennet said flatly, because some man he barely knew, no matter what help he'd offered, couldn't absolve this black cloud of guilt.

"Why? Because you're involved with her?"

When Bennet didn't respond in any way, because yes

he *had* been involved with her but he wasn't so certain he would be from here on out, Jaime continued.

"Been there, done that, buddy. It's really not different. Not when you've both survived relatively unscathed and have a chance to build a very nice future."

"She was knocked out, tied to a chair and seconds away from being killed. We must have different definitions of *unscathed*."

"We don't get out of life unscathed. Not a one of us. Alyssa's tough. She's had to be. If you think she's going to wither away—"

"I don't think that. I know she's tough. She's tougher than she should have to be, because she's had shit thrown at her her whole life."

"Then how about this? Don't be more of the shit. I didn't get to save Gabby when she was in trouble. She mostly saved herself. I didn't like it, but you know what I did like? Getting someone I loved and wanted to marry and have a family with out of the deal. So. Stop being a dumbass."

"Thanks for the pep talk," Bennet muttered as the paramedic reappeared.

"Go to the hospital. I'll let Alyssa know you'll be by when you're released. Don't disappoint her, or you'll have a whole slew of intimidating women to answer to."

Bennet nodded absently as Jaime went over to talk to another FBI agent and the paramedic started leading him out of the house.

He *was* being a dumbass, feeling sorry for himself, blaming himself, and as much as it felt right to wallow in that, Jaime had a point. This was over now, and Alyssa *was* safe.

There'd be fallout to deal with. His father was a part of this, and Bennet... He didn't know how to absorb that, or how she would. How anyone would.

But Alyssa was safe. Alive and safe and able to go home, and maybe she hated him a little bit now. He could deal with that. He could deal with any range of emotions she had toward him, but that didn't mean he had to sulk and give up and stay away.

Not when he'd fallen in love with her, and damn it if she wasn't tough enough to take it.

Alyssa had showered as much of the day off her as she could. She'd been fussed over by Gabby, had a newborn baby shoved into her arms and been plied with tea.

She hated tea, but she hadn't found her voice. Not since Vaughn had ushered her away from the house she'd been tied up in and driven her to his house.

Natalie and Gabby had done *all* the talking since then. It was nice, all in all, since Alyssa didn't know what to say or what to feel. Her entire body felt cold and numb.

A knock sounded at the door, and Vaughn disappeared to answer it. When he returned, Jaime was with him.

Alyssa had approximately eight thousand questions she wanted to ask him, but in the end she just looked down at the baby sleeping in her awkwardly positioned arms. The little girl was so tiny, her face all scrunched up in sleep.

Alyssa's chest felt too tight, her eyes too scratchy. Everything ached and hurt and didn't make any damn sense.

She swallowed at the lump in her throat, still watching the baby in her arms. "How is everything?" she managed to ask, her voice squeaky.

"Everyone has been transported to the hospital. In Bennet's and Oscar's cases that's more of a precaution than a necessity. I arranged to have your bike brought here, and it's out in the driveway." He placed her keys on the table next to the couch.

"Wait. You didn't give her a chance to talk to Bennet before you brought her home?" Natalie demanded, turning toward Vaughn.

"Bennet was a little busy. Would you sit down? You shouldn't be up around pacing."

"I'm not pacing, I was getting Alyssa more tea, and I will not sit down. Is your memory faulty?"

"Alyssa hasn't drunk the tea she's got and my memory is fine," Vaughn replied, pressing Natalie into the chair.

Natalie whipped her accusatory gaze to Jaime. "You, too?"

"He needed to be transported to the hospital. The entire place was crawling with law enforcement. That's not exactly the time to talk."

"Even though you both know talking after these kinds of ordeals is important?" Natalie returned.

But Alyssa had been glad. She didn't want to talk to Bennet just yet. Not when all she felt was this horrible numbness interrupted only intermittently by the need to cry. She wouldn't cry in front of him in the aftermath. She needed to be strong the next time she spoke to Bennet.

Strong enough to pretend she didn't care that they didn't have a future together.

"Bennet will be by once he's released," Jaime said. "They'll be able to talk in a calm, comforting environment instead of in the middle of a crime scene."

"Unless that's not what you want?" Gabby said, sliding onto the couch next to Alyssa. It was the first time in this conversation anyone had talked to Alyssa directly.

Which Alyssa wanted to shy away from. She wanted to live in this numb bubble for right now. She didn't want to think about Bennet or the impossibility of their future. She didn't want to think about Oscar or what he'd been willing to do. She didn't want to think of CJ killing her mother or any of it.

She just wanted to stare at a sweet little sleeping baby who would always know her parents loved her.

"We can tell him not to come, sweetie. Until you're ready." Gabby squeezed her arm, and Alyssa barely felt it. She wasn't sure she'd ever feel ready. What had she ever been ready for in her life? She'd only ever had things happen to her and learned to deal, or learned to fight, or learned to be the victim. Time and time again.

Something poked through all the numbness. Anger. She was so damn tired of being a *victim*. So tired of things happening to her and her having to learn how to fight, how to survive.

When was it going to be her turn to live? To make choices without worrying if she was going to inconvenience someone or get them connected to something they shouldn't be connected to. When did she get to have a *life*? With ups and downs and successes and failures and…

"Can you take her?" Alyssa asked abruptly, nodding toward the baby she was still afraid to jostle.

Gabby obliged and Alyssa stood as soon as she was free of the baby. "I have to go," she announced to no one in particular.

"You're not going anywhere, Alyssa."

Alyssa ignored Gabby. "What's happening with Gary Stevens?" she demanded of Jaime.

"He's been arrested. He has a team of lawyers working to get him released, but there's a lot of damning evidence to him being an accessory. Including Oscar's throwing him under the bus."

"And Dominguez?"

Jaime shoved his hands into his pockets, rocking back on his heels. "Died en route to the hospital."

"Good. And my brother?"

"Oscar is being checked out, and once he's fit for confinement, he'll be transported to jail. We're also applying for warrants on your brother CJ in the murder of your mother."

"Oh." Alyssa cleared her throat. "Good. Good, I'm glad." They should all pay for what they'd done. Every last one of them. "I need to go then."

Jaime glanced at Gabby as if asking permission. Alyssa scowled. "I don't want to wait for him to get here. I have some things to say to him. I'm not waiting. I'm done with waiting."

Jaime inclined his head. "I can't argue with that. Can you?" he asked pointedly at Gabby.

Alyssa looked back at her friend, her *sister*—more her family than any of the horrible men related to her—and Gabby sighed heavily.

"Just drive her to the hospital."

"I can handle myself," Alyssa retorted.

"We all can, but it doesn't hurt to let the people who care about us take care of us either. Got it?"

That numbness receded further. Care and taking care. *That* was what she wanted out of her life. She crossed back to Gabby and gave her a hug. "Thank you," she whispered, then did the same to Natalie. "Thank you for being my family," she said firmly. Damn if she'd ever be afraid or hesitant to say that again.

"And I appreciate the taking care," she continued. "But this is something personal and I want to drive myself. Okay?"

Gabby gave a nod. "Just keep us informed on where you are so we don't worry, okay?"

"I will." Because that's what family did, and she was most definitely part of a real family now.

Chapter 18

Bennet signed the paperwork to get him the hell out of the hospital. It shouldn't take that long to stitch up a little bullet wound, Bennet thought.

Captain Dean had debriefed him on the status of Alyssa's mother's murder case, including a warrant for CJ Jimenez. Bennet couldn't begin to guess what Alyssa would think of that when she'd been so certain her brothers hadn't done it.

But no matter how she took it, he wanted to be the one standing by her as she did. Now, he just had to hope she'd let him.

The nurse ushered him out of the room he'd been in, and when Bennet stepped into the waiting room, he stopped short. "Mother."

Mom stood from the chair she'd been sitting in. She'd changed out of her gala finery, and in fact looked pale and as mussed and bedraggled as he'd ever seen her in his entire life.

"Have you been released?" she asked as if she was asking him how the weather was.

"Yes."

Mom swallowed, clutching her purse in front of her. "The police are crawling all over my home and guest-house. I'd relish the opportunity to stay away and drive my son back to his house." She swallowed, and Bennet realized no matter how calmly she spoke, she was as affected as her appearance might suggest.

Bennet sighed. "They arrested Dad?"

Mom nodded tersely. "Obviously his lawyers are working overtime to find some loophole."

Bennet didn't know what to say to that. Didn't know what to do with this. What he wanted was to see Alyssa, to talk to her, to sort things out, but maybe this was as important to sort out.

"I had no idea," Mom said, her voice more a whisper than that cool politician's tone she'd been employing. "Apparently his assistant was the only one who did. I don't know why he'd risk it, Bennet. Working with a cartel, no matter what the money, is political suicide."

"Unless no one finds out and you can use it to aid your cause."

Mom shook her head. "It's unconscionable. Maybe you don't believe me, maybe he could have convinced me otherwise, but I swear to you, if I had known… I would have had to have turned him in. My career is everything to me, Bennet. It always has been for better or worse, but I never could have condoned this kind of…" She shook her head, a tear slipping over her cheek.

It was impossible not to believe his mother at this point. She wasn't an emotional woman. She hadn't even cried at her own mother's funeral. For her to be this distraught, she had to be caught completely unaware, and he supposed as separate as his parents had been conducting their lives, it was more than possible.

"I'm sorry you got caught up in it."

Mom nodded jerkily. "You, as well. I hope Alyssa wasn't hurt."

"Not physically."

"Good. I… Well, I suppose I wasn't overly polite when I met her."

"Are you going to apologize how you treated a woman in my life, Mother?" Bennet asked incredulously.

Mom sniffed. "Well, it perhaps took my life being ruined before my eyes to get me to that point, but yes. And, though I'm sure you'll think it makes me cold and callous, your father's ruined our name completely now. It doesn't really matter what women you consort with at this point."

Perhaps it shouldn't be funny, but after this long-ass day, Bennet could only laugh. He laughed and did something he hadn't done for years, maybe over a decade.

He hugged his mother.

"Oh, well, it turns out you might be busy," Mom said after giving him a quick squeeze back. When he pulled away, his mother pointed to the doors of the waiting room.

Alyssa stood there, arms crossed over her chest, looking beautiful and pissed off. And for the first time since she'd shown him the gun strapped to her thigh just *hours* ago, he finally relaxed again.

She was here. They were both all right. If they could both survive a kidnapping plot orchestrated by members of each of their families, they could probably figure just about anything out.

"Go to my house. Stay there until the police clear out of yours. I have…business to take care of," Bennet told his mother absently.

"Bennet, I'm going to tell you something I'm likely never to admit aloud again."

"Yeah?"

"I quite like her."

He managed to tear his gaze away from Alyssa and stared at his mother, who shrugged and began walking for the exit. She paused as she approached Alyssa, said something, and then she was gone.

Then it was just the two of them. And a handful of people in the waiting room, but he barely noticed. He walked toward her, and she didn't move. Just stood there staring at him as though they were about to fight.

"They stitch you up?" she asked.

"Yes."

"And you're okay?"

"Aside from a bruise the size of Jupiter on my back and some stitches on my arm."

"Well, you got something to say to me?" She lifted her chin, all brave defiance, and he grinned.

"Yeah." But he didn't say any of it. He kissed her instead, tangling his fingers in her hair, drowning in the taste of her he'd never be able to live without no matter how he might fail her in the future.

* * *

Alyssa had not come to the hospital to make out in the waiting room in front of a handful of people, but now that Bennet's arms were around her, his mouth on hers, it was hard to remember what she had planned to do.

She wanted to stay here, in this moment, for good. They were safe. They were together. He was *kissing* her regardless of her last name or his.

"Bennet," she murmured against his mouth. She'd come here with things to say. Things to demand, and he was dismantling it all because this was all that mattered. All she wanted. Him, him, him.

His hands moved to cup her cheeks, his mouth brushing across her mouth in between his words. "If you're going to yell at me, can it wait?"

"For what?"

He pressed his forehead to hers, his eyes still closed. "My wounds to heal, the case to be over, fifty years— take your pick."

"No, I didn't mean wait for what, I mean what would I yell at you for?"

His eyes opened, blue and vibrant. "You didn't come here to yell at me?"

"No, I came here to tell you that I'm tired of waiting and being pushed aside and we will talk about everything on *my* time, and when *I* want to."

"Okay," he returned all too reasonably.

"And I don't want to do it in this damn waiting room with all these people listening to me."

"Okay."

"And stop saying okay!"

He grinned at her again, and she didn't know whether to laugh or cry, tell him she loved him or kiss him a million times over no matter who they were in front of.

"All right," he said, feigning seriousness. "This is where I point out I don't have a car or any way of getting us out of here."

"I guess you'll have to ride on the back of my bike. If you think you're up to it."

"I guess it's fitting punishment all in all."

She frowned at him. "Why do you think I'm going to yell at you or you need to be punished? You recall saving my life earlier, right?"

"I'm the reason you were in that position. I let my father convince me to do something I knew I shouldn't. I didn't want to leave you with him. It went against every gut feeling I had, but I let it go because..."

"Because he's your father. You think I don't understand the way loyalty and family love can screw with you? I trusted Oscar. I trusted CJ. They... Bennet, you want to love your family, and it's an awful thing when they don't deserve it. But it's not our fault."

His thumb brushed her cheek, back and forth, and all she wanted was to be in a bed somewhere with him and shut the world and their families and this awful day away for good. But his next words made her breath catch.

"I love you," he said in the middle of a hospital waiting room, earnestly and looking her right in the eye as if there was no greater truth in the world.

Alyssa tried to make sense of those three simple words. Except, she hadn't expected them, and they were anything but simple. "Wh-what?"

"'What' as in you didn't hear me or you don't believe me or you don't want me to?"

"I…"

"Because I'm not sure how to talk you into loving me back without knowing which objection I'm fighting."

"You don't have to talk me into it," she managed to say through her tight, scratchy throat.

"I don't?"

"I may not have had very good luck with the kind of love a person is born with, but I've been pretty good about finding it myself these past few years." With shaky fingers, she traced the impressive cut of his jaw. "I love you, Bennet."

"Just took a week, a few kidnapping attempts and successes, a dramatic shootout."

"Don't forget the involvement of family members."

"No, who could forget that?" He inhaled deeply, then let it out. He looked at her so intently Alyssa wasn't sure she'd ever get used to it, but she'd gladly spend a very long time trying.

"We managed to turn today around, I think," he murmured, still touching her face, still looking at her in that heart-melting way.

Alyssa glanced at the clock. "It's after midnight. It's tomorrow."

"Even better."

Then he was kissing her in the middle of this waiting room again, and she didn't care anymore at all.

Epilogue

One Year Later

"The timing is so funny," Tawny said, attaching a golden hairpiece to Alyssa's impossibly perfect updo. "I swear we were just doing this a year ago."

"We were," Alyssa returned. "Except I was wearing black."

"And now you look positively radiant in white." Tawny stepped back and studied her handiwork. "Please wear the heels. Please. I beg of you."

"Sorry. Tennis shoes are tradition."

"So is kidnapping. I'm hoping we avoid that this time around."

"You and me both."

Tawny pouted at Alyssa's feet. "Well, at least they're

white. But everyone is going to see them when you walk down the aisle."

"They'll survive the shock."

"Ready for the great unveiling?" Tawny asked.

Alyssa took stock of herself in the mirror. It was no different from how she'd felt a year ago getting ready for a Christmas gala, and yet it was completely different. As uncomfortable as she felt all dressed up, she was going to her wedding this time.

And that made all the difference in the world.

Tawny opened the bathroom door and ushered her out into the bedroom where the photographer and her bridesmaids waited. Natalie and Gabby were both dressed in beautiful forest green, Nat holding pretty little Sarah dressed in red toddler finery on her hip, Gabby lying miserably on the bed.

But both looked at Alyssa as she entered the room, brown eyes shiny.

"Oh, you look like a princess," Natalie said with a little sniffle. "It's perfect."

"You look great, Lyss," Gabby added. "I've got a bet with Jaime that Bennet cries, so do your best for me, okay?"

Alyssa managed a laugh, feeling a little teary herself. "You going to make it down the aisle?"

"Do you want me to go get you some ginger ale?" Tawny asked.

"No, I'd prefer a time machine so I can fast-forward out of morning sickness land," Gabby replied.

"You're getting there," Nat offered.

Gabby simply groaned, but Alyssa had to grin. She'd spent much of her life alone and isolated, and now she was getting married surrounded by her surrogate family. Her sisters, her friends. And soon enough she'd be walking down the aisle to the man she loved.

She swallowed at the lump in her throat, because she did not want to go through the arduous process of redoing her makeup.

A knock sounded at the door, and when Tawny opened it she screeched and slammed it right back shut. "You are not supposed to see the bride, Bennet Stevens," she scolded through the door.

"I'm not superstitious," Bennet returned from behind the closed door.

"Well, I am," Alyssa said, crossing to the door. "So get the hell out of here."

"Open the door."

"No."

"Just a crack. We don't have to see each other. I just want to give you something."

"If it's jewelry, I don't want it."

"It's not jewelry. Open the door and hold out your damn hand, woman."

She looked at the door, unable to stop grinning. How she'd gotten here, she'd never know, but she was so happy. So, so happy, and what's more, she knew she darn well deserved it.

She cracked the door open and stuck her hand out the crack. Bennet placed something in her palm, and she curled her fingers around the slim piece of metal and pulled it to her.

When she uncurled her fingers, she was staring at a Swiss Army knife. A *monogrammed* Swiss Army knife, with her soon-to-be initials on it.

"If I'm not fishing that out of your dress later, you're going to be in very big trouble," Bennet said from behind the door.

Tawny peered into Alyssa's palm and wrinkled her nose. "What kind of gift is a *knife*?"

Alyssa slid the knife into the top of her dress, making sure it was secure before she flashed a grin at Tawny. "The perfect gift." She cleared her throat and peeked out the crack in the door.

Bennet was standing there looking all too pleased with himself, polished and perfect in his tux.

She kept her body hidden behind the door, but stuck her head out the crack.

"Hi," he offered.

"Hi," she returned. She stuck her finger out the crack and crooked it at him so he'd step closer.

"If I come closer, I'm going to kiss you," he warned.

"On the cheek," she said, offering her cheek, but as he moved closer, he only cupped her face with his hands and bent his face close enough their noses were touching.

"Not the cheek," he whispered, touching his lips to hers. It would ruin her lipstick, but she was a little too happy to care. She kissed him right back.

There were protests from inside, but Alyssa didn't care. Today she was marrying the man she loved, and no luck—good or bad—could stand in her way.

"I love you, Ranger Stevens," she murmured against his mouth.

"And I love you." He pulled away, that charming grin firmly in place. "See you soon, wife," he offered, heading back down the hall toward the grand staircase.

They would be getting married at the bottom of it, then having their reception in the huge living room decorated with the giant gold tree she'd admired last year.

Bennet hadn't loved the idea of getting married at the Stevenses' house, what with his father being in jail, but Alyssa thought it was fitting. It was where they'd had their first real kiss, where they'd made love for the first time, where they'd spent all that time together that had led them to this wonderful moment.

Yes, it was perfect, even in all its glitz and glamour, and when they went home tonight to Bennet's less flashy house that he'd insisted she help decorate over the past few months, they'd have their low-key, very naked wedding night, and celebrate the start of a very wonderful, *loving* life together.

And if everything in her life had led her to this wonderful point, she wouldn't trade any of it and risk missing out on that. Because the life she'd built in her newfound freedom wasn't perfect, but it was full of love, and love, it turned out, wasn't a weapon.

It was freedom.

* * * * *

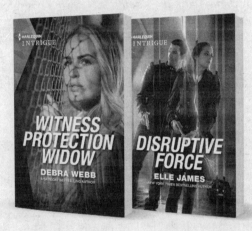

"So, tell me who you *think* is stalking you," he said in more of a statement than a question.

She shrugged her shoulders. "I don't know. That's a tough one. There's a guy in one of my classes who creeps me out. I'll be taking notes furiously in class only to get a weird feeling like I'm being watched and then look up to see him staring at me intensely."

"Has he come around the bar?"

"A time or two," she admitted.

"Is he alone?"

"As far as I can tell. He never has worked up the courage to come talk to me, so he takes a table by the dance floor and nurses a beer," she said.

"Any idea what his name is?"

"Derk Waters, I think. I overheard someone say that in a group project when his team was next to mine. By the way, there should be no group projects in college. I end up doing all the work and have to hear complaints from everyone in the process," she said as an aside.

Garrett chuckled. "Maybe you should learn to let others pull their own weight."

She blew out a sharp breath. "And risk a failing grade? No, thanks. Besides, I tried that once and ended up staying up all night to redo someone's work because they slapped their part together."

"Sounds like something you'd do," Garrett said.

"What's that supposed to mean?" She heard the defensiveness in her own voice, but it was too late to reel it in.

"You always were the take-charge type. I'm not surprised you'd pull out a win in a terrible situation."

Well, she really had overreacted. She exhaled, trying to release some of the tension she'd been holding in her shoulders. "Thanks for the compliment, Garrett. It means a lot coming from you. I mean, your opinion matters to me."

"No problem." He shrugged off her comment, but she could see that it meant something to him, too. He picked up his coffee cup and took another sip. "Okay, so we have one creep on the list. What about others?"

"I wouldn't classify this guy as a creep necessarily, but he has followed me out to the parking lot at school more than once. He's a TA, so basically a grad student working for one of my professors. He made it known that he'd be willing to help if I fell behind in class," she said.

Again, that jaw muscle clenched.

"Doesn't he take a hint?"

"Honestly, he's harmless. The only reason I brought him up was because we were talking about school and for some reason he popped into my mind. He's working his way through school and I doubt he'd risk his future if he got caught," she surmised. "Plus, this person is trying to run me off the road."

"You rejected him. That could anger a certain personality type," he said. "What's his name?"

"Blaine something. I don't remember his last name." Up to this point, she hadn't really believed the slimeball could be someone she knew. A cold shiver raced down her spine at the thought. "I've been working under the assumption one of the guys at the bar meant to get a little too friendly."

"We have to start somewhere. I believe my brothers would say the most likely culprit is someone you know. I've heard them say a woman's biggest physical threat is from those closest to her. Boyfriend. Spouse. Someone in her circle." He shot a look of apology. "It's an awful truth."

She issued a sharp sigh. "I can't even imagine who would want to hurt me."

Don't miss
Texas Stalker *by Barb Han,*
available November 2021 wherever
Harlequin Intrigue books and ebooks are sold.

Harlequin.com

HIEXP1021

Love Harlequin romance?

DISCOVER.

Be the first to find out about promotions, news and exclusive content!

Facebook.com/HarlequinBooks

Twitter.com/HarlequinBooks

Instagram.com/HarlequinBooks

Pinterest.com/HarlequinBooks

YouTube.com/HarlequinBooks

ReaderService.com

EXPLORE.

Sign up for the Harlequin e-newsletter and download a free book from any series at **TryHarlequin.com**

CONNECT.

Join our Harlequin community to share your thoughts and connect with other romance readers!
Facebook.com/groups/HarlequinConnection

HARLEQUIN

Heartfelt or thrilling, passionate or uplifting—Harlequin is more than just happily-ever-after.

With twelve different series to choose from and new books available every month, you are sure to find stories that will move you, uplift you, inspire and delight you.

SIGN UP FOR THE HARLEQUIN NEWSLETTER

Be the first to hear about great new reads and exciting offers!

Harlequin.com/newsletters